BRAZILIAN PSYCHO

Joe Thomas

First published in Great Britain by Arcadia Books in 2021
The paperback edition published in 2022 by

Arcadia Books
An imprint of Quercus Editions Limited
Carmelite House
50 Victoria Embankment
London EC4Y 0DZ

An Hachette UK company

A CIP catalogue record for this book is available
from the British Library.

ISBN (MMP) 978 1 91135 084 2
ISBN (Ebook) 978 1 91135 096 5

This is a work of fiction. All of the names, characters, places, incidents,
organisations, and events portrayed in this novel are either products of the
author's imagination or are used fictitiously. Where real-life figures appear, the
situations, incidents and dialogues concerning those persons are fictional.

For legal purposes, the Afterword constitutes an extension of this copyright page.

10 9 8 7 6 5 4 3 2 1

Typeset in Minion by MacGuru Ltd
Printed and bound in Great Britain by Clays Ltd, Elcograf S.p.A.

For Martha and Lucian;
and dedicated to the memory of Marielle Franco

Contents

Author's note

'The reader may ask how to tell fact from fiction. A rough guide: anything that seems particularly unlikely is probably true.'

Hilary Mantel, *A Place of Greater Safety*

Brazilian Psycho introduces and completes the São Paulo quartet. Like each of the other novels – *Paradise City*, *Gringa* and *Playboy* – *Brazilian Psycho* is a standalone work. The books are in conversation with each other: there are echoes and repetitions; plot lines intersect; characters, themes and ideas recur. Quite deliberately, certain passages in *Brazilian Psycho* have previously appeared, in altered form, in one or more of the other novels.

Brazilian Psycho is a work of fiction based on fact: the historical-contemporary context is recognisable. The quotations that begin each chapter are attributed; fictional quotations are attributed to fictional characters. There are a number of articles, documents and transcripts included in the text, some real, some fictional. An Afterword follows the main text which acknowledges sources consulted and includes a list of all quoted material.

The favela is not the problem. The favela is the city. The favela is the solution.

Marielle Franco

Once upon a time in São Paulo –

1930: Getúlio Vargas takes the presidency of the Brazilian republic by coup d'état. He rules by decree, unbound by constitution, in a shaky, dictatorial, provisional government. The coup erodes state autonomy.

They don't like Getúlio Vargas in São Paulo. Four students are killed by federal troops in May 1932, protesting against the government.

São Paulo's motto: *I lead, I will not be led.*

In July, São Paulo responds. São Paulo rises, bears arms, goes to war, rebels –

It doesn't end well.

The state government is counting on the solidarity of the political elites of the two other major Brazilian states, Minas Gerais and Rio Grande do Sul.

Solidarity that does not materialise.

Some allies.

Eighty-seven days of fighting; nine hundred and thirty-four dead; cities left reeling –

Surrender.

It doesn't end very well at all.

But São Paulo learns a hard-earned lesson:

Rely on no one but your own.

V FOR VICTORY

São Paulo

7 October 2018

There's fuck all to do, thinks Beto. Sunday night blues.

Nothing, nada, zip, which is why he's bouncing about with his mates Andre and Fat Pedro on the day of the first round of the presidential elections.

The results are coming in already, and though Beto doesn't much care for politics, he's pleased that Bolsonaro appears to be killing it, romping home.

Killing it is a good phrase for old Bolsonaro, Beto thinks.

He's heard he's got a psycho edge to him, Bolsonaro, a killer instinct.

Ten years in the Military, a paratrooper in the 80s: Beto's heard this means he's hard as nails. He survived that stabbing attempt for a start, a few weeks ago.

Beto's seen him on TV in the hospital, giving it the *come on then*.

Hard as nails –

Brazilian psycho.

Beto is wired tight, tense. And he's afraid, too, frightened of something, something he can't quite put his finger on.

Not that he's showing it, mind.

His mates have a year on him, but he's top boy in their little gang of three.

Sixteen years old and king of the jungle.

The Bixiga Boys.

Bixiga, the bladder of São Paulo. An old-school neighbourhood either side of Avenida Paulista. Born and raised there, and now out of school and on a retainer to keep the peace. That's the remit: police the area for undesirables. Fat Pedro's older brother got them the gig.

Beto's not sure who got him *his* gig, but there's money coming in from somewhere.

Beto thinks it's likely a neighbourhood-watch scheme approved by the Military Police.

They're all three bumming smokes and kicking rubbish round the back of that junkie, faggot haven, the park off the avenue.

Looking for a hophead to roll, a rent boy to scare. Do their job *right*.

Fat Pedro's prattling on about the election, the protests that have been going on for weeks, who's right and who's wrong, and what happens now our man's in charge, or soon to be.

He doesn't have a clue what he's on about, Beto thinks.

Fat Pedro's talking about getting organised, joining some skinhead mob or other, something about his brother's connections, showing these lefty fucks what's what.

Beto's not listening. This new president-elect means there's a green light to work, that's how Beto sees it.

His eyes open, and wide, and looking.

It's on now, anything goes, and that's why he's scared, a little jazzed, if he's honest about it. The sense of power.

And yes, he is wound right up.

It's been a miserable few days and he's got the hump.

Life can piss you off in the bladder, in Bixiga, is what they say.

And doesn't Beto know it. His mum on his case to get a real job, his dad beaten down and a shell of his old self, a sad sack who now clears tables and washes dishes at one of the Italian canteens up the road.

He used to *be* something, Beto's old man. At least that was what it felt like, to Beto. Perhaps that's the point: it *was* only Beto who thought he was something.

He picks up a rusting aerosol can. He grabs Fat Pedro by his fat throat.

He sticks the nozzle in Fat Pedro's face.

Will you shut up? he says.

Fat Pedro's got his hands up, trying to push Beto off him.

Leave it out, you twat, he says, you'll fucking blind me.

Beto's laughing, wheeling Pedro around, pressing down on the button.

I'm a graffiti artist, Beto is saying. Ele não! Ele não! he yells, laughing.

Ele não, meaning *Not him*, meaning vote anyone but Bolsonaro, a graffiti protest that's popped up all over the city in the last few weeks. You see it sprayed on bridges and walls, inside tunnels and on the side of buses.

Beto's laughing and Fat Pedro's spitting, covering his eyes, but the aerosol's not working.

Nada, fuck all – *nothing*.

A hiss of air is the only thing it produces.

Beto pushes Fat Pedro away and tosses the can.

Fuck this, he says.

Then: something to do.

The air crackles. There's a shift. Beto can smell it.

He nudges Andre.

Hang about, he says.

What?

Queer.

Where?

Walking down the side road, see him? Carrying shopping bags, the thieving little cunt.

Where?

There, you twat.

Beto points.

Oh yeah.

Well then? Come on.

What?

Come on, you know the rules: see a queer and you have a go at him. See what he's got for us in those bags. Come on.

All right, slow down, I'm coming.

And then Beto sees the queer's T-shirt:

EleNão

And that does it. You've got to stand up, he thinks, you've got to represent your boys, your *side*.

And they're all three of them across the park and the queer sees them and he quickens –

This is not the first time Beto and his boys have gone after a flash-looking gay lad.

These queers need to know.

But it's the first time one of them is sporting the **EleNão** business.

Which is really not on.

They need to know their place and it ain't here.

Bolsonaro's all about getting rid of these scumbags, ruining our great country and blah blah blah.

And Beto is moving quicker now and the lad's done a right and gone into the park hoping he'll lose them round the back of the hedges, so Beto sends Fat Pedro gasping off round the other way, and Andre loops round, and a couple of old drunks grunt encouragement from a bench, lift their cans, but Beto ignores them, he's wound tight, he's let loose, and then they spring the lad three-ways, all of them on him in a moment, and he drops his bags and Beto's head is on his nose, and there's a crack and a yelp, and Fat Pedro and Andre are sticking it to him in the ribs, thump, thump, crack, and Beto pulls his steel and he sticks it to him, right in the neck, he feels it go in smooth, and he watches it go in and then he watches it come out, he slides it out, and Fat Pedro and Andre look at him like what the fuck and they're shaking their heads and they're primed to run but Beto's not going anywhere, he thinks, and he watches the lad bleed out, watches him stagger, watches him bleed, watches him stagger, and he gets a few yards, a couple of steps, and then Beto watches him fall.

And then, calmly, Beto walks over to him.

He lifts the queer's T-shirt. He lifts the T-shirt with its slogan: **EleNão**

Fat Pedro is hissing at him to come the fuck on.

He waves him away.

Beto lifts this T-shirt, and he takes his knife, and he scratches lines on this dead faggot's skinny chest.

He scratches two lines.

V for Victory.

He then scratches more, the six lines of a swastika, a clear, bloody swastika.

And he laughs and he laughs and he laughs.

Junior has been in the Military Police for six years now.

This doesn't quite make him a veteran, but it does mean he's been around, he's seen some shit. Like any Militar who has lasted this long, Junior has trodden a few fine lines in his time.

He stands, now, next to the flashing lights of a police motorbike. He watches the road, listens to his younger colleagues talk big. They are on duty off Avenida Paulista, top end of Rua Bela Cintra.

Today was the first round of the presidential elections and it is Sunday night quiet. They've been placed here for a specific detail –

There's been talk of a lefty protest, a gathering of students and radicals and other do-gooders on the main drag.

And if that happens, then the anarchist black blocs will turn up.

And they always enjoy a spot of decorating.

Smashing the windows of corporate businesses, spraying paint, *throwing* paint, leaving tacks on the road, smashing traffic lights, breaking into the secure cashpoints, sticking rubbish bins through the glass-fronted shops of the malls.

That kind of thing.

'Anyone does show,' one of Junior's colleagues is saying, 'it's on, right? We use whatever means necessary to bring them in, certo?'

'Whatever means necessary?' says another.

'Yeah, dickhead, *force*. We can use any appropriate force. It's a green light. It's done. We can do what the fuck we want to any mouthy prick who breaches the peace, entendeu?'

Junior says nothing. They've got enthusiasm at least, and the lad's right, too, mais ou menos.

More or less.

Bolsonaro is romping home in this first leg of the election and this gives them a bit more room for manoeuvre. He's got a pretty much hundred per cent approval rating with the Militars, unsurprising given his military career and his position on handling the criminal elements of society.

Which is: get the big Militar dogs to eliminate them.

There's an old saying in São Paulo when a crook is ironed out by a policeman or a private security guy with a gun.

It is spoken with a shrug, with indifference.

The saying: Menos um.

Meaning: *ah, well that's one less then.*

In a town like this, the only good bandit is a dead bandit.

Bolsonaro has that message nailed on, Junior thinks, and it's no surprise São Paulo is voting for him. Despite all the lefties and students and radicals and do-gooders, Bolsonaro will get this city too.

And the reason for that, Junior knows, is because a good number of the liberal, left-leaning types here are so utterly fucked off with the Workers' Party, with Lula and Dilma and all that went with it; they'd rather vote for the man Jair Bolsonaro or not vote at all.

Junior doesn't understand this, himself. Voting is a legal obligation. Not voting is a bigger admin and bureaucratic ball ache than *voting*.

It is really making a point.

They're going to regret doing that, Junior reckons.

His boys are still rabbiting.

'Point is, right, the country's ripe for change, this is a protest vote. This is a fuck Brasília vote, sabe? It's a vote for us, for the systems that exist *outside* of politics that keep the country in any sort of fucking order, yeah?'

Junior's listening and not listening, but he also thinks his younger colleague might be onto something. The lad's name is Felipe and he's a clever little fucker, and a ruthless one too.

He'll go far.

'See, what the lefties don't get is that the attempted assassination of Bolsonaro, that nut with a knife who went for him at the rally, will make him stronger. What doesn't kill you, entendeu?'

Junior reckons this is true too.

'Bolsonaro is many things,' Felipe's saying now, 'but he ain't any good in a debate, in a formal chatter with other politicians. This way, he doesn't even need to do it. It's golden. And it shows how fucking serious he is.' Felipe's laughing. 'No one can stop him. God, no less, has chosen him to rescue Brazil.'

'You don't believe that, do you?'

'Doesn't matter, a lot of people will.'

Junior sighs, shakes his head.

He's senior man here and he's decided to let them get on with it.

There's no one about. The bars are all closed, the malls were done hours ago.

It's a big space, Avenida Paulista, a monument to the financial muscle of the city, a great fuck-off symbol of power and wealth.

But on a Sunday night it's deserted.

Junior can just about make out movement at the top of Rua Augusta across Paulista, the trendy end with the decent bars and padarias, wop canteens and pizza joints probably doing a bit of business. Further down the road it's your street walkers and strip clubs, your students and your noias, those paranoid addicts.

Down a parallel road to Augusta on Junior's right is the notorious bender's paradise, the neighbourhood of Consolação. They'll very likely be in mourning tonight, he thinks, in 'Gay Caneca' the shopping mall in the area, real name Frei Caneca.

Junior chuckles at this.

Funny thing is the nickname is used with affection by those who go there and as an insult by those who don't.

Junior's not sure what that means.

It's not a neighbourhood he spends too much time in. He can't afford the swank condos that dot the hill down from Avenida Paulista, all curved glass and painted concrete. And the roads around the mall – tighter, street-corner greenery, low-rise bars and clubs – are filled by drag shows and karaoke if they're legit; and rent-boy pick-up joints at the seedier end if they're not, neon signs flashing American Bar, or, the tell tale Americana, the feminine ending indicating that this is very much a man's world.

And the mall itself is just a fucking mall, so while Junior's an open-minded young man, there ain't much for him in old Consolação.

It is what it is.

Of course, now, either way, Bolsonaro's made his stance on the

LGBTQ community, as Junior's now been told he has to call it, very clear.

The gist being parents should beat the gay out of their effeminate sons.

And yet, Junior's seen there are gay groups publicly voting for him.

It is a headscratcher, all right.

A fucking mess.

Felipe's still banging on. 'Mark my words, lads, we're in the right game at the right moment. We're – '

'Okay, chega, ne, Felipe?' Junior says. *Enough already.* 'Why don't you and your adoring audience of one take a turn round the block, eh?'

'Calma,' Felipe says.

Junior glares at him.

'We're going, Senhor, no need to get your knickers in a twist.'

Junior ignores this and watches Felipe and the other lad, Gilberto, wander off.

He's left behind with the fourth member of their detail, Rubens, nickname Chatterbox, as he says fuck all.

'You know what I like about you, Rubens?' Junior says. 'The fact you never shut up, falou?'

Rubens says nothing. Junior laughs at his little joke.

The gloom thickens a touch, cusp of night. Junior sniffs at the air. Faint dusting of smoke from fireworks, that trace of exhaust ever-present in the city –

Sunday night blues.

The evening flat, the odd sound of desperate people trying to gee themselves up a bit and finish the weekend on a high.

Good luck.

Junior turns and looks down the hill at the roads that make up leafy Jardins, an area that was as foreign to him growing up as anywhere in Europe. Swank restaurants and stores selling thousand-dollar jeans. Sedate streets. Rich couples ambling around with their tans and their smart clothes. Fast cars parked under roadside trees. The smell of decent food wafting about, Junior always notes. Not like the stench of fried meat and potatoes where he grew up. The place, Junior always thinks, smells like countryside. He wonders which way the political wind blows in the hotels and posh high-rise condos that flank the streets like a row of dominoes.

Maybe Bolsonaro is the guy to flick one and watch them all tumble down, one after another.

Domino rally. Political rally. Junior will work on this little joke, he thinks.

Then: shouting.

Junior turns and sees Felipe and Gilberto pulling a figure dressed in black: hooded top, trousers, shoes, rucksack, all black –

And Gilberto is holding up an aerosol can.

Junior sighs. Why did they bother picking this clown up? The paperwork will be a fucking ball ache.

'Senhor,' Felipe says, 'we found this bitch defacing a prominent landmark with the words Ele Não.'

Bitch. Huh.

Felipe pulls the balaclava off. The woman's eyes flash defiance.

'You'll see, Senhor, that she's also carrying political leaflets and other contraband in her backpack.'

Contraband. Junior has a rummage inside. It's kid's stuff – knocked-off cigarettes. This is a total waste of time.

He rubs his eyes. 'And you caught her in the act, did you?'

Felipe nods.

'Where exactly?'

'Two blocks down. She was giving the bookshop in the mall, Conjunto Nacional, a paint job.'

Junior nods. He doesn't exactly trust Felipe.

'She know anything about a gathering here tonight?'

Felipe shakes his head.

Junior breathes, heavy. 'Okay,' he says, 'you two take her in. I'll go and verify the damage to public property. Rubens, you wait here.'

Felipe smiles.

Rubens says nothing.

One hour later and back at base. Junior stalks the corridors. He's looking for Felipe and Gilberto. They didn't return to their position on Bela Cintra, disobeying orders.

There's no sign of them anywhere.

Where the fuck have they got to?

He tries the locker room.

He tries the rec room.

He tries the canteen.

No one's seen them, no one knows where the fuck they are, not since they brought that tasty anarchist back with –

And then that's when it hits him.

He takes the stairs double quick.

He ignores the shout of the duty officer –

He's down the line of holding cells, opening and slamming doors.

Last cell on the left.

The door closed.

The blind down.

Junior tries the handle.

The door locked.

Junior hears words –

You'll do what we say, you miscreant bitch. Hear that? Nothing. Your cowardly fucking subversive no-good friends aren't going to help you now.

Junior hears sobs –

I'm going to enjoy this.

Slaps –

That's coming off. It's all coming off.

He hears struggles –

This is V for Victory, sweetheart.

Junior shakes. Jams the door.

Barges, kicks –

The door splinters.

It gives –

Junior sees Felipe, his fingers forming a V, his tongue flicking between this V –

He sees the woman, naked, sobbing, in a ball.

There's Gilberto, his head down.

Felipe, smiling.

Last night, hours after confirmation of Bolsonaro's victory in the first round of the presidential elections, a young woman was caught by the Military Police spraying graffiti near Avenida Paulista, São Paulo. Her message: *Ele Não.* 'Not Him', a protest against candidate Bolsonaro. Meaning: *anyone but him.* She was arrested. At the Military Police headquarters, she was, allegedly, refused a phone call or lawyer, stripped naked, violently abused, thrown in a cell and left with no food and water for over twenty-four hours.

With a clear triumph in the first round now under his belt, the far-right, populist Jair Bolsonaro is campaigning to be elected as president of Brazil ahead of Fernando Haddad, the left-leaning Workers' Party candidate, a former mayor of São Paulo, and the successor to Lula and Dilma. Bolsonaro holds deeply abhorrent views on women, race, the LGBTQ community, Brazil's former military dictatorship, the use of firearms; these views are on show for all to see in his statements over the years. He is promising to unite the country, purge the corrupt leftists and fight crime with a ruthless and brutal no mercy, no leniency policy. Just weeks before the first round of elections, Bolsonaro was attacked and stabbed while speaking at a rally. He survived. It is predicted that he will win the second, and definitive, election in a landslide.

What, you may ask, is the connection between this situation and the fate of the poor woman in a Military Police cell? Or, perhaps, the answer is obvious enough.

More importantly, this question:

> *How did it come to this?*

More to follow.

Part One

WHITE DEATH

São Paulo, 2003–2006

1
Money talks

January 2003

---

*What was São Paulo like in 2003? Like it is every year: filled with
a grandiose sense of its own worth, its own self-importance. Yeah,
so Lula and the PT were elected and the left-wing buoyed, flying
on the wings of hope and optimism, and the students and the
unions and the lefties and gays and the anarchists and addicts and
the dealers and pimps and the artists and aristocrats were pretty
hopped up too. It was a good time to have a social conscience; it was
a good time to be young and forward-looking. Who knew that the
socialist paradise would mean cash-money and credit for all. Well,
not all. There was still the little something known as the São Paulo
elite, and they held the keys to the safe, a fortress in the jungle.*

Assis, 54, businessman

Detective Mario Leme is on his way down to the swank old neighbourhood of Jardim Paulistano to figure out who has whacked the headmaster of the British International School in his own home.

Leme is green and he is apprehensive.

He knows the school; who doesn't? It takes a serious amount of dinheiro, *cash*, to even consider sending your kids there.

The monthly fee is well over what Leme earns as a rookie detective in the Civil Police.

It is a closed community, in many ways, protective of itself and its interests, and he reckons they won't be tickled pink to have him poking about the place, asking awkward questions.

And on top of this, Leme's superior – Superintendent Lagnado, a squat man with a mean streak – has made it clear how this whole investigation is going to go.

'Now, Leme,' he said earlier that morning, 'I think it's pretty obvious this is a robbery-went-wrong scenario. Rich white guy tragically iced by nasty, opportunistic street thug. You shouldn't need more than a few days to sort it out.'

Leme has a feeling that this won't be the case, and he's not sure why.

Ricardo Lisboa, Leme's old friend and partner, drives. 'This is lose-lose, son.' He keeps his eyes dead ahead. A big man in a slovenly suit, he's funny, Lisboa. 'A couple of Catholic priests at a kid's party,' he says, 'is what we'll be.'

Leme doesn't doubt it and says nothing.

'Know who goes to this school?'

Leme shakes his head.

'Maluf's grandkids for a start. Mick Jagger's boy. I think the word I want is *elite*.'

Leme nods.

Paulo Maluf: one-time São Paulo mayor.

They coined a phrase for old Maluf: *Roba mais faz.*

He steals but he gets things done.

It's what São Paulo has voted for time and again.

It's more important that the city runs – the rubbish gets picked up, the metro works, the roads are repaired – than to worry about the kickbacks and shakedowns at City Hall.

But, of course, most of these kickbacks and shakedowns relate to the contracts that *enable* the city to run.

Though this might change, Leme thinks, with lefty Lula installed in office only the day before. It *might* change, yes, but when it comes to social transformation of any sort, São Paulo is a fucking mule.

'Do me a favour,' Leme says. 'Don't start.'

'It's a new beginning,' Lisboa declares.

Leme shakes his head.

Lisboa continues, 'The Workers' Party begin their reign with a hard-on for rubbing out inequality and whatnot. And the very next day, a symbol of the, you know, the *elite*, is the victim of a nasty-looking snuff job.'

Leme nods, tries not to smile.

'All I'm saying,' Lisboa says, 'is that it's poetic, know what I mean? Symmetry.'

Lisboa pulls off Alameda Gabriel Monteiro da Silva and into the low-rise, green spaces of the roads behind the school. There are women power walking, clad in expensive Lycra, dogs trotting beside them on leads. Maids and nannies dressed in white, shoulders hunched, scurry between shops, home, school. Kids kick footballs. Kids fuck about. School is *out*.

Lisboa ghosts round shallow bends, eases past glittering SUVs.

Leme spies the private security booths on every corner.

It is this kind of a neighbourhood.

Security is business, after all, and whether or not the guys stationed in the booths have any idea how to prevent crime – and it certainly hasn't helped in this case – the booths themselves, and the camera systems that flow from the booths, tend to be a pretty good deterrent.

Leme notes different security company names on different booths.

Leme clocks the house where the headmaster lives. It is *big*. The gate is green, heavy. Barbed wire bunched on top. Leme clocks the uniforms and the tape, the flashing lights and the neighbourhood gawpers, the local rubbernecks.

He points at a space. Lisboa nods, pulls over –

'Deep breaths, old son,' Lisboa says. 'Walk in the park.'

Leme spears his door. 'More like the fucking jungle, mate.'

Work. The sun beats down. Large trees form shadows on the uneven pavement. Leme runs his hand over his neck, under his collar. He wipes sweat; grime clings to him.

Leme flashes his badge. A uniform steps aside. Leme steps inside.

A dark hallway. A rectangle of light from the door. Keys on a small table. Silver cufflinks. Tasteful paintings on the walls. A small coat folded up on a chair.

Leme moves through. The back door is open. It is taped off to show *this is how it was found*, undisturbed by anyone since the night before.

Back garden. Chairs clustered around a metal table with a glass top. A barbecue in the corner, ash collected in the bottom. Leme runs his finger across the grill. Still greasy. Leme looks for signs of activity. There are light dustings of dried mud. There are small living quarters on the other side. The maid's, he assumes. To his left, a side entrance from the street. This door is locked, from the outside, Leme thinks. No sign of a key.

A helicopter buzzes overhead. Leme lights a cigarette.

Lisboa stands in the doorway to the garden.

Leme nods upstairs. 'What are they saying?'

'Early hours. Single blow. Blunt instrument, most likely. Something heavy.'

'No weapon then?'

'No sign, as yet.'

Leme nods. 'Who found the body?'

'The maid,' Lisboa says. 'She's in a fair old state.' He gestures across the garden. 'Her room.'

Leme nods. 'Anything missing?'

'His wallet is still on the dressing table.'

'Full?'

'For now.'

Leme snorts.

Upstairs. Three men in white flit around the body. They step back.

Elegantly furnished, the room is calm. The bed is ruffled. There are clothes scattered over it. On the dressing table is an open notebook next to a Louis Vuitton wallet. A stylish wooden chair lies on its back.

The light is on in the en suite. Damp towels hang over the shower rail. Toothbrush bristles damp. Clean and uncluttered.

Bedroom –

The body face down on the carpet.

A crumpled red dressing gown, slashed open and untied, revealing a pair of white Y-fronts. Thin, hairless legs bent like question marks. Arms halfway to his face.

His legs bound by a red tie at his ankles.

His hands bound by a blue tie at his wrists.

He wasn't able to protect himself.

A pool of sticky blood from a wound to the back of the head. A hairy, rounded belly, a concave chest. An odd air of virility.

Leme is green.

What hair is left is matted and stuck down, plastered over the wound. Thin strands of it are stiff, as if they would snap like icicles.

Footprints in the spilt blood clotted on the carpet.

Leme is apprehensive.

Nausea hits and Leme doubles up.

He examines something on the floor.

The sickness eases and Leme straightens.

He scans the room. He notes angles, positions of limbs. He measures, with his eyes, the distance from doorway to bed, how far the victim has fallen. With a pen pulled from his shirt pocket, Leme turns pages of the notebook. Scribblings in English, what look like dates, to-do lists. He jabs the pen into the wallet, springs it open. There are swank-looking credit cards, a fairly hefty fold of notes. Not too shabby. The wallet's clean lines and the smoothness of the leather suggest it's new. There are no identifying features, no photos of loved ones, no business cards or memberships to any clubs, nothing like that.

Leme notes how the chair landed. It was, he thinks, pushed back as the victim stood. Supposing it was the victim who was sitting there.

He nods and heads back downstairs.

Kitchen. Lisboa fiddles, bent over a coffee machine.

He looks up. 'How does this fucking thing work?'

Leme says, 'No idea, mate.'

Lisboa shakes his head. He flicks his eyes at the ceiling. 'What do you think?'

'I think the intruder came through the side entrance,' Leme says, slowly, deliberate. 'He then came through the back door. It wasn't a forced entry, though he might have jimmied the door without causing obvious distress to it. He goes upstairs. The victim is at his dressing table, writing in his notebook, or doing his makeup, counting his money, whatever the fuck he does before bed. Clothes all over it, so maybe he's having some kind of a wardrobe spring clean, you know, as you do. The intruder steps into the room. The victim stands quickly, his chair falls behind him. He takes a step or two towards the intruder, who comes towards *him*. Maybe they exchange a blow or two, or tussle, though nothing too violent, nothing too forceful, entendeu? Maybe not. The intruder threatens him. Grabs the ties from the bed. Secures his hands and legs. Perhaps he has a weapon, uses it to keep him quiet. Perhaps he simply overpowers him. Then the victim turns to try to get away, flight instinct, and the intruder nails him with a heavy blow.'

Leme pauses.

Leme is green.

Lisboa says, 'If he tied him up *before* the blow. Could have done it after.'

'Yeah,' Leme says, 'though why he'd do that, I don't know. Maybe he pulls the clothes from the wardrobe afterwards too, a cover.'

They stand, quiet.

'So, victim falls,' Leme continues, 'bleeds out, and intruder retraces his steps to leave. Either the back door was open when he arrived and so he leaves it, or he forgets to shut it in his panic. That might tell us something about the cunt's experience of breaking and entering. We'll check with the maid what the lock-up procedure is exactly.'

Leme is apprehensive.

'She says door's normally locked, but sometimes it's not.'

'Helpful. Anyway, the intruder goes out the side entrance, locking the door from the other side. Though I haven't checked for the key to confirm this.'

'No sign.'

Leme sighs. 'That sound about it?'

Lisboa nods. 'Yeah, it does, once he's in. Question is whether we can get any visual of him *getting* in.'

'You can start with those private security booths out on the street then, mate. They're looking at the CCTV back at the ranch.'

'And what are you going to do?'

Leme leans over the machine, pulls the plug and grins.

'I'm going to get us some coffee.'

Leme marches up onto Alameda Gabriel Monteiro da Silva. On the opposite side of the street, a padaria. A group of manual labourers hunched over coffee and shots of cachaça. Exhaust fumes from trucks, shunting through gears on the busy road outside. Leme orders two coffees pra viagem – *to go* – and sits tight, up at the counter. The waitress makes small talk in response to which Leme grunts. The waitress shrugs, Leme takes the coffees and leaves her a fat tip.

He crosses the road, the school on his left.

There are shouts, the sounds of children playing.

They don't even know yet, he thinks.

Whose job will it be to tell them? Well, *his*. Or at least his job to decide who does.

This is a helluva first case, he can see that already.

Not so much a fish out of water as gutted, deep fried and served up on a platter with batata fritas.

He scoots past the school.

He notes the private bodyguards outside.

The kids are kidnap targets, many of them.

They are the sons and daughters of media moguls and politicians, of businessmen and construction magnates, of lawyers and hedge fund managers, of philanthropists and rock stars.

They are the sons and daughters of an awful lot of money, of an awful lot of wealth, inherited and made.

A bodyguard half-turns, faces Leme. Leme steps to one side to avoid him. The bodyguard shapes up to speak and Leme stops.

The bodyguard holds his hands over his crotch. He's wearing aviator sunglasses. He smiles at Leme, a mean little smile. 'You're the detective, right?'

Leme nods. The bodyguard nods.

Leme holds a coffee in each hand. He gestures: *I need to get on, son.*

'Do us a favour?' the bodyguard says. 'When you get anywhere with it, give us a shout. We're all well up for helping out, yeah? We liked Senhor Lockwood.'

Leme nods. Leme scoots on. The coffees spill foam.

Paddy Lockwood, the man's name. Sounds Irish, but without the luck.

Miami airport and Ray Marx sidles onto the concourse. Ray *slides* into a seat. The hall echoes – chatter and suitcases, heels clicking on the hard floor. Ray looks right and left, checks his watch. He sees: couple minutes until the handover, a good hour before his flight –

Ray settles and checks his pockets. Money, keys, passports, a first-class ticket, one way, São Paulo. A leather grip by his feet – stylish. Travel light, light on your feet. He shapes up into the middle-distance posture, the *stare*, of international flight mode. His shoulders back, his stomach flat, his chest – firm. He eyes the arrivals board. Flights look prompt, weather tasty, disruption minimal, flight conditions – picturesque. Sun floods the hall. Clouds thin. Ray scopes shifty holidaymakers. Their trolleys weave, heavy with boosted electronic goods. On their way home, Ray thinks. Late Christmas presents for the extended família, the dozens of tías and tíos, all their feral kids, all *their* kids. Or fence the lot out the back of a dirty van. The board flashes, blanks, rearranges itself. He clocks a name: Mexico City. Landed, on time.

Ray places a newspaper on the seat next to him. No one fancies asking Ray if it's free. He's perfected that look of *don't even think about it, cabrón*. He needs the room.

Then someone picks up the newspaper, takes the seat. A squat man, sweating bullets. The man's body odour *sings* enchilada.

'Holá, Big Ray,' the man says. 'All good?'

Ray smiles. *Big Ray*. He's not small, Big Ray, but he's not big, either. He's tall – at a push. But compared to his compadres south of the border, the Sinaloan cowboys and trigger-happy beaners like the young man now sitting next to him, Ray is a fucking giant. Slim as a bean and tough as old boots – and always looking down on you, is Ray.

'Don't say that,' Ray says. 'Don't say *all good*. You're not in a fucking movie.'

'Okay, Señor Marx.' The guy makes a face. 'Como está?' he asks.

Ray cricks his neck. 'It's all there?'

'It's all good, Ray.'

Ray smiles. 'You're a heartbreaker. Now beat it, mi'jo.'

The beaner punk beats it. Ray looks down. A leather grip, the same leather grip, except a different leather grip, is now at his feet. This new, same but different, leather grip has a false bottom, and under this false bottom is stored exactly two hundred and fifty thousand US.

Seed money.

Ray's going to São Paulo to plant some seeds. And to plant these seeds, he needs some of the untraceable, out-of-circulation product that is not currently available at home. And as a former CIA operative, current associate, and now freelance fixer, Ray has ways of getting hold of uncut seed, as he calls it. Clean cash.

Ray's two martinis in and digging the view from his window seat.

'What brings you to São Paulo, hun?'

Ray turns his attentions to the stewardess. Ray is aware of what this scene looks like. He glances at the leather grip stowed at his feet. He grins. 'Money,' he says.

The stewardess fixes him another drink.

'So you're, what, a finance guy?'

'Consultant,' Ray says. 'I make things happen.'

'Huh.' The stewardess hands him his drink. She dawdles, leaning over his seat.

'How about some more of those peanuts?' Ray says.

'Coming right up, money man.'

Ray slurps martini. His teeth buzz with cold. The view stretches out and slips down –

The Atlantic coast pops.

Ray fast-tracked through gate and customs. The grip feels good, soft handles, well-balanced, nice ballast to it – excellent packing.

The airport hums. Ray's name on a placard held up by a mean-looking young man in a decent suit. Ray digs his style. He clocks the other men holding up signs with names written on them. A slovenly crew. Great big fat guys with squat foreheads and thick monobrows. Oversized peaked caps and industrial cologne. Cheap-ass suits mean shit-heap transport. You pay peanuts, you get apes, Ray thinks.

Ray says to the driver. 'Hotel Unique, amigo.'

The driver nods. Ray knows the traffic. Ray knows the route. This is opportune shut-eye time, and Ray leans back in his seat –

The Hotel Unique is aptly named.

Ray scopes the outside view. It's the shape of a ship. Ship-shape. Curved round, a flat top and portholes for boudoir windows. Ray's smiling as he checks in.

'So you'll be staying with us – ?'

'Indeterminate,' Ray says.

The receptionist looks a little panicky at this, perhaps she doesn't understand the word, can't find the right answer in front of her on the computer, her colleague frowning –

'I –'

Ray keeps smiling. 'Don't sweat it, sweetheart,' he says. 'It's all good.'

A manager appears. The manager smooth-talks the receptionist out of the way. She furnishes Ray with an embarrassed, apologetic smile. Ray appreciates this. He appreciates the effort, appreciates the acknowledgement of her mistake. It says something.

'If you'll follow me, Senhor Marx…'

Ray's room is made up. The cupboards are full. Shirts and jackets. Some jeans. T-shirts and shorts. Bathing costume. The right sort of footwear. The bathroom is kitted out exactly as he likes it. The bed is pulled tight, white and crisp. Ray stows the grip in the back of a cupboard, behind the false panel and pulls it shut with a click, feels for the lock and slips out the tiny key. He pockets the key.

Cocktail hour. The deck is teeming. Night moves –

A narrow swimming pool runs down one side. A red-purple underwater light-show gives it an exotic feel. An expensive feel.

Ray strolls the deck, which is, for once, actually a deck. A ship's deck. It's also a roof, and Ray gets his bearings. He's in a low-rise, high-cost neighbourhood. North, he sees the high-line of Avenida Paulista, skyscrapers and electricity towers flashing warnings – incoming choppers, short-hop internal flights, a row of lighthouses on helipads. To the east, a dark patch of dark green: Ibirapuera Park, he thinks. West, swank-looking pads with pools and tennis courts, outdoor spaces. South, only thing he can see is the hotel sushi bar.

He finds a seat. He orders a caipirinha. Night settles. Ray *breathes*.

Back in his room, Ray slides open the cupboard door. Ray's ready for bed, but he needs –

He has needs. He pulls the leather grip. He removes the false panel. He feels beyond the bricks of cash. There. He pulls a smart leather wash bag. He unzips it. Ray's had three caipirinhas. The alcohol *melts*. Inside the leather case: a bottle of pure-grade, medicinal-level Mexican heroin – very high quality, very hard to get hold of, very strong, not for amateurs. Ray's no addict, but he has needs, he *uses* –

This stuff is gourmet, right up Ray's alley.

Ray inserts the slim syringe into the bottle. He loads. He removes it. He squirts. He takes a rubber tube from the leather case. He wraps it around his left arm. He finds a muscle and pulls the trigger –

That'll do, son, Ray thinks.

Ray sinks into an easy chair under the porthole window. Ray feels very comfortably at sea, the waves lapping gently, the wind soft, the night air –

When Ray slips into bed, he wonders: Where am I going to find anything this good over here? He reckons he has a month – maybe three weeks – until he needs to start thinking about it.

It isn't the first time that Renata Sanchez has been into a favela, but it is the first time she's had to lie to her boss about it.

She stands outside a por kilo restaurant at a crossroads at the top end of Paraisópolis, a block down from the main road Avenida Giovanni Gronchi. She isn't hungry – she's had an early but substantial lunch with a client in Itaim not long before – but the smell of rice, beans and stewed pork is mouth-watering. She checks her phone; she is on time. The estate agent should be along any moment. He reassured her that she wouldn't have to wait for him, and that, anyway, at this time of day it's safe, of course, and, wait, don't worry, safe any time of day, really, and what, you've said you've been here before so you know, right?

Well, she *is* waiting – standing outside the restaurant as it was friendlier than the bar across the road. Rusting tables and gnarled old men with blood-eyed persistence; mangy dogs batting fleas. Not a great spot for a quick coffee. The restaurant owner glares at Renata. She is a large woman with a no-nonsense expression and a grease-spattered apron. She stands with her arms crossed, shaking her head, clicking and sucking her teeth.

Renata smiles.

'Quer alguma coisa?' the woman asks. *You want something?* 'I've got lunch, snacks.' She gestures at the plastic tables on the sidewalk. 'You can sit down then, too.'

'I'll have a coxinha,' Renata says, nodding. 'And a Coke.' She digs into her handbag for change. She thinks: yes, chicken, cheese and potato pastry with Tabasco.

The woman raises a palm, shakes her head. 'Sit down. I'll bring it over. You can pay after.' She smiles – ironic. 'You look trustworthy enough.'

Renata sits down at a table that is dangerously wobbly. She watches maids and nannies dressed in white, carrying céstas of rice and beans. Are they going to work or back home? The céstas look small, which likely means going home. These are big enough baskets for a small family; a bit threadbare for a house up the hill.

'Here.'

The restaurant owner dumps a tray with the coxinha, a bottle of Coke and a glass with a straw on the table.

'Obrigada.' Renata smiles. 'You don't have any hot sauce, do you?'

The woman raises an eyebrow and grunts.

A car is parked nearby, music blaring, and Renata glances at the flip-flopped men in dark glasses who stand around it, keeping an eye on the five dirt roads that join at the junction.

'Here.'

Renata smiles. She picks up the snack with a rough napkin from the dispenser on the table. The pastry is stringy, and warm only in parts – it has been softening and stiffening up for a good hour on the hot plate, she reckons. It's tasty though, the salt and crunch from the deep fryer, and the melted catapiry oozing, just about enough. She swallows Coke and the bubbles fizz inside her. This is pure hangover fuel; but she doesn't have a hangover.

She watches as roadworkers heft by from the bus stop, trudging home beyond the tyre shops and burnt-out cars. They carry their white helmets, their orange overalls knotted round their waists. The stink of rubbish wafts. A cloud seems to hang above where she sits. Dopey-looking, long-eared dogs nose about in the garbage, pulling out scraps. The owner growls at them, lifts a broom in an unambiguous threat, and they soon lope off.

Renata wipes her mouth, checks her phone again. The estate agent is now fifteen minutes late.

Trucks rattle past up on the main road and Renata catches the scent of the heavy exhaust fumes. Two Military Police officers stand next to motorbikes, lights flashing, hands on the guns at their sides.

It is a shortcut, this favela thoroughfare, when Giovanni Gronchi – the main road – is jammed with traffic. A shortcut for the middle class, so there's always a Military presence.

Renata isn't sure this makes the place any safer.

The Military Police is rife with bad apples. A well-armed group of corrupt enforcers, they are as naughty as the drug gangs, if the stories are to be believed.

Renata doesn't know if this is true, but the idea for the work she wants to do in the favela will certainly need cooperation from both sides.

It leaves her in an interesting position.

Life seems to unfold around her, to unwind –

Carrossos laden with rubbish, boys rolling tyres down the hill, men unloading wooden cases of fruit and beer from rusty, double-parked vans, school children meandering, slapping the bonnets of the better cars, waving into the darkened windows. Washing on lines drooped in the breeze, yellow and blue bin bags sweating, the low hum of hijacked electricity. Kids poking their heads through car windows, tongues sticking out.

She wonders if she could really come here every day. She wonders where she'd *park*. She pulls cash from her purse and gestures at the woman. The woman ambles over, less resentfully this time, Renata thinks.

'Keep the change,' she says, smiling.

'Valeu.' *Cheers.* The woman half turns, decides better of it. 'What you doing here, anyway?' she asks. Her smile is wry.

A man in a white shirt and black tie hurries towards them, waving an apology.

Renata nods at him. 'I think that's my appointment,' she says.

'Ha, good luck,' the woman says, stuffing the notes in her apron pocket.

Renata watches the man in the white shirt and black tie sweat. The shirt looks cheap and the collar and armpits are doing some serious work.

'Sorry,' the man is saying, 'this should be the right key.' He mutters: vamos, porra. *Fucksake.*

They're on the first-floor landing, and the sweating man is struggling to get them through the door.

Renata smiles, shakes her head lightly. 'Worry not,' she says.

'And I'm sorry for being late. Traffic, ne? Nightmare.'

'I know,' Renata says. 'I drove here from Itaim myself. Not far from your office, I think. Or did you come from the branch across the road?'

The man's forehead *shines.* His cheeks drip, coitado. *Poor lamb.*

'Yeah, I mean, of course.' There is a click. 'There. Got it.'

He opens the door, holds it for her.

'This way.'

He smiles, flustered.

Renata steps in and immediately thinks, yes, this'll do –

From one window the view rolls down the favela, down the crater of it, then back up to the highest point.

It is crawling, Paraisópolis, it seems, *swarming*.

The concrete, brick and wooden shacks bake in the heat, seething.

The place simmers, shivers in the fat sun, like a desert mirage, she thinks.

It is, this place, exactly what she'd imagined, hoped for.

From the other side, she looks down on the junction and up to the main road. It is like a conduit; she feels like she's standing at the frontier, the final outpost before the wild west.

She feels, immediately, that she can help people, help *someone*, from here.

'Wonderful views,' the estate agent says.

'Really are. Remind me how long until it's available.'

'Oh, a month, now.'

'And remind me why not any sooner.'

'Well,' he says. 'We call it local administration processes.'

'You mean clearing it with the police and thieves, right?'

He nods. 'That's a good way to say it.' He has regained a little composure. 'You work for Capital SP, don't you? The private bank?'

Private bank is one way of putting it. Renata is a lawyer in one of the biggest financial hitters in South America.

The reach of the hedge fund is legendary; they broker deals with private investors to secure involvement in lucrative public works, including the biggest construction projects on the continent.

Renata looks at him, sharply.

'Oh, I looked you up. Agency policy, entendeu?'

'Right.'

'Funny thing,' the agent is saying, 'one of my friends works there, same department as you, and she said, so I thought – '

'One of your friends?'

'A legal secretary, a coincidence, I mean – '

Renata nods. The only legal secretaries at Capital SP work, one way or another, for *her*.

That settles it –

'I'll take it,' she says. 'You can start getting the paperwork together.'

Rafa watches the posh, fit, white woman leave the building with a spineless-looking fuck in a suit. He's fairly sure they haven't been inside boning. He doesn't look like he's got it in him, Rafa thinks, and, besides, the chick is way out of his league.

She's world class, Rafa reckons, stylish and elegant, effortless –

You don't get ass like that in the favela.

'Rafinha! Fala aí, mano!'

Rafa turns. It's his boy Franginho asking what's up. Rafa jumps down off the pile of tyres he's sitting on and they slap hands. Franginho follows Rafa's eyes and nods down the road.

'Who's that?'

'No idea. Pulled up about a half hour ago. Had lunch at Dona Regina's. Went inside with that scatty-looking lad. Came back out.'

'E daí?' *So what? What gives?*

'Nada, you know, just keeping my eyes peeled, entendeu?'

Franginho understands. They both go to school in the mornings, which means they're done by one, which means that they can earn a little loose change as lookouts for the bosses in the afternoons. It's a piece of piss: you take note of everyone that comes and goes, you report it at the end of your shift. And if it's an unsolicited visit from the Military Police, you beep your lineman and set off a couple of fireworks.

Rafa has been doing this work since he was eleven years old, two years almost to the day, and he's never had to set off any fireworks.

He's been thinking, in fact, that things have been pretty quiet lately.

They've not seen a raid in a long time.

And there's not been any punishment meted out by the boys up the hill for even longer, Rafa thinks.

It used to be a fact of everyday life –

Some moleque pulls some shit he shouldn't, bit of thieving, maybe a drunken fight, maybe skimming a little from an income that wasn't strictly his, maybe he's bothered the wrong bit of skirt, either way, he'll end up beaten to a pulp on the street, just about breathing, if he's lucky, or dumped in the sewer, black and charred from a premature cremation, if he's not.

Happy days.

'You wanna help me out here?' Rafa says.

'Why not? I'm avoiding my grandmother.' They hop onto their tyre-pile thrones. 'That's the only pressing engagement in my diary, I believe.'

Rafa laughs. 'Well, you can just as well do that here as anywhere, ne?'

'Ain't that God's honest.'

Rafa laughs again. Franginho has always made him laugh. His way with words, his bate papo – his *chat* – is world class.

'You think I need to find out a bit more about the chick in the car?'

Franginho considers the question. 'If it means you paying Dona Regina a visit, asking a couple of questions, picking us up a couple of coxinhas, then, yeah, I'd say that's the correct protocol.'

Rafa sucks and clicks his teeth. 'Fine. You stay here.'

Franginho stretches out, lies back. 'I'm just kicking it at the beach, baby.'

Rafa jumps off the tyres and crosses the junction.

Yeah, Franginho makes him laugh, that's for sure. His nickname, Franginho – Little Chicken – was one Rafa came up with himself, years back. They were playing football in the street when Franginho dropped a shoulder, sold a stone-cold dummy, an outrageous shimmy past this fat lad Jorginho, who was left face down in the dirt. When Jorginho eventually stood up, muddied and laughing, Rafa said, 'He did the chicken dance on you there, mate. Cluck, cluck, cluck!' flapping his arms and making pecking movements with his neck, imitating Franginho's moves.

That and his stringy-looking chicken legs too, of course.

So Little Chicken it was. And here they still are, together.

A couple of old drunks at the bar wave hello, shout at him to stay out of trouble, cackle with laugher. He nods, yeah, yeah, pipe down, old man, fake smile, head lowered, flip-flops slapping on the rough road –

The little mercado is busy with women buying supplies for dinner. Even though he knows his mum won't be there, he looks out for her. Anytime he sees a group of women he looks out for her face, something he recognises, a glance of affection, of love, a smile, a gesture, a movement that might be her –

But, of course, he knows he'll never see her again. He's not stupid, he misses her is all, and it's been six years now, and his dad is doing his best and his grandma comes back to the favela every Saturday and Sunday and sorts out their little house and cooks for them and leaves their food portioned out for the week, so he's pretty well set, it's just it's not always easy –

It is *hard*.

No time to think about all that now, though.

Rafa arrives at the little restaurant. The owner is nowhere to be seen.

He bangs his fist on the counter.

'Dona Regina, bonitinha!' he yells. 'Where are you?'

She materialises, like a grumpy genie, in front of him, apron spattered with grease, hair pulled aggressively back.

She says, 'Ah, leave off, Rafinha. Not in the mood, sabe?'

Rafa smiles. 'You know you love it, Dona Regina.'

'Hmm.' She makes a face, crosses her arms. 'Get you anything?'

'Actually, Dona Regina, old Franginho and myself are in the market for a coxinha. Any chance?'

'Don't be cheeky, young man. That all?'

'Well, a tasty tin of Guaraná to wash it down with seems a good plan, wouldn't you agree?'

'Shouldn't you be in school?'

Dona Regina fishes two coxinhas from her hot plate and places them on napkins. She pulls two cans of Guaraná soft drink from inside her fridge.

'School's out for the day, ma'am.'

'You should get on with your homework,' Dona Regina points at Franginho with her chin, "stead of working with that layabout for those malandros up the hill.'

Up the hill. The bosses tend to keep themselves well out of the way, right in the thick of the favela maze. Which is why the likes of Rafa and Franginho are needed down at ground level. The chain of command, Rafa realises, literally runs up.

'They don't set us homework anymore,' Rafa says. 'It's child abuse.'

Dona Regina shakes her head. 'Can you manage all this or am I going to have to lend you a tray?'

'I can manage.' Rafa winks. 'Deep pockets.'

Dona Regina raises her eyebrows, makes a face. 'You better have, son.'

'Here.' Rafa hands her the right money. 'Keep the change.'

'Vagabundo,' Dona Regina mutters.

Rafa turns to go, stops. 'One question. Who was that woman having lunch here earlier, you know who I mean? Just now. She was *fine*, entendeu? I would like to see her around a bit more often.'

Dona Regina's expression hardens. 'I don't know.'

'Come on, you weren't talking to her?'

'She asked if I had any hot sauce.'

'That reminds me.' Rafa picked up a bottle of Tabasco from the counter. 'I'll bring it back.'

'You better.'

'No idea why she was in the neighbourhood? Didn't look like she spent too much time in the ghetto.'

'I have no idea.'

'Okay, good to know.' Rafa turns away again, looks back. 'So I'll just pass that on, yeah? That they might need to ask you themselves?'

Dona Regina sighs, shifts from foot to foot. 'Cheeky so and so,' she says. 'How old are you? Thirteen, fourteen? Too smart for your own good.'

'Thirteen. I'm in my prime.'

Dona Regina snorts at this. She softens. 'Look,' she says, 'the guy she met is an estate agent. The building they went into has vacant office space. You do the math.'

'She didn't say anything about what she wants this office space for?'

'She did not. She likes hot sauce with her coxinha. That's pretty much all I can tell you.'

'Dona Regina bonitinha, you're world class. A true heartbreaker.'

'You bring that Tabasco back and tell your friend to get his scrawny ass over to his grandmother's. She was looking for him earlier, *that* I can tell you.'

But Rafa is already walking away, his arm raised in farewell, thinking about the next bit of the day, his mouth watering at the thought of his snack and his drink, and excited to explain to his pal quite how clever he's been in his investigative work.

Dona Annette, Paddy Lockwood's maid:
  Listen.

We work with knives, gutting the small gaps between the paving, cleaning up the dirt that has gathered there. Small pieces of mud and grass lifted out and swept away as we work. We need to finish before seven o'clock and the first arrivals at school; teachers and students don't want to have to see the reality of our routine. Kitchen staff cross the enclosed area carrying large pans and singing love songs about Brazil.

'Annette,' one of the other cleaners, Maria Elisa, says. 'How's your son doing?'

I am bent over the concrete, my back aches. 'He's fine,' I say. 'Well,' I qualify, 'it's been a little while since I've seen him. He was working for a time, but he lost his job.'

'What happened?'

'He fell asleep when he was supposed to be watching the store. He was fired.'

'That's a bit harsh.'

'Well, there's plenty of people who could do the job and not fall asleep.' I feel guilty for not defending my son.

'Where was he working?'

'A shop on Teodoro. A music place, sells guitars.'

'Well, I suppose you can't fall asleep at a place like that.'

'No, you can't.' I want to continue, to feel pride, but it is impossible.

I blunder on. 'He got the job through a connection with the band he was in. Now his friend won't talk to him as he messed up the opportunity, so he has no band and no job.'

I don't mention how talented he is.

'He was playing?'

'Occasionally. Bars in Vila Madalena, the odd free show in the Centro, nothing major, but it brought in some money.'

'Samba?'

'Yes. He plays guitar and Cavaquinho. They were good. Well, I thought they were.'

Maria Elisa nods. 'Not much you can do then...' she says. 'And the kid?'

She's asking me so I can feel better about myself.

I'm grateful and smile, though she can't see me, bent over the ground as we are.

'He's great,' I say.

'Graças a Deus, my two are okay,' Maria Elisa says. 'I'm blessed with two responsible kids, adults now. Making their own way. Three beautiful grandchildren, God protect them.'

She fingers the effigy around her neck and crosses herself.

'You're blessed,' I say.

She nods and we continue in silence.

Listen.

I've worked at the school for eleven years and for the last four I have cleaned the headmaster's office as well as his house. We're told not to talk to the staff – well, not to disturb them – but Professor Lockwood is always keen to chat. He's very tidy, so there isn't a great deal for me to do. He keeps his desk free of loose papers; I often see him filing things away in the wooden cabinets at the end of the room. His desk is glass-topped and often covered in small stains at the end of the day: fingerprints, drops of ink, larger areas where he has wiped his sweaty hands. The sun pours in through the open window in the afternoons, and I can see faint yellow traces on the underarms and collars of his white shirts. He must get awfully hot rushing around the school as he does.

He rarely sits still, fidgeting at his desk. On the phone, typing at his computer, writing notes with the old-fashioned pen he keeps in the top drawer of the desk. He's amazing, they say. And I can see it. We've all heard the stories: the time he helped out a teacher with some money to pay legal fees during a difficult divorce; the administrative assistant he helped with a university place and offered to keep on as she studied; the understanding he showed at the death of another teacher's father; the regular contributions he makes to leaving presents and baby showers; the dinners he throws for the staff, even us, the funcionarios; the politeness and respect he shows to everyone who works for him. Dashing about from classroom to meeting, talking to kids, parents, teachers, administrative staff, he is always cordial, always has time to listen and never makes you feel like you're imposing. Of course, that's only what I hear and what I see. My dealings with him are minor indeed. I clean his office, keep his house tidy, cook for him, that's all.

But I'm proud to say that I do.

Nothing prepares you for death. The angle of the head. The nature of the wound. The shocked, disbelieving expression on a face. The pooling blood. The way the strands of hair and the crushed skull mat together –

A blur of procedure. Forensic reports, transcripts of interviews with the security guard and the maid, brief initial interviews with the Deputy Headmaster and Bursar at the school. No one able to illuminate very much. *Private*. That was the word they all use to describe Lockwood.

Leme thinks:

I wanted to investigate murder out of a sense of justice to the victim, doing what was right to honour their memory.

The victim is in no position to worry about all that jazz, it turns out.

The fact of death is brutal in this case. Brutal and final.

Autopsy. The doctor carves open the old man, inspects body parts, pulls him this way and that. Death is simple, relatively. Single wound to the back of the head, the blow strong enough to provoke massive haemorrhaging. Time of death placed at a little after 1 a.m. No signs of recent sexual behaviour. No signs of a violent struggle. And yet the deep marks on his wrists and ankles where he was bound by his own ties. No skin under the fingernails. No bruising. No relevant pre-existing health condition.

'He was tied up after the blow,' the doctor tells Leme. 'It's a quite different thing,' the doctor says, 'being struck when you're already on the ground. This man died on the way down.'

Leme boosts his car and heads home. The clouds thicken and the sky darkens. An oppressive heat. Dampness in the air. Leme takes Cidade Jardim and the tunnel that runs underneath Faria Lima before the heavens open. Motorcyclists careen down the middle of the two lanes, beeping and shouting. Leme out of the tunnel into thick sheets of rain. Raindrops bounce violently, windscreen wipers unable to keep up. Lanes of traffic shuffle right and left over the bridge. Leme picks left, staggers forwards. The lights from the procession of cars headed down the six-lane Marginal endless. He brings up the rear, shunts forwards into an outer lane, accelerates quickly and brakes hard as some snide fucker in a silver Merc cuts him up. Leme beeps, shouts. They all crawl forwards.

Buses loaded with passengers, faces locked into grim smiles. In the pouring rain, men hanging from the outside doors. Men eat stringy meat on sticks, sheltered from the rain under inadequate cover. Leme passes the new, unfinished bridge. Great cables run down from its top, lit up by coloured lights flashing through the rain. The bridge is a fuck-up. Leme's sure it won't do a thing to ease the traffic, will worsen congestion, in fact. Looks good though. Leme queues and thinks empty thoughts. The radio plays classic rock. Leme engages, shunts forwards, brakes.

He passes hypermarkets and building supply stores. Scores of people soaked in queues for buses. Rain runs down from the favela onto the Marginal. The water level rises. Lightning flashes above the new hotels on the other side of the river. Helicopters are blown like flies in the wind. Leme does a right, heads off the freeway, joins another queue into Panamby. Expensive apartment buildings strut their stuff, peacocking about, towering over Parque Burle Max. The rain comes down. Cars wind up the slope past the park. Leme, favela-bound, swerves right in the darkness, the car jolts, jumps on the dirt road. Almost home. He's into the garage as the rain eases. He nods at the condominium guards. He takes the elevator to the fifth.

Pulls a beer from the fridge and sits out on the balcony, watching the rain ease.

Another day.

The next morning, the sky bleeds.

Lisboa conducts interviews at the school.

Leme back to the crime scene.

No body. The space marked by dried blood on the carpet.

The clothes on the bed a crumpled heap.

In the wardrobes: clothes neatly lined up, spaces where others have been strewn about the bed. Looks like the old man was having a sort through, Leme thinks. He wonders why. If it means anything at all, new chapter, that kind of thing, like a drastic haircut.

Or the perp was using a form of misdirection, trying to confuse the scene.

Next to the bed a small table, an alarm clock and a book. The book lies open, spine out. Leme picks it up. A photograph falls from between the pages. Three young boys look up at the old man, smiling.

On the chair facing the bed, more clothes, ties. The wallet and notebook still on the dressing table next to the expensive after shaves and lotions. In gloves, Leme picks up the notebook. Numbers scribbled down on the first page.

He slips it into a plastic sheath, pockets it.

In the bathroom: faint dusting from fingerprints on the side next to the sink.

Downstairs –

The bookshelves bulge. Biographies and history; fat things with broken spines and yellow pages. The hallway dusty and empty.

Leme cracks the door. The sun pours in, heat on his face and neck.

A woman walks a dog. She stares, brazenly, into the space behind the door.

Leme glares at her, shakes his head. She looks away and hurries on up the road.

Leme and Lisboa sit in the headmaster's garden. It is becoming an office from the office. They drink coffee at a glass-topped table. The garden is neat but lacks love: it doesn't look like gardening was a hobby of this Lockwood fella. The plants look sad, the flowerbeds cleared –

'It's miserable over there,' Lisboa says. He gestures towards the school. 'I thought your British sensibility was all about a straight bat on a sticky wicket, keeping your pecker up, and that – what's the phrase?'

'Stiff upper lip.'

Lisboa sips coffee. 'There's a lot of wailing and gnashing of teeth going on.'

'Mate, most of the students and at least half the staff are Brazilian.'

'Still, you know, British imperialism.'

Leme smiles. 'They know what happened yet?'

'Do we?'

'Fair point.'

'And no,' Lisboa says, 'they don't, not exactly anyway.'

'Not exactly?'

'Put it this way, I've not been shouting about the state of the old man's bonce.'

Leme nods.

Lisboa says, 'Though they might not be letting on, entendeu? Tricky balance, that – curiosity and fear. I'm not sure I'd be asking tricky questions, put it that way, if the boot were on the other arsehole, entendeu?'

Leme smiles, shakes his head. 'You learn much else?'

'Not really.' Lisboa examines his notebook. 'He was popular. He was good at his job. He lived alone. He didn't socialise much outside of work or work-related events. His family never visited him. He had a good relationship with pretty much everyone in and connected to the school. No one seemed to know what he got up to in his spare time, his extracurriculars, as they say.'

Leme smiles.

Lisboa says, 'General consensus is that when he wasn't working, he was at home, living a quiet life.'

'Your basic workaholic.'

'É isso aí.' *Exactly that.*

'There's got to be something more.'

Lisboa makes a face.

Planes crawl across the sky. The heat thrums above them. The garden remains cool. There is a crackle of electricity. Kids playing nearby.

It is, Leme thinks, peaceful.

Leme says, 'Strikes me we've two places to start. First thing is find the murder weapon.'

'Not turned up here?'

Leme shakes his head. 'We're going to have to widen that search.'

'Yeah, they probably took – '

'Do me a favour,' Leme says.

Lisboa raises his palms. 'You're right, not helpful. Just thinking authorisations, departmental resources, all that palaver.'

Leme ignores him. 'Second thing is find out why local private security didn't see anyone going in or coming out.'

Lisboa nods.

'And more than that, even,' Leme says, 'why no one can find anything on the fucking CCTV, both on the system *inside* the house and our public guardian outside on the street.'

'Huh.'

'Some sense of these questions and start thinking about motive, entendeu?'

'What *is* missing, do we even know that?'

Leme nods. He cocks an eyebrow, nods at the back door. The maid approaches.

She's wearing white and brandishing a piece of paper.

She keeps her eyes down and her back hunched.

'She's been doing an inventory,' Leme said. 'We'll find out right now.'

'Maybe we don't widen that search, after all, ne?'

'Yeah,' Leme says. 'I'm hoping item one is the family cricket bat.'

The maid leaves the inventory with Leme and goes back into the house to make coffee and pão de queijo – cheese bread – and then

---

comes back and sits quietly, her hands in her lap, her head bowed, waiting to do what she is told.

Leme picks up one of the cheese breads. 'It's kind of you, but, to be honest, I never liked pão de queijo.'

'I'm sorry, Senhor, I didn't know.'

Leme smiles. 'Of course you didn't.' He tosses the cheese bread to Lisboa. 'Not to worry, they won't go to waste.'

'Easy, son,' Lisboa says.

Leme continues. 'No, I've never been partial. Part of the reason might be I had a friend once who didn't like them either.'

'Sim, Senhor?'

'Yeah, we nicknamed him Pão de Queijo he hated the smell so much. Funny kid, he was, moleque, entendeu?' A *cheeky punk* is the implication.

'Sim, Senhor.'

'Any time anyone had any, we'd chuck it at him.'

Lisboa laughs.

'Rub them under his nose, that kind of thing. Drove the moleque crazy.'

'Sim, Senhor.'

'He was a good kid, gente boa, a real close pal.' Gente boa: *good people*. 'You know how it is when you're kids. When you've got a little gang going, ne?'

'Best time of your life.'

'We ruled our neighbourhood. At least we thought we did.'

'Sim, Senhor.'

'Thing is, I moved schools, right. And we drifted, our little gang. You know how it is, it happens.'

'It is what it is, porra.'

'Sim, Senhor.'

Leme leans forward. 'But I didn't leave the neighbourhood, not exactly. And one day, when I was about thirteen, my old friend Pão de Queijo tried to rob me, mug me, sabe? Um assalto. He was with a new little gang and that was their thing, apparently, street crime. What they thought they'd get from a kid like me I do not know. But you know, something to do, ne?'

'What happened?'

Leme looks at Lisboa. 'Nothing, he recognised me in time. We had a good laugh about it.'

'It's a funny story.'

'Yeah, it's funny, it's also profoundly depressing.' Leme eyes the maid. 'Know why?'

'No, Senhor.'

'We grew up near the favela, Paraisópolis. Know it?'

The maid nods. 'Sim, Senhor.'

'Well, you likely know they don't appreciate petty street crime in or around Paraisópolis as it disrupts the rhythm of the rather more lucrative, and therefore rather more important, drug trade.'

'Sim, Senhor.'

'And you know who I mean by *they*, ne?'

The maid nods.

Leme takes a sip of his coffee. 'Last I heard, old Pão de Queijo was relieved of his duties. Ironed out.'

'A shame,' Lisboa says.

Leme eyes the maid again. 'I mean, you think you know someone, sabe? Then that happens, turns out your old pal is a two-centavo thug. People change; or perhaps they don't.'

'Sim, Senhor.'

'Paraisópolis, sabe?' Lisboa says.

The maid looks down.

The distant growl of heavy traffic. Sunlight clear, yellow skies. The judder of construction, the weighty cough of a heavy drill. Shadows move inside.

'Cheap-ass favela kicks, what are you going to do, ne?' Leme says. He shifts in his seat and faces the maid, square on. Jaw set, eyes dead ahead. 'You're from the favela. When did your patron here move you out?'

'Four years ago, Senhor.'

'You've lived here since then?'

'Sim, Senhor.'

Stewed pork wafts. Onions sizzle.

'Where's your room?'

———

The maid points across the garden.

'And that's where you sleep, where you live?'

'Sim, Senhor.'

'What time do you normally finish in the big house?'

'I cook dinner and leave it on the stove. I'm out of the house before Senhor returns from work. Six o'clock, most days, I'm in my room.'

Leme nods. 'And in the mornings?'

'I wake at 5 and straighten the kitchen and make breakfast. Senhor comes down at around 6.30. Yesterday morning – ' she chokes back a tear ' – he didn't.'

'So you went upstairs?'

'Yes.'

'But you wouldn't normally.'

'Not when Senhor is in the house.'

'From your room,' Leme says, 'can you hear anything? Is there any way of knowing if there's anyone else in the house, if he has guests, parties, entendeu?'

The maid shakes her head.

Leme nods. 'Well,' he says, to himself, as much as anyone else, 'we can test that out, of course.' He pauses. 'What about weekends?'

'Weekends I visit my son, my grandson.'

'He didn't mind?'

'Senhor insisted.'

'Good for him.'

The maid heaves dry sobs.

Leme says, 'And where does your son live?'

'Paraisópolis.'

'Alone?'

'With *his* son.'

Leme breathes. 'Well,' he says, 'I don't want to seem insensitive, querida, but I suspect that you might have to move back to the jungle.'

The maid nods. Lisboa passes her a tissue.

'But for now you stay put, certo?'

The maid nods again.

'We're going to need to talk some more. I'll let the school know you're not going to compromise the – the big house, okay? That way you're on hand for the next couple of days, at least. Make sense?'

The maid nods.

They sit in silence for a beat.

Leme says, 'How well did you know him?'

The maid looks down. 'Senhor was very kind to me. That's all I know.'

Leme nods. He glances at Lisboa whose expression says: *it checks out*.

'Get some rest, eat something. We'll talk again later today, go through the inventory.'

'Sim, Senhor. Obrigado, Senhor.'

The maid shuffles off towards her room.

Lisboa says, 'If she has any idea whatsoever about what might have happened, then I'm an Irishman.'

Leme laughs. 'You hungry?'

'Does the Pope shit in the woods?'

Ray's first day is a cinch. The hotel breakfast: abundant –

They send a car and Ray sits back and enjoys the fifteen-minute commute. They set him up in an office and fetch refreshments. Twenty-third floor. The view *spins*.

Ray's examining the refreshment tray when his point man and Capital SP region head Dave Sawyer walks in.

'Hello, Huck,' Ray grins.

'I haven't heard that one for a while.' Dave nods, smiles – broad. 'Everything okay, guy?'

Ray nods at the tray. 'Not sure there's quite enough pastries.'

Dave laughs. 'You oughta be careful, the food here, I must have put on fifteen pounds.' He runs his hand over his belly. 'Well, you know, maybe a half dozen. It's quite a spread. Wait until you see lunch.'

They both face the window. The city rolls away from them. Gridlock and chaos. Ray thinks: *concrete jungle never felt so apt*.

Dave says, 'You get your bearings?'

Ray points. 'Hotel's down there.' Ray points again. 'My desk's over there.'

'It's good to see you, Ray.'

'Why am I here, Dave?'

Dave gestures at a meeting table and two chairs. 'Coffee?'

Ray nods. Dave fixes them two espressos and they sit.

Dave says, 'Why do you think you're here, Ray?'

'I'd say it has something to do with the shift in government that this fine country has recently undertaken.'

'And?'

'And you wanna know whether this change in direction is going to work, cash-wise.'

Dave nods.

Ray says, 'My question isn't so much why I'm here, it's more like who's idea was it.'

'What do you know about the new government?'

'Left-wing messiah, this Lula. Trade union guy, like a Teamster with a conscience. And some serious clout. Wants to change the world. He gonna?'

Dave takes a sip of his coffee. The a/c hums. It's cold as a mother-fucker. Though Ray is not ungrateful. The brief walk from hotel lobby to car – all of six or seven paces – caused his neck to prick with sweat and his crotch to melt.

'He made a lot of promises. People make fun of him as his Portuguese is pretty, what would you call it, rustic, I guess. But he's got the popular touch, that's for sure. And his big beef is inequality.'

'Which means cash.'

'Yup.'

Ray nods. He fiddles with his coffee cup.

Dave says, 'There's word he's going to implement a big anti-poverty scheme, a conditional transfer type of deal.'

'Cash for the poor in return for what?'

'School attendance, vaccination, I don't know what else, civic responsibility.'

Ray shrugs. 'Clever plan.'

'Maybe.'

'It won't cost much to make a lot of desperate sons of bitches feel pretty special.'

Dave grunts.

'And,' Ray says, 'the conditional aspect – the *terms* – has some serious long-term growth potential.'

'What we're thinking.'

'So why do you need me?'

Dave smiles. 'It's not your first rodeo, Ray.'

'It is not. But that doesn't answer the question, cowboy.'

'We want you to solve poverty in Brazil, soldier. Why the hell else you think we brought you here?'

Ray laughs. 'So the answer to my real question is it was you.'

'Yup.'

'And a left-wing messiah doesn't preclude some heavy business, some major bank. You wanna know the cash ramifications in response to whatever political currents are flowing. And how we – how *you*, excuse me – can keep a step or three ahead.'

'Like I say, it's not your first rodeo.'

'And I got complete access in here and deniability outside?'

Dave opened his arms. 'You're a consultant, Ray. A numbers guy, no one understands what it is you do exactly, you're Russell Crowe in that movie.'

'*Gladiator?*'

'Ha,' Dave stands. 'Let me know there's anything you need.'

Dave heads to the door. Dave turns back and says, 'See you at lunch, on twenty-four, big dogs only. Trust me, the spread, it's something else.'

Ray nods. This first day, he thinks, is a cinch.

Ray decides to skip the big dog lunch and scope the neighbourhood a little. Ray's a wolf, after all. He's only half-joking, but he knows it.

He pockets shades. The elevator whisks him down. He waves away reception's offer of a car. Ray wants to figure his beat. He likes to vibe the street. Ray's looking for a beer and a snack, and a sense of what they'll make of him over here. The sun hits like the flash of a torch in the eye on a black-night tail-job. Ray-Bans on, Ray's shades: Ray's *Rays*.

He makes a left out of the office. He's on Avenida Paulista, the financial artery of São Paulo, of Brazil, of Latin America. Glass and girder. Towers of power. To his right, the spider-legged red frame of the art gallery he's heard about. People scurry underneath, selling tat, begging. Wide-berth it. He makes a left, aiming for a parallel road, trying to find some neighbourhood. He passes a dingy-looking park, thick trees and crap all over the ground. Looks a likely hotspot for cover-of-darkness deeds, not Ray's bag that, though. He makes another left and heads so he's pretty much facing the backside of the beast, the Capital SP building. He looks up. It is a *long* way up.

The first thing Ray's noticed: people on the street do not look up.

Ray sweats. His white shirt is loose, cotton, two-buttons shy of the neck, sleeves rolled neat. And yet. It's the kind of heat is the thing, Ray thinks. Comes from all sides, the smog and the sun, hits from the ground up. Concrete, Ray knows the science. Makes for a pretty fucking far from refreshing lunch break.

Ray spies a bar on a corner. There are red plastic tables outside, maybe four or five. Red plastic chairs. A handful of office workers lounge. Inside, the lights bright, harsh. Ray's shades stay on. There are a couple of sour-faced drunks slurring in the corner, picking at a plate of fried something or other. Everyone's drinking from these tall bottles. A greasy waiter in a dirty white smock appears.

'Senhor?' he asks.

Ray jerks a thumb. 'Fora, okay?' *Outside.* 'Cerveja. Obrigado.'

The waiter mooches. Ray steps back out and nestles into a red plastic chair. The legs feel ominous. There's a definite bend to them. Big Ray does not want to come a cropper at this early stage of proceedings, he thinks, only half-joking with this little running commentary, this calling of the game.

The waiter leaves a large beer and a tiny glass on the table. The table wobbles. Ray serves himself what is little more than a fucking shot of freezing lager. It tastes *good*. Ray pours another shot, lets it settle, tips it back.

Ray watches. There's a light buzz in the heavy air. Laid-back chatter. That sacred hour off, Ray thinks. They hit the office early in this city, Ray's learned that. A lunchtime beer to take the edge off seems a fair trade.

Ray clocks a Capital SP lanyard on the next table. The table seats two men, late-twenties, Ray guesses, though hard to tell these days, and a woman of around the same age, perhaps older: it's hard to distinguish youth from *actual* youth, he thinks.

Ray pulls his own lanyard from the top pocket of his loose, cotton shirt. Ray holds it up. Ray says, 'Speak English?'

All three at the table examine Ray from behind their own expensive sunglasses. The woman says, 'Only American, actually.'

The two men laugh. Ray laughs. The power dynamic is clear, given Ray's age and the distinction he carries about – and *in* – his person, so it shows some style, this woman's joke.

Ray points at his bottle. 'This the right one to drink?'

The two men jabber something about different beer brands. Ray doesn't listen.

'This a standard sort of a lunch?' he asks.

'Only when it's hot,' the woman says.

Ray smiles. He gestures at the street, the buildings. 'The sun shines long on the concrete jungle.'

They all sip their drinks.

The woman says, 'You're Ray Marx.'

'I am.'

'We've heard about you.'

'Have we?' Ray says. 'I wonder why.'

The woman smiles. 'We were told to keep out of your way.'

'Were you told why?'

The woman and the men shoot each other looks.

'I suspect,' Ray says, 'it was a well-intentioned piece of advice.'

One of the men says, 'Can you tell us why?'

Ray shakes his head. Ray grins. He fingers his pockets for change. He leaves a few notes on the table.

He kills his beer and stands. He tips an imaginary hat. 'See you next time it's hot out,' he says.

Back in his office, Ray rifles desk drawers. He pulls a strip of tablets. No-nonsense prescription meds. Serious heft to these boys so he does a half. He'll take the other half pre-drinks. He's heard the pharmacies stock these babies at a premium rate, half the dollar you'd need on your health insurance. Happy days.

The sweat on his back cools with the ferocious a/c and the meds-beer lunch he's enjoyed. The refreshment tray has been refreshed. There are – what are these – empanadas? Ray pops two: one meat, one cheese.

Ray's chair is one of those ergonomic things. He plays with the settings. He adjusts to low-rider. The chair accommodates. The chair *welcomes* Ray. He spins and takes in the view. The sky shimmers. The heat makes waves. *Make hay while the sun shines*, Ray thinks. He's here to plant seeds, after all. Harvest the fuck out of the place. You reap what you sow, young man, do you not?

Make Ray while the sun shines.

Ray's examining the two reports he had delivered that morning, reports that he requested. The first is a simple list of all entities – individual and corporate – that hold Capital SP private finance privileges in the region. The second is a basic overview of the deposits and withdrawals that these individual and corporate entities have made over the last five years. Ray joins dots. It's not a complicated pattern to discern. Money arrives in entity form; but a lot more of it goes out on a no-name, numbered account, individual basis. Ray's weighing these fluctuations against the whole country's economic performance, as measured by the World Bank, at year-long intervals. And he's measuring *this* against political polls, as well as unemployment statistics.

It is grunt work, but Ray digs it. The numbers flash and roll –
The office is a fish tank.
Ray swings, Ray sways in the a/c current –
The window glass so thick the outside world is an idea.
Ray's wrapped in numbers –
Numbers wash over Ray.

Ray's conclusion: when the country is objectively worse off, Capital SP investment and dividend payments spike.

Roughly speaking, that is. Right-wing or left-wing, it doesn't seem to matter too much which way the wind blows, on some levels. But conservative with a small 'c' is definitely a factor, in terms of the interests of his fine employer, Capital SP.

Ray sees where he might fit into this picture.

2
Police and thieves

January 2003

---

*The only thing you need to know about São Paulo in 2003
is that the TV sexologist we voted in as mayor, not two years
before, turned out – surprise, surprise – to be a whore.*

Maria, 38, administrator

Anna's first day in her new job is confusing. Technically, it's the
first day of her *first* job, she thinks, and wonders if that's why it's
confusing.

What she's actually wondering is if she belongs here at all.

Here being City Hall.

Here being assistant to chief political aide to São Paulo's new
mayor, Marta Suplicy, representing the Workers' Party.

Here being the first day that this administration – which has run
São Paulo City Hall since 2001 – will work explicitly in tandem
with the president of the country, Luiz Inácio Lula da Silva, 35th
President of Brazil, and leader of the same Workers' Party that Marta
represents.

What's confusing is that you'd think this would be a day of
celebration.

You'd think that a clear, united front between the capital of South
American finance, the economic heartbeat of the country, and the
corridors of power in Brasília would be a moment to cherish, a
moment to effect real political and social change.

Anna certainly thought this. She was geared up to start.

But it's mid-morning and so far all she's done is listen to her colleagues bitch and gossip.

And she's trying hard to keep up.

It seems that most of the chat is about sex.

It's an open plan office and Anna sits at an island of three desks right in the middle, no window nearby, so no view, and no peace and quiet as the island is on pretty much everyone's route to the kitchen on one side of the office, or the bathroom on the other, and there is a constant stream of traffic.

Anna shares the island with her two colleagues, Franco and Martina, and neither of them is yet to speak more than six words to her. Anna's boss's secretary has provided Anna with login details and a paper database of party members and supporters that Anna is to input into an Excel spreadsheet.

It is not inspiring work.

'I'm telling you,' Franco is saying, 'I don't think she's doing the right thing. Marrying Rasputin is, like, not an option. She just can't.'

Martina makes a face at this and shoots Franco a look that says: *not here.*

Rasputin, Anna has gathered, is the nickname of Marta Suplicy's new lover and, now, husband-elect.

He is known as Rasputin as he is a behind-the-scenes guy, a shadowy campaign advisor and former aide whose name, Luís Favre, betrays his Argentinian provenance.

This has not enamoured him to the Brazilian public.

Marta was elected in 2000 and took office in 2001. She was inspiring and poised and beautiful. As soon as Anna graduated college, she volunteered for Marta's team, distributing leaflets, filing, that kind of thing.

And after Lula and the PT won the presidential elections, there was room for Anna to get a real job.

She looks now at the transcript of the first words she heard Marta speak, the night of her victory:

In the last eight years São Paulo was pulled apart, filth permeated all parts and the city became the image of abandonment. Its people were

*humiliated by corruption, demoralised by lacking education and
health, disillusioned by their capacity to rein in the destruction of all
places of civilised community life. I am a woman and people are very
disillusioned with men. I am known for being frank and honest. Our
research is saying that the men have had their turn, let's see what the
women can do. I thought that I would only be a candidate in 10 years'
time, because I thought people would have to get used to the issues
that I was campaigning for. But these issues gave me great visibility.
They gave me an image of someone who would fight for rights.*

Martina hisses at Franco to shut up. Franco is badmouthing Marta's
ex-husband, Senator Eduardo Matarazzo Suplicy.

Martina thinks this is a bad idea, that it's not their place and if
someone overhears them, well, it's not going to be her fault.

'Pussy,' Franco says.

This puts an end to the conversation.

Anna knows it's not been an easy year for the mayor.

The fact that her career started in the eighties, on daytime TV,
giving advice on erectile dysfunction among other things, has not
made it especially hard – forgive the pun, Anna thinks – for the
media to really go to town on her marriage breakup.

Mr Suplicy remains a powerful senator and Marta's political
sponsor.

He has presidential ambitions, everybody knows that.

So when Marta announced presidential intentions of her own and
made it clear she was staying neutral in her husband's race, a lot of
people figured their marriage was more Hillary and Bill than Sonny
and Cher.

Though it was exactly this kind of thing that made Anna want to
work for Marta.

And it's hardly new, this brand of political treachery.

Marta's predecessor, Celso Pitta, was ruined when his wife left him
and accused him of overseeing a network of corruption.

The city was something like ten billion in debt when Marta took
the reins.

And it didn't help when her municipal sanitation officer was caught greasing the wheels – and his own palm – so his former employer could win a major garbage collection contract.

And which senator do you think endorsed the investigation?

Yep, that's right, the former Mr Marta.

Bit snide, that, at the end of the day.

One thing Anna reminds herself, now, sitting at her desk, tapping numbers into boxes, is the very important fact that it was Marta who left the marital home, Marta who abandoned the powerful and extremely wealthy Senator Eduardo Suplicy.

Yes, Anna thinks, Marta really is an inspiration.

And Anna is very happy to be here.

Anna saves her work, stands.

'Where are *you* going?' Martina says.

'Bathroom, querida.' *My dear.* 'Need anything?'

As Anna walks away, she hears Martina mutter, '*Querida*? Punchy.'

Ray takes the lift from high up in Capital SP towers down a few floors to the lesser mortals. He's got a zing in his step thanks to the meds and a clear head thanks to the pure espresso shots he's been nailing at ten-minute intervals for the past hour.

And he's got an idea.

He locates legal, floor nineteen. He's looking for a secretary Huck Sawyer recommends. He doesn't want to speak to any of the actual lawyers –

He wants the word to get back to them on its own.

He scans the floor layout, scopes an obvious underling sitting far enough away from the glass-fronted offices of the three or four key members of the legal team.

The underling looks busy. She's bent over paperwork and sighing, passive-aggressive. She doesn't look like she gets much help from her colleagues, which Ray thinks is perfect for his intentions.

Ray stands in front of the desk. It takes her a moment to realise he's there.

'Hi,' Ray says. 'I'm Ray Marx. How's your day going today?'

'Um,' the underling is confused, it amuses Ray to notice, by the question. 'It's... going, ne?'

'It's going,' Ray repeats, nodding, trying out the phrase.

The underling smiles. 'Sorry, a translation from Portuguese. If something's "going" it means it's, well, it's *going*, nothing else to report, entendeu?'

'Eu entendo,' Ray says, smiling. *I understand.*

'Oh, you speak Portuguese?'

'Only a little. Your English is very good.'

'I studied in the States.'

'Oh yeah, where?'

The underling smiles. 'Dartmouth.'

'Huh,' Ray says. 'Go Big Green. What's your name?'

'Fernanda.'

'I was thinking you might be able to help me, Fernanda,' Ray says. 'Bit of legal research.'

'That's my job.'

'And you know who I am?'

'I know that it's part of my remit now to help you with legal research.'

Ray grins. 'Key thing is you don't tell anyone else exactly what you're doing for me.' Ray rolls his neck, narrows his eyes. 'That something you'd have a problem with?'

Fernanda nods at the space around them, the quiet. 'Does it look like I get consulted on much, asked for my opinion?'

'Outstanding,' Ray says. 'What I need is a profile, a thorough profile, of Luís Favre. Know who he is?'

Fernanda nods.

'As much as you have on him, professional and personal, okay?'

Fernanda nods again.

'Just a single typed page, keep it concise, and don't save the file on your computer, for heaven's sake.' Ray grins. 'I'll be back later to pick it up.'

'It'll be sitting on my desk.'

'Good woman,' Ray says.

Renata watches Ray Marx talking to Fernanda from the elevator. *What the fuck does he want with her?*

Fernanda, Renata is now sure, is the colleague who knows her real estate guy. She needs to find out how much Fernanda knows. Watching her talking easily with *Senhor* Marx, she wonders if her strategy – bluff, misdirection, disingenuousness – is the right one, and perhaps she should just pull rank and threaten her.

Ray's walking towards her. Renata pretends to examine her phone. She doesn't want Marx to see that she's going to be the next person to speak to Fernanda.

Ray's smiling as he approaches her. 'Well, well,' he says, 'you again.'

'Hello,' Renata says. 'I didn't expect to see you this close to the ground.'

Ray looks out the window and whistles. 'Pretty high up,' he says.

'They don't open for a reason, querido.'

Ray's nodding. 'I guess we won't know then, what with the a/c and whatnot.'

'Know what?'

'Whether it's hot enough out for a lunchtime beer.'

'I guess we won't.' Renata puts her phone into her handbag. She smiles at Ray and gestures at the lift, arms wide. 'Which floor, Senhor?'

Ray grins. 'Very good,' he says. He pushes twenty-three.

Renata sees Fernanda see *her*, and then duck her head to her work. She doesn't want me to ask her about Big Ray Marx, she thinks. Well, I'm not going to – yet.

'Hello, Fernanda,' Renata says. 'Tudo bem?' *Everything well?*

'Tudo, você?' *Everything is well, yes, you?*

'I am very well, thanks.'

Renata and Fernanda are a little wary of each other and Renata knows why. They are roughly the same age – Renata is thirty; Fernanda just shy of – have similar backgrounds, a similar sort of education, and yet, technically, Renata is Fernanda's boss.

Truth be told, neither of them especially likes this fact.

Renata finds it awkward asking Fernanda to undertake tasks that she knows are administrative at best and menial at worst. She knows that, sometimes, these tasks are an insult to Fernanda's intelligence.

But what is Renata supposed to do? It wasn't her decision to employ someone clearly overqualified to work as a legal secretary. It's a bind.

Though she knows that Fernanda doesn't blame her. Fernanda's frustration is saved up for Renata's bosses, but, of course, a little of it spills over for Renata too. From time to time. It's awkward for them both.

All of this is in Renata's mind, and in the drab little exchange they're now having – you okay? I'm okay, you okay? – a solution presents itself.

'So,' she says, 'something I wanted to discuss with you.'

'Okay.'

Renata glances around the office space.

It is quiet, no one around, doors closed. She can hear muffled phone calls, the tap-tapping of computers, the buzz and beep of printers, the ringing of phones.

Fernanda looks a little tense, Renata thinks, like she's making too hard an effort to appear nonchalant.

But that's likely the Ray Marx business, whatever that is.

Which will have to wait.

Just say it.

'I think I might have met a friend of yours,' Renata says. 'Works in real estate.'

A look flashes across Fernanda's face, her eyes widen a touch. Renata thinks: she knows *something*, but she doesn't know what she knows – yet.

Fernanda says, 'Yeah, I think so. Aurelio, ne? Nice guy.'

'He seems to be.'

'He is.'

Renata nods. 'Did he tell you how we met?'

Fernanda shakes her head.

Renata knows this is a strategic white lie and she appreciates it. She leans in a little closer.

'I went to visit a property he represents, office space, in Paraisópolis, the favela, sabe?'

Fernanda nods. 'The favela,' she says. 'This something for work?

I didn't know we had any dealings in that kind of thing, pro bono and whatnot.'

This is a clever way of phrasing it, Renata thinks.

She's always been sharp, Fernanda.

Renata has been at Capital SP for seven years, straight out of law school, worked her way from trainee, to junior, to associate.

Fernanda joined four years ago and hasn't been promoted, still sits at the same desk.

The first time the two of them found themselves at a social do, an out-of-office-hours client dinner, Fernanda said to Renata: 'We're not going to be friends, you know. Colleagues is quite enough. In a nice way, claro.' *Of course.*

Thing was, she did put it in a nice way, it was a friendly remark, and in the context, quite funny, enough irony for them both to laugh, but not too much that they didn't acknowledge the truth contained within it.

And clever that she'd said *colleague*. Renata had admired that. Really established how this working relationship was going to work.

Renata smiles. 'You're right to think that. Why would we involve ourselves, ne, in something like that? I don't suppose there's ever been anything you or I have done here that would suggest that we might.'

Renata feels herself rambling, her words tumbling out too fast. But she's pleased with the idea of collusion, of partnership, that she has implied.

'I guess not.'

Renata is, of course, telling the truth, too. They are the legal department of a prestigious and inordinately wealthy private investment bank and hedge fund. One that maintains a sort of exclusivity and mystery due to its relatively small size.

And while Capital SP is well-known for its philanthropy, it's a philanthropy that is measured out in donations, lump sums of cash, and not in community outreach programmes, or anything, in fact, that takes its employees outside of Capital SP towers for any reason other than the further generation of wealth.

'So I suppose you're wondering why I was there?'

———

Fernanda nods. 'I mean,' she says, 'only in the sense that you seem to want to tell me.'

Renata smiles. 'Well put.'

Fernanda smiles and settles a little.

'I'm looking into an opportunity,' Renata says, 'and I think that, consequently, there might be an opportunity for you.'

'What kind of an opportunity?'

'A job.'

Fernanda raises her eyebrows. *Go on then, I'm listening.*

'Put simply, I am looking to leave Capital SP and set up a legal-aid office in Paraisópolis. I have the seed money from a couple of our clients who are looking to diversify, an investment which includes a fairly significant amount for salaried employees.'

'*Diversify*? Interesting term.'

Renata does not miss the tone; she is well aware that Fernanda knows all about the tax benefits of ploughing money into socially conscious projects like this.

What Renata doesn't add is that Capital SP has a very profitable sideline in private equity, too, the old mortgage-the-company-and-flip-it approach – offset interest payments against tax, borrow billions to buy underlying companies, while securing the loans on the underlying company's own assets –

Successful NGOs are ripe: they offer mortgageable property, plus regular cash revenue payments.

The cleverest way that Capital SP has found is if this regular cash revenue, this *income* – which is tax deductible in a philanthropic loophole – comes from a different wing of the same company that is mortgaging it to the hilt for short-term profit.

It means Renata is secure, and that means she can do good, so, in the end, she can turn a blind eye here.

She's not even really supposed to know.

Renata shrugs. 'It is what it is, and the benefits…'

'Are risky.'

'Yes, there's risk. But it's worth that risk. I'm done with processing contracts to help people get even richer.'

'We do more than that.'

'You know what I mean.'

'Right, I think so. You told anyone else about this yet?'

'Nope.'

'Interesting.'

'Here's the thing, Fernanda,' Renata says. 'Well, two things. You keep quiet about this and I can recommend you for the position I'm vacating.'

'Recommend?' Fernanda laughs, but not in an unpleasant way. 'I suppose you might have some influence, I'll give you that.'

'Point is I'll use all I do have, you keep this to yourself.'

Fernanda draws two fingers across her mouth. *Lips. Sealed.*

'You said two things,' she says.

'Yeah, well, the other thing is you come and work with me.'

Leme and Lisboa are back at Lockwood's house talking to the maid.

The maid, they've discovered, is called Dona Annette.

Dona Annette is nervous.

Leme thinks this is most likely as she is shortly going to have to move out of her cushty little set-up and go back to her family shack in the favela.

Leme is doing his best to be sympathetic.

The problem is, he has to be realistic, which means that Dona Annette has to face up to this unfortunate fact.

At least she has somewhere to go, Leme thinks.

Being straight with her is a form of sympathy –

Tough love.

Of course, there is another reason she should be nervous: with family in the favela, who's to say she wasn't the one who unlocked the front door?

Lisboa's convinced this is not the case.

'You see her face? Mate, no way,' he said. 'She's as loyal as a bloodhound, entendeu? And if she's been leaned on, she would've cracked by now.'

Leme is of a mind to agree with him, but he also realises that Dona Annette must understand that she is, in some ways, a suspect of sorts.

And that will terrify her.

Lisboa's right, though, Leme's pretty sure.

But it doesn't mean they can't use the fact she's scared to ask some difficult questions. They're on the same page, he and Lisboa.

They normally are.

The two of them go back a long way. Teenagers and men together: not a bond that's easy to keep, actually, but if you do, it's one that's near impossible to break.

They joined up on the same day and made sure they partnered up at each stage after that.

Lisboa's father was a detective in the Polícia Civil.

'It's a worthy and rewarding profession,' he said a good many times more than once, when they were kids. 'You use your head, you think, but you're out and about, *doing*. Not many careers offer that combination. Solving other people's problems is a fine way to live.'

Leme and Lisboa were in – in for a penny, in for a pound.

Neither college nor a desk job for them, nem fodendo. *No fucking way*.

And the Polícia Civil was not the Military Police.

They wouldn't be on the front line in an endless firefight with the traficantes – the dealers – in the favelas.

And they wouldn't be spat on in the street.

They work hard and have built a good reputation as both competent and fair. What they're discovering, though, after their last promotion, is that competence and fairness means there's a ceiling on how far you can rise up the ranks.

A low ceiling.

And it's this realisation that has left Lisboa a touch disillusioned.

He has a family now, two young children, and the job takes second place.

Leme tries to understand.

For now he puts all this out of his mind.

He and Lisboa are sitting on one side of the kitchen breakfast bar, the maid on the other.

There's a plate of ham and cheese and sweet breads between them.

No one's touching it. They sip at coffee. The maid's drinking nothing.

'Dona Annette,' Leme says, 'I know what the favela is like. I was a kid there, like I said. I know how the place works, entendeu? And I'm sure you must be thinking, at least a little bit, that *I'm* thinking that you might have something to do with all this.'

Dona Annette looks both appalled and terrified.

'I'm not saying,' Leme says, 'that you did anything on purpose, but, you know, there are some heavy guys out there. And if there's something you need to tell us, it's better you do so now, rather than seeking us out when you're back living there, sabe? Which will be sooner rather than later.'

Dona Annette starts to cry.

Leme knows why.

He grew up near the Paraisópolis favela, yes, spent his childhood in the hood, so he knows something, but he was born in Bela Vista, Paraíso, spent a lot of time there, too.

It was another story, in Paraíso.

Old-school neighbourhood, run by stand-up immigrant families, Italian, mainly. Close to Japatown in Liberdade, and the Asians kept things clean, family-oriented, a sort of criminal neighbourhood-watch scheme.

Everyone looked out for everyone else.

The goal was to keep the kids away from the drugs

Or keep the drugs away from the kids.

As Leme's dad used to joke: Paraíso to Paraisópolis –

From Paradise to Paradise City.

Growing up as a teenager, he had three different names for Paraíso:

If he was with a girl, he was from Jardins, playing at being more sophisticated, giving out the promise of wealth and taste.

If he was with a student, a hipster-type, it was Bela Vista.

If he was with a mano, a brother: Bixiga.

Bixiga: the bladder of São Paulo.

Quite different to life in the jungle, Leme thinks. Poor old Dona Annette: she's wound up and worried, and rightly so.

Leme says, 'But first let's talk about this inventory.'

'Sim, Senhor.'

'We're not especially curious as to what's on it, you understand, more that if anything *should* be on it and isn't.'

'I understand, Senhor.'

'Wonderful.' Leme looks at Lisboa. 'Ricardo?'

'If this were a robbery,' Lisboa says, 'then we'd expect a few things to be gone, entendeu? TV, stereo, laptop, you know what I mean? It doesn't look like any of those have been lifted. Our impression the correct one, you think? That none of these are missing?'

'I think so, Senhor.'

'That we're correct, you mean, that none of these are missing?'

'As far as I can tell, Senhor, none of these are missing, that's correct.'

Lisboa nods. 'Grand,' he says. 'What about the safe in his bedroom? Do you know what he keeps in that?'

Dona Annette shakes her head. 'Não, Senhor.'

'No reason why you would, I suppose.'

Leme knows, of course, what he keeps in it. *Kept* in it.

Documents, and a couple of pieces of jewellery, look like heirlooms. Grandmother's wedding ring, an antique watch, that kind of thing.

They got inside it easily enough and forensics seem to think there was nothing else in there – dust traces and whatnot – so unlikely to be a targeted cash heist this one.

'Então,' Lisboa says, *so*. 'You must have cleaned this place a thousand times. That about right?'

'Sim, Senhor.'

'Fact is you likely know better what's in here than the old man. That fair?'

'Perhaps, Senhor. I wouldn't like to say.'

'I don't blame you,' Lisboa says. 'All I mean is that *Senhor* is an expat, and as an expat a lot of the things in the house aren't actually his, so, I wonder how personal the interior design really is. You understand?'

'I think so, Senhor.'

Leme's not sure he understands, but he knows where Lisboa is going.

———

'So, I mean the artwork. His?'

Dona Annette shakes her head. 'The photographs are his, but not the paintings on the walls. They were here before he arrived, Senhor.'

'You're sure?'

'I was part of the team that prepared the house for his arrival, Senhor.'

Lisboa nods. 'What about the books?' he says. He smiles at Leme. 'They look British enough, at least.'

'Many of the books are his, Senhor.'

'*Were* his,' Lisboa says.

Dona Annette looks down, wipes an eye. 'Yes, Senhor.'

'Not a lot of clutter about the place, is there?' Lisboa says, sweeping his arms in a circle. 'He liked to keep things clean, simple, would you say?'

Dona Annette nods.

'So would you say that the inventory is complete? Of the objects, paintings, that kind of thing. Things that can be stolen, I mean. Stuff that might be worth nicking, entendeu?'

Leme shifts slightly in his seat. The kitchen is sterile, functional. Gadgets look box-fresh. Pans and cooking utensils *gleam*. Knives flash light as the sun sneaks, in slices, through the blinds, their edges aligned perfectly on a magnetic strip above the hob, either arranged every day with unnecessary care or basically ornamental.

'Sim, Senhor,' Dona Annette says.

'The inventory is complete?'

'I believe so, Senhor.'

Lisboa nods. 'Good,' he says. 'That's good.'

Dona Annette tries a slight smile.

Leme sees relief.

Leme sees a frightened woman a *touch* less frightened.

She is not, Leme thinks, going to enjoy the next part of this interview.

'Very good,' Lisboa says. 'Really very helpful.'

He looks at Leme. Leme nods.

Dona Annette flashes a startled look from one to the other.

'There is one other thing, though,' Lisboa says. 'Our forensic team thinks that there's a fairly good chance something was taken from Senhor's desk, the desk downstairs, in his study. You know the one I mean?'

'Sim, Senhor.'

Lisboa nods. 'You know the desk or the study?'

'Both, Senhor. Sorry, Senhor, I didn't understand the question.'

Lisboa waves this away. 'Don't be silly. Can you show us the study, the desk? I think it'll be useful.'

'Sim, Senhor.'

Leme stands. Lisboa stands. 'After you,' he says.

'What a gentleman,' Leme says.

Lisboa ignores him.

The study is old-school swank.

Leather chair in the corner, reading lamp peering over it like a crane. The desk is vast, polished oak, a green mat — leather? Probably — across a portion of it. Gold handles on the drawers. Two fountain pens sit in custom-made holders. There's even a blotter, for fuck's sake.

Leme wonders where the snuff box is.

Dona Annette stands with her head bowed, her hands held over her lap, waiting for the next questions.

Point is, she knows, *now*, that they're not messing about.

She knows that she can't hide anything for old Lockwood's benefit.

If she knows something, anything that she might have kept quiet, for the sake of his reputation or whatever, she ain't being discreet anymore.

Not now she knows her favela family might be investigated, leaned on.

And we all know what that might mean, Military Police and all that.

The heavy mob. Violence.

Leme will never understand the unquestioning loyalty of the service class to the very rich.

They don't show Leme and his sort the same deference, that's for sure.

Funny that.

Must be the natural authority that comes with years of privilege.

The sheer entitlement that makes giving orders effortless, charming even.

Not something Leme can do. His own maid tells *him* what to do.

Lisboa points at the desk. There is a chalk circle about the circumference of a large glass. 'What used to be where that space is, Dona Annette?' he says. 'It's really very important that you tell us.'

'There was something, Senhor.'

'And what was it?'

'A… I don't know how to say it, the name. A thing to keep documents in order, you know, stop them blowing away, in the wind, Senhor. I don't know the name.'

'A paperweight,' Lisboa says.

'Isso, Senhor, that's it.'

Lisboa looks at Leme.

Leme thinks: heavy enough.

'Can you describe this paperweight?'

'Sim, Senhor. It was clear, with a blue pattern, supposed to look like the ocean, sabe?'

Lisboa nods. 'Any other distinguishing features?'

'There was some writing on it. In Portuguese, Senhor.'

Lisboa gestures for Dona Annette to go on.

'The writing said something, I don't remember.'

'I think you do.'

Dona Annette turns to Leme. Leme gives her a stony look.

Leme sees Dona Annette begin to fluster, to panic.

'What does it have written on it, Annette?' Lisboa says.

She hesitates. 'It –'

'Go on.'

'It was a gift.' She nods, face now set, determined. 'It was a birthday present. It said happy birthday.'

'Who was it from?'

Dona Annette gives a quick shake of the head. 'I don't know.'

Lisboa looks at Leme.

Leme gives Lisboa a look that says: time out.

Leme's thinking that the maid likely doesn't know who the gift was from, but that she might be able to provide something like a shortlist.

Leme says, 'You would have met, or at least seen, many of the old man's guests. We're going to need a list of people who visited more than once, entendeu?'

'I don't know any names, Senhor.'

'We do though. We know some names. You put your mind to it while we go and talk to your son and grandson in Paraisópolis.'

But they don't go to the favela –

Course they don't – not yet.

They go for a beer, leaving a uniform to make sure Dona Annette stays in her room thinking things through.

And when they come back, an hour or so later, they find Dona Annette sitting with her coat on, a bag packed and piece of paper by her side.

On the piece of paper: the description of a man that Dona Annette has seen visit the big house.

The thing is, the description is hardly revealing –

A young man, dressed in a dark-coloured, hooded tracksuit and white plimsolls.

Dona Annette is adamant she has nothing else on this man, no name, no contact, no real visuals.

Leme believes her.

'How do you know the paperweight was from this man?' Lisboa asks.

'Because,' Dona Annette says, 'there was a spelling mistake.'

Leme nods.

'And I think Senhor's other friends know that anniversario has more than one "n", entendeu?'

'And you have no idea why this man would come round?'

Dona Annette shakes her head.

Again, Leme believes her.

'I'd like to go home now,' she says.

Leme nods.

———

Lisboa calls in the uniform and they arrange for him to give Dona Annette a lift.

Leme says, 'We best give admin a poke for that CCTV footage.'

Bocão, Big Mouth, *former escort:*
Look.

You'll probably call me a liar, but it was him that approached me. He came over and invited me to have a drink. He was alone and older than most people there, but he was charming, tall and strong-looking, a lovely smile, clearly very educated and his Portuguese was impressive and he offered to buy me dinner and I accepted.

At the end of the evening he steered me by the elbow into a taxi.

'Come back with me,' he said. 'It'll be worth it.'

I wasn't sure what he'd meant by that.

When it was all over, he said: 'Stay as long as you want.'

We had breakfast together in his garden. He read a book afterwards while I sat in the sunshine. Later, we ate grilled meat and salad and drank wine. He showed me around the house: flicked through art books that were on his coffee table. He told me about the painting on the wall in the hall. It was by someone called Jackson Pollock, an American. 'You see, there's a frieze of figures beneath the swirls,' he said. 'It's a direct application of the subconscious. The colours are a part of the abstraction. How does it make you feel?'

'Good,' I said. 'It makes me feel good. I like it.'

He smiled at me, laid a hand on my shoulder. 'Yes, it does have that effect.'

I was talking about how he had made me feel: the way he was telling me about the painting.

'It's what is called a drip-painting.' He said the phrase in English. 'Always reminded me of blood dotted on a carpet. All instinctive.'

'You know a lot about it.'

'Just a few things a girl once told me long ago. A different life.'

'A girl?'

'Yes. Like I say, a different life.'

Then he told me a story about a place in England where he grew up, a lost dog.

Like he said, a different life.

That was something we had in common, past lives.

We both wanted to move on.

Well, I did.

He seemed happy about his own. Or at least he accepted it. Not that I wasn't happy about mine, only that I was improving myself so much. I didn't want to lose sight of that: of who it was that was helping me.

Look.

One night I had to work late.

I left the office feeling proud of myself. I was making a difference, however slight, to other people's lives. I was walking along Alameda Santos, coming up to the park behind Paulista when I heard a shout and noticed a young man in a baseball cap and smart tracksuit running through the traffic across the road.

I flinched.

'E aí, Bocão,' he said, an unpleasant smile on his face. *All right, Big Mouth.*

Big Mouth. I felt my heart quicken and my shoulders tense.

'That's not my name.'

'Ah, meu. Puta que pariu.' *Fucksake, mate.* 'You don't have to act like that with me.'

'It's not my name.'

He sneered: his jaw jutted forward. 'Fuck you, Bocão. You're no better than me.'

'Come on, leave me alone.'

'Meu. I just saw you, wanted to talk. It's been a while. You disappeared. Don't pretend you don't know me.'

He sniffed. Rubbed his nose, which had red patches under each nostril. His eyes were wild. He was gaunt: his handsome features ravaged, bone where there had been muscle.

'Look at you now, all fancy clothes. A blazer. What's that you're carrying?' He reached out to touch my briefcase. I pulled it away from him. 'A fucking briefcase, man.' He laughed. 'You think you can get away from what you used to do? Porra.' He jabbed me in the chest with a finger. 'You're still a fucking michê, a hustler, you're just doing it in a different place.'

I shrank in fear and shame. 'Leave me alone.'

'So why are you around here then, if not to rub our noses in what you've got now? Huh? You think you're special? Is that why you're here?'

'It's on my way home. I was working late.'

Cars crawled slowly past, their headlights bright eyes boring into us. Each a brief inquisition and then gone.

'Working? Is it that old fuck I used to see you with? Is that gringo bicha paying your way now so that you can play with his wrinkled cock every night? You going to fucking leave, go to Europe? That's a joke.'

He sucked air between his teeth. Pushed me and I stumbled backwards, my hands raised in defence.

He laughed. 'Mate. I'm not going to hit you.' He backed away, pointing. 'Just don't you forget where you come from. Babaca.' *Arsehole.* 'We'll never forget, even if you do. You're one of us, you prick.' He turned and laughed again. 'Next time you meet a rich old man,' he shouted, weaving his way between cars, slapping their bonnets and gesturing at the drivers, 'make sure you let me know.'

I got halfway down the next block before I had to stop and vomit. I wiped the sticky tears from my face. He was wrong. But he was right too. I lay awake all night, scratching at my legs and arms, my pulse racing. I rocked back and forth, moaning quietly. There was no one I could talk to.

If it were that easy to come face to face with what I'd done, by simply walking down the wrong road after work, then maybe I'd never escape it, sabe?

Rafa likes to skate.

He's got a reputation with the manos, the brothers, as the quickest thing on four little wheels. His nickname with the older boys is Rapido. *Speedy.*

'Oh, Raf-Raf-Rapido!' they call out when he zips past, effortless.

The day after he saw the sexy white woman and passed on the news up the chain, he was summoned by his line manager.

Line manager. That always made him and Franginho laugh. The dealers imposing a corporate structure.

Selling lines, line managers.

It's a mug's game, Rafa thinks, too dangerous.

But for now, working as a messenger boy, running errands, making a little bank while he figures out how he's going to get out of the jungle for good.

'We need you on your board, son,' the line manager told him. 'Bit of recon work, understood? Need you to run a tail.'

Rafa nodded. He didn't know what the lad was on about.

'That woman you spotted other day. She's coming back tomorrow, visiting the same building, six o'clock. You're going to follow her home.'

'On my board?'

Laughter. 'Yeah, more discreet that way, son. Here's how it's going to work.'

And so Rafa finds himself now crouched over his board in one of the bocas de fumo, a little side entrance to the favela, waiting for the woman's car to come past.

He's standing next to a lanky teenager who he knows is an experienced drug-slinger. He's blazing away on a hefty-looking joint, this lad, which he now offers to Rafa.

'Want some, kid?'

Rafa shakes his head.

He needs a clear brain for this mission.

He's not happy here in the boca de fumo, the mouth of smoke, so called as it's one of the little half-hidden pockets at the edge of the favela where rich playboys and lefty student types can swing in and buy drugs quickly without having to get too deep into the jungle.

He's not happy as he knows if any Military Police come by, they'll shoot first and ask questions later. Only the pushers hang out where he's waiting.

And the Militars like to drive by and spray bullets from time to time for a little light diversion. They've got a name for it, apparently.

Duck hunting – if you don't duck, you're dead.

Or some such hilarity.

Just being here has Rafa's teeth on edge.

It's what Franginho would call a precarious situation.

As soon as the woman's car pulls up outside the vacant office building, Rafa ankles it down to the boca, where Lanky is waiting for him.

The boca is set next to a steep road that runs parallel to the northern edge of the favela. The road runs down from Giovanni Gronchi, the main avenue, which the woman will have to take to leave.

One of the other scouts saw her arrive via this steep road, the estate agent is on it, MRV Engenharia after all, so the thinking is she'll go back that way. It's a risk, but Rafa reckons there'll be another kid on a board or a bike waiting on Giovanni to follow her if she takes a left instead of a right and doesn't go back the way she came.

But no one's actually going to tell Rafa this, as they want him primed, under pressure.

And there's no pressure like thinking it's all on your shoulders.

And Rafa knows why he's been positioned here:

The hill is steep and he will fucking fly down it.

At six o'clock the traffic will be chocka. Absolutely rammed.

The woman, more than likely, will crawl along.

There's a lookout across from the boca and up the road and when the woman's little red Volkswagen Golf goes past he's supposed to give this lanky streak-of-piss dealer a buzz, and he'll tell Rafa to get cracking.

But old Lanky is puffing away with a real urgency that is at odds with the requisite urgency he should be giving the task at hand, and he doesn't seem especially bothered about his role in this little escapade, Rafa thinks.

And Rafa can't say anything, no Senhor, as that would be cheeky, would be a direct querying of the chain of command.

So there's not much he *can* do except think, porra, this is what I do now? This is what I have to *do* to get ahead?

He's pissed off.

But he's also jacked up and he supposes that's the point. He just wants the whole thing to happen. He wants to feel his board move underneath him, to act, not to have to think anymore.

***

'You sure you don't want a hit, Rafa-Rapido?'

Rafa shakes his head again.

'Good boy. Professional.' Lanky laughs. 'You'll go far, son,' he says, only half-joking.

The other reason Rafa is pissed off is the message stuffed into his shorts.

He is, basically, fine with following the woman. He's clever on his board, black lightning, and he's discreet, too, and he's young enough and clean enough and just about cute enough – yeah, he knows it's important – that he's unlikely to be mistaken for a thief, a pusher, a gangbanger.

And following someone, by definition, means you're keeping your distance.

He has no idea what the message says, he just knows that he has to deliver it, tell the woman to read it and give him her answer, yes or no.

And it's that part that's worrying him: what might happen, what she might do when she's reading the message, if she even does.

Who might be around.

How he's going to give her the note, let alone speak to her.

She must live in the kind of condo where you drive past security and straight into the car park, ne?

What's he supposed to do if she does? Follow her in? Fucksake.

Yep, Rafa is in well over his head with this part of the job and doesn't he know it.

It is certainly what Franginho would call a precarious situation.

The boca is *tight*. Rafa's not sure he's ever really appreciated how tight. The shacks are miserable, little more than tents. There is rubbish *everywhere*. Rib-thin, one-eyed cats, and dogs with weeping sores and missing limbs.

It is, he thinks, literally a dump.

Who the fuck lives here?

He's heard the rubbish is part of the disguise to allow the dealers to work with something like cover. There are bullet holes, he thinks, in the little wood that does protect these homes. There is very little light. A makeshift blue plastic canopy is stretched over the road from the roofs either side. Road? Well, the *track*. And alongside the track, there is a trench for the shit-filled, stinking water to run out into the wider world.

It's not making very quick progress, Rafa thinks.

'Who lives here?' he asks.

Lanky laughs. He gestures. 'Who you think? Who gonna live here? Kid, look around. You see anyone?'

Rafa shakes his head.

'There's a reason for that,' Lanky says.

Rafa nods.

Lanky doesn't elaborate.

Rafa reckons there's likely a reason for *that*.

Lanky checks his watch. They don't know how long the woman is going to be.

Rafa is alert, his board under his feet, he's marked a clear run to the road. His plan is to get down to the bottom of the hill before she does and figure out where she's headed next.

Thing is, at the bottom of the hill there are about half a dozen options.

And if she picks one of them, lives down in the basin of smart-ish low-level houses, or up one of the crescent-shaped side roads that head towards the swank sports club Paineras, then Rafa's likely fucked as the traffic won't be so bad off the main drag, it'll be tough to keep up, and there will be little green security huts and plenty of condo seguranças, the security *guards*, to do the heroic thing, and yeah, Rafa knows what'll happen there –

He knows that shrugged phrase 'menos um', one less, meaning one less malandro, one less crook, so what? Some condo security firms advertise their willingness to bear arms – and use them.

The smart money though is that she'll take the big avenida, Morumbi, down to the Marginal that runs alongside the river, and if she does Rafa's fucked, as no matter his nickname, a skateboard ain't keeping up with nothing on the fucking motorway.

In fact, Rafa thinks, if this chick don't live pretty much round the corner, he's pretty much fucked.

Waiting in the boca with Lanky is not helping.

The time he has to reflect is not proving at all helpful.

Lanky's radio beeps. He flicks a look at Rafa. 'Embora, cara,' he says. *Go.*

Rafa pushes off and weaves between piles of sweating rubbish bags, the rips in the plastic like wounds, oozing. The smell –

The smell would make a lesser man gag, Rafa thinks.

Then he's out and onto the road.

It's two-way traffic and he was right about one thing: it is absolutely ram-jammed with cars, barely moving.

He skids right and tucks himself in close to the cars shunting down the hill to his left. The other side of the road, the cars queue for Giovanni Gronchi on the slope, each vehicle doing a little shuffle down then up as the drivers crunch into first gear and pump the gas to stop from stalling.

Rafa's got time, he sees now.

The little red Volkswagen Golf is about a quarter of the way down and Rafa is well ahead and keeping an eye over his shoulder.

He's coasting, pissing about, doing turns and tricks, showing off to anyone who has their window open. Busking, is the idea, seeing if anyone will chuck him a few coins, maybe a note, and this helps him stay under the radar as a PCC drug gang messenger and bounty hunter.

Anyone makes him for even a small part of the biggest organised crime syndicate in São Paulo, the PCC – First Capital Command – then this little jaunt is game over, early doors.

Across the other side of the road an expensive tennis facility stretches down the hill and he can hear the thwack of players hitting. The courts are buried in the trees, camouflaged by their green covering, keeping prying eyes out. It's not a private club, but it is so expensive to play it might as well be. When Rafa was younger, he was a ball boy for a couple of the coaches, fetching mishits and bottles of water, taping grips and delivering racquets for restringing. He and Franginho both did it for a couple of years and it was fun, and the tips were okay, but really it was chump change compared to a lookout's salary, and then there were suspicions in management that some of the kids might be lifting small bits of equipment from the clients' bags and selling it on cut price to other clients, and the company simply fired all the ball boys and girls, and started again.

The real shame was that working there meant the guys in the burger place next door at the top of the hill would let them in to spend their hard-earned cash on a burger, or a burger to share at least, the thinking being they could trust these *favelados* not to fuck around too much as they were working so close by.

Well, they stopped letting them in after the kids were fired so that was that in terms of a decent burger – and they were *so* good, thick meat and buttery onions, mounds of fries and buckets of milkshake – and it was back to stringy meat and stale bread sandwiches at Zé Bolacha's padaria and market, outside of which Rafa now waits for the red Golf to catch up.

Zé Bolacha – Joe Biscuit – has that street-food stink to it.

Three men in dirty overalls stand outside with glasses of beer and a little grill fired up, burning cheap meat on sticks.

Filet miaow, is the joke: cat barbecue.

The embers in the grill glow and headlights begin to appear in the early gloom.

Rafa needs to keep an eye and work out exactly when to take off again as there isn't too much hill left to gather the speed he needs to get up the other side. It is much shallower but some serious momentum is necessary to keep him from getting left behind.

Rafa clocks the car edging forward and decides to go for it; he'll get across the first junction by the petrol station and make it in time to the second with a view of which way she goes.

He hopes she follows him.

If she doesn't, takes one of the side roads, it's a bit of a maze down there, quite private, a lot of houses with high walls and barbed wire fences, a low-level condo development on one side, which is, Rafa knows, well looked after, security-wise, and a small government office on the other, and though it's small, it's still a *government* office, *entendeu*?

And then Rafa's flying, passing cars, knocking on their bonnets, on their windows –

He gets thumbs-up, cheers, the odd beeping horn, which usually, in a traffic jam like this one, is reserved for when a woman crosses the road and a driver chooses to show his appreciation.

Rafa's loving it, for a minute, loving the way his speed breaks the thick, evening air, creates that breeze across his dirty, clammy body, through his dirty, greasy hair.

He's arrowing straight for the gas station when he sees an old codger bent double, yoked, dragging a carrosso loaded with crap between cars –

Fuck.

Rafa measures the distance and feels the speed he's going and understands that stopping, or trying to stop, will lose him a whole bunch of momentum, momentum he very much needs, and swerving into the road proper is not an option, the cars are jammed right up each other's backsides, and he reckons he will hit this man unless –

He weighs all this in a beat and thinks, fuck it, and puts his head down and lets out a yell for the old geezer to look lively and watch the fuck out –

He slides by.

The codger yells back at him to respect his elders.

Rafa's arm is raised in farewell, in salute, in celebration.

And he skids around the cars, the petrol station to his right, and the cars ripple forward, and he spies a gap, and realises he'll have a smoother run up the middle of the road, and he swerves, and climbs and climbs, cars edging past either side, and he kicks down and gathers speed, and realises he's like one of those motorbike couriers, the old moto-boys, who tear along between the traffic, hugging the markings on the road, and one of them dies every day –

He comes to a stop at the top of the next junction.

He looks down and sees the little red Golf making something like progress towards him.

His lungs feel clean, his legs pumped, his mind clear.

The road here is pretty level, and with the traffic as it is, keeping an eye on this chick's motor without being made for a tail should be easier.

Unless she takes the Marginal highway.

If she does, he's going to have to admit defeat.

He goes back to turning tricks in the traffic, spinning his board, doing little one-eighties and the odd outrageous ollie, busking, hand out for change, and he picks up a little here and there from the friendlier drivers whose windows are down –

The real money is in the cars with the blacked-out windows that are very firmly up. Shut-up-shop type of scene, Rafa thinks.

Yeah, he's not getting anything from anyone in any of them.

Doors locked, windows down, much less chance of a carjacking, or some moleque like Rafa leaning in and lifting your handbag or phone or whatever other bit of kit you keep next to you that likely costs more than a month's minimum wage.

The red Golf meanders, accelerates, slows, keeps on towards the avenue –

Happy days, Rafa thinks. Piece of piss, this bit.

Then she turns left and Rafa follows, but she opens up a bit and Rafa can't quite stay with her.

And then, without warning, without even indicating, she does a sharp left into a car park, a good twenty yards up the road.

Fuck.

A car park that Rafa cannot turn into, nem fodendo. *No fucking way.*

The car park for the restaurant Casa da Fazenda.

Posh.

And, he knows, with about half a dozen guys on the perimeter making sure the likes of Rafa are kept well away.

Casa da Fazenda was the big house when Morumbi was a farm, some years ago. It was, Rafa learned in Geography, all green fields and rural goodness once upon a time.

The funny thing is, it wasn't *that* long ago.

Rafa's seen the place change even in his few short years.

He fingers the note in his shorts.

He'll wait, he thinks.

He doesn't really have a great deal of choice, after all.

It's hard to imagine that once upon a time Morumbi was a farm, Renata thinks. It takes its name from a traditional Portuguese expression meaning 'green hill'. It's difficult to call anywhere as populous as this part of São Paulo undulating, but the roads are pretty steep, dipping up and around the luxury sports club Paineiras, the seat of the State Government, the stadium of São Paulo FC and a number of well-preserved parks.

Nicer than that shortcut that runs alongside the favela, that's for sure.

Not fun when a group of boys in vests and flip-flops laugh and point – hey, check out the chick driving!

Renata is sad at how intimidated she felt.

Determined this feeling will end.

Sure she is doing the right thing.

Renata learned a lot in school.

She loves how you can twist São Paulo history into something relevant for today. Jesuit priests, she remembers now, first founded São Paulo as a college and village at Piratininga in the mid-sixteenth century, but it was the bandeirantes who turned it into a city. They struck out from the coast into the unforgiving interior searching for precious stones, gold, diamonds – and Indians to enslave and sell. This was História lesson one, basic local history.

And, of course, the names of many of these fuckers adorn major roads in the city.

The old entrance to the farm is preserved and Renata notes this with some pleasure as she drifts into the car park of the restaurant where she's meeting her, well, her boyfriend, she supposes.

Or at least he'd like to *believe* he was her boyfriend.

There's a distinction there somewhere and she wonders on whom it reflects best.

Worst.

The Casa da Fazenda, his choice. *The Farmhouse*, which is predictable.

Even more predictable is that it's bloody expensive.

Pulling into the car park, the air seems thinner, fresher to Renata. Thick vegetation blocks the view of the traffic jam she has just escaped, grinding its way down towards the river one way and the favela the other.

Valet parking, but of course, and Renata hands over her keys to a good-looking, grinning young man who may very well live in Paraisópolis, which is neither here nor there, she thinks, but it's not really, is it?

She smiles at the man, thanks him.

If she is going to work in the favela, if this project is going to be a success in any way at all, she needs to stop seeing everything as black and white, as either of the favela or not.

Black and white feels pretty fucking apt.

She goes inside. She's early and there is no sign of her boyfriend.

The dining room is all colonial elegance and high wooden-slatted ceilings.

Her train of thought proceeds backwards. The county lines in and out of São Paulo are paved with cash, historically. Those roads named after thugs.

Rodovia Raposo Tavares runs from the centre of the city and through most of the state to the southwest. António Raposo Tavares was a seventeenth century-brute, who treated the indigenous population in one of two ways – he either killed them or made them slaves.

Rodovia Bandeirantes runs from the city towards Minas Gerais, following the route of the pioneers in the gold rush in 1690. And it was this influx of money that transformed the village into a city, the bandeirantes eventually expelling the Jesuits. After the gold ran out, they made their money from sugar cane and then coffee. Brazil won its independence and São Paulo became the regional capital.

Money talks.

Looking around this colonial throwback, Renata's not sure how much has changed.

The higher ground always does the business.

The maître d' greets her, and when she explains her companion has not yet arrived, he invites Renata to take a quick turn around the gardens.

The air really is fresher. The place is slap bang in the middle of the Morumbi maze – at the top of the 'green' hill, really – but you would never know it.

There is a sort of cave with peculiarities and original memorabilia from the farm, an ox's yoke, dusty jars with faded labels, thick, ridged paintings of brightly coloured parrots.

Candles flicker in the dusk and couples cling to each other and mutter knowing comments.

The men are dressed *well*. Their shoes *shine*. The *buckles* on their shoes shine.

There is little intimacy here, she realises.

No one seems to acknowledge the existence of anyone else.

The default São Paulo setting is distance.

A dehumanising experience, it often is. Even here in this faux forest, this throwback, this exercise in nostalgia or aspiration.

Renata finds herself composing a rant, narrating what this all means.

We live in our cars and shopping malls, block out the realities of the city with our tinted windows, she thinks, avoiding mundane, everyday routines by paying someone else to do them, then taking sensory pleasure in the artificial – mood lighting, air-conditioning – and *consuming*.

Dinner is slow, several courses, several different bottles of wine opened, none of them finished.

'So it went pretty well today, did it?' her boyfriend asks her, finally, over dessert and coffee.

'It did, yes.'

'You really are going ahead with this nonsense? You're sure?'

Renata nods.

He considers this. 'Might have to cut back on this sort of thing, of course.' He gestures at the room. 'Pro bono don't pay steak dinner wages, querida.'

Renata smiles. She stands. 'I think I'll leave the bill to you. *Querido*.'

Ray rings Fernanda and tells her there's a change of plan, let's meet in the cafeteria on eighteen in twenty minutes, sit yourself down and I'll come over and hit on you.

Fernanda doesn't laugh.

Ray slides into a seat.

The cafeteria is post-lunch quiet.

'I was joking about hitting on you,' Ray says. 'Cover story and whatnot.'

Fernanda smiles. 'I know you were. I just didn't find it very funny.'

Ray nods. 'Point taken. It won't happen again,' he says. 'I'm a fast learner. What do you have for me?'

Fernanda pushes a single sheet of paper across the table.

Ray gives it the once-over.

A pretty comprehensive biography, he thinks. This Favre guy has a chequered past. Born in a Buenos Aires ghetto to Polish Jewish immigrants. Fleeing Argentina in 1969 to avoid arrest for illegal political activity. Moving to France where he became Latin American director of the Trotskyist Fourth International, married four times, set up an Internet company, and developed a serious wine and cigar habit.

Now he's married to the mayor of São Paulo who left her pretty major political player of a husband for him.

Quite a character.

'Okay,' Ray says. 'But what's *not* on this rap sheet? What can *you* tell me?'

'Well, Lula got the nomination, not Marta's ex-husband,' Fernanda says. 'And Lula won, so it was vindicated, ne?'

Ray nods.

'The thing is that Senhor Suplicy reckons it was Marta – and Favre – who fucked him over.'

'It does seem that way, doesn't it?'

Fernanda nods. 'Thing is, of course, this unwanted, attendant attention that the Workers' Party, São Paulo mayor's office, has been getting is not good for left-wing business.'

'So they're looking to cut her out?'

'Let's just say that Lula owes Marta, but no longer needs her.'

'That is well put. Does she owe him?'

Fernanda smiles. 'She *needs* him.'

'Very good,' Ray says. 'We need to flip someone in City Hall.'

'One step ahead of you,' Fernanda says.

She pushes a smaller piece of paper across the table.

On it: a name.

Anna Something, Ray sees.

'Who's this?' Ray asks.

'Someone young and gullible. And in need of cash.'

Ray laughs. 'Maybe I'm going to take back that thing about it won't happen again, after all.'

'Very funny.'

Ray smiles. 'So this time it *is* funny?'

Renata sits in her car and is dawdling.

The engine's off and she's pretty much blocking the entrance – and exit – to the restaurant but she doesn't really care. The *fucker*. The absolute fucker. She knew that he wouldn't be exactly supportive of this idea, this venture, this new path she was taking, but she hadn't expected him to be outright hostile. This is not exactly a true-colours type of thing, she thinks; she knows what he's capable of. But he'd made noises that suggested he thought it was a good idea.

The diversifying fund aspect of it, for starters.

Doing good and making serious money did not have to be mutually exclusive, they both knew that.

And she'd played up that angle to make it easier to get him on board.

Well, she thinks, it looks like he's abandoning ship. Not that it matters, she doesn't need him, he's not invested, it would just make it easier at home.

Home.

She is yet to really call his apartment home, despite the fact she's technically lived there for six months. One of those your landlord needs her apartment back and we spend enough time at each other's places anyway, so why don't you just move in here?

And it's very convenient for work, no real rent, and she can always find her own place –

But once you're all moved in, you're not finding your own place unless you split up. Which is a harder proposition than she thought it would be, if she's honest.

She's not sure that she loves him. She used to love him. She's known no one else, really. They've been together since she was twenty-one. He was very charismatic. There was real chemistry.

He's four years older and that seemed significant – in a good way.

Now it feels like he's got her where he wants her. Dependent.

But it also feels very much like he's established that it's *he* who needs *her*.

So she can't leave. And anyway, where's she going to go?

It's a fucking pickle, is what it is, she thinks now. A conundrum.

She has loved him. But what does that even mean?

She's aware of movement outside, near the entrance to the esta-cionamento, the car park, just out on the street. She sees it's a kid on a skateboard, pulling tricks, showing off, spinning his board, jumping, his hand out for change.

She remembers the feeling she had earlier, the kids pointing and laughing, the powerlessness. She remembers how she needs to get a handle on that feeling. She thinks this might be a good chance, get straight back on the horse as it were.

She starts the car and rolls forward a few metres so she's just poking out onto the pavement. She opens her window.

'Eh, moleque,' she calls out. 'Vem aqui.' *Come here, kid.*

The boy slouches over, and he is a boy, she can see now, about twelve or thirteen, a little kid busking for change.

She pulls a few loose, low-denomination notes from the pocket by the handbrake. She keeps them there in case she needs to mollify someone with quick cash; it's common practice.

'Here.' She hands him the money. 'Having a good night?'

Then the boy does something she is not expecting. 'Read this,' he says, and thrusts a piece of paper through the window at her. 'Then tell me yes or no.'

Shocked, she takes it, unfolds it, reads. Autopilot.

Though the handwriting is a scrawl and the spelling a little off, the gist is that if she wants to set up shop in the favela, she needs to meet with some of the community elders to explain what it is she's doing, and does she understand that this is not a request?

'Quick,' the boy says. He gestures at the heavy-looking secu-rity guy by the valet point who's noticed something and is coming towards the car. 'Yes or no?'

Renata hesitates.

The boy's eyes flash panic.

She realises something is at stake for him, almost certainly, so there is only one answer she can give.

'Yes,' she says.

The kid nods and scarpers, fast, down the hill.

The security guy leans in her window.

'Everything okay?'

She nods. 'Tudo bem,' she says.

All good.

Though it's definitely not all good.

She needs to let this sink in.

She pulls out and heads down Avenida Morumbi towards Real Parque –

Home.

She's never felt it less.

Rafa rounds the corner and there's the little Red Golf just stopping in front of a smart-looking condo in Real Parque –

He swoops behind, knocks on the window and sees her see him.

She looks startled.

He smiles.

She nods, understanding.

Job done.

Leme and Lisboa sit outside Superintendent Lagnado's office. Lagnado – their superior.

Their boss.

Lisboa holds a copy of their brief report.

Leme hears voices in the room; serious, low tones rumble through the door.

On the fifteenth floor, the traffic is a faint growl beneath. Lagnado's secretary – a stout woman of indeterminable age – ignores them.

Leme takes the report from Lisboa and scans it.

Leme hands it back to Lisboa. A masterpiece of suggestion, nothing concrete. Squares with everything they've found out, which isn't much. Storybooks the likely chain of events given what they *do* know.

Progress hinted at without assertion; no attempt to pin down motive.

Should pre-empt questions and buy time.

Leme remembers the autopsy: a rare treat that was.

A vision of the old man's twisted face.

I don't want to be here.

The door opens. Lagnado waves them in.

They settle in chairs in front of his desk.

A tall, imposing man stands behind Lagnado, his back turned, looking out at the view, the skyscrapers of Avenida Paulista: a panoply of interests. Something in his bearing communicates importance and Leme's shoulders tense.

Redness creeps up Leme's neck despite the chill of the air-conditioning. His armpits, two damp enclaves.

'You look like shit,' Lagnado says, looking at Leme. 'You need to get out more, do some exercise.'

He turns his attention to papers on his desk. A squat man, he is in good shape, with the fresh face and tight chest of a regular athlete.

The room drips money.

A dark wood desk dominates, cabinets filled with books line the walls.

The carpet is thick, a darkish blue, and the chairs Leme and Lisboa sit in are green leather. A family portrait sits on the corner of the desk, Lagnado smiling at the camera, flanked by wife and children.

'So...?' he says, looking up from his desk. The other man turns and Leme immediately recognises him.

Porra.

Lagnado makes introductions.

'This is Dr Leonardo Magalhães, Director General of the Polícia Civil. Dr, this is Detective Inspector Ricardo Lisboa and Detective Inspector Mario Leme. Dr Magalhães will sit in on our briefing.'

A show of nodding consent.

'Dr Magalhães has a personal interest in the case you're working on. He'll explain. We're keen for a swift and discreet resolution. I don't want any reports of heavy-handedness. I know I can rely on the two of you.'

Lisboa hands over the report.

He starts to speak.

Lagnado waves him quiet.

Magalhães reads over Lagnado's shoulder.

Leme feels drops of perspiration form on his forehead, imagines it glistening in the sunlight that streams into the office through the generous windows.

A minute passes.

Lisboa twitches in his seat.

Another minute.

Lagnado looks up at Magalhães.

He raises his eyebrows and they share a private interaction.

Magalhães comes round from the back of the desk and leans against it.

He crosses his arms and exhales slowly.

He is immaculately dressed in an expensive suit, a dappled pink tie over a white shirt.

His hair is slicked back revealing a high forehead.

He smiles slowly, lines retracting around his eyes. His skin is pulled tight over his face like a leathery mask. The sharp odour of his aftershave narrows the distance.

Despite the well-groomed appearance, ratty features taper off into a thin, pointed nose which sniffs at the air.

Leme thinks of whiskers, of scavengers preying on a fresh corpse.

A passing cloud blocks the sun and for a moment Magalhães is vampiric in the dull light.

'I don't usually pay visits to any of the delegacias, as I can rely on my superintendents to work efficiently without me breathing down their necks,' he says. 'But today I decided to come. Paddy Lockwood was a personal friend of mine. My son studies at his school.' He pauses, leans forward, eyes Leme. 'I wanted it to be very clear to you both that there can be no insensitivity in this case. None at all. Lockwood was a great man; he accomplished much for our school and our community. Your investigation needs to reflect this legacy.'

He turns to look at Lagnado who nods, reassuringly.

'I know I can count on you,' Magalhães says, warmly.

This little speech, the show of collusion, wakes something in Leme.

Magalhães straightens and steps towards the door. His confidence, his years of privilege disguise the stoop in his back, the awkwardness in his movement.

Sem graça, Leme thinks. *No elegance, no grace.*

No precision, no economy.

Lagnado rubs his eyes. 'Robbery gone wrong, end of. See to it, right? I don't need the old man in here again, entendeu?'

Lisboa starts to say something and Leme shoots a look that says not now.

Lagnado says, 'The maid. She's got connections in Paraisópolis.'

Leme nods.

One of the uniforms has said something. Fuck.

Always the way.

'That's our angle, certo?'

Lisboa exhales. Leme, again, silences him with a look.

'The CCTV,' Leme says, 'is proving hard to locate.'

'Our angle,' Lagnado says, 'is this favela business. We've had a chat with our colleagues in the Military Police. They'll help us – help *you* – find our man. That clear?'

'Crystal.'

'Don't be a cunt,' Lagnado says. Then, 'Good lads.'

Signalling the interview is over he goes back to the papers on his desk.

Lisboa and Leme stand and shuffle out.

Leme curses under his breath.

I don't want to be here.

But I am.

And there might be a good reason for it.

'I'll tell you something for free,' Ray says. 'If I eat up here again this week, I'll be shitting the spicy tuna.'

'Charming,' Fernanda says. 'What a romantic.'

'You said this wasn't a date.'

'It's not. You're old enough to be my ancestor.'

Ray laughs. He points at the menu. 'The spicy tuna's outstanding.'

They're sitting in the top-floor sushi restaurant of Ray's hotel, the Hotel Unique.

A hotel that Ray is really beginning to enjoy.

It is seriously well endowed, facilities-wise. It is very much a place for a big swinging dick, a big dog like Big Ray. And the staff are all over him like a cheap suit. Yank charisma in spades. They *love* Big Ray, the staff. Ray tips like a king and asks questions, is friendly and polite. He treats everyone the same, and they like it, they see it.

Yep, Ray is all set here at the holiday inn. It's business and pleasure.

'I didn't come for the food,' Fernanda says.

'Why did you come then?'

It hadn't been especially difficult to get her there.

'You should come and have dinner with me at my hotel,' he said.

'You're paying.'

And that was that.

Ray didn't invite her to hit on her. That was a bonus. He invited her as he decided that someone in the organisation should know what it is that he's doing. Might be helpful if a bit of misinformation needs spreading, a bit of gossip needs starting – or clearing up.

Ray reckons Fernanda might be just what he needs. She's quite clearly undervalued and underpaid, working well below her level of expertise –

He can make her feel special.

He doesn't need to hit on her to do that.

He suspects any attempt at hitting on her would have quite the opposite of the intended effect. He doesn't envy the young men that must be queuing up to try and fuck her, that's for damn mustard.

The waitress arrives.

'I'll have the spicy tuna,' Fernanda says – straight face. Ray smiles. 'Cold sake. A salmon temaki. And some of that fancy eel thing I hear you do here.'

Ray raises an eyebrow. 'I thought you didn't come for the food.' He looks at the waitress. 'I'll have the same. And a beer.'

'Two beers,' Fernanda says.

The food really is, Ray thinks, outstanding.

They try not to wolf it down but it's hard not to and they order more. They try something called a dragon roll, then a dynamite roll, some straight up salmon sashimi, a third portion of the spicy tuna.

'Thing about Japa food,' Fernanda says. 'It's designed for much smaller people.'

'That's grey-area racist, young lady,' Ray says.

'You not seen the advert?'

'I don't watch TV.'

Fernanda makes a face at this. 'How stylish of you.'

Ray opens his palms.

'It's an advert for, I don't know, Hitachi or Panasonic or whatever,' Fernanda is saying, 'and it's set in a lab, you know, where they're building electronic goods, a load of Japanese in white coats and clip-boards, right? Everything is going well, it seems, they're innovating or whatever. And the punchline: our Japs are better than their Japs.'

Ray roars.

'Biggest population of Japanese outside Japan, São Paulo,' Fernanda says.

'So it can't be racist?'

'Something like that.'

After dinner they go through to the bar to drink espresso martinis.

'If it's mixed well,' Ray says, 'it's dessert, coffee and a line of good coke in a glass.'

Fernanda looks at the waitress. 'I'll have two.'

After their third, Ray makes his play. 'I imagine you wanna know what it is I'm doing here exactly, why I'm asking you to do a little research for me.'

'I think I know what it's about, Ray. The gist, entendeu?'

'And that's why you're here tonight.'

'Uh-huh.'

Ray nods. 'That's good. You wanna tell me why you think I'm here?'

'Cash, Ray, you're here to help us all make money.'

Ray's grinning. 'Good woman. Wanna tell me how?'

'I'm guessing that your arrival coinciding with pretty much the first day of our new left-wing government is not unrelated.'

'That's a solid guess.'

'You're here to figure out if an ideological, political shift will affect our investors, our investments, the nature of our contracts, our syndicates, our potential – bottom line, our bottom line. Am I wrong?'

'You are not wrong.'

'I suspect that this little investigation into Marta's playmate Favre is about comparing the São Paulo political landscape with the rest of the country.'

'Go on.'

'And seeing if there's money to be made from Lula's first big initiative.'

'From what we *think* will be Lula's first initiative.'

'The Bolsa Família.'

Literally, *the family allowance.*

Ray nods. 'Conditional cash transfers, social welfare, federal assistance. It's a noble idea.'

'More importantly, with the Fome Zero aspect, it might be a profitable one too.'

Fome Zero: *zero hunger.*

Ray knows: a poverty reduction programme and key part of the Bolsa Família.

'Rumours have it,' Fernanda says, 'that Lula plans in part to fund this using the CPMF tax, which is primarily supposed to finance public health.'

Ray grins. 'Robbing Peter to pay Paul.'

'There'll be a lot of critics. The church won't like it. Some people will say it will discourage people from looking for work. And, well, it's a money-transfer system. And this is Brazil. You do the math.'

'I already have.'

They sip their drinks. Some anonymous dance music plays. The deck is lit by the underwater purple lights of the empty pool. The lights throb, the lights dance. Beautiful people chatter. In São Paulo, it's easy to be beautiful if you're rich, Ray thinks.

'I ask you to do more jobs for me, you do them and keep it to yourself,' Ray says. 'That's how this works, entendeu?'

Fernanda grins. 'Jobs, Ray.'

Ray has the concierge order a cab and they say goodnight at the door.

Back in his room Ray fishes his bottle and his apparatus and shoots himself up and the moment is pure simplicity.

He doesn't know if Fernanda would have come back with him if he'd put the moves on her, but he wasn't going to push it, and there'll be other dinners.

Right now, he's glad he's all alone.

He wonders how much longer this bottle will last.

He is very high functioning, is Big Ray.

This city never sleeps, he thinks. It's caught in the throes of its own death rattle.

Leme doesn't want to go to a party but Lisboa isn't letting up.

What a surprise.

The point is it's clear the Lockwood murder is being cleaned up now without them. They're getting the credit, they're golden, but it's with the Militars now, they're flushing the favela to find the mark, which they will, and it all feels like false praise, fake recognition.

Leme knows it's above his pay grade, that there's nothing he can do, but it sticks in his craw all the same.

He knows they're finding a patsy. Scapegoat city.

The PCC will likely offer some poor sod up to take the heat and life goes on.

Best-case scenario for the boys at the top is always the best case.

Question is why they give a fuck about this old gringo?

It's a question Lisboa doesn't want to answer.

He's all about the weekend, the party.

'Mate, it's at mine, barbecue. Will be fun. You need a break, we're up against the fucking wall, you know this, take some time off.'

Leme does know this, but he can't help feeling he doesn't fancy talking to people he doesn't know. He tells Lisboa exactly this.

Lisboa laughs. 'Well, in that case, you're fucked, son. Stay at home and wank into your sock, for all I care. You won't have to talk to anyone you don't know.'

Leme relents and turns up at Lisboa's with a case of beer and some spicy sausage.

'Good-sized crowd,' Leme says. 'Your wife's got a lot of friends.'

Lisboa pushes him into a conversation with a guy who grew up in Morumbi.

Turns out they lived round the corner from each other for a bit.

The guy's come with a friend, Renata. She's just set up a legal aid office in Paraisópolis. Leme should meet her. She could do with some more local knowledge, the guy says. That's her just over there.

Then Lisboa hustles this Renata over to chat.

It's immediate, what happens.

Something stirs inside Leme. Something deep.

'So, pro bono?' he asks.

He's not entirely sure what the phrase means, but he knows it has something to do with helping the less fortunate.

She laughs. 'Sort of. I do actually earn some money. I am lucky though. My partner works in the private sector, so we get by.'

'Your business partner?'

'No, my… well… boyfriend, I suppose.'

Leme thinks: I *suppose*. What the fuck does that mean?

My boyfriend. Two stinging wounds.

Leme feels his insides empty, all excitement and optimism drain away and he's faint and lightheaded, as if from a physical blow.

He recovers himself, takes a long pull on his beer.

'I live nearby,' he says, 'if you ever fancy a drink?'

'That might be nice.'

'Might?'

'Here's my number.'

He gives her a card.

'Ah, of course. You're the famous Detective Leme. Ricardo has told me a lot about you.'

She offers her own card.

'We should definitely meet,' she says, 'I want to pick your brain. We can grab a drink.'

They have more than one drink the first time they meet in a bar in Morumbi.

They go outside for a cigarette and Leme is sure the evening is coming to an end.

'Well, we could get the bill or... one more? *Saideira?*'

'I probably should get home.' She looks at him, her arms crossed, cigarette to the left of her mouth. 'But I want another one.' Leme smiles. 'You have to stop being such good company,' she says. 'Bad, bad influence.'

He's never been called that before.

She said something: that emotionally things were simple, practically not.

So there is some hope.

The next time, as he watches her approach, notes the fresh makeup and smile of recognition when she sees him, the way she greets him from across the room, he knows that something is going to happen.

They kiss, that's all, but it's enough.

'My situation is complicated,' she writes in an email, 'and the last thing I want to do is hurt you. Maybe this is bad timing. I want to wait until everything is resolved, but I can't imagine not seeing you.'

'Bad timing is an excuse,' he replies.

'It's not an excuse.'

That hurts, feels demeaning.

He struggles to sit still. Restless, his feelings veer from optimism to despair.

He thinks about her constantly. It's new.

It's a distraction from things he shouldn't be thinking about, anyway.

Or that he should be.

'There's not a moment when I'm not thinking about you,' he tells her.

Lisboa's no help. 'Birds, mate' is pretty much all he can muster.

They see each other. Spend a week together when she takes time off.

Afternoons in bed, bars, and shared pizza.

He tells her he loves her.

She says she felt it the first moment she laid eyes on him, that her stomach had dropped and settled and a physical understanding had dawned on her: this is the man I will marry.

This is the father of my children. This man is the rest of my life.

But at the end of each day, she went home. To him.

He believes she'll leave him.

But she doesn't.

He sends her messages in the knowledge that he's trying to elicit certain responses.

But she never responds in the way he hopes.

And then when he isn't expecting it, she writes something truly disarming.

It is all so hopeless. And yet he doesn't stop.

Months pass. They continue to spend time together, walking, talking, drinking.

She tells him she doesn't love the man she lives with. Feels trapped, she says.

'So leave him,' Leme says. 'Live with me.'

'I want to, silly,' she says. 'You know that I love you.'

'That's enough,' Leme says. 'The rest is details.'

But even as he says it, he fears it isn't enough, that he's wrong.

He becomes demanding, confused. Tries to tell himself it isn't his fault, that the situation is making things impossible, intolerable.

But he doesn't know if he's asking too much or if she's promised too much.

She stops answering his messages, leaves his calls unreturned. He begins to feel stupid. He wonders what he's done wrong other than try to be honest, try to be understanding.

All he's done is fall in love with her and believe in her.

'I can't do this anymore,' she writes in an email. 'I need space.'

Space? You're living with someone you don't love. What about everything you have ever said to me?

She ignores his questions. Tells him, simply, she loves him.

It feels cruel or confused – he isn't sure which.

Perhaps, when it comes down to it, she simply doesn't love him enough.

He doesn't know what to do, and so leaves it, leaves her, walks away.

It's harder than he imagines, because he never thought he'd walk away.

But confusion settles, wounds heal.

And then, she calls him.

She'd decided to leave her partner but needed to make the decision without feeling that Leme was an undue influence. She needed the time to do it. Her partner was suspicious and she needed him to know that it was more than just an affair, that there were deeper, more final problems.

Just like that. An analysis and a decision.

Very her, he thinks, smiling at her terminology. Undue influence. That's what he's been.

Later, she tells him that the practicalities were overwhelming, that ending a chapter of her life was harder, took more time, than she envisaged.

He tells her he understands.

She wants to take things slowly, but she wants to see him.

He agrees that's what he wants too. It is. All he ever wanted was to be with her.

He's like a magpie, engaging totally with the world, collecting things to share with her. Every little shiny nugget in his life has a new purpose: to make her smile.

To make her love him more.

Document record: Article in newspaper *Cidade de São Paulo*
by
Francisco Silva, Crime Correspondent

Friday, 3 January

In the early hours of Thursday morning, a Caucasian man of
approximately sixty years of age was murdered in his house
on Rua Coronel Bento Noronha in the Jardim Paulistano area.
The man was discovered by his maid at 0730 in his bedroom
after he had failed to get up at his usual time. He was
identified by the maid as a Mr Paddy Lockwood, a British
national, who had been headmaster of the British School
for the past ten years. Mr Lockwood lived alone but had
a rich social life in the city. The police are currently
waiting on forensic evidence before issuing a description
of the attacker(s). At a press conference on Tuesday
evening, Chief Superintendent Lagnado could not confirm the
number of suspects involved. He did confirm that death was
caused by a violent blow and that they were proceeding
with a murder enquiry. The police appealed for witnesses
in the area between 1200 and 0300. The police made a clear
suggestion that it was a robbery gone wrong, and they are
pursuing leads in Paraisópolis, the favela where Lockwood's
maid is from and has family. The Polícia Civil is confident
that the case will be resolved in the next few days. The
investigation continues.

Document record: Article in newspaper *Cidade de São Paulo*
by
Francisco Silva, Crime Correspondent

Monday, 17 March

Police have confirmed they have apprehended and charged a
suspect in their investigation into the murder of Paddy
Lockwood, the late headmaster of the British School in
São Paulo. Owing to delicate aspects in the nature of the

case, the identity of the suspect will not be released. A source close to the investigation suggests this is due to the potential for gang-affiliated reprisals. The source confirms the murder occurred during an attempted robbery. The Polícia Civil has thanked the Polícia Militar for their assistance in finding the suspect. The source believes all are very confident of a quick conviction.

Part Two

BLACK RIOT

São Paulo, 2006

1
What's love got to do with it?

April 2006

---

*What's that joke? There's two Brazilians on a desert island
and they form three political parties. There's only one way
to keep a coalition together, and that's through the oldest
form of political donation in the book: a retainer.*

Wilton, 53, teacher

*Bolsa Família has already become a highly praised model
of effective social policy. Countries around the world are
drawing lessons from Brazil's experience and are trying
to produce the same results for their own people.*

Former President of the World Bank, Paul Wolfowitz

*I travel a lot around Brazil and see many places where the average
monthly income is BRL 50 (approximately US$ 26.32). In these places
the Bolsa Família comes in and adds an extra BRL 58. It makes all
the difference in the world and adds a lot for the needy population.
What is more important is that it promotes a virtuous circle. If
there is more money in circulation, the local market heats up, the
purchasing power is increased and the effects spread throughout
the whole economy. But only to give money is not enough.*

Senhora Renata de Camargo Nascimento (heir to the
Brazilian multi-billionaire Camargo Correa Group)

Rafa ain't a lookout no more.

No, Senhor, he's gone up the ranks a touch these last few years, and he's well aware of how he's looked at differently in the favela, by the younger boys and the old guard too. Part of this is because his dad's gone away for a stretch, he knows. He's now looking after himself and his grandma; he's on the road to becoming a big man.

His old man's inside, but Rafa's not exactly sure why.

It's been nearly three years. Rafa didn't even know that his dad was a part of the organisation. It always seemed like he didn't approve of how the community was run, like he was better than it all. He didn't exactly forbid Rafa from earning a little change, but he definitely did not encourage him.

'You're a smart lad,' he said. 'Don't forget, there are plenty of ways to leave Paraisópolis. The trick is to make sure your heart's still beating when you do.'

Rafa supposed that in some ways his dad was following his own advice.

Point is though he'll be back, all things even. Word is he took a voluntary fall for a manslaughter beef for a hefty wad of cash, that it was a five to ten stretch and he'd be out in time to see his boy become a man. Which, knowing the old man, has a plausible ring to it. He's a belligerent fucker.

Heroic, really.

Rafa's grandma will neither confirm nor deny this.

'Who gives a fuck?' is Franginho's nuanced take on the whole thing. 'You're up the ranks and you've got a steady mensalão coming in too. Happy days, mate.'

Mensalão. A monthly payment. A salary, really.

'More like a retainer,' Franginho says when he suggests he's on the payroll. 'Difference is it means you're a part of the team when *they* want you to be.'

And very much excluded when they don't, of course.

He's definitely not excluded now, is Rafael, no Senhor.

He's at the mid-level HQ. It's a room above a shit-can bar where the mid-level boys drink. A few old-timers. A few two-centavo whores sitting outside between tricks. They're not much older than

Rafa. He's like a coiled spring, sexually, is young Rafa. Full of tesão. He wouldn't mind a go on one or other of them if it was under different circs, but he knows that these girls are on a tight leash and no quick spunk-job is worth the complication of treading on the pussy of someone who's higher up the food chain.

Besides, he doesn't have the dinheiro to spunk, as it were.

The mid-level men are a few years older. They've earned their position halfway up the hill. Rafa respects that.

He's waved up the stairs at the back of the bar. Dingy, damp and crawling with roaches it is. A stale-beer stench. The place reeks, an odour not unlike the gang of cackling, toothless mendigos that lie around the cemetery across the main road poncing change for pinga, Rafa thinks. It brings the memory of his mother sharply into focus and he shakes his head. Smell can do that, take you somewhere, Franginho once told him. He's not exactly thrilled that it's this particular smell that conjures his mother; or her place of rest, at least. Same difference now, he thinks.

The room's tight. There's a heavy cloud of dope. The mid-level men are splayed about on seats – *in* seats – that barely contain their long, skinny limbs.

Rafa stays on his feet.

The tallest of them, a dude in shades and shorts known as Garibaldo after the big bird in *Sesame Street*, beckons Rafa. He is folded, Garibaldo, elegantly into a deckchair. How the fuck he can see anything in here in sunglasses Rafa does not know.

'E aí, Rafa-Rapido. Beleza, mano?'

Rafa nods. Yeah, things are beleza, *beautiful*. It's tudo bem, *all good*. 'Take this.'

Garibaldo hands Rafa a mobile phone. Rafa has never held a mobile phone before. It's heavy, heavier than he expected, it's got heft, substance, like a gun, he imagines.

This is status, he thinks. Or something like it.

Better than setting off warning fireworks when the Militars come to town.

Or running the whispers, what they call delivering messages right into the ears of the line managers.

'Only person has the number, Rafinho,' Garibaldo is saying, 'is your old man, certo? And no one else will get it, got it?'

Rafa nods. Garibaldo takes back the phone. He holds it up.

'When you get a message, right, it beeps, like this, you press this button, you read it, you remember it, you delete it – this button – and then you come directly to me – directly, sabe? – and tell me exactly what it says.'

He hands the phone back to Rafa.

'Show me.'

'Okay.' Rafa points at the buttons.

'You understand, kid?'

'Yeah, message comes in,' Rafa says, 'I find you.'

'Don't get cocky, moleque.' Garibaldo shapes as if to get up. 'What else?'

'I delete the message.'

'Good boy.' Garibaldo grins. His limbs unwind and he stands. 'Now scram.'

Rafa scrams.

Next day, Rafa gets a text.

Filho. Saudades. Pãe

Son. I miss you. Dad

What, Rafa thinks, so I have to deliver *this*?

He knows the answer to the question is yes.

Renata looks out at Paraisópolis from her office window.

It *teems*. People everywhere, first thing. Just noise and people.

Hustling, getting in each other's way.

It's why she's here, she supposes, to help people get what they need without treading on anyone else's toes.

Or something like that.

'Oh Fernanda,' Renata says, 'what you working on this morning?'

'Bolsa Família applications. There's a mountain of them.'

'Right.'

Renata nods. Lula's family allowance scheme is thriving. Interrupting the transgenerational cycle of poverty, apparently, is the idea.

Renata has seen it make a difference in the favela. Put simply, there are more people buying more food.

More work for her and Fernanda, too. Every application has to be rubber-stamped and notarised, checked, and legally all above board before the government will release the Citizen Card to the female head of the household, so she can start withdrawing cash and spending it.

There's an awful lot of applications coming in for them to process.

Paraisópolis is a very big place and a very poor place, but still, it's a lot.

'Can you give me a hand?' Fernanda asks.

'No can do, querida,' Renata says. 'Not until this afternoon. I'm chasing something on the Singapore Project, sabe? Our old friends at Capital SP. Doing a bit of consultancy or something.'

Fernanda laughs. 'You mean trying to work out where their money's gone.'

'Something like that.'

Renata looks at her notes.

Singapore Project

Mid-90s public housing program based on urban renewal strategies – population surge due to large scale in-migration from the impoverished northeast – housing deficit by 2000 estimated at 1 million units – substandard housing occupied about 70% of São Paulo, 1,500 km, roughly three times the size of Paris – failure of the Mutirões (funding given to community groups to build or renovate) led to adoption of the Singapore model based on slum removal and 'verticalization' of the favelas – '94: R$7.5 million targeted – '95: R$67.5 million – '96: R$206.5 million – '97: R$300 million – this amount of funding should have provided for almost 100,000 units – most apartment blocks constructed in areas immediately adjacent to the favelas to provide support for the residents and enable them to continue with their working lives – ownership passed to COHAB, municipally managed, charging rents of R$57.00 a month.

Serious challenge 1 – funding: simply never happened as promised with credible accusations of diverting allocated funds to other areas – escalation of unit costs from R$15,000 to R$25,000 made it impossible to sustain – only 14,000 of the projected 100,000 were built.

Serious challenge 2 – program management: became clear that the state government was using the project as a propaganda exercise and was never serious in its intention to genuinely solve the substandard housing issue – blocks were built in visible areas (e.g. major roads) where middle-class voters would see them – nothing constructed in Freguesia do Ó, the most significant area of substandard housing – favouritism and potential for political corruption in terms of selection of construction companies – the housing secretariat apparently demanded compliance with the wishes of the Inter-American Development Bank – government turned a blind eye to companies using substandard construction materials and practices – in one instance there were hollow blocks found instead of concrete-filled pillars – according to an unnamed former employee, companies used the state-allocated materials for work in luxury building projects and brought in the cheapest material and labour for the Singapore buildings – construction companies received undeclared financial incentives to finish quickly, with large bonuses if the projects were completed in half the predicted time.

Issues over quality of life for residents – inadequate living space – no education in apartment-style living in terms of garbage, equipment, responsibilities, etc. – livestock brought in (goats, etc.) to help with livelihood of residents but created huge problems for other residents – enforcement of no-animal rules led to deprivation of livelihood – black market developed with unauthorised sales and unit-sharing – resentment of favelados who were selected for the project – restriction of commercial activities in the buildings – social workers ran the committees for day-to-day management in an aggressive, dictatorial style – protests against lack of utilities spread into street violence, road blocks, tyre-burning and violent police reaction.

Now a new system of Mutirões implemented – financed in part through a syndicate put together by Capital SP. Payments into Capital SP's business accounts throughout the mid-late '90s with the state government reference prefix which means the bank doesn't ask any questions when it comes to declaring it. Must be linked to the Singapore Project.

The short version, Renata realises, is that the companies made money and the housing crisis remained.

She's unsure why Capital SP is asking her to look into it.

Their involvement, it appears, is a little embarrassing at best.

And probably far worse than that.

'I'm going out,' she tells Fernanda. 'Have a look at the new building down the road, see if there's anyone about, sabe? Need anything?'

'Only that you be careful.'

Renata shrugs. 'They know me here, now. I'm one of the boys, sweetheart.'

'I don't doubt it.'

Renata pulls on her coat and heads for the big Singapore Project contribution to Paraisópolis or what the locals call a fucking building site.

Dona Annette, Paddy Lockwood's maid:

Listen.

Lunch is early.

We have to eat before the teaching staff and children, and I am sitting with a couple of cleaners, their plates piled high with rice, beans and grilled meat. The sound of cutlery on china. Heads down, we tuck in noisily.

The men nap for half an hour round the back of the kitchens after their heavy lunch, lying on bits of cardboard in the shade. The afternoon drags longer than the mornings and I envy them – it's harder for us women to switch off. Chatter fills the room, competes with the clatter of knives and forks.

'When do we get the Césta básica?' someone asks.

'Two weeks.'

The Césta básica, a basket of basic foods – rice, beans, oil, sugar, biscuits, pasta – arrives every month and sets us up for our simple family meals at home. Can't complain at how we are treated. A free lunch every day, coffee, tea, a snack in the morning and afternoon and the Césta every month. We're lucky and we know it. Our superiors often remind us of it, though they needn't.

'I need mine now,' a cleaner called Rafaela says. 'My boys are eating us out of house and home. I've hardly got anything left. God willing, I'll make it last. If,' she laughs, 'I don't eat anything and fill up here at school every day.'

'That's what I do,' Maria Elisa says. 'D'you think I could eat this much twice a day?' She points at her plate, rice scattered on her tray like birdseed. 'I'd be the size of a house. I catch my husband sneaking extra portions from the fridge most nights and look at him. Gordão. *Fatso*. And he complains when we don't have any dessert.' She forks in another hefty mouthful. 'I should get myself a young namorado. A nice playboyzinho who could take me out to dinner a few times a week.'

'He could do more than that,' Rafaela winks.

Maria Elisa shakes her heaving chest. 'Stop by at one of those motels on the Marginal on the way home,' she laughs.

Rafaela laughs. 'Amiga,' she says. 'It's our right, ne? If I let my husband lie on top of me, I'd get squashed.'

'Last night,' Maria Elisa says, 'when I got home, my husband was fast asleep on the sofa, a half-empty bottle of pinga on the table and a bunch of cans on the floor. Twenty years ago… well,' she smiles, her eyes twinkle, 'twenty years ago, I wouldn't have had to go out in the first place.'

They egg each other on. I laugh, saying nothing.

'Twenty years ago,' Rafaela says, pointing with her fork, 'is exactly the problem. You let one guy sleep with you, and the next thing you know you're pregnant and waiting to be married. I tell my boys, use condoms. They look at me like they're only fit for animals. Well, I say, it's your choice, but there's no way we can afford an abortion, not a safe one, at least. And I'm not taking that risk, breaking the law for a vagabundo who can't look after his own cock. Boys will be boys, and, thanks to God, they've been told for years that contraception is wrong and we have no choice in the matter. They're too horny to take care, too stupid to think of the consequences, and have too little self-control to wait until the time is right. And that's my boys too.'

I feel uneasy.

Think of my own son.

We brought him up right, took him to church, taught him to fear God, to respect women.

I think of my husband.

He was a good man, a reasonable role model, wasn't he?

Maria Elisa speaks softly. 'Fa fa, you're right, but we do our best. If we don't educate them, who will? I have grandchildren and they are a blessing and I thank God for them every day. But you're right. We have to have faith in our children as much as ourselves.'

'I have faith in mine,' Rafaela sniffs. 'But they need more guidance than I can give them.'

I know where they should go for guidance.

But I don't say it.

Sometimes with Fa fa it's easier to let her vent.

She wouldn't agree with me, anyway. She's lapsed and it's sad, but there's nothing anyone can do except pray for her. So I do.

I look up at the clock. I fetch us three coffees and sit back down.

We all started at the school at the same time. It was an easy decision to become a professional cleaner. My mother needed help around the house as she got older, and I left school at fifteen to give it. I got work as a maid in the big condominium near Paraisópolis, Portal da Cidade. I worked for a young family, helping the mother look after her small child, taking care of the apartment and cooking meals. Santa Maria, she called me. They paid well. It was pleasant work and there was always time to chat. They gave me a Césta every month, and once or twice a year I holidayed with them at their house on the beach in Guarujá. The simple pleasures of family life, even if it wasn't my family, made me happy.

The child grew up and I felt a special bond with her when her mother went back to work.

Treated her like one of my own.

After five years they moved away from the city to live in the suburbs and it was too far to commute.

They wanted me to come and live with them, but my son, you know, then he had a son and, well, my priorities changed. I was sad to leave them, especially their little girl.

Praise Nossa Senhora Aparecida, I heard of a job at the British School through a friend who used to work here. Too bad she'd been fired (complaining about your pay is one way to lose your job). That's when Rafaela, Maria Elisa and I were employed. Best friends ever since.

'You're very quiet today, Annette,' Rafaela says.

I smile at her. 'Just tired, that's all.'

Maria Elisa's eyes narrow. 'Are you sure?'

'It's been a long week. I need an early night. Not that I'm going to get one.'

'We're lucky,' Maria Elisa says. 'There's worse things we could be doing.'

'We could be dustmen,' Rafaela points out.

'They're the happiest people in Brazil!' Maria Elisa laughs. 'They run after the trucks, singing. They run. They're crazy! They must be the happiest dustmen in the world, so we must the happiest nation in the world.'

'Carrying shit and still smiling: that's the Brazilian worker,' Rafaela says and we all laugh.

'Never seem to reach us though,' I say, quietly.

I think of the heap of rubbish by the bus stop at home.

The mangy dogs scavenging scraps.

'Well, there's no money in it,' Maria Elisa says. 'The Prefeitura aren't going to waste their time on you. It's this lot,' she waves her arms about, indicating the school, 'that they're worried about.'

Rafaela starts to say something but thinks better of it. I look again at the clock, scrape back my chair and the others follow me. Sighing, we place our trays on top of the bin and leave the dining room, just as the first shift of teachers arrive to take their lunch.

Later, I walk down Gabriel Monteiro da Silva to pick up my bus on Faria Lima. Lightning flashes above Shopping Iguatemi. Thunder cracks. I feel the first drops of rain as I join the queue for the bus outside Clube Pinheiros. (Fifty thousand reais just to join, they say at school, can you imagine?)

I squeeze onto the bus just as the heavens open.

I stand, squashed between two men.

Rain drips through the window, down my neck.

The traffic on Cidade Jardim doesn't move.

I look at my watch. At this rate, in this rain, in an hour and a half I'll be home.

Ray's phone rings. Fernanda.

'Hello gorgeous,' he says.

'You're back in town then?'

'Uh-huh.'

'Been in long?'

'Put it this way,' Ray says, 'I am not yet shitting spicy tuna.'

Fernanda laughs. 'You inviting me to dinner?'

'Yep. Tonight?'

'Sounds perfect, Big Ray.'

'Easy.'

Ray twirls in his chair. The city shimmers soundlessly in the heat, many floors below. He pops his desk drawer. He shoulders the phone. He pops a med from a plastic packet. He slams it and swallows it dry. He chases the med with a good slug of sparkling water.

'She's not here, Ray, I can talk.'

'You got the most recent paperwork?'

'Yep.'

'Stamp it through, no questions, no digging.'

'You surprise me. What's this Singapore Project business you've got her on? She's practically wetting her knickers.'

'Misdirection.'

'Misdirection.'

Ray hears Fernanda sigh. He smiles.

'She'll learn something and she'll want to act on it. When she does, let her.'

'Very helpful.'

'See you tonight, baby.'

'*Baby*? Thanks, old man.'

Ray hangs up. Ray *grins*.

Anna still works for Marta Suplicy. It's been well over a year since Marta lost the mayoral election. She did five years in office and what's she remembered for –

Outside of her sex life, a few things actually.

She did a fair bit, did Marta.

And Anna was involved in it.

There were changes to the city's bus system, a new ticket valid for a period of two hours, a bilhete único. That made a real difference to your manual workers, your cleaners and labourers, many of them travelling for hours across several buses to get to and from work. A late shift at a swank international school – the kind of place that resolutely did *not* support Marta – tidying up after a late dinner or something, and you might only get three or four hours at home before you had to get up again.

Talking of schools, Anna played a key role in Marta's overhaul of the public educational system, overseeing the establishment of large schools and cultural centres, the so-called 'CEU', built in the poorest districts of the city. This was very much in line with old Lula's attempts to eradicate poverty first, and then inequality.

Marta was right in the frontline there.

Anna was too.

Towards the end of Marta's administration, she turned to another key São Paulo gripe: traffic. She green-lit construction of underpasses and bridges at major flash points.

They were popular, these initiatives, in theory at least.

Problem was it was in everyone's interest to keep the building work going as long as possible.

It was when Anna learned the word kickback, understood the phrase greasing palms, watched the old euphemism of the cafézinho – the quick coffee, the bribe – really play out.

Maybe it wasn't a surprise Marta wasn't re-elected.

So for the last year, Anna's worked as a mediator, an assistant, focusing on positioning Marta in the big project, the Bolsa Família.

First thing this morning, Anna got on the phone and called a legal aid office she's heard is based In Paraisópolis.

An office that contacted her a few years ago, but she didn't bite, didn't get involved.

Making great strides with the Bolsa Família registrations, this office is, now.

A whole community energised and given hope.

'Come and have a look for yourself,' the woman in this legal aid office told her. 'Today if you like.'

Marta green-lights it. 'Could be quite a photo-op,' she says. 'Go on and scout locations.'

They laugh at this, what with Marta's TV experience.

Anna hasn't been to Paraisópolis before. Anna hasn't been to any São Paulo favela, truth be told.

She's no princess, no patroçinha, no trust fund chick, nothing like that, just she's never been in.

She has in Rio. Who hasn't?

One of those baile funk parties, which claim to be edgy and authentic as they're hosted up the hill, up in the twinkle of the favela lights. But really the only danger you might get in at one of those is being hit on by hipsters claiming they're edgy and authentic, or by boys who actually *are* edgy and authentic, and frankly, if you don't wanna get hit on, it's all the same difference, really.

'You be careful, querida,' Marta says. She grins. 'I'm kidding. A nice girl like you? They'll be falling over themselves to look after you.'

Marta's still laughing when Anna leaves. 'Be careful. What a hoot.' She shakes her head, cackling. 'Bring me back an idea.'

Taxi all the way, obviously.

The woman from the office, Fernanda, meets her when she arrives. 'Welcome,' Fernanda says. Her eyes dart. 'Come on in.'

It feels, to Anna, like she's been hustled inside, which is hardly very welcoming.

It's quite something, the favela. The view from the office is *real* impressive.

Fernanda is giving her the tour, which does not take long. The room has two desks and a kettle, Anna sees is the extent of it.

'Coffee?' Fernanda asks.

'Please. No milk, no sugar.'

Fernanda smiles. 'Good answer.'

Anna's not entirely sure why.

Coffee made, Fernanda's pointing outside, the view is pretty much 360 degrees, and Anna is getting a real sense of what it means to work here.

Fernanda is saying, 'The area, you know, is the same as anywhere else, sabe? There is all the gentrification and the social cleansing that inevitably goes with it. There is the sense of a political elite and then the rest, and *then*, the disenfranchised. There is the tragic failure of social housing projects, the Singapore Project is a mess, right, the fact that these projects barely get off the ground at all. There are acid attacks, nasty, nasty muggings, everyone knows someone who has been a victim. There is a construction industry that fucking *thrives*, which we see all around us, ne? And yet a deepening housing crisis, luxury buildings empty. Entendeu? Have a look. They're all around us. The favela, and the area that surrounds it, is no different from the rest of São Paulo, I swear.'

Anna nods. 'Yeah, I get that.'

'What a city though, ne?' Fernanda says. 'São Paulo is indisputably the capital of South America. Think about it, menina, rich in culture, dripping with cash, undermined by political corruption, marked by a rich-poor disparity that fuels desperation and a life-is-cheap criminal ethos. Yet, São Paulo is so full of life you feel energised, politicised, important. At least I do, entendeu?'

Menina, Anna thinks. *Girlfriend.*

Strange pitch this, that Fernanda is giving her.

Sort of chummy tour guide, she's playing at. Doesn't she realise that Anna works for the fucking mayor? Well, the former mayor.

'Yeah, yeah, exactly. Exactly how I feel, sabe?'

'Pois é, ne? É isso ai.'

Exactly all that.

Anna nods. She waits for Fernanda to wrap up her pitch.

'Look, here's the thing,' Fernanda says. 'Morumbi is the new São Paulo suburbs. It's not the traditional areas around Paulista Avenue with their neighbourhood bars, old-fashioned apartments and canteen restaurants. It's somewhere to move to and have children or move to when your children have left home. It's dangerous outside the condominium gates, you know? Here in Paraisópolis, look, you can see the harried faces, the slouch of rubbish and mess, the half-naked children and the condensed, improvised houses, like an approximation of a home, at least in our narrow conception of one. *Our* conception, that's middle class, certo? And that's what we're doing here, we're educating both sides – and helping the side that needs it most.'

Anna looks out the window, turns and takes in the panoramic.

Paraisópolis is set low, in a crater, a settlement built in the hole of an explosion.

A settlement on Mars, maybe, Anna thinks. The colour, the dust. The people scurrying about like ants, up and down the hill.

Except the explosion is everything that surrounds.

An explosion of wealth, of property, one that's just kicking off now.

Helicopters, the size of fat flies, hover silently not five kilometres away.

'I bet you're wondering why I'm here,' Anna says.

'You work for Marta.'

'I do.'

'How did you hear about us?'

Anna smiles. 'There's not many like you, you know that.'

'We're not a political organisation.'

'At the moment,' Anna says, 'neither are we.'

'Ha, yeah, very funny.'

Anna raises an eyebrow. 'I could respond the exact same way.'

'Fair enough, that's true.' Fernanda smiles. 'Então?' she says.

So, get to the point, eh?

'We know something about your funding.'

'Funding? We're not exactly an NGO.'

'No, but you know the expression, if you stop pedalling,' Anna says, 'the wheels fall off.'

'Nicely put.'

Anna sips at her coffee. 'São Paulo has no past, I've heard that somewhere.'

'That's a good line,' Fernanda says, 'but I suspect it's just that, a line.'

Anna smiles. She pulls a piece of paper from her bag. A piece of paper with numbers scribbled all over it. 'Bolsa Família is worth roughly 0.5 per cent of Brazilian GDP and roughly 2.5 per cent of total government expenditure, okay?'

Fernanda nods. 'That sounds about right.'

'It's going to cover, by the end of this year they reckon, roughly 11.2 million families, which equates to, mais ou menos, 44 million Brazilians.'

'Those numbers are estimates, right, based on the last three years and how registrations and so on are going so far in 2006, that fair?'

'Exactly this, menina.'

Menina. This time it's Fernanda's turn to smile.

'And you're not a political organisation,' Anna says.

'Go on.'

'That's a lot of voters indebted to Lula's government, don't you think?'

'It's not a cash for votes programme, Anna.'

'Nothing's for nothing, Fernanda, not in this world. No such thing as a free lunch and a trip down the zoo.'

Fernanda laughs. 'Very good.'

'Point is it strikes my boss, who is currently not in office, of course, that it wouldn't hurt the newer recipients of the generous and life-changing PT government's family allowance to know the political provenance of their good fortune.'

'You do have a way with words.'

'You see what I mean?'

'Your boss wants to take another run at the mayor's office, that it?'

Anna shakes her head. 'There's no specific goal here. Just a question of alignment, entendeu?'

Fernanda nods. 'And what do we get out of it?'

'The World Bank provided our generous government with a hefty loan to help manage the programme. That new ministry for social development and tackling hunger was formed, which meant easier administration, everything was expedited straight through City Hall, skipping the level of federal government. My boss was a big part of that.'

Fernanda is nodding.

Anna goes on, 'You can't do what you're doing and not nail your colours to a mast, Fernanda, you must know that.'

Fernanda says nothing.

'A lot of benefits available, keep your business clean-looking and wholesome.'

'What does that mean?'

'Capital SP and the diversification of its portfolio.'

'It's an above-board, well-documented investment.'

Anna smiles. 'We're keen to couple up. Talk to your colleague, you have my number, ne? And either way, maybe we can have a drink some time.'

'You're a sharp one, menina, I'll give you that.'

Fernanda calls a cab and sees Anna downstairs.

The journey back and the a/c hums in the car, the leather seats smooth. The city soundless, removed.

'They genuinely seem to believe in what they're doing,' Anna tells Marta. 'They seem to love it.'

'What's love got to do with it?' Marta says.

They both laugh.

Key thing about Rafa's new position and status in the organisation is that he's not slinging dope in a boca de fumo.

He is very keen to avoid that particular promotion.

He now finds himself in a sort of managerial capacity.

He is, and it feels pretty ridiculous to say it, in charge of a little supermercado at the civilised edge of the favela, just down from the main road, Giovanni Gronchi.

Sixteen years old and running a business!

Except of course he's not exactly running the business.

He's supervising the queue, working out who gets what and collecting cash.

Nominally, the old geezer Zé Roberto and his bustling shrew of a wife still run the place.

Except of course they don't.

They just receive deliveries, fetch goods for customers, make sure the place is as clean and welcoming as it can be, stack shelves, cut and package meat, stocktake, and at the end of every day, they hose down the aisles, make sure any perishables are secure in the fridges, pull down the grille and lock up.

They do everything except collect money – from anyone.

Rafa quickly brings in Franginho to help with logistics and numbers and *he* explains it all to Rafa.

'They're earning a salary from up the hill, certo? It's their business, they own the store, right, but they're earning a salary.'

'Not a retainer?'

'Don't be cheeky, filho.'

'Well that doesn't sound like too good of a deal, given the roaring trade we've been doing.'

'It's not. It's a terrible deal. The boys upstairs pay them a reasonable amount for a monthly turnover, that's true, you know, so they can live all right and they won't grumble. But, in the end, they're accepting the salary and the arrangement to protect themselves.'

'Protect themselves from who?'

'From the same people who are giving them the salary, you div.'

Rafa gets it, of course he does. 'Right.'

'Ever think about why we're holding the money, why all of the customers, every last one of them, rather than paying for what they buy simply give us a wad of cash?'

Rafa nods.

'Ever think about why each of them hands over the exact same amount?'

'I have thought about that, yes.'

'And what about the brand spanking new fifty or so Caixa bank cards you're given every week, bank cards you hand out to the young lads here to traipse around the city and withdraw as much cash as they can. Ever think about what that means, amigo?'

Rafa has thought about all this.

'And the fact you then kick this money up the chain, up the hill. What you reckon that means, eh?'

'You know what, *Little Chicken,* how about giving me a fucking break? I'm not stupid, porra, in fact quite the opposite: I'm doing what I'm told. And so should you. Ever think about what *that* means?'

'Easy, porra, I'm just laying things out, telling it like it is.'

'Yeah, yeah.'

It takes Rafa a little longer than it took Franginho to figure it out.

Bolsa Família.

The family allowance scheme is a favela scam from start to finish.

The organisation gets the cash; the favelados get the food; the mercado owners get a wage.

It's win-win.

But the number of Caixa cards is confusing for Rafa –

There are a shit-tonne coming in every week.

He decides that this is a case of mouth shut, eyes averted.

The work they do is basically crowd control. And it ain't hard. They don't even need a weapon, even the threat of one.

The mobile phone Rafa carries is quite enough.

It represents power.

And doubles as a radio, which means if anyone decides to make trouble, the cavalry are right around the corner.

And everyone knows it.

Happy days.

Rafa's grandmother does her shopping on Tuesdays. There's an orderly queue and a system in place to ensure fair distribution.

It's Franginho's idea.

'Mate, everyone comes on a fucking Monday. Mondays are a nightmare, it's stressing everyone out. There's got to be a smarter way. It's the same food every day, after all. Why does it have to be a Monday, entendeu?'

'You wanna tell the boys up the hill you've got a better system?'

'No. But you could. Trust me, you'll be golden when you do. Here, listen carefully and tell them exactly what I tell you, certo?'

Franginho's plan is to follow the same system as the citywide, municipal rodizio – a vehicle registration scheme – for driving in the centre, or what is roughly marked out as the central district.

Which is in fact pretty much anywhere anyone ever needs to go.

Rodizio days are a massive ball ache. But, in the end, the city benefits.

This is Franginho's principle.

The rodizio is organised by number plate, meaning every day only cars with a specific number at the beginning can go into town at rush hour, between seven and ten in the morning and five and eight in the afternoon.

'We could use the number plate system,' Franginho says, 'but hardly anyone in the hood has a car. So we got to think of another way.'

It's Rafa that has the idea. 'Pretty much everyone that shops here is using the Caixa cards, right?'

Franginho nods. 'Clever cookie.'

'And there's a kind of sequence, right, that's standard?'

'Not much escapes you, my friend.'

'Don't be a twat. You see where I'm going with this?'

Franginho does see.

They use the unique variations on the cards to deliver a system in which one particular combination means Monday, another Tuesday, and so on until Friday. Weekends are for stragglers and cash purchases only, if anyone has a little change to spare. Which isn't often, but it does happen, and by assigning the weekends to this alone, it gives your average favela dweller a little incentive to earn a bit more, which pushes coin into the favela economy, which means more dinheiro for the boys up the hill, which means everyone is happy.

It's a fucking masterstroke.

They're playing on an existing system. Everything in Brazil can be bought in instalments or parcelas, and that's their model, more or less.

Franginho thinks the whole thing is a scam to fuck over the poor.

'The more people are encouraged to buy beyond their means,' he says, 'the more household debt builds, falou? It's a fucking racket.'

Rafa thinks that sounds about right.

'So you're left owing every fucker, every which way. Which is why what we're doing is, *basically*, ethical, sabe?'

Rafa's not so sure about that.

It's working out though.

The boys up the hill are *very* happy.

Rafa really is golden.

Paraisópolis is buzzing.

Paradise City is turning into a money metropolis, they're saying.

There's a whole bunch of graffiti going up about the eye of the needle, a rich man and the kingdom of God, the gist of which is that, hey, if music be the food of love let's eat.

Rafa and Franginho are making bank.

Their percentage take is upped, and they employ a couple of the young lads to keep a daily eye on their original supermarket branch while they put the bite on a couple of other small mercados, forming a sort of franchise.

Happy fucking days.

And on Tuesdays, Rafa's grandmother does her shopping, so Rafa always makes sure he's around so she gets exactly what she's owed – and more – as the grandmother of one of the sharpest business brains in the jungle.

'I'm glad you're working, Rafael,' she tells him. 'Keep out of trouble, eh? You're a good boy. Don't forget that.'

They're standing outside the market.

A young lad in shorts and vest and flip-flops waits patiently to carry Rafa's grandma's groceries back home. There's a bustle to the place this morning. Men unload crates of beer at the corner bar. There's an awkward, haphazard queue of half-rusted cars parked up on the sidewalk outside the tyre shop. The owner prowls in oil-soaked T-shirt. His men slide under the cars and out again. The line at the bus stop snakes down towards them. Grim-faced workers and empragadas stoic. Nothing they can do but wait. A bus arrives, its doors pour similarly grim-looking people onto the street. Night-shift tired. The bus fills up. The driver yells. He guns the engine. The bus wobbles past the tyre shop, riding the sidewalk. Kids wander half-heartedly to school, laughing, kicking a flat football about the place, pointing and yelling, enchendo saco, *taking the piss.*

Rafa notes all this in a flash. Not his life, not anymore.

'Deus te abençoe, Vó,' Rafa says. *God bless you, gran.*

He feels a touch awkward as his grandmother has no idea quite what his job entails. He's supposed to be the big man but he can't do his job with her hanging about.

'My dad sends his love, Vó,' he says.

'Your dad?' She looks at Rafa sharply. 'And how does he do that exactly?'

Rafa's sheepish. 'Ah, you know, I hear things.'

'Hear things? Filho, you want nothing to do with the guys your father had far too much to do with, certo?' She jabs at Rafa with a crooked finger. 'You don't hear things from them. You stay away from them.'

The young lad with the groceries turns away. He stifles laughter.

Rafa cuffs him. The kid yelps. Rafa's grandma shakes her head.

'Vó, relaxa, ne? Ta tudo bem,' Rafa says.

Rafa feels the mobile phone buzzing in his pocket.

He needs to ignore it. His grandma mustn't find out.

But it's persistent. It vibrates against his skinny leg.

And he knows the drill, all right.

He should be halfway to Garibaldo by now.

'Vó, I'll see you later, okay? I need to get back, you know?'

Rafa's grandma nods slowly.

Rafa watches her turn a full circle looking at the little mercado, taking in the orderly queue, the respect her grandson has achieved is clear, he can see her see that.

She smiles. 'Good boy, God bless.'

She clasps his hand in hers.

It feels cold, like bone.

Leme has been looking at cold cases on and off for three years. Sort of a spare time thing.

'Bit of a macabre hobby, mate,' Lisboa says. 'You should get out more.'

One thing that Leme doesn't really want or *need* to do is get out more.

After the initial confusion, the initial headfuck of it all, he and Renata have never been happier.

Marriage, it seems, suits Leme.

Stability and contentment came at a price – those months of desperation, the wonder that he could ever feel satisfied without her – but they came, and he realised he *could* live without her, which made living *with* her even more joyful, somehow.

'You know why I'm doing it,' Leme says.

Lisboa nods. 'Waste of fucking time.'

The Lockwood case rankles.

Leme is pretty fucking sure they dug up a favela fall guy to take the rap and keep everyone sweet. The lemon was identified only by a nickname: Big Daddy.

Someone had a sense of humour. It wasn't clear where the nickname came from, but what *was* clear was the message from up top that the nickname was in place for a very good reason: an alias to prevent any comeback from police or thieves.

Hush hush, then. It happens. And Leme's fucked off about it.

The murder weapon never turned up.

The maid's connection to Paraisópolis was enough; no one gave a fuck about the paperweight business.

'It's at the bottom of the river now, Mario, regardless,' is Lisboa's take.

Which is as good a way of looking at it as any other.

So since all this, they've been doing grunt work, mainly. Not explicitly out to seed, but not exactly getting the Hollywood cases.

Lagnado is keeping them happy enough. Which, of course, is part of the deal.

You keep shtum, lad, and you'll get on, yeah?

Nice one, thanks, wink wink, but not *too* big of a wink, entendeu?

Leme has a mate in the Military Police. Carlos is his name.

They met a year ago on a classic vice beef – old Carlos works the dealer end, the roust-them-first-and-ask-questions-later type of scene.

They get on well, have the odd beer, make each other laugh. Not easy to make friends in their line of work. Too many bad apples souring the pie, got to know who's straight up and who's bent as hell.

Tends to be one or the other.

Leme waits a while before asking his help. He needs to know he can trust him, rely on some discretion.

Carlos might have an inside track on the Civil/Military quid pro quo that leads to a favela gang offering up a patsy for a crime that needs solving double-quick time.

If Leme's honest with himself, it's not only the injustice that sticks in his craw, it's professional pride – that feeling he's being used; he does not like it one bit.

'Come and have a word, I'll show you around,' Carlos tells him.

So Leme pops along to the Militar HQ down by Paraisópolis.

'Quickest way to find out anything round here,' Carlos says, 'is call your beak and mock up an arrest, sabe?'

Leme understands.

Carlos calls his snitch and arranges a meet at the edge of the favela, a boca de fumo alongside a steep road that runs down from the avenue, Giovanni Gronchi. Carlos and Leme take a marked Militar vehicle; Carlos calls ahead and arranges for two boys on motorbikes to get in the mix.

It's all for show.

It's as important for Carlos as it is for the informant that any meeting looks like your basic police brutality and harassment. Hardly an uncommon scene, after all, so no biggie.

'Maybe leave your mate Lisboa at home,' Carlos says.

Leme thinks that's a good idea, all things considered.

Mid-morning and the traffic is light. They reach the turning and Carlos pops the siren and they charge a hundred metres down the hill. The Militar SUV bumps. Leme hangs on.

Carlos is on his radio. 'Now, porra!' he's saying.

He swerves onto the shit-strewn excuse for a sidewalk and powers into a gap.

Carlos is out the car, gun raised.

A skinny lanky lad turns to do one.

Two police bikes block his way into the favela. Lights flash.

Carlos grabs the kid by the scruff of his neck. He pushes him against a crumbling wall. He takes a pen from his pocket and jabs deep into the lad's mouth.

The lad vomits small plastic bags.

'Bingo,' Carlos calls out.

He forces the lad into the back of the SUV.

The motorbikes edge out into the road.

Carlos gets into the back seat. He holsters his weapon. He grins.

'All right?' he says.

The lad is pissed. 'Ah, Carlão, que isso? That fucking hurt, caralho.'

'Settle down, son.'

The lad is a tall drink of water, Leme sees. He's rubbing at his throat.

'What now, eh?' he asks. 'Anyone sees, what, I tell them I wasn't pinched?'

'Tell them I nicked your product, mate, and took a commission while I was at it.'

Carlos rifles the lad's pockets and pulls a wad of notes. 'Slow day, then?'

'Porra, meu. I'm going to be light now.' The lad is shaking his head. 'What do you want, Carlão?'

'Stop whining and listen up.'

Carlos shifts in his seat. Softens. Leme looks down the road. Notes a couple of men drinking in front of a makeshift bar. He sees them point up the road. A couple more join them. Leme sees shaking of heads, hostile gestures, middle fingers up, forefingers wagging disapproval.

'Right,' Carlos says. 'What do you know about who went inside for that snuff job in Jardim Paulistano? Old British man, a while back. Nickname of the perp: Big Daddy.'

'Man, I don't remember, years ago it was.'

Carlos narrows his eyes. 'You want to play nice or you want to play nasty?'

'Porra, you know I don't know fuck all. Me deixe em paz, Carlão.'
Leave me in peace.

Unlikely, Leme thinks.

Carlos tries again. 'Think. I'm sure I can jog your memory. Who is Big Daddy?'

The lad is shaking his head, looks pained.

Leme thinks he's telling the truth. The name itself is absurd.

'Believe me, porra, I know jack-shit.'

Carlos nods. He looks at Leme. Leme shrugs.

'Okay,' Carlos says, 'you can't help on that. Maybe you ain't lying, maybe you are. If I find out you are, mate, then that pinch you're concerned about will be the least of your worries. Entendeu?'

The lad nods.

'So tell me this,' Carlos says, 'what's new in the hood? Who can I talk to might be able to help me out, eh?'

The lad breathes. He looks left then right then left again.

'Easy, chief,' Carlos says. 'No one can see through these darkened windows.'

The lad coughs. 'Yeah, I get it, Carlão.'

'Então?'

'Not much is new, things pretty quiet.'

'And?'

'There's a couple of young lads running the market now, that's new. But it's logistics, sabe? They're not muscle, not high up the food chain.'

'Who are they?'

'Kid called Rafa and his buddy Franginho.'

'Which one should I lean on, you reckon? You know, diplomatically speaking.'

Leme smiles at this.

'I'd say Franginho. He's lower profile, helping out is all. Other kid Rafa carries a phone, understand?'

Carlos nods, looks at Leme. 'Little Chicken it is, then.' He turns back to the poor lanky fuck sitting next to him. 'You know where the kid is?' Lanky nods. 'Right,' Carlos says, 'you tell Franginho to hit Burning Burger in half an hour. Got that?'

'And how am I supposed to make sure he does, porra?'

'I leave that to your twisted imagination. You just make sure you do.'

Lanky shakes his head. Whistles through his teeth. 'Burning Burger, half an hour. Fine, I'll sort it.'

'And make sure you let the boys up the hill know about your run-in with the law. How you don't got all their money today.'

Lanky nods.

'Now fuck off,' Carlos says.

Lanky fucks off – sharpish.

There are whistles and cat calls from down the street.

Carlos holds the money up. 'Let's treat ourselves to a burger lunch, my friend.'

Leme laughs. 'All this police work, I'm starving.'

Carlos jumps out the back seat. He takes a step towards the boca de fumo. He has a word with one of the Militars on the bikes. The guy dismounts. He pulls an evidence bag and, gloves on, fishes Lanky's vomit-flecked plastic wraps and seals them inside.

Carlos swings into the driver's seat.

He holds up the bag.

He grins. 'Time to get a little leverage on Little Chicken.'

Leme and Carlos chow down.

The burgers are meaty, juicy, the cheese sharp, the onions just the right amount of butter –

They both neck cold beers.

They drink from large, frosted glasses with hearty handles. They *chug*. It's called Bavaria, the beer brand – faux-German festive situation.

The fries are dusted with salt.

Carlos is meticulous with his condiment deployment. Before each bite, he squeezes a careful, thin line of mustard, then mayo, then ketchup directly onto the meat. He works like a craftsman, Leme notes. It reveals, Leme thinks, a rigour to the man, shows he likes to do things in a certain – the *right* – way.

Leme's more of a mustard covering when the meal arrives and leave it at that.

Concentrate on the eating. Still, he sees the benefit in Carlos's approach.

'Top burger,' Carlos says.

Leme nods. 'Been coming here for years. I know one of the cooks a bit.'

'Yeah?'

'And he often knows what's going on up the hill, entendeu?'

'Yeah.'

They munch on.

Leme says, 'You think your boy will come through?'

'If he knows what's good for him, he will.'

Leme snorts. 'And then what?'

'Wait and see.' Carlos smiles. 'Fact is nothing's going to happen too quick, but we'll get another ear on the ground, if we play it right. And to groom a beak, it's slowly slowly catchy monkey the way we *do* play it.'

'We?'

Carlos grins. 'Good point.'

He waves at a waiter, signals for two more beers.

'Look, old Lanky is an established face,' Carlos says, 'a low-level dealer, reliable at what he does, does it well, I gather, but he's not going anywhere, know what I mean?'

Leme nods.

'He's pondlife, to a point, certo? And he knows that to keep his head above the dirty stagnant water that runs through his neck of the woods, he needs to play nicely with us, and be very careful with them.'

'Nice turn of phrase, mate.'

'They call me Shakespeare in the locker room.'

'Do they really?'

Carlos grins. He swallows the last of his sandwich. He wipes his mouth with a theatrical flourish. He nails the last of his lager. He checks his watch.

'Should be here any minute,' he says. 'Remember, good chance this whole thing has been buried deep, certo?'

Leme nods. He's clutching at something, he knows that. It's peace of mind. It's this naïve idea of justice, of his fucking job.

The door swings open.

Lanky walks in with a geeky-looking kid.

The kid looks wary. His legs are stick-thin, but he's got a chubby little pot above his shorts and he also looks, Leme thinks, happy he's about to fill it.

They take a corner table.

It's a mixed clientele, Burning Burger.

It's a twenty-four-hour place so you get your playboy types swinging by at the end of a long night, and your young families too, all sorts, as it's affordable, and cops eat here, mainly Militars. You get your suited working men, mainly alone, sitting at the counter, and then, if they've got a bit of change, you might get some favelado kids –

But they keep a low profile.

They're watched like hawks.

The security is always poised to kick them out, and give them a kicking too, it's been known.

Militars turn a blind eye to that.

Course they fucking do.

Carlos nods over at Lanky.

Lanky gets up, goes towards the toilets, disappears through the door.

Carlos stands. 'Come on, let's get this done.'

Franginho's studying the menu when they sit down next to him.

He registers what has happened –

His eyes flash confusion, anger, disappointment, resignation.

'Hello, Franginho,' Carlos says. 'Can I get you a burger?'

Carlos doesn't wait for an answer.

He waves a waiter over. Points at Franginho.

'Get him the works, burger with everything on it, an X-Tudo, you know the one? A plate of fries and a milkshake. What kind of milkshake you like, kid?'

'Strawberry.'

'Good choice.' Carlos look at the waiter. 'Don't hang about with it, entendeu?'

The waiter moves fast.

Franginho studies his hands.

'Know why we want to see you?'

'No, Senhor.'

'Course you don't.'

Leme sits back in his chair. Give Shakespeare the stage, he thinks.

The waiter brings a strawberry milkshake.

'Tuck in, son,' Carlos says. 'And don't fret, your mate Lanky legs isn't getting any dinner, sabe?'

Franginho takes a gulp.

The milkshakes are good here, Leme's had one or two in his time and they are big, thick, serious –

Franginho cannot help but smile, lick his lips.

'Good, ne?' Carlos says.

Franginho nods.

The burger arrives.

Carlos points at it. 'Crack on, I'll do the talking. You just nod you understand. Got that?'

Franginho nods.

'Good lad.'

Leme watches as Carlos leans across the table, narrows the distance between him and the kid.

The kid eats like it might be, if not his last meal exactly, then his last burger at least.

He savours it *while* he demolishes it. Face right in it, eyes down.

'How's the burger?' Carlos asks.

The kid pauses, looks up. 'World class.'

Carlos says, 'We hear you're helping the boys run the old supermarket, top end of the favela. You and your buddy, some moleque called Rafa.'

Franginho says nothing, keeps eating. He's using both hands, one on the burger, the other cramming fries.

'What we want to know,' Carlos says, 'is why Rafa has a phone and you don't.'

The kid nods.

'Seems like he's the boss. You know why?'

The kid shakes his head.

'But you'll find out?'

The kid nods.

'See, the thing is, Little Chicken, a bunch of people in here have seen me buying you a meal. Old Lanky will testify to that, I'm sure. I need a guarantee so I can put the word out I was just fucking with you, entendeu?'

The kid nods.

Leme looks on.

Carlos pulls the plastic bag of cheap, favela product.

'The other way this goes is that I'm having lunch with my good friend Mario from the Polícia Civil, and we see something suspicious with you and Lanky and we recover this... evidence. Okay?'

Franginho nods again.

'Here, same time, in three days. Certo?'

Franginho nods.

Carlos looks at Leme. 'Let's leave the kid to enjoy his lunch, shall we?'

Rafa's phone is still buzzing when he gets away from his grandmother.

A call, which is not common.

He hits green.

'Moleque.' It's Garibaldo. 'I shouldn't have to wait for you to pick up.'

Rafa grunts.

'Woman from the office you know is on the move. She's just walked past Casa Bahia, headed towards Batata Suiça, you know the place?'

'Yeah, the baked potato is world class.'

'Don't be cheeky, son. Get after her.'

Rafa jumps on his board. He's not gone a dozen metres before he feels that vibration again against his leg.

Garibaldo.

'And filho,' he's saying, 'you follow the bitch back to her office and then after that you follow her home, entendeu?'

Rafa sucks his teeth. 'Porra, I done that already, cara.'

'She's moved, dickhead.'

Renata decides to walk to the site.

It's not as risky as it used to be, she thinks.

Her office has been up and running in Paraisópolis for a few years. It's over three, in fact, she realises. She's helped a lot of people over these three years. She quickly made a name for herself as someone who can be trusted, someone who is one of the good guys, on your side. Most of the work she does is sort of upmarket notary work, getting documents in order, drawing up contracts, family law, weddings, funerals, inheritance, probate –

Which is not always easy in the favela.

Who owns what is the big question in any case, in any disagreement.

Short version: the family might own the shacks, own the bricks and mortar and wood and plastic, but more often than not the state owns the land on which it was, technically, illegally built.

And when it's not owned by the state, it's the property of the leaders of the favela community council, as the organisation somewhat ironically refers to itself.

And the organisation in this case is the PCC, the First Capital Command, the biggest organised crime syndicate in Brazil.

Renata knows all about the PCC.

She had to get their approval to open her office.

A sit-down, with a couple of vaguely senior figures who told her she would be watched, but that they understood she'd be doing good for the community and anything that keeps life smooth in the favela is a good thing for the organisation. Basically.

The gang's key figures gave the thumbs-up from prison, where most of them are and continue to run the organisation from it. She's been accepted, so she's fairly comfortable walking the streets of the jungle.

'Don't trust anything anyone from the organisation ever says to you,' Mario's told her more than once. 'They're slippery as fuck, they're serious, heavy criminals and they'll never be your friends.'

Some of that seems pretty obvious to Renata.

She's told Mario more than once not to ever tell her what to do.

It's a good system, so far.

Renata has begun to wonder what the organisation would think if it were more widely known that her husband is a detective in the Civil Police.

The question of land ownership and the Singapore Project business is complex. Renata has seen that Capital SP put together a syndicate to assist the state-run department in terms of costs –

A loan.

But where exactly the money has gone is not especially clear.

Certain payments seem to have been made into accounts associated with businesses in and around Paraisópolis.

Renata's hunch is that these are 'permission payments', known as 'accessibility charges' that have gone to the PCC to secure the location for the build. Disguised, effectively, in local investment, and as a form of transferred property ownership.

If the state does own the land, then the administrators of a state-run social housing project working for the state can't really buy the land from itself.

Not even in São Paulo have they got the gall to try that.

Renata's problem is that Capital SP and its investors are important in the funding of her pro-bono legal aid NGO. She's not sure how useful it is to find out. And this is not something she can talk to Mario about.

She passes Casa Bahia. She doesn't know the names of the streets, never remembers where, in terms of the charter, one ends and one begins, only thinks of them in terms of work she's done. So, here, two doors down from the supermarket, she helped secure a driving licence for the mother of a family of three. A year after that, she helped the same woman buy the car outright that she'd been paying for in extortionate instalments. A year after *that*, only three months ago, in fact, the same woman came to Renata as her eldest son was arrested for assault.

Renata couldn't help with that, no matter what the kid's mother thought, no matter what Renata had done for her in the past.

The main problem Renata has in her job, emotionally speaking, is the inevitable fact that she often ends up letting people down. Their expectations of her, and not unreasonably, given the huge amount she achieves for her clients, are unrealistic.

They imagine Renata as some kind of superwoman.

No pressure then, she often thinks.

The site she's headed for fringes the favela on its eastern side.

When she started the office, the Military Police kept an eye out for her, kept an eye *on* her. They called it protection, keeping a respectable member of society safe, ensuring her welfare and all that jazz, but Renata was never sure what it was they were looking out for. It became clear, pretty quickly, that they didn't approve of Renata's efforts to help the disenfranchised.

She was branded a do-good cunt.

'They ought to stay exactly where God saw it fit to put them,' is the gist, meaning keep the poor poor, let the weak and needy remain weak and needy.

Do not cede the higher ground.

In the context of a favela in São Paulo, the Paraisópolis crater, this is an apt metaphor.

Renata's finding out that an empowered community means less economic and political reliance on the gang that runs the place. The gang the police are looking to contain. Renata's finding out that her work might be helping the police keep the peace.

If that's what the police are trying to do, of course.

It's pretty fucking far from likely, to use Mario's phrase.

She concedes she might be being naïve.

You know the right people, can make the right connections, have the right product for the right occasion, and there is a lot of money in the game.

Mario's told her the authorities turn a blind eye to the racket.

Renata reckons the authorities *are* the racket.

She reaches the edge of the favela. The sun is piercing.

She squints, watches traffic crawl past.

She scans the road, left then right, then left again, and crosses over to the site.

The area is marked off by temporary, ten-foot high barriers. At the entrance, there's a Portakabin office. The windows are murky, dust-rinsed, and there is every appearance that no one is at home.

She knocks on the door and waits.

Rafa sees the woman cross the road and head towards the fucking building site, as it's known.

Fuck.

He knows that she does not want to go in there.

He's not only heard the rumours, but he *knows*.

You go in there, it spells a significant amount of trouble.

Seeing the woman – *his* woman, as she's now known, to a few – on the brink of going in, leaves Rafa in a pickle.

He hesitates.

He sees her outside the cabin. He sees there's no one inside.

Which is a spot of luck.

He feels a rush of something he doesn't quite recognise.

Fact is, ever since he tailed her to the swank restaurant, delivered the message and followed her home, he's had a bit of a soft spot for her. He sees her around – he looks for her, if he's honest, and why not, she's fit as fuck, after all – and he knows she sees him. They exchange something every time they see each other. A look, nothing more, but there's a sort of tight half-smile she does, like she's grateful, which is odd, considering the formal context of their relationship, as Franginho once put it.

It's enough to make Rafa skate fast as he can past Casa Bahia, through the traffic, not stopping, and across the road after her.

Renata peers inside the cabin, hand cupped above her eyes.

There's definitely no one in there.

Beyond the cabin is an open sandpit of a space about the size of a half dozen tennis courts. It's empty. It's clearly been worked on, dug up, flattened, but there's no machinery. It looks abandoned.

At the far edge, there are more cabins, either side of which are parked two vans, and two other cars. She can't see anyone, but it looks like there's movement behind.

It's a bit of a walk, it's very open. She's vulnerable, exposed, and she hesitates –

She simply wants to know why so little has happened here up to now.

There must be a supervisor, or at least a security guy or two, who can help her.

She sets off across the open space.

Rafa's too slow.

She's halfway to the other side before he reaches the entrance.

What she doesn't know about, and can't see, are the lookouts posted along the walls that surround the site.

Rafa reckons they'll hear the warning whistles at exactly the same time.

Renata is twenty, thirty metres from the cabins and vehicles.

She's wearing sunglasses, has her legal aid office card, her briefcase, and she steadies herself, takes a deep breath –

Which is when she hears whistles. She spins. They're coming from all sides, high up, she can't see anyone, they're loud, insistent –

Two men with automatic weapons come out from behind the cabins, pointing the guns at her, jogging towards her, snarling looks on their faces like angry dogs, shouting something.

Renata stops, stands dead still, puts her briefcase down – *slowly*, spreads her arms, opens her palms, just as Mario has shown her in case anything like this ever happened.

The men – in vests, shorts, flip-flops, sunglasses glinting in the sun – stop ten metres in front of her and raise their weapons.

They're saying nothing now. Renata does nothing.

Then –

A voice behind her, yelling to the gunmen it's all right, not a problem, relax, she's with me, it's all good.

It's all good, the voice repeats.

Another man comes from the cabins. He seems to be listening to this voice.

He waves the gunmen away.

'Oh, Rafa, que isso, cara?' he shouts. 'Embora, moleque.'

Rafa, mate, what the fuck? Get out of here, kid.

He goes back to the cabins.

Renata turns. She sees the young man she's known for a few years now.

The boy with the skateboard.

'We really should go,' he says to her.

She nods, gives a tight half-smile.

Rafa's walking back into the favela.

He can hardly follow the woman home now, so he's left her, told her this didn't happen, end of, and she seems okay with that.

As he mooches home, slow, despondent for some reason, his phone buzzes.

Fucking what now? he thinks.

This phone is a fucking cross to bear.

A message.

Whatever you're doing, don't. Stop it, deliver this right now.

And then:

A date.

May 12.

2

Rebel yell

May 2006

___

The police are totally outgunned. They try to
protect us, but really they're unprepared.

Lúcia Sousa da Silva, 46, greengrocer, Paraisópolis

It is barbarity against barbarity, truculence against truculence,
firepower against firepower. Down this path, only chaos can be sowed.

A group of prominent lawyers, law professors and bar association leaders

We don't bargain with banditry.

Cláudio Lembo, governor of São Paulo State, 2006

We are prepared for much more and have the ability for much more.
The authorities have declared war but are forgetting that they are
leaving society defenceless. The two sides have firepower, and those
who lose out are those who don't belong to either of the two sides.

Marcola, leader of the PCC, First Capital Command

Ray's been busy up in Brasília.

He's been cultivating.

His seed money has come in *very* useful.

The introductions were arranged by a certain Luís Favre, Rasputin to his enemies. Or, Mr Marta, as he's known in congressional circles. Just another emasculated klutz, some think. Look at her ex-husband. Others reckon Rasputin's got more reach than, well, Rasputin, Ray supposes.

___

No one seems to be able to end the analogy very well.

Ray doesn't mind. He's happy to be back in São Paulo.

Brasília is summer camp. The digs are like dorm rooms. The streets they're on arranged by number; every block looks the same. The police are heavy-handed camp counsellors –

It doesn't feel like a place for grown-ups.

Ray's been insinuating himself into the congressional group charged with investigating organised crime activity. This group has been inviting a number of senior people – police, mainly, federal, civil and military – to give evidence as part of the inquiry. Closed-door sessions.

Ray's way in: Capital SP has an even longer reach than Rasputin.

But Ray hasn't actually been *in*. Doors remained closed.

But he made a friend, a friend he's now meeting in an old man's bar in Vila Madalena.

Ray pops meds. Ray gulps beer. Ray eyes the door.

It's late-morning quiet.

Ray's got a bowl of Canja de Galinha on the go. A chicken broth that makes him feel less bothered about the pre-lunch beers. The chopp, the glasses of draft lager that the waiters dump in front of him before he's even finished the last, is outstanding. Creamy, smooth, cold, crisp –

Ray's nailed a few in the half hour he's been waiting.

He arrived early for that reason.

The broth *soothes*.

His new friend told him the place, Bar Filial, was old-style decent. It's got a black and white checked floor, cheap linoleum, Ray thinks, wipe-clean. The tables have off-white stone tops and sturdy black legs. The chairs are stiff-backed and uncomfortable, encourage an edge-of-the-seat vibe, encourage activity, which in this case means more eating and drinking.

There are two vast fridges with Bohemia printed on the front; a small rectangular window reveals rows of brown bottles. Ray likes a Bohemia: it's a stylish brew, touch of class about it. Frosted glass hides the kitchen, and Ray makes out the shapes of large men, frying shit behind. Stacks of cachaça bottles up the walls, whiskey, too,

Red and Black labels, the amount left in each marked with a line. Whiskey club, is what it is: you buy your bottle and keep it behind the bar, note how much you've had with each visit. Loyalty scheme, Ray thinks.

At night, the street here teems. No discerning type would think of coming before it gets dark.

Ray digs a Saturday night in Vila Madalena.

It's a low-down, dirty mess. Bars on every corner, bands competing to be heard, the smell of barbecuing meat, a mass of bodies swaying across the roads, weaving between honking cars, the drivers knocking beer cans as they crawl past each other.

Ray's friend has chosen well. Bar Filial hits all the right spots.

Aside from the guy Ray thinks might be the owner eating a champion's breakfast – spicy sausage, sliced, on a bed of yellow rice – Ray's all alone.

Then he's not.

'Bom dia, Rayzão.'

Ray looks up and his friend is standing over the table.

Rayzão: Big Ray.

'I'm not sure that nickname quite works, amigo.'

'Ha, it's a compliment, porra. Grande Ray, sabe? You'll learn.'

Ray laughs. He waves over a waiter. 'The chopp here is outstanding.'

'I know.'

Ray's friend takes a seat. 'Funny how much doing business with you is doing business in bars, sabe?'

Ray grins. 'I'm a nomad, son. No office, no problems.'

The waiter dumps beers.

'Saúde.'

They knock glasses and drink.

'Have some soup,' Ray says. 'It's a real comfort in this heat.'

Ray's friend laughs. 'Let's get to it, shall we.'

Ray nods. 'I'm hoping you have something for me.'

'I do.'

Ray nods again.

He knows he can rely on this new friend.

This new friend is a sort of concierge to the political world, works closely with old Favre from time to time, basically freelance, knows how to hook people up. And takes a fee – a decent enough percentage cut – for it. Brasília is run by coalitions; a man who knows how to synthesise interests is valuable. Ray knows this new friend by his professional name: Joãozinho, *little Johnny*. It's ironic, apparently.

Ray pushes his soup to one side, raises his glass of chopp.

Ray grins. 'Cheers, I'm all ears.'

Joãozinho takes an envelope from his pocket and places it on the table. He pushes it towards Ray. Ray picks it up, weighs it in his hand. Ray's eyebrows shoot upwards.

'It's a recording, made on a pen drive, dead simple,' Joãozinho says. 'But it's clear, and obvious who is doing the talking.'

'Okay.'

'The congressional inquiry you're interested in, one of those closed-door sessions.'

'Outstanding.'

'Don't blow your load yet, Big Ray, you don't know what it is.'

'I'm an excitable guy. An optimist.'

Joãozinho smiles. 'So a couple of days ago the inquiry called in two very senior police officials.'

Ray nods.

'Closed doors, like I said, attempt to shut off any leaks.'

'And yet you're here.'

Joãozinho shrugs. 'It is what it is, porra.'

'And what is it?'

'An attempt to disrupt the influence and power base of the PCC, the biggest organised crime syndicate in the country, as you well know, amigo.'

'I do know that very well, yes.'

'And you also know, I suspect, that the leaders of this syndicate, and a good number of their associates, are currently behind bars in São Paulo state prisons, from which, thanks to mobile phones smuggled in past guards who are more than happy to look the other way at the right price, they run the organisation with impunity.'

'Yeah, I know the scene.'

'But what you don't know is what's on this recording.'

'Enlighten me, mestre.'

Joãozinho smiles at this.

'A plan, in some detail, to move the leaders of the PCC and around seven hundred other members to a maximum security unit that is, oh, hundreds of miles from São Paulo city, with the stated aim of fucking up the syndicate's stranglehold on dozens of prisons all over the country.'

'They'll enjoy that idea.'

The two men consider this for a moment, drink beer.

'You want this recording, Ray?'

'I certainly do.'

'And I don't suppose I should bother asking why?'

Ray grins. 'Ask me no questions, little Johnny, and I'll not have to answer any.'

'You've a way with words.'

'I know quite a few of them.'

Joãozinho smiles. 'You interested in provenance?'

'This the only copy?'

'It's the only *copy*. Original recording still exists.'

'And you got it where?'

'Sound technician.'

'He play hardball?'

'Not really.'

'But you will.'

Joãozinho grins. 'I will be asking for considerably more than he did, yes.'

'And I respect you even more for doing so.'

'You know the drill.'

'It's not my first rodeo.'

They shake hands. Ray pockets the envelope.

'Saideira?' Ray asks.

One for the road.

'Be rude not to.'

Ray signals to the waiter for another round by circling his finger over their table. He adds a bring-the-check flourish.

The waiter dumps glasses. He drops a metal ashtray with the bill.

The saideira is on the house.

'Good lad,' Ray says. 'Saúde.'

Again, they knock their glasses. Their glasses spill foam. They drink deep.

'I do got one question for you, Ray.'

'Shoot.'

'The senior police officials captured on your new recording make reference to a whole load of passes for prisoners across the state to visit their families over the Mothers' Day weekend.'

'That ain't a question, Johnny boy.'

'You know what they say: talk or get into trouble.'

Ray smiles. 'But you do have a question.'

'Yeah, I do. Apparently a legal aid office in São Paulo is helping to process a good number of these passes, expedite them, that kind of thing.'

'Every little thing needs to be notarised in this country. Red tape and whatnot.'

'Tell me about it.'

'Getting my driving licence was a bitch.'

'You should've said. I know people who'll take the test for you, practical and theory, for a very reasonable fee.'

'Yeah? My name on the licence?'

'Senhor Ray Marx, first class.'

Ray smiles. 'You wanna know what exactly, Johnny? If I've heard this weekend pass story or if I *know* it?'

Joãozinho opens his palms. 'There just seems to be something fortuitous about the timing, falou?'

'Big word, fortuitous.'

'Yeah, same number of syllables as coincidence.'

Ray grins. 'You deal in information, in bringing people together.'

'So I don't worry about the consequences of what happens when I do.'

'You've hit the nail, as they say, square on the cabeça.'

'Amigo, I ain't counting on being left to pay the duck here, take the blame for something I didn't do.'

Ray smiles. 'He who doesn't have a dog,' he says, 'hunts with a cat.'

'Well played, amigo.' Joãozinho kills his beer. He stands. 'I'll be seeing you, Ray.' He smiles. 'Or not.'

Ray tips an imaginary hat.

Little Johnny leaves.

Leme's listening to Lisboa tell him a few home truths.

'Fact is, querido, you've been so obsessed with thinking about who *didn't* kill Lockwood, you haven't been thinking about who *did*.'

It's a fair point.

Turns out that Lockwood had an interesting past. He worked at a school in England, was popular and caring. His murder made the news, low-level. The head of the school where he taught from the late 60s, was quoted: 'He was a much-liked and respected teacher. Noted for his generosity, the power of his personality, his capacity for friendship and his sense of humour. He will be much missed by his many friends at the school.' Another friend, too: 'He was tremendously gifted and energetic. You would find it hard to get anybody to say a bad word about Paddy – he was that type of person.'

But that wasn't all. No, Senhor, he went the extra mile for his pupils. He helped save seven kids from the Moonies, for fuck's sake. In 1981, parents told him how their two sons had been brainwashed and taken to America. He took out a bank loan and flew to San Francisco. Lockwood mobbed up with a local chaplain, a lad called Richard Hullah, and the two of them convinced the cult that the brothers needed their education, to let them go without any fuss. They secured the freedom of another five lads while they were there. The Moonies have form, after all, were involved in the abduction of an Irish kid, Phillip Cairns, in 1986, so this is a tasty bit of knowledge.

Leme's impressed by it.

Add to that all the glowing testimonies from the staff at the school, the kids, the parents, and it's not too hard to see Lagnado's perspective –

Let sleeping dogs lie.

Lisboa's still talking. 'Naïve, too, mate, to think you didn't let this happen. You colluded – *we* colluded – to an extent, falou? And the clever thing is we can tell ourselves we had no choice.'

Leme's nodding.

'And at almost exactly the moment,' Lisboa says, 'that we might have kicked back against it, exactly the moment we're told nice one, thanks, but we'll take it from here, you met Renata and, mate, frankly, your priorities changed.'

It really is a fair point.

They never ascertained what was in Lockwood's safe, so, technically speaking, they didn't know if anything valuable had in fact gone missing.

The security guys in their little green booths claimed they never saw anyone go into the house, so there was no corroboration with the maid's version, which of course squared with the idea that it was all about her favela connections.

When Leme did see the CCTV footage, it showed in very grainy black and white a man entering by the side door, without using force, which, for their narrative purposes, meant he had got hold of a key.

Favela connection again.

And the kicker was to play it like the maid was a victim too, not her fault, not her responsibility, tragic, that's all.

So the narrative worked, then it was a case of finding a likely face to fit up for it. Easy pickings finding a villain in Paraisópolis, so Carlos tells him.

Scenario was most probably a powwow with a Militar go-between and a top boy from up the hill. A name and an address, and Bob's your uncle and blah blah blah, medals and honour and the uneasy peace in Paradise City is maintained.

It all made sense.

'It's fucking utilitarianism,' Lisboa says. 'Think about it: greatest good for the greatest number, that was the outcome. So if we did collude in leaving off a little, then fair play to us, mate, we did the right thing.'

Leme nods.

'And who's to know it wasn't this Big Daddy anyway, entendeu? The alias is in place for a good reason.'

'Utilitarianism,' Leme says. 'You going to night school?'

'Don't be a cunt, Mario.'

Leme smiles.

Thing is, he hasn't told Lisboa two important developments.

One, the fact that he is helping Carlos groom an informant in young Franginho.

Two, he was recently paid a visit by an ex-employee of the school where Lockwood was headmaster.

The first development is out of his hands, a part-time thing, he's dependent on Carlos and is waiting for the nod to go back down to Paraisópolis.

The second involved a tawdry but illuminating conversation.

Leme had left his details with the school. He had a call from a teacher there a week ago. He isn't sure what to do with it.

It seems the British school has its share of scandal.

The teacher, a thirty-something bloke called James, does not speak highly of the place.

'It's a finishing school, that's all,' he tells Leme. 'The kids believe they're the bees' knees as it's all they've been told all their lives. The teachers are either washed up on their fat salary and pension, sub-par Brazilians, or wasters off the international circuit.'

Leme raises eyebrows. 'Not the reputation I heard.'

'Nah, well,' this James says, 'money is everything, isn't it? Mutton dressed as lamb, overall. Most of these international places are.'

Leme shrugs.

'Put it this way,' James says, 'if you work on the circuit for too long, you'll never get a job back in England, and definitely not at any sort of management level. Schools don't trust you. It's indicative.'

'Right.'

Leme isn't sure why he's having this conversation. He was piqued by the call, the promise of information. Now he's sitting outside a corner bar in Pinheiros listening to a bitter man rant.

'You sure you don't want any?' James says, waving a bottle of Original in Leme's face.

Leme shakes his head, arms crossed. 'Why don't you tell me why we're here?'

'Yeah, yeah, course. Hang on.' James waves the bottle in the air and another appears. 'Sorry, I'm really hungover.'

'It happens.'

'Yeah, this city drives you to drink.'

'You know what,' Leme says, 'I will have some.'

'Good man.'

James splashes beer into small glasses.

It is a fairly textbook Pinheiros haunt. An old-school joint, near the turnoff to Vila Madalena. At this point, the neighbourhood is all pretty basic: you have standard corner bars with their regulars, plastic awnings, plastic tables and chairs bending under the weight of the customers. Leme has seen casualties on this kind of seating. These places do standard burgers, leathery steak beaten tongue-thin, cheap cachaça and beers in bottles. The street is home to a few brightly lit buffet restaurants with their piles of day-old feijoada and gleaming butter-heavy veg. Further down the whispers of gentrification: trendy chains and concept breweries, a posh French restaurant, live music venues selling R$20 glasses of Guinness. The street is a symbol now, Leme's heard: it divides old-money Jardins and hippie Vila Madalena.

Gentrification: a new word for Leme. He wonders when Bixiga, the bladder of São Paulo, his old stomping ground, will get a makeover.

It'll need a new nickname.

'Let's have it then,' Leme says.

'It's simple,' James says. 'Lockwood was gay.'

'Huh.'

'Worst-kept secret in the school.'

'Why are you telling me this?'

'Because I suspect no one else has.'

He's right there, Leme thinks. 'And why haven't they?'

James gulps lager. 'Well, it doesn't match the school's carefully curated squeaky-clean image. And you well know, detective, in Brazil homo teacher means kiddie fiddler.'

Leme shrugs, makes a face.

'So Lockwood wasn't exactly open, right? And we all have needs, don't we? So there was the odd rumour of how his needs were met.'

'And?'

'Late-night visits, professional services, that kind of thing.'

'Can you corroborate any of this?'

'I don't expect anyone else will say the same thing. It's just what I heard.'

Leme lets this news sink in.

'Why did it take you so long to contact me?' Leme says.

'I am no longer employed by the school. I liked Lockwood, he was a good lad, fair, decent boss. The guy that took over, not so much.'

'And this is your revenge?'

'Something like that. The new head has got one of the teachers up the stick, right? Well, let's say there may have been an overlap in our amorous activity.'

Leme smiles, makes a face that says, nice one Cyril.

'The place is pure hypocrisy.'

'And now you're a crusader for the truth,' Leme says.

'Yeah, I'm a regular fucking Batman and Robin.'

Leme smiles. 'Go easy on the lager, son,' he says.

What Leme decides to do about this is contact Vice and figure out where a rich man might find a companion.

'Like looking for a rent boy in a haystack,' they tell him. 'We can help you get laid, if that's what you want.'

Sense of humour in Vice. Leme reckons you'd probably need one.

Vice tell Leme about some interesting correspondence they've had with a man calling himself 'Evandro' living in the northeast, Recife. Some sort of garoto de programa. *Boy on the game*. Looks like he turns tricks in a sauna. Dreams of leaving and setting up home with a rich gringo. Some revealing photos. An advert, really, the Vice boys suppose. The last message a plea to see some shrivel-cocked old man. They tell Leme about a report from the NGO, Programa Pegação, from the mid-90s. Straight men posing as gay to earn money from tourists. Still all the rage, apparently.

Leme's heard sex tourism is ruining the northeast. European men are paying large sums for the company of young girls and boys. Ruthless gangster-types are exploiting these workers, luring them from the slums and forcing them into prostitution with false promises of a better life.

This doesn't sound like the experience a fella like Lockwood would go for at all.

Not when you factor in his heroic saving of those kids.

Leme reckons he seems a bit classier.

Vice tell Leme that the young men are well-mannered, dapper, urbane. They're considerate. They work in relatively sophisticated places. They understand the benefits of striking up a relationship. They are driven – many of them – by material desire, certainly, and this whole thing is simply a transaction cost in their particular mode of capitalism, an exchange: one asset for another. There isn't the vulgarity you see when you walk the streets. There's the promise of something more.

'Though perhaps you just went to the right places.'

The Vice boys howled at that one.

'That sound like your man at all?'

Leme has no fucking idea.

They also tell Leme that tourists in São Paulo tend to start near Praça Alexandre de Gusmão. The park there is a notorious hotspot for perverts and paedos. A line of underage rent-boy cocksuckers available to those who seek it. Dropout schoolgirl pussy for hire for your less than discerning nonce.

Charming, Leme says.

'They come out to play at dusk,' the vice guys say. 'Feeding time at the zoo.'

Leme heads up there one evening. He's not sure what he's looking for, or what he wants to know, but he figures the answers will present themselves when he's had a poke around, as it were.

'Kerb crawling, mate,' the Vice guys tell Leme. 'All the cool kids are doing it.'

Leme doesn't feel cool ghosting down the side of the park looking for a lad to pick up.

It's not a great look, kerb crawling, Leme now sees.

You feel like a right cunt.

First thing he thinks: they're very young.

Second thing is: there must be a better way than this if you have any cash at all.

Though, of course, perhaps this aspect is part of the allure.

On his second pass, a scrawny lad – gold earrings and a ripped vest – leans into Leme's window. He's chewing gum. Leme admires his haircut. He's got a spring to him, too, a bounce.

'Can I do for you?' he asks Leme. 'I ain't seen you here before. No time like your first time, querido.'

Leme grins. He likes the lad's style. 'Get in, cowboy,' he says.

The lad pulls the door open.

'And buckle up, buttercup,' Leme says.

The lad smiles. 'Buckling up is extra.'

Leme pops the gas and they pull away.

'Nice wheels,' the kid says, flirting. 'Where are you taking me, eh? I bet your pad is smoother than a homo wax job.'

'What's that, top and tail?'

The kid laughs. 'Back, crack and sack, old man.'

Leme smiles. They drive in silence for a moment. He flips a button and all the doors lock –

'I'll get to the point,' Leme says. 'I need to speak to someone who's been on the scene for at least three years, falou? You know anyone who can help.'

The kid raises his palms, leans back against the door, guard up. 'Who are you?'

'Don't get your knickers in a twist, big boy, I'm Civil Police, detective, and this is very much off the record.'

'And – what – I can just trust you?'

'You ain't got much choice, son. You don't cooperate, however, and maybe I make a call, entendeu?'

The kid relaxes. 'Yeah, okay.'

'So you know anyone can help me?'

The kid looks down, examines his hands.

'I can help.'

'You?'

'Yeah, me, I've been around a few years, okay.'

'You don't look old enough.'

'You'd be surprised. In some circles, I'm already a bit too old, you understand?'

Leme swallows. 'And you've worked here how long?'

'Four years, on and off.'

'On and off?'

'Ah, this isn't full-time employment. You don't get a dental plan, chief.'

Leme smiles. 'Okay, and when you're off?'

'When you're off it's because you've got some patsy on the hook, right? You get a retainer sort of thing.'

'That the career goal, is it?'

'Beats working.'

'Yeah,' Leme says, 'this don't look much fun.'

'It's not.'

'You fancy a bite?' Leme asks.

'Yeah, why not?'

'There's a sweater on the back seat,' Leme says. 'Put it on and I'll buy you a sandwich.'

The kid does as he's told.

They sit up at the counter in Padaria Bella Paulista on the corner of Rua Augusta and Haddock Lobo.

They're next to the patisserie section, the fridge full of cakes and desserts.

The kid drools.

TVs show sports and news channels. It's early and apart from a few post-work drinkers, it's quiet. The lights are bright, the tables are simple.

And yet –

The joint jumps in the small hours. Twenty-four-hour place, popular with all sorts.

Clubbers and clients, white-collar, blue-collar, cops.

'I been brought here by a John more than once, detective,' the kid says.

'Play like I'm your big brother, moleque.'

Leme orders a beer for himself, a Diet Coke for the kid.

Leme scans the menu. All the classics.

He chooses the turkey cheese for himself and the Italian mortadella for the kid.

Leme watches the counter servers work.

Mortadella is sliced, stacked, then griddled crisp.

The cheese melts and floods the stack.

The sandwiches are ample.

Crusty white bread heavy with filling. Leme counts a good half-dozen layers. The meats are packed in tyre-thick. The cheese is like lava. The onion and salad crunch.

The kid has a field day with the condiments –

He really goes to town. Mayo, mustard, ketchup, chilli sauce –

The sandwiches are *beasts*.

Leme lets the boy chow down. He's finishing his mortadella as Leme polishes off the first half of his turkey cheese. Leme signals the waitress he wants his leftovers wrapped. He hands the package to the boy.

'There's your dessert, pal.'

'You're a gentleman.'

Leme wipes his mouth. Plucks a toothpick from a plastic dispenser. Jabs and scrapes with it. Gets a little tooth-groove on.

'Would you say your scene is pretty tight?' Leme asks.

'Ah, more or less, certo?'

'But you know each other?'

'We do. We're in competition, you know, theoretically speaking, but it doesn't work out like that.'

'No?'

'Clients are regular. Tastes are specific.'

'So you don't tread too much on each other's tails.'

The kid smiles. 'Yeah, not too much.'

'And you know the guys that work the other streets?'

The kid nods. 'Most of them. There's not too many spots.'

Leme nods. 'I'm looking for a guy that likely went AWOL about three years ago. January 2003. Though he might have left the scene before that.'

'Three years?'

Leme nods. 'Good chance he had a regular fella. Not sure if it was quite your retainer level, but there's a chance.'

The kid thinks. 'How old you say he is?'

'About your age.'

'Ha, you're funny.'

Leme smiles. 'I'd say mid-twenties.'

'About my age, then.'

Leme sips at his beer. 'Have a think, kid, but don't take too long. Don't want your dessert to get cold.'

'Maybe someone I can think of. Not from round here, kept himself to himself. Started up across the road, you know, informal, around Frei Caneca.'

'Yeah?'

'He walked the beat about a year, then didn't.'

'No one figured something might have happened to him?'

'Something always happens to someone.'

'Fair point. What was his name?'

'Bocão.'

Big Mouth.

'His name was Bocão?'

'Look, what can I tell you? We're on a professional-name basis here.'

Leme nods. He can run the alias by Vice, see if they have anything. This was beginning to feel exactly like looking for a rent boy in a haystack.

'Why don't you settle down with one of your old Johns, rapaz?' Leme says. *Young man.* 'Go straight, legit.'

The kid stands. 'I'm rent, not bent.' He laughs. 'I'm not looking for a nice boy. I'm already straight, mate.'

Leme watches the kid leave, smiles.

Of course, what happens next is Leme runs the name with Vice, who check it out for him, but they also hear about Leme's ride and dine with the kid, and what with the sense of humour they have in Vice –

Word in the precinct is Leme's out looking for a homo hook-up and Lisboa hears the jokes doing the rounds and next thing is Leme's having to explain himself.

'I'm staying well out of it,' Lisboa tells him. 'I've got your back when you need it, you know that. Crack on, if you can forgive the pun.'

So that's okay, Leme reckons. If he can joke.

Next thing is that Carlos gets in touch. Tells Leme that the Franginho groom is on, that Little Chicken is squawking.

'Chickens don't squawk,' Leme says. 'They cluck. They peck, they gobble and they cluck.'

'Either way,' Carlos says, 'it's winner-winner chicken dinner – for us. I've had a word with the lad. His buddy Rafa has the phone as his old man is in the joint and he gets messages from him, that's it. Which is obviously not just it.'

'No?'

'Phone distribution doesn't normally work on the basis of paternal love, put it that way.'

'Right. So Rafa's pop is a player.'

'He's low-level, I gather. Most likely Rafa's not getting messages from him at all. And the messages he is getting are going straight up the hill.'

'Franginho tell you this?'

'He didn't have to. I kept him clean. He told me enough.'

'You want to use him again.'

'My grandma always taught me that if you want to make good broth, you got to use the bones, entendeu? Stretch it out, use the whole bird for as long as you can.'

'Yeah, I get it. Go easy on the analogy, son.'

'Anyway, Mothers' Day weekend,' Carlos says. 'Friday May 12th, a whole load of passes out of prison, visiting family and whatnot, have been green-lit. Rafa's old man is one of them. There's going to be thousands on furlough, I hear, so don't make too many plans to see the old dear.'

'She's dead, mate.'

'My sentiments. You'll be free then.'

'As a bird.'

'You're getting the hang of this.'

Leme snorts. Leme ends the call.

He wonders what this is going to mean for his weekend, what he's going to tell Renata.

For now, nothing.

Bocão, Big Mouth, *former escort:*

Look.

I was born in the northeast. At least that was what my mother told me. No father – I never knew him anyway. We lived in a simple house in a shithole shantytown on the edge of Fortaleza and my mother scraped a living working as a maid. My sister, as soon as she was old enough, left school to help her. I don't remember that making much difference in terms of our income. I just left school. I spent my time on the street, keeping out of trouble, more or less, sheltering from the sun.

The light in Fortaleza is piercing white.

In São Paulo the sun is strained through the pollution, the fumes, the crap that fills the air: streaks of piss-yellow paint.

Down on the city beaches, there were tourists to fleece. I watched friends sell knocked-off tat like it had some Afro-Brazilian heritage; sometimes these friends procured certain things that the tourists asked for – certain things that they couldn't ask for back home, or didn't want to. Drugs, I found out, and girls and boys. I was scared of drugs, of the men that slung them in corners of the favela and the slicker areas where the gear was better, more expensive. I wasn't going to get involved in any of that.

'Filho, you're a layabout,' my mother would say. 'Se Deus quiser, God willing, you'll find something. But how, I don't know, with all this not looking.'

'But, Mãe, there is no work. Why look?'

And she'd shake her head, suck her teeth, wag her index finger.

'You're a good boy, you're just afraid. One day you'll understand that this rice and beans don't come for free, querido.'

There were other good-looking boys who were whisked off, pockets full of cash. So I'd heard. They were mercenaries, I thought, savages. Love isn't to be played at, I believed. I still do.

'Your cousin in São Paulo has written to us,' said my mother, one afternoon. 'You can stay with her until you find work.' She was washing clothes, beating them with her hands in soapy water. She didn't look up. 'I think you should go. God will see clear whether or not you use this opportunity and I have faith.'

I never saw my mother again.

My cousin was kind, but much older than me. We had little in common; we didn't talk much.

One night, I ended up in Consolação, near the shopping centre at Frei Caneca. The people were nice to me there. There were boys like me. I soon found out I could make good money. I told my cousin I had found a job working nights and a little while later I moved into a tiny, roach-infested, one-room apartment close to Rua Augusta, near the centre. The darker end: where a boy like me could make a living, sandwiched between the mirrored bars that flashed 'American' in red neon, the students laughing and drinking at plastic tables in cheap botecos, the whores, threatening in their explosive underwear and vicious heels, the strip-club bouncers meting out punishment to badly behaved gringos in piss-stinking alleys, the theatre bars and traditional Italian canteens that waved me away whenever I approached.

A year after that I met him. I got settled. After a short illness, my mother passed away and my sister came down to live with me.

Like my mother said: I'll be whatever God makes me.

Look, see.

My sister and I go shopping for food and sometimes clothes. We have a small television and we watch the reality shows and laugh and pretend that we'd hate the attention. We've become friends. We were always close, but we only talked about the big, important things. Now we swap little stories about our days.

Just the other night, I went out. With friends. It was the first time.

My colleague Manuela dragged me for drinks after work. She's persuasive.

'Dude, you're too young to play househusband to your sister. A gatinho like you, a hot stud, should be out and about.'

She slapped on lipstick at her desk, pouting into her handbag-mirror, pulling her top down a touch.

We piled into a bar close to the office. I sat quietly, listening to the noisy chatter, the mock arguments, a dopey grin, my face an alcohol flush.

I stopped worrying about my sister at home.

Manuela smiled, blew smoke at me.

'Coitado,' she said. *Poor thing.* 'You're sweet.'

'You're beautiful,' I said, with a sloppy, beery smile.

'Ha,' she laughed. 'Você nem tem idéia!'

You have no idea.

It felt good. Compared to what I'd been through, this little embarrassment was sweet. It was normal.

I'd arrived.

Look again.

Most mornings I work out, doing sit-ups and push-ups, exercises to strengthen my core: I want to keep my old teenage body. I study myself in the mirror while getting dressed. My jawline is slightly thicker and I can pull a little flesh away from above my hips, but I am the same fit young man I was when he first noticed me. And the new clothes suit me: tailored shirts pinched at the waist, a neat 'V' across my broad chest.

'You're my beautiful boy,' he said early in our relationship. 'Such beautiful eyes, beautiful skin. You're confident, but vulnerable. I don't know what you see in me. Don't ever change.'

I wasn't used to flattery. I didn't know how to answer.

'I won't,' I said. 'I don't deserve your attention.'

He laughed at that. 'My boy,' he said, 'you'll never lack for that.'

Rafa's getting more messages than ever.

He's been wondering for a while why he's the one with the phone.

'Deniability, mate,' Franginho tells him. 'It's all code, innit? Law get hold of it, it ain't a problem, look at what the messages say. Nothing incriminating, is there? Course, your old man will be up the creek if some Militar pulls you.'

'Why's that?'

'You really are slow sometimes, mate. Considering your nickname, Rafa-Rapido.' Franginho laughs, warms to his theme. 'You think they're giving out handsets and line-rental plans when you turn up at the gates to do your time? Here you are, sir, and enjoy these silk pyjamas while you're at it.'

Rafa feels stupid, but relieved that Franginho is with him.

'All right, settle down, I'm only saying.'

Franginho punches his friend on the shoulder. 'And what would sir care for at dinner this evening? Our steak special is world class.' He grins, sees Rafa is hurt. 'I'm just taking the piss, you know I love you.'

'Leave it out.'

Yeah, it's true, Rafa is relieved Franginho is with him in all this. Except, he's not with him in *all* this.

Rafa hasn't told him about following the woman down to the building site the other day and what he reckons he saw. Stockpiling. Though for what, he has no idea.

And May 12th is approaching fast. Not that he knows what that's about either.

Rafa asks Garibaldo, in roundabout terms, about the phone.

'Never you mind, filho,' he's told. 'Not your business, falou?'

Rafa shrugs. He makes a face that says, Well, you know, what if, sabe?

Garibaldo sees this look and Rafa watches him as he processes its meaning.

Rafa's serious and Garibaldo sees he's serious.

He takes him to one side. 'You're not stupid, lad, so I don't need to tell you your papa is not playing nice and checking in with his only son.'

'Yeah,' Rafa bristles, 'I know that.'

'Well, then. Point is more phones we have receiving, less chance they've got of putting the wiretap on us, entendeu?'

Rafa nods.

'Militars,' Garibaldo goes on, 'been tapping, using the information to shake us down, sabe? Bribes, son, *cash*. And not just the wire, kidnapping, too. Holding our kin to ransom.'

'Right,' Rafa says.

'So you're one of many, son. Take it easy.'

'I'm cool.'

Garibaldo laughs. 'There'll be a reckoning, is the point. The Militars aren't playing the game.'

'What's the game?'

'The game is cooperation and everyone's a winner. They fucking us over, playing outside the rules. And they bringing family into it is out of order.'

'Yeah.'

'Yeah? You understand?'

'Yeah.'

And then Rafa finds out his dad has a pass to get out over the Mothers' Day weekend. And everything else sort of feels less important.

He tells his grandma, who doesn't seem thrilled by the news.

'Franginho says it's likely as Mum died, compassionate-leave type of thing. Franginho says.'

'He says a lot, your friend, Little Chicken, doesn't he?' Rafa's grandma says to that.

It's true, to be fair.

But his grandma's indifference doesn't stop Rafa cooking up a plan, of sorts.

He's heard what it is that the woman he's now followed twice, and rescued once, actually does.

And Rafa plans to pay her a visit at her office on the day itself, May 12th, just before his daddy gets home.

He reckons she'll see him.

Morning of Friday May 12th and Ray is keeping busy.

There's a lot of Capital SP numbers tied up in the Singapore Project.

There's a lot of Capital SP product tied up in the enormous loan that went to the government to help fund the Bolsa Família.

There's a lot of outsourced legal work going into notarising and rubber-stamping the movement of these numbers and this product, as well as ascertaining where the human capital involved is to be found.

Friday May 12th, 2006, and São Paulo is a moderate city, politics-wise.

Marta is no longer top cat, and while lefty Lula has a loony grip on the country as a whole, São Paulo remains staunchly ambivalent to his gyppo charm.

What Ray senses is opportunity.

Ray's moving numbers and product to capitalise on some righteous chaos.

What Ray reckons is that by the end of this weekend, the Mothers' Day weekend, São Paulo will not be quite so moderate.

Ray vibes construction legalities.

São Paulo is subject to zoning laws drawn up in 1972, he reads.

These laws divide the city into 'Z1' and 'Z3' areas. 'Z1' areas were designated as 'elite residential' and carefully managed. 'Z3' were 'mixed', i.e. everyone else. In the first half of the twentieth century, the city developed on a principle of 'demolish and rebuild' before these zoning laws were brought in for a degree of control and order. The effect is not obvious except that now the principle simply seems to be build, build, build and has been for some time. The Basic Plan for Integrated Development of São Paulo (a state-run sustainable urban development plan to manage the city's extraordinary growth) was put together in 1968 and from this came the Zoning Laws.

The language is interesting.

'Integrated' is not how anyone would perceive the city, Ray reckons.

The buildings may provide homes and represent opportunity, but it is an inorganic, segregated approach perpetuated by private investors, competitive companies, bottom-line social responsibility.

Irresponsibility, really, Ray thinks.

People like us, my friend.

Ray grins. This is all a cake walk for Big Ray.

It's not his first rodeo, after all.

Morning of Friday May 12th and Leme is pouring coffee for Renata.

'I'm going to be knocking about your neck of the woods today,' he tells her.

'Oh, yes?'

'Bit of informant grooming going on.'

Renata raises her eyebrows. 'You do that now, too?'

'Working with a Military guy, guy named Carlos.'

'Huh.'

'Connected to… well, it's connected to the Lockwood thing, actually.'

'Mario.'

'No, not like that. It's complicated. Might be a lead, I don't know.'

'Well, don't get your hopes up, querido.'

'You wanna have lunch, maybe? I reckon I'll be right in the neighbourhood around then.'

'Why not.'

Leme smiles. 'See you later, alligator,' he says, in English.

Morning of Friday May 12th and Renata drives to work worrying about Mario visiting her for lunch.

Renata is hoping no one will see him with this Military guy Carlos and then with her. It wouldn't be very helpful for anyone.

She decides to take a detour. She has time.

At the top end of Morumbi, off the main Avenida, on a road that snakes its way down to the Marginal freeway, lined by tight, elegant houses, sits the chapel. It's her favourite building. It's unassuming – rust-red, low sloping roof, circular dark wood forming a neat porch – but distinctive in its simplicity in an area so dominated by ostentation. A number of the houses nearby are alpine in style with roofs designed to facilitate snow removal – not something required in São Paulo, she thinks. Idiots. What's that expression? In the States it's better to be educated than beautiful; in Brazil it is better to be rich. In São Paulo, status is everything. And everything in São Paulo moves quickly – apart from the traffic.

Renata drives past and, as usual, slows down. She stops. The chapel appears to be bleeding. Red thread spins from its walls, covering the grass and flowers outside. She gets out to investigate. Inside, there is a loom at the altar, a long red carpet, and more thread angling its way outside. She skirts the edges of the chapel. The red is a sharp contrast to the greenery but calming. The chapel seems to throb with life, as if the thread grows, thickens imperceptibly while she looks at it.

Quite something. But what, she doesn't know. She finds an information stand and reads a leaflet.

Turns out this is Penelope, an installation by artist Tatiana Blass.

Based on Homer, and Penelope's twenty-year wait for Odysseus, warding off suitors by dedicating herself to the funeral shroud.

Patience of a woman, Renata thinks. She wanders over to her car. From where she's parked, she can see, through the trees, the Marginal down by the river. The traffic is unusually light. She can see smoke.

She walks to the edge of the car park.

She sees, she thinks, a bus stopped in the middle of the highway, people milling around it.

She sees, she thinks, a bus in flames.

She shakes her head. Sad. As if the commuters don't have enough problems. That'll mean even more delays for the poor sods.

She goes back to her car.

She puts it to one side.

She pulls away and up towards the favela, her work.

Morning of Friday May 12th and Rafa's outside the supermarket, working, but he's also spent most of the last two hours zipping up and down the hill on his board, passing on messages.

And he gets another one, so off he goes.

Rafa cannot wait to see his daddy.

Leme's in the back seat of Carlos's vehicle at the business end of Paraisópolis. One of Carlos's boys is driving. He doesn't say much. All aviator sunglasses and attitude. They park near the top of the favela scrum.

Franginho is late.

A group of young women saunters by.

They stop to talk to Carlos and he makes them laugh.

They examine Leme like an exhibit and raise their eyebrows, suck their teeth, slap hands. Carlos tells Leme they're hookers who come to dance samba on Saturday afternoons in the grotty garage bar opposite the condominium where Leme lives.

'I'll give it a go,' Leme says.

Carlos laughs – long. 'I'll be out the back, having a lie down.'

One nice thing about Carlos, Leme thinks – he doesn't judge, will befriend anyone, it seems.

Young men in shorts and flip-flops pass by, calling out across the road to someone Leme can't see.

They look more hostile.

The young men are joking and laughing at something.

They're speaking in a rough slang.

Leme sinks into his seat.

There is a light breeze.

It's that rare thing in São Paulo when the heat dissipates and the freshness is, for a moment, cool, comforting.

Shacks bend over the vehicle in the tight street, their irregular shapes jutting out at odd angles, corrugated extensions hanging low, seeming to sway with the wind.

There is a constant crackle of electricity in the wires criss-crossed above him, straining to carry the current around the Paraisópolis labyrinth.

The girls amble down the street and the young men swagger behind, laughing at them, flip-flops slapping on the bumpy road.

'Oi, oi,' Carlos says. He gestures with his chin up the road at the supermarket. Franginho has arrived with three other kids of roughly his age.

Carlos grins. 'Let's do this the old-fashioned way,' he says. 'You sit tight.'

Leme sits tight.

Carlos pops the siren, one flash, one wail. He bounces out from the passenger side and his goon does the same from the driver's.

They unclip their weapons but leave them holstered. They rest their hands on their weapons in a clear show of intent. Carlos barks instructions at the four boys.

'Turn around, lads, hands against the wall, slowly.'

The four lads do as they're told.

'Don't move. Legs spread. Keep any helpful thoughts or suggestions to yourself, certo?'

Leme smiles. He's got style, Carlos, a bit of flash to him.

Carlos nods at his heavy who rifles pockets, ruffles feathers, manhandles.

When he reaches Franginho, he pulls a wallet, flips it open, rummages for show and nods again at Carlos. He pats down Franginho's back pockets and pulls a hefty-looking package, a thick envelope. He holds this in the air for all to see.

'Bingo,' old Carlos fairly sings now, in delight. 'You three, scram. You,' he says to Franginho, 'you're coming with me.'

Carlos grabs Little Chicken by the scruff of his wattle.

Leme leans out the window. 'Shakespeare, mate.'

'All the world's a stage,' Carlos says.

He bundles Franginho into the back.

They tear off up towards the main road, get the fuck out of Paraisópolis.

Renata gets to the office and there is a stack of work to do but no Fernanda to do it.

She's surprised: Fernanda's normally in first.

There's a red light flashing on the answer machine.

Renata hits playback.

There's a crackle, a long ugly beeping, then:

'Oi, querida,' she hears Fernanda's voice saying, 'I'm not well, I'm sick. I don't think I'll make it in today, sabe? I'll call you in a bit? Desculpe, viu?'

Yeah, Renata's sorry, Fernanda got that right.

They're on a tight deadline and these Bolsa Família applications are not so straightforward to expedite.

There's something in the air. Rafa feels it. Tension, frayed nerves, a certain amount of worry, fear even, seems to be flooding the mid-level boys' HQ this morning. Unlike them, Rafa thinks. There's not much he's worried about, to be fair. He just wants to do what he's got to do to see his old man –

He didn't realise he'd be this excited.

He tries not to be. He can't show it as it'd show weakness, and Paraisópolis is a jungle, as he well knows. There is a distinct food

chain in the jungle and Rafa's well set for now, but weakness is det-
riment to ambition. And caring about something at all is a sign of
weakness. Life-is-cheap, easy-come-easy-go, live-fast-die-young, but
leave a good-looking corpse or three in your wake before you have
your coat buttoned –

These are the PCC slogans for your up-and-coming drug slinger,
your aspiring gangbanger. Rafa's a supermarket supervisor, that's all.

Straight player.

Garibaldo huddles with his crew. Garibaldo whispers orders. The
crew leave one by one. The crew look focused, business-like. The
usual hash cloud is nowhere to be seen. Today is a clear-head scene.
Must be serious, Rafa thinks.

Garibaldo beckons. 'Vem ca, Rafinha.' *Come here, son.* 'Job for
you, certo?'

Rafa nods.

'You in a little trouble, filho, but nothing a hard day's work won't
fix.'

Rafa's not sure what he's talking about. He nods.

'You followed the bitch from the legal office. Remember?'

Rafa nods.

'But you ain't stopped her from reaching The Factory.'

The Factory. So that's what was going on down the bottom of the
favela. Stockpiling weapons, cash, drugs. A kind of ironic name as
no production goes on there, which is the point.

'I tried, porra,' Rafa says. 'I got her out.'

Garibaldo slaps Rafa, hard, across his left cheek. He steadies Rafa's
head, gripping his chin between forefinger and thumb. He slaps him
again, harder, across his right cheek.

'You don't try, kid,' he says. 'You fucked up, you listen, sabe?'

Rafa nods. His cheek stings. His eyes water. Hold it in. His eyes
redden. His lip quivers. Shape up. Show nothing. He shoots a look
round the room. Only a couple of no-marks kicking about so the
humiliation is lessened. Stay stylish, he thinks, and this'll get out okay.

Point is, he's done something really wrong and this conversation
isn't happening, no Senhor. He's done something really wrong and
he's already burning in a coil of flaming tyres.

Rafa gives it the contrite underling. Brazens it out a moment, shows his face –

'Look, Rafa, I like you,' Garibaldo says, 'and I know it weren't your fault, but needs must and someone has to put their hands up and say fair fucks, it was me.'

Rafa says nothing. Juts his chin, plays the big man who understands, the big man who will put things right, like the big man he is.

It's working.

'Point is, Rafa-Rapido, the bitch was seen, you were seen, but the big boys want to know what she did or didn't see. And depending on what she saw, actions will be taken, okay?'

Rafa nods. He sees where this is going. It feels odd, it feels *indecisive*. Very much *not* the PCC MO.

Rafa sees Garibaldo see this thought flash across his brow.

'She's a civilian and she helps us out. She's on the books, mais ou menos, okay? Community shit, don't even sweat it, but it does mean we need her on side, sabe?'

Rafa thinks he understands. It won't look too good if they whack a legal aid representative for going about her business in the favela.

'You go and see her, and you find out what she saw.'

How the fuck is he going to do that?

'And if she does know something, something will be arranged. Something you're going to be a part of. Bala perdida situation, sabe?'

Bala perdida. Stray bullet. Caught in the crossfire.

'And you don't bullshit us, right? Otherwise something's going to be arranged for you.'

Now, this is *great* news, Rafa thinks. What a fuck-up.

'You go and get that done, then you come back. Big day today and you're going to be very busy, young man.'

'Doing what?'

'You'll see. Shit is hitting the fan, filho.'

Rafa nods. Rafa frowns. Garibaldo laughs.

He says, 'Keep your phone on, your board close and your wits sharp. You're going to be a runner, a messenger. And things are going to move pretty fast.'

———

Rafa can't help disappointment leach out of him. Garibaldo, who is not stupid, sees this. He puts his arm around Rafa. Says, 'Your daddy is on his way. Him and a fucking small army have got out over the weekend. You'll see him, I suspect, tomorrow, Sunday lunchtime tops.'

Rafa nods.

'Keep your pecker up, kid,' Garibaldo says. He gives Rafa a little push.

Rafa leaves.

Ray's phone rings. Fernanda.

'Fala, querida,' he says.

What's new, pussycat? is the basic gist of his tone. The sigh at the end of the line speaks volumes. Ray waits, smiling.

'Your accent's no better, big man.'

'Must be the company I'm keeping.'

'You mean financial imperialists and gringo sex tourists?'

'There's a lot of them about.'

Fernanda clears her throat. 'I'm not going to work today, Ray, just like you told me.'

'Good woman.'

'You wanna tell me why I'm taking a duvet day?'

'Nice lingo, real Ivy League English.'

'Ray.'

'Yeah, sure, why not. This weekend there's chaos on the cards, is what I'm hearing, and Paraisópolis is just one place of several I wouldn't necessarily want to be.'

'So you're just looking out for me.'

'Exactamundo.'

'That's not Portuguese, Ray.'

'Neither are you. Come to the hotel tonight and I'll fill you in.'

'Sounds delightful.'

'Turn of phrase, sweetheart. You wanna know or what?'

'I'll see you at seven.'

'Good woman.'

'Ray?'

'Yeah?'

'My colleague, Renata, you remember her?'

'I do.'

'I should tell her to go home early then.'

'I'd say that is not a bad idea, yes.'

'You seem very well informed for a hedge-fund numbers guy.'

'Money gets everywhere, querida. It's like sand that way. If you're not careful, you'll be digging it out of your crotch for weeks.'

Fernanda laughs. 'I'll be careful then. See you tonight.'

'I'll be the guy at the bar nursing a cocktail, looking like he's missing you,' Ray says.

Fernanda hangs up.

Carlos tells his driver to keep his foot to the floor.

'Pedal to the metal, son.'

Leme smiles. Leme's getting back-seat comfortable with Franginho. The lad's got his hands in his lap and his eyes down. Moping. His bottom lip protrudes.

Carlos looks over his shoulder. 'Stop sulking, moleque,' he says. He taps Franginho's knee with his handgun. 'And don't forget to smile, bicho, it may never happen.'

Leme chuckles. Carlos howls.

Leme says, 'Where we headed?'

'We're taking young Franginho here to someplace quiet so we can have a word, undisturbed.'

Leme nods. 'You're a poet, Carlão.'

'And don't I know it.' He points up the hill beyond the shopping mall Jardim Sul. 'Up there. Perfect spot. Nice romantic view of the city, no one around.'

'Lover's lane,' Leme says.

'Well,' Carlos snorts, 'one way or another, one of us is going to get fucked.'

Renata's phone beeps. Text from Mario:

lunch isn't going to work, my love. I won't be in your hood after all

Renata's not unhappy about this. If she could, she'd put off introducing him to life at the office indefinitely. She's busy, too. Lunch is looking increasingly unlikely full stop. Fernanda's left her somewhat in the lurch. The forms, it turns out, do not expedite themselves. Renata's cursing Fernanda when she gets a text from *her*.

leave early today, querida. I've had word something's going to happen

That's nice, thanks, Renata thinks, tossing the phone. Easy for her to say, tucked up in bed no doubt. Something's *always* going to happen in Paraisópolis, querida. She shakes her head. Whatever's going to happen, it's not happening *now*.

She keeps at it.

Leme clocks Carlos's radio crackle.

Something about buses on fire on the Marginal ring road. Something about approach with caution there may be an ambush. Something about all units drop all you're doing and await orders. Something about an informant's bleating, a major PCC move to fuck with the city in general, and the Military Police more specifically.

Carlos picks up, turns away from Leme. Carlos speaks terse code. Leme catches the nub: we don't got long to play chicken with Little Chicken.

Carlos leans back over the seat. He says, 'We better make this quick.'

Leme's not sure if he's talking to him or Franginho.

They creep up the hill past the Extra supermarket and the houses get rougher the higher they climb and at the top there is a patch of grass, a sad-looking tree and a car park that is empty, clearly disused. A standard, off-the-books interrogation spot. Anyone sees a Militar vehicle go in, they sure as eggs is eggs won't follow. Leme's mind fogs. Something's going on.

They come to a stop at the far corner of this concrete playground. They're pretty much level pegging with the top of the favela hill. About two miles east as the chicken flies. Craters spread out after the main road ends. Bricks and dust. Fast-food joints flash neon signs. They tower above the traffic. Clouds sit heavy, swollen in thick blue skies. I wouldn't move either, Leme thinks. No one wants to do anything much. Pull down the blinds and have a quick wank and a nap is about all anyone can see themselves achieving in his heat. Tropical ambition.

Carlos and his goon jump out. Carlos pops the back door and drags Franginho by the hair. Leme gets out the other side and follows. So it's like this, he thinks.

There's a thin brush of dried-out and dying bushes littered with beer cans and drug paraphernalia. Carlos drags Franginho all the way over to it. Franginho's legs move double quick trying to keep up.

'Kneel,' Carlos tells him.

Franginho does what he's told.

The kid's in shock, Leme thinks. He had a mouth on him, he remembers, last time, and was sharp, clever. Likely never had to bother with this kind of scene. Likely thinks – or thought – he was above all this gangster shit. His face is white. His face is *green*. Leme thinks that he's not all that far from pissing himself.

'First thing,' Carlos says, 'what the fuck's all this?'

He thrusts the envelope his goon lifted from Franginho into poor Franginho's scrawny little face.

'Bank cards, Bolsa Família programme,' he says. 'All legit, I swear, serious.'

'Yeah?' Carlos turns away. 'Then why the fuck have *you* got them?' he says.

A beat, then Carlos turns back to face Franginho, pivots, and backhands him across the jaw, right hand, in one fluid movement. Terrific leverage, momentum, purchase. Franginho's neck snaps sideways. Carlos steps in close. Backhands the other way, left hand, his right to left. Franginho's neck snaps backwards.

Leme thinks: nice one two. Keep your guard up, kid.

Carlos nods at his goon. The goon pulls a plastic bag and then pulls it tight over Franginho's head.

Leme thinks: well that somewhat alters the odds.

Carlos steps over to Leme. 'We got to be quick as something's happening all over town. It's connected to those Mothers' Day free passes I told you about. What you're seeing here – ' he points at Franginho gasping and struggling, spitting blood into the clear plastic, speckling it ' – is pretty much textbook. No one minds too much, no harm, no foul, if you'll forgive the pun.'

Fowl. Leme raises an eyebrow.

'Thing is, some of our boys are bent for the wrong side. There's been some unauthorised shakedowns across the state. Young bandit Militars who don't have the dignity and decorum to play by the rules have been making a profit at PCC expense. And in very unpalatable ways.'

Carlos's goon lets Franginho breathe a moment. Carlos nods. The goon gets back to work.

'I understand,' Carlos says, 'why their boys are unhappy. It's not on to kidnap family and ransom them. No class. We don't do that shit here, but it's going to bite us in the behind all the same.'

Leme nods.

'There's an equilibrium, right, and it's a tricky fucker to keep balanced. And if you're clean, like I am, it's even harder to know what's what.'

Carlos waves his goon away from Franginho.

'We'll get some answers now and then we best fuck off.'

Leme nods. Good plan.

Carlos pulls a weapon. He's down on his haunches, more or less eye level with Franginho. He wipes blood from Franginho's mouth. He wipes sweat from Franginho's forehead. He taps the barrel of his handgun against Franginho's jaw.

'Okay, filho, I think that's enough, ne?'

Franginho nods.

Leme looks on. This Carlos is clean, so he says. Leme reckons it's true. Brutal don't mean dirty, apparently. If it's done in the name of the law, in the interest of the people –

'Let's start again,' Carlos says. 'Tell me about the bank cards.'

Franginho sniffs. He spits blood and phlegm. 'We get a batch like this every week and we dole them out to whoever's in the supermarket queue and they go and withdraw the cash and bring it back to us.'

'And what do you do with the cash?'

Franginho breathes deep. He shudders like he might cry. Leme wonders what will come first, tears or urine.

Franginho says, 'Some goes to the supermarket owners, some we keep, most of it goes up the hill.'

'Right. And the groceries from the supermarket are just handed out.'

Franginho nods.

'Clever,' Carlos says. He straightens up. 'Eh, Mario,' he says to Leme, 'that's clever, ne? Inventive, wouldn't you say?'

'They ought to win the Nobel Prize for Economics,' Leme says.

'I'd nominate them.' Carlos turns back to Franginho. 'It's a lot of cards. You get this many every week?'

Franginho nods.

Carlos shuffles through them like a deck. 'Same names every week?'

Franginho shakes his head.

Carlos is nodding. 'Interesting.'

Franginho lets out a groan.

'You keep track of the names?'

Franginho lets out a whimper. He shakes his head.

'So, what, you're just doing your job, falou? Like a cog in the machine.'

Franginho nods. 'We get the cards, we run crowd control, basically.'

'Who is we?'

'Me and my buddy Rafa.'

'Ah, the kid with the phone.' Carlos looks at Leme. Carlos raises an eyebrow.

Carlos turns back to Franginho. He kneels. He knocks his handgun against Franginho's forehead. He flicks a look at his goon. His goon sidles behind Franginho, grabs him by the throat. The goon prises open Franginho's mouth. Carlos takes his handgun and inserts a good deal of the barrel into Franginho's mouth. Leme looks away. Leme hears Franginho squirm, hears Franginho's muffled protest, hears the muffled groan of a child. Leme smells ammonia – urine.

Leme sees Carlos stand.

Carlos says, 'What sort of messages has your buddy Rafa been getting?'

Franginho chokes. He dry-heaves. Spittle drops. 'I don't know.'

Carlos grins. Carlos nods at his goon. His goon kicks Franginho, from behind, with his pointed-toe boots, squarely in the kidneys.

Franginho gasps. Chokes back spit and blood. Heaves vomit.

'We want this over as much as you do, son,' Carlos says.

Franginho sways, eyes flutter, close. Carlos nods at his goon. His goon pulls a two-litre bottle of water from the vehicle and soaks Franginho.

'Last time, kid. I'm not asking again.'

Franginho nods. 'Today, May 12th.'

'And?'

'The messages have been about today, May 12th. Rafa is just a go-between. The messages are written like they're from his daddy. It's code, ne? Please.'

'So he doesn't know what they mean?'

Franginho shakes his head.

'His daddy coming home this weekend? Can you tell us if that's true at least?'

Franginho nods, says something they don't catch.

'Speak up, moleque.'

Franginho coughs. 'I hope so,' he says.

'You know why his old man went away?'

Franginho shakes his head.

'Does Rafa?'

Franginho shakes his head.

'You can likely guess where we're going with this, clever kid like yourself.'

Franginho, again, shakes his head. His head, to be fair, is lolling forward now. It's not making it any easier to understand him, Leme thinks.

'Where do we find Rafa on this most auspicious of days?'

Franginho coughs. Carlos hands him a handkerchief. Carlos hands him a smaller bottle of water. Franginho wipes sweat and blood, drinks deep.

'He'll be on his board,' Franginho says. 'Up and down the hill.'

Carlos makes a face. 'That's not hugely helpful, young man.'

'I –'

'You're going to have to do better than that.'

Franginho looks panicked. Leme sees his brain racing. Carlos makes another face. The gist: urgency is imperative.

Then Franginho's nodding. 'Wait, I know,' he says, 'I remember one place he's going, about his daddy, I think.'

'Go on.'

'There's a legal aid office, top end of the favela. A woman there. He's going to see her.'

Leme freezes. Carlos clocks Leme freeze. Leme's mind jumps forward three steps. Carlos stands, waves his goon over.

'Son, you can walk home.' Carlos hands Franginho a ten-note. 'Get yourself something to eat and clean yourself up.'

Leme's already in the car.

Tyres shriek.

Renata works to a mid-afternoon rhythm –

Drowning in paperwork. Rubber-stamp grunt job. A window-open breeze. Outside street-chatter seems normal. Maids and nannies heading home. Men gathering at the bar, clinking glass, group cackling. The shunt of delivery trucks abrupt, periodic. The splutter and growl of engine tests at the grease-monkey garage. The net curtains flap. Radio's playing stirring classical music – Shostakovich. A coffee-flask buzz staves off the post-lunch slump –

Renata is surprised to look up and see the kid with the skateboard standing in the doorway to her office.

There is a moment as they both look at each other. Recognition is immediate. There is history between them, but they are hardly on first-name terms. The few words they have ever exchanged now flash through Renata. She is, she is surprised to realise, settled by this young man's presence. There is in the air a sort of inevitability to this, like something has been building to it for some time.

A fault line is being reset.

Renata puts down her pen. She closes a document on her computer. She pushes back in her seat. She gestures for the young man – the boy – to come in.

'You,' she says, simply. There is a beat. 'What can I do for you?'
The young man shuffles forward.

'Here.' Renata pushes a chair towards him. 'Sit, go on. Sit down, please.'

He is tentative. He sits down. He uses his board as a shield. He cradles his board, hugs it to his chest. His eyes downcast. His shoulders hunched. 'You remember,' he says, 'the other day?'

Renata nods. Of course she remembers. It's her secret. She put it down to the reality of working in the favela. Collateral consequence. She was embarrassed at her own naivety.

'You didn't see anything, did you?' the boy asks.

Renata shakes her head. 'Nothing,' she says.

'You were just taking a walk, ne?'

'Yes.' Renata smiles – soft. 'Exactly that.'

The boy is nodding. 'That's good,' he says. 'So you didn't tell no one?'

'I didn't tell anyone I went for a walk, no.' She smiles again. 'Porque? Não faz sentido, ne?'

Why would I do that?

The boy nods.

The truth: how *could* she tell Mario and expect him to allow her to keep on working in Paraisópolis?

Allow her. She wouldn't allow *him* to allow her to do anything – or not. But this is what she'd told herself, slipping into the machismo stereotype that she knew their marriage was not.

It made it easier in this particular case.

And she hadn't seen anything.

The boy is still nodding. 'Okay, that's good.' He smiles. It is a smile that drips relief. 'I was worried,' he says. He looks down. His feet twitch. He looks up and smiles again.

Renata thinks she understands why he's here. She, too, is feeling a good deal of relief. There is a lot, she realises, that is best left unsaid.

She says, 'Is there anything else I can help you with?'

The boy nods. He hugs his board.

Renata leans, a touch, towards him. 'Do you know what it is that we do here?' she asks.

'I think legal work, like bureaucracy? Like a notary, ne?'

'Pois é,' she says. *That's it.* 'Though it's a little more complicated, too.'

'Okay.'

'Best way to explain is to say that I help people who need it with legal matters. Maybe it's securing a loan, maybe it's doing the paperwork to buy a house, maybe even renewing a driving licence. Maybe it's more.' She smiles. 'You never know what you're going to need help with, that's one certainty.'

The boy nods. 'My father – ' he says, and then stops. He looks down. He clutches his board to him.

'Your father.'

'He's... not at home.'

'Where is he?'

'He's... in jail.'

'Okay.'

'And I don't know what he did.'

'Okay, I understand.' Renata takes a pen, a piece of paper. 'It's okay,' she says, 'you can talk freely here.'

'I want to know what he did and if you can help.'

'What's your name?'

'Rafa.'

'Rafael?'

'Yes.'

'Rafael what?'

'Rafael Nascimento.'

'And your father's name?'

'Sergio. Sergio Nascimento.'

'I'll need documents. Do you have your RGE, your CPF?'

The boy shakes his head. Renata nods. It's not a surprise. No ID means you're not in the system, which can have its benefits. Though you can't claim *actual* benefits, of course, for a child that doesn't technically exist.

'Do you have your father's RGE or CPF?' Renata asks.

'They're at home, I think. I'm not sure where. I'm sorry.'

Renata smiles. 'You think you can find them?'

The boy looks animated, excited. 'Yes, I can look. I can go now if that helps?'

'I mean the sooner you find them, give them to me...'

The boy is smiling, nodding. 'He's coming home this weekend.'

'He's coming home?'

'Mothers' Day weekend. He has a pass.'

Renata's eyes narrow a touch. 'Right,' she says. 'Of course.'

The boy takes the plunge. Renata can see his eyes widen and chest expand in hope as he asks, 'Will you be able to meet him?'

She makes a face – weighing it. 'I'm here until six, then it's the weekend.' She looks at the boy. She feels something for this boy. Their history weighs more. 'I can be here tomorrow morning, between ten and midday. You can bring him then. Okay?'

The boy smiles – wide. 'Yes, yes, thank you. Thank you so much, Dona – '

She hasn't told him her name. She smiles. 'Dona Renata,' she says.

He stands. 'I'll go now and find the documents,' he says. 'I'll bring them here before six.'

Renata smiles. 'There's no rush, Rafael.'

He stops. 'Only my grandma calls me Rafael.'

'It's a nice name.'

The boy looks embarrassed. That gawky adolescent posture, that gratitude, that not knowing how to act.

'Goodbye, Rafael,' Renata says. 'We'll talk.'

The boy leaves, happy.

Carlos's goon pops the siren and they bounce down from Avenida Giovanni Gronchi. Heavy ride, heavy mob.

Carlos is on the radio. 'We're coming *in*, porra, so shape up and game faces on. Rua Dr. Laérte Setúbal. Clear the road. You've got about two minutes. Follow us down and flank, certo?'

A crackle of roger that.

Leme sits tense. A/C cool fights the nerve sweats. He fidgets, chews his cheek, grinds his teeth.

The Militar SUV swings wide and loud. Two motorbikes rev their engines and flash blue-red. They pull in alongside. Both sets of helmets and aviators nod at Carlos. They nod at Carlos's goon. They pick up speed. Favelados jump back out of their way. Arms raised, teeth sucked, insults fly.

They jam through the junction. They rip past the corner bar. Tables scatter, men duck, kids scarper –

They expect gunfire and arrests.

Carlos's goon jams on the brakes. Motorbikes skid to a halt alongside. Motorbike riders unclip their holsters and adopt the position: don't fucking think about it.

Leme's out the door and in the building and up the stairs in moments. Carlos follows a tad more circumspect.

Leme skips stairs. He sees the office door open. He slides through, he skids in, he sees –

Renata, alone, at her desk, pen in hand, radio on, coffee on –

'Querido,' she says, 'what on earth are you doing here?'

'I –'

Leme huffs. His breath shallow, hot.

Renata stands. She places a hand on his shoulder. 'Remember to breathe, Mario,' she says.

Leme's nodding. 'Come on, get your things, lock up, we need to go.'

Carlos is in the doorway. He's nodding. Leme points. Renata sees him, understands.

'Mario?' she says.

Leme makes a face. Meaning: trust me, sweetheart, *please.*

Renata nods.

She closes windows. She shuts down computers. Leme hovers, smiles through a grimace. She picks up her coat, her bag.

'Right,' she says, through a tight smile. 'Let's go.'

Rafa finds his dad's ID at home but when he gets back to Dona Renata's office, she's not there and the doors are locked. He thinks about a cheeky B&E, just for a moment, leave the document on her desk to speed things along a touch, a nice helpful surprise for her when she clocks in tomorrow morning. He thinks better of it; he doubts she'd appreciate the gesture, the good intentions. He doubts the boys up the hill would like it. He has, after all, passed on the message that she doesn't know anything about The Factory, that the deal they've brokered with her, even if she doesn't exactly know about it, is ongoing.

It's early evening and Rafa's work is in full flow. He can't find Franginho anywhere; he doesn't have time to worry.

His detail: ferry messages between Paraisópolis and a square triangle of a few miles or so that includes the Militar base near Jardim Sul, Avenida Morumbi up to just before it crosses the river, and from Giovanni Gronchi down to the stadium at the bottom.

His detail: support what he now knows is a sustained citywide attack, coordinated by the leaders of the PCC from prison, on the Military Police.

His detail: keep his eyes open for potential incursion into the favela by Military Police, or any other unwanted guests for that matter, within his designated triangle, and report back sharpish if any incursion looks like it might occur.

His detail: ferry ammunition and light weapons to any group of PCC gunmen in need.

His detail, as he assigned himself: keep his head down while doing all this. No point trying to help out his dad if he's going to catch a stray bullet on the weekend he's home.

It's turning out to be quite a day.

Leme's into the fridge. He pulls three beers. He takes them onto the balcony. Renata and Carlos stand. They look out. Leme doles cans. They crack their cans, drink thirsty gulps. They knock their cans together. Say nothing. There is a distant sound of fireworks – warnings – coming from all directions. There is smoke – winding, wispy – visible some away across the favela. There is a quiet in the air, a stillness. Calm before the storm, Leme thinks. Electricity buzz and generator hum – cables sweep down from above. They are surrounded by other smaller buildings. Daylight fades. Dusk is muito grey, unforgiving. Apartment windows lit up – there are a lot more people at home than usual on a Friday.

Carlos downs his lager. He shakes the can, ascertains it's empty.

'I'm off, mate,' he says to Leme. 'You two stay put. Don't leave the condominium, certo?'

Leme nods.

'They won't call your mob out. There's a three-line whip on all of us, so I need to make tracks.'

Carlos nods at Renata.

Leme says, 'Take care, mate.'

Carlos smiles, leaves.

Pushing midnight when Rafa thinks things have eased. He's spent the last four hours close to home. He's seen no violence yet. He's heard there's been a lot of it. He's helped load weapons into cars, cars that carried PCC troops across the city, troops that used these weapons. He's heard there was a gunfight at the 55th precinct. He's heard the Militar traitor who sold out the organisation to cover his own back has been offed outside his front door. He's heard half a dozen police vehicles have been routed. He's heard there are scores of burnt-out buses all over the place. He's *seen* three himself.

Still no sign of Franginho.

Rafa's phone beeps. Again.

The message is telling him to get to the boca de fumo for a small pick-up. It's the same boca he knows well after tailing the lawyer woman not that long ago. Small pick-up likely means an envelope of cash. He's supposed to take the package, whatever it is, back to the Portakabin. The code ain't too hard to crack, let's be honest, he thinks.

He sets out. It's dark. The roads are shadows. The roads are empty. Road lights flicker. House lights are off. People cowering behind darkness, Rafa thinks, and good for them: it's mighty sensible given the fucking state of the city in general, and anywhere a gangbanger with a grievance might likely be lurking in particular.

Favela demographics is an economic reality, Franginho says. Ninety-nine per cent hard working, poor and honest; one per cent taking advantage. Pure right-wing capitalism.

The lights close to the boca are out but for one naked bulb right at the end. Rafa sees it straining, glowing faint, swinging on a stringy cable a good few feet above anyone underneath.

Rafa approaches dead slow. His work all night has been predicated on a bit of care, a good dollop of caution. He sticks to the left-hand side as the track narrows. Shadow-skulks his way along. He's got his board in his hands now. The roughness of the track kicks up noisy.

Rafa hears voices. Three or four of them, he thinks. He hears Garibaldi. He hears Lanky's laconic assent. He hears a gruff, older voice. Another grunt. Rafa moves slow, steady. He creeps and peeps; he prowls.

He can see them now. He knows better than to interrupt. He crouches between wooden crates. The bulb illuminates little.

He sees that the other voices belong to two Military Police. He thinks: hello.

He sees one of the Militars – bald, handsome like a bull – hand an envelope to Garibaldo.

He sees Garibaldo go *yeah, nice one, no need to count it, porra*, then, *nah, only joking*, and count it anyway.

He sees Lanky tense up.

He sees the two Militars give it the all right then, son, please yourself. They're smiling, Rafa sees, relaxed.

Rafa is maybe a dozen metres away, well hidden. He feels invisible.

He sees Garibaldo nod, grin, slap hands with the bald Militar.

He sees Garibaldo and Lanky turn to move away, towards where Rafa waits.

Rafa thinks, right then, stand up now, don't want to be accused of being late.

Rafa in a half-crouch sees the two Militars draw weapons and shoot Garibaldo and Lanky in the backs of their heads.

They go down, messy.

Rafa goes down. He sees the Militars flip the bodies. He sees them empty rounds into chests. He thinks: covers up the whole snide execution-from-behind business.

He sees the Militars rifle pockets. They commandeer cash. They pull handguns from both Garibaldo and Lanky.

They place said handguns in the dead men's hands. They fire rounds towards the entrance to the boca, the exit too, in fact, Rafa thinks.

Laughing, they drop the dead men's hands. They do a quick look around; they see they're all alone. They amble off. Baldy divides cash and hands over a wad to his mate.

Rafa sees all this, waits five minutes, then he fucks off, sharpish.

He's sitting up on the tyres outside the supermarket when his phone buzzes. Okay, chega, he thinks. *Enough already.*

He unpockets the phone and flips the lid. One message:

sorry, son. I won't be coming home

It takes Rafa a moment to digest this. He shudders, he heaves. He knows what it means, he knows the code and he knows this is news he does not have to pass on up the hill.

It's for him.

It's his dad.

Rafa's chest tightens. He *howls*.

The bar on the deck at the Hotel Unique is in full swing. It's fin de siècle debauchery. The low-light precautions mean blackout morals. There are couples *copulating* in the pool, on the loungers, up against the glass. Least it looks that way to Big Ray.

'Civil unrest is a helluva aphrodisiac,' he says to Fernanda. 'Let's fiddle with each other while Rome burns, baby.'

Fernanda laughs. 'What I like about you, Ray, is your optimism.'

'First thing you do Monday morning, querida, is you destroy those files you took from work.'

Fernanda nods.

'Only people know what you've been doing is me and you,' Ray says. 'Yeah.'

'Until then, keep your head down.'

'Like everyone else?' Fernanda says, gesturing at the deck.

'Ha,' Ray laughs. 'I'll get you a room.'

'One key, Big Ray.'

'Trust me,' Ray says. 'Safety first. I'll take care of it.'

Ray signals the concierge, secures a room.

The chaos feels miles away out across the darkness of the city. But it's there, this chaos, they all know it.

Ray smiles, goes downstairs, shoots up.

Ray *glows*.

Outside his soundproof window, the city simmers.

Ray can see it shiver, silently.

He feels good, Ray does. He takes a long shower.

As he dries his hair, snug in his soft robe, there's a knock at the door.

It's Fernanda, two cut-glass tumblers of whiskey in her hand.

'That looks like good stuff,' Ray says.

Fernanda makes a face: *I'm here, aren't I?*

She says, 'My room was too big.'

'Outstanding,' Ray says.

Document record: Military Police incident report

Thursday, 11 May

The intelligence branch of the São Paulo Military Police department intercept phone calls between members of the PCC — wiretapping of key members — and it becomes clear that there will be a major incident over the weekend involving hundreds of PCC members including a large number released for the weekend to celebrate Mothers' Day. This information was classified as need-to-know basis. The government announce the transfer of 765 members of the PCC to the high-security Presidente Venceslau prison, to disrupt the group's leadership and prevent such an occurrence.

PCC leader Marcos Williams Herbas Camacho, *Marcola*, requests 60 televisions, to watch the 2006 World Cup. He also requests more frequent conjugal visits. The government ignores these requests. Intelligence branch believes that the requests are a smokescreen for the major incident and a public justification for the violence. The true cause is the government attempt to dismantle the PCC leadership.

Friday, 12 May

Marcola and seven other leaders of the PCC are taken to the headquarters of the Departamento Estadual de Investigações Criminais for interrogation. Marcola refuses to make any statements regarding planned action or otherwise. He simply repeats his desire to follow Brazil in the World Cup.

During the morning and afternoon, buses are hijacked, the passengers evacuated, and then the buses set on fire at six key traffic hubs in São Paulo. Congestion problems are immense. Rumours spread of civil unrest. Workers are sent home early. As a result, said congestion is exacerbated beyond all levels previously experienced in São Paulo. The city is, for several hours, effectively paralysed.

At 8 PM, attacks against police officers begin. The 55th Police department is attacked by a convoy of 15 cars filled with armed gang members. A police officer is killed outside his home, in what appears to be a pre-meditated assassination in the eastern part of São Paulo. Four Civil

Police officers, a prison guard, four civil guard members
and a military serviceman are killed, and nine people
injured, in 19 separate incidents before midnight.

Saturday, 13 May

A major, coordinated rebellion takes place in PCC-
controlled prisons across the state. There are 24,472
prisoners in 24 prisons involved in active rebellion and
violence. They take 129 hostages. The police arrest 17
suspects. Prison authorities effectively powerless.

State governor Cláudio Lembo mobilises the entire police
force to confront the criminals and end the violence.

In a press conference, Cláudio Lembo and Saulo Abreu, the
Secretary for Public Safety, state that the PCC reaction to
the transfer of its leaders to maximum security facilities
is 'predictable'.

The number of separate incidents of violence reaches 69, 44
in the metropolitan area of São Paulo. Thirty-two people
are killed: 22 police officers, 5 prison guards, 1 civilian
and 4 criminals. The situation in the prisons remains
critical with hundreds of hostages still being held.

Sunday, 14 May

Police patrols identify and contain key PCC strongholds.
Fifteen criminals are killed in 33 separate incidents of
Military police-led operations to reinstate order. Over 70
arrests are made.

In response, a further 47 prisons in the state of São Paulo
receive a PCC order to rebel.

Violence and major disruption continue in the southern and
eastern areas of the city where buses are hijacked and
set alight and, using these attacks as cover, banks are
held up and robbed. Two traffic police depots are attacked
with Molotov cocktails.

**Document record: From *Cidade de São Paulo*,
16 May 2006, article by Francisco Silva**

According to a source close to the Chief of the São Paulo
Polícia Civil, officers, who were shot at during the violence
are entitled to receive danger money. On hearing this, as
the violence peaked and then subsided over Saturday night
and Sunday morning, a number of officers shot at their own
police headquarters, the bullet holes used as proof they'd
been attacked. These officers too, the source states, are
claiming danger money.

**Document record: From the *New York Times*,
17 May 2006, article by Paula Prada [Redacted]**

São Paulo: Government officials dismissed local news reports
that the police had used the crisis to kill suspects they
had previously singled out as gang members. A police
crackdown during the battles led to the arrest of more than
100 suspected gang members and the killing of 71.

While most of the dead were suspected of being criminals,
some 40 police officers were also killed, and the scale of
the fighting has prompted many to question an already shaky
faith in Brazil's public security forces.

The federal government offered to send troops to support
the state forces, which by law are those charged with the
state's security. But Cláudio Lembo, the acting governor,
declined the offer on Monday, calling it unnecessary and
arguing that the violence was 'under control'.

The decision prompted a wave of criticism that the refusal
was politically motivated. Mr Lembo's predecessor, Geraldo
Alckmin, recently stepped down as governor to run for
president, and any failure of state policies could easily
be used politically in what is expected to be a re-election
bid by President Luiz Inácio Lula da Silva.

'The government should spend more time trying to stop
this kind of activity instead of trying to keep itself in
office,' Noélio Alves Ferreira, 62, a shopkeeper in Conjunto
dos Metalúrgicos, a western suburb of the city, said in

an interview. 'We get shot at while they make political calculations.'

Afraid of a possible attack, Lúcia Sousa da Silva, 46, a grocer who lives across the street, shut her shop early on Monday, losing the evening's sales. 'The police are totally outgunned,' she said. 'They try to protect us, but really they're unprepared.'

Document record: From the *New York Times*,
30 May 2006, article by Larry Rochter [Redacted]

São Paulo: The police have acknowledged responsibility for some of those deaths, which they said had resulted from exchanges of gunfire or resisting arrest. But relatives and witnesses said some of the victims had not belonged to gangs at all, and were killed either on their way to or from work, or were simply executed by armed groups wearing ninja masks.

According to lawyers and medical groups whose members saw some of the bodies, many had numerous bullet wounds to the head, back or heart, and some also had wounds to the hands that appeared to indicate that they had been trying to defend themselves. Some of the victims' bodies also had gunpowder residue, indicating they were shot at point-blank range.

The authorities indignantly deny that they negotiated a truce, with the governor of São Paulo State, Cláudio Lembo, saying he found the suggestion 'offensive' because 'we don't bargain with banditry'. But President Luiz Inácio Lula da Silva encapsulated widespread public doubts and dismay when he commented that 'it seems that the police and the bandits were in collusion'.

Part Three

THE COMMUNIST MANIFESTO

São Paulo, 2011

1

The horror

January 2011

---

*2009: we all watch President Lula make his speech. YES! Brazil gets
the Olympics to go along with the World Cup. This is BRIC-affluence
at its cash-leverage peak. In São Paulo, my friends are unanimous.
Clusterfuck: this is another cheque that lefty-thief Lula can't cash.
Order and Progress claims the heart of the Brazilian flag. Yeah, right.*

Joe, 32, expat teacher

*Brazil was the second big surprise for us, at least in monetary
terms. Including it among the BRICs was my biggest gamble,
but by 2010 it had overtaken Italy to become the seventh largest
economy in the world, with a GDP of $2.1 trillion (£1.3 trillion).
I never imagined Brazil could grow so big so fast. Our [analysis]
did not suggest that it would reach that stage until after 2020.*

Jim O'Neill, Goldman Sachs economist, creator
of the BRIC economic concept, 2011

*I shall attend with utmost care to the weakest and most needy
– but I shall govern for all! A notable Indian leader once
said that you cannot shake hands with a clenched fist.*

Dilma Rousseff, 36th President of Brazil, Inaugural
speech to the Brazilian public, January 1, 2011

Happy fucking New Year.
Not long past five in the morning on the first day of 2011. Early

---

doors. Leme's phone ringing and ringing. He's been asleep for about an hour. Lisboa's words echo: *Happy fucking New Year!*

Leme dozes. The phone rings and rings. He feels a Renata-groan. Hot soured breath on his neck.

He drifts to pounding beers and pinga shots, to music and shouting. Leme yelling joyous salutations and promises of commitment and fidelity in Lisboa's ear.

Leme tastes garlic and salt, pork fat and stale cigarettes. Crisps stuck between his teeth.

Who the fuck is calling?

Leme picks up. Lisboa. What the fuck does he want *now*?

Lisboa says, 'Get out of bed, garanhão. There's a body with our name on it. Happy fucking New Year, mate.'

Garanhão. *Stud.* Quite a remove from the present situation.

Leme sits up, groans. His head spins. Full brain lurch. Change of plan. Five more minutes and I'm up, he thinks. Leme prone, dozes.

Ten minutes later, he comes round. Face down, head in the pillow.

He clocks hangover damage. With each heartbeat-thud, dust is lifted from the floor of his empty cranium before settling back down again.

Leme breathes, assesses a churning stomach.

A faint groan. Leme's left hand brushes the carpet. A foot. A presence rears up over him. It leans down, plants a kiss on his forehead. Renata.

A glance upwards. The clock reads 0537.

He fumbles in the top drawer for Neosaldinha. He finds it and pops two pills.

Leme scopes the nightstand, clocks a glass of water. He tosses both pills into his mouth. Murderous effort. Leme gasps, yells. It's not water, it's vodka and he gags as he swallows it down.

Happy fucking New Year.

He drifts to singing along to Tim Maia and Cazuza. Full-on sofa straddle, air guitar and Jagger shuffle. He grimaces. Kitchen swaying, kitchen spinning on regular beer-fridge reconnaissance work. He remembers looks from wives and friends of friends which said: woah there, you all right, mate?

He shrugs them off. Yeah, I'm fine, and with Renata and Lisboa he's golden. Another pinga with your can of lager? Brother, hit me. I love you, man.

Yeah, yeah. Too old for this.

Early doors.

Happy New Year.

Lisboa's got the heating up and the windows down.

Leme's head is dog-prone, stuck out in the cool breeze, tongue hanging. He tastes burnt coffee and soap. Lisboa, sensibly, keeps his trap shut. It's too early for the city heat, the concrete sauna.

Saturday January 1st, 2011, and there's no one about at this ungodly hour – and anyone that is still lives in 2010.

The streets are festa-filthy.

The streets are a damn shame.

Cans everywhere, rubbish spewed. Broken bottles. Bins knocked over. Dogs licking themselves in the mess, yawning. Happy days.

First thing in the morning, all-nighter noise spills from one or two balconies. Slurred laughter. Sad music. Joy and desperation in an even mix. The city exudes a just-one-more-drink vibe, but no one's gone home.

The park, Ibirapuera, sweeps away from them to the right. Fountains spunk jets of water at ten-minute intervals from the lake. They shoot high above the trees. Leme thinks it looks refreshing. The park is gated and locked.

They drift round the edge, move left across the lanes in front of the Monumento às Bandeiras. It is immense, the monument. It glorifies a conquistador impulse.

Leme likes the monument. It is *huge*. Eleven metres high, eight or nine metres wide and forty-odd metres deep. All granite. A serious heft.

Granite horses lead a party of men pulling a boat. The monument *gallops*.

Leme remembers the caption.

The gist: *Glory to the heroes that seek our destiny in the geography of the free world. Without them Brazil would not be what it is today.*

197

Cheers, lads, Leme thinks. Thanks a lot. Then: *what even is Brazil today?*

The statue depicts imperial pecking order: the Portuguese at the head, then the mameluco slave-hunters, that first generation the product of initial European and Afro-Brazilian copulation. Behind are slaves, and behind them the indigenous workers, crosses round their necks.

Granite horses nay and bray, they rear up. The granite boat looks *way* heavy. The hunched figures at the back push. The leaders at the front stand tall, jut their chins –

It's all very frontiersman.

Leme knows his history. It's about the settler expeditions into the far-flung and hostile interior of Brazil. São Paulo leading the way, as usual. *I lead, I will not be led.* City-motto relevant. Searching for gold, for cash, for a place to stick their flag, their *Bandeira*.

And now, today, he thinks, we inaugurate our first-ever female president.

Dilma.

Change. Order and Progress. It's all good.

Lisboa says, 'Fun night, ne?'

Leme grunts.

'You wanna know where we're going?'

Leme shakes his head. It *hurts*. 'Just tell me how long until we're there,' he says.

Lisboa jams into a low gear, slides into the car park by the swank concert venue. Brakes hard. 'We're there,' he says.

Leme sighs. 'Happy fucking New Year.'

There's a cordon in place behind the concert venue. The park stretches out into manicured lawns and well-kept paths and ponds of carp. Here though, it's wasteland-rough. Uniforms are spread out and prevent rubbernecker access. A plastic tarp has been erected like a windbreaker on a beach. Men in white coats hang back. The head honcho doctor has a look on him Leme's never seen before. The look: disbelief. Men stand facing outwards, protecting the cordoned area. Their faces are white. Their faces are green. Leme thinks they look relieved to have their backs to the scene, whatever it is. They look vomit-ready. Late-night, early-morning shift is a fucker. Lisboa makes nice with the cavalry. Official pecking order established. Leme looks wistfully at the Bandeirantes – the explorers, the founders of this fine country – parading and swaggering on their monument. What he wouldn't give to be off on a fucking expedition.

Leme doesn't much like the look of all this palaver.

Lisboa nods, gestures with this chin. 'This way.'

Leme nods.

The cordon is opened out. Men stand aside. They don't look Leme in the eye.

In long grass and thin brush Leme sees a body.

He sees the face of a woman. Long dark hair frames this face. Leme blinks, steadies himself. The face has been erased, damaged. It is recognisably a face, but one whose features have been flattened. Like someone has scribbled with a dark, blood-black marker all over it. The blood is thick and crusted. The eyes and nose are missing. The mouth is smashed. The horror, Leme thinks, is not this, not this devastation, this endgame discovery; it's that someone can do this to someone else.

Leme heaves empty vomit. He chokes back bile.

Lisboa places a hand on Leme's shoulder. He knows Lisboa isn't looking.

The corpse is twisted, in the recovery position, unclothed. The body is dirtied by soil and scratched by brush and long grass. She has been dragged to this place, Leme thinks.

He bends over the body, sees a hole in the victim's chest. A dark, rough, black hole.

To the right of the body, Leme sees what has been pulled from this hole. He sees the victim's heart. Dark, rotting. Butchered.

Leme inspects the corpse waist down. Genitalia indistinct, wiped out.

His head spins, he lurches forward, breathes. Leme crouches and recovers his composure.

The doctor is at his side. He says, 'Looks likely the victim was killed and mutilated close by, early hours, and dumped here not long ago. I'd say an hour, maybe two.'

Leme's nodding. Lisboa is coughing.

'I'll need to do a full autopsy – '

Leme nods more.

'It's not the place to – '

Leme straightens.

'Point is,' the doctor says, 'you need to see what's been found.' He gestures at the ground a few feet from the victim.

Leme gloves up, studies evidence.

There is a small pile of jewellery. Secured on top, tied on with a shoelace, is a business card. It reads: *Pereira Modelling*.

Next to this, there is an ID card. The name: Gerson Anderson. The name: *male*.

The ID card is held in place by a paperweight.

Leme's eyes flash, his head zips, his head clears.

On the paperweight is an inscription: *Feliz Aniversario*.

The misspelling *screams*.

Leme's head spins. He gestures at Lisboa. Lisboa gloves up. A few moments later, Lisboa says, 'Jesus.'

The doctor is sweating.

Leme nods at Lisboa who issues forensic clean-up instructions. Men comb the surrounding area. Leme is sure there is nothing left to find.

He walks back to where the vehicles are parked. He talks to a uniform who skedaddles to locate the poor sod – a park gardener – who stumbled on the body.

A man hovers. Leme thinks he knows him, isn't sure. The man approaches Leme. He has his notebook out, pencil ready.

Leme says, 'No fucking way, mate.'

The man nods. 'Fair enough. Here.' He gives Leme his card.

Francisco Silva, Crime Correspondent, Cidade de São Paulo

Leme studies this Silva. He reckons Silva has come direct from a New Year soirée.

Leme says, 'At this point, son, you don't even want to fucking know.'

Silva smiles grim. 'When you want to talk,' he says.

'I'll keep you in mind,' Leme says – sardonic. 'You tell me how you got here so fast, I'll at least consider it.'

'Oh, I don't reveal my sources.'

Leme spits. He glares at Silva. 'You best fuck off then,' he says. Silva agrees.

Late morning and Silva's at his desk opening the mail. Silva's desk is his dining room table. Silva's dining room table would be considered untidy if you stumbled across it on a building site. He is fairly sure that he has never used his dining room table to eat dinner at. He has never had anyone over to share the privilege.

Silva eats his meals on the hoof. Which is a good phrase for him as many of Silva's meals involve bife à cavalo, cowboy-style steak, à la horse, which means two slabs of beef and two fried eggs on top with a side order of fried potatoes. He's started ordering fried potatoes rather than fries, which, though it makes him feel better, makes no difference to his plate of food. It's become a joke at his local eatery: would you like fried potatoes with your fries, mate?

It's nice to be known some place, Silva reckons. And besides, he was joking when he first did it but now it's his thing, his shtick. Bit like when he wanted to order calabresa acebolada, grilled sausage with onion, but drunkenly asked for cebola calabrezada – onions with sausage. The waiter laughed. Silva doubled down. I'm not joking, he said. The waiter shrugged. Brought it over. Silva remembers now how it tasted. Fucking glorious. And so another of Silva's things. Onions.

Silva sips cold coffee. He dips pão na chapa. He's a fan of the old-school breakfast – bread fried in butter.

He surveys his desk. Piles of paper. Dog-eared magazines. Back copies of *Cidade de São Paulo*, his own venerable publication. Leaking biros and deadened pencils. Half-empty coffee mugs. A computer that won't turn on. He uses it as several paperweights. He smiles, because today it is with some pride that he surveys his workplace. And this is due to the package he is opening. The draft of a report he has co-authored in which his investigative work has been instrumental. It's been something of a crusade for Silva. For all his egg-stained ties and sloppy suits, his piles of fried breakfasts and liquid lunches, his dusty bachelor apartment and solo drinking sessions, Silva is a crusader, a bull-headed game-changer who takes real pleasure in fucking over the system that allows the endemic corruption and violence that blights his town.

São Paulo is his town all right. Silva is a *real* product.

He tears into the package. It's a press-release draft.

Report by Harvard's International Human Rights Clinic and Brazilian NGO demonstrates central role of police brutality, corruption and prison mismanagement in major security crisis of May 2006 and today

Silva's role has been on the ground, frontline interviewing, digging, using his contacts and his muckrakers, his IT guy has been *way* helpful. Hacking has never been so easy, so Silva gathers. He reads:

Five years ago, a series of coordinated uprisings in 74 detention centres and attacks on police stations and public buildings left 43 state officials and hundreds of civilians dead and brought South America's largest city and financial capital to a standstill. São Paulo streets were deserted as residents stayed at home in fear. After the violence coordinated by the organised crime syndicate the 'First Command of the Capital' (Primeiro Comando da Capital, or 'PCC' by its Portuguese initials) stopped, police killed scores of civilians in a wave of reprisal attacks, targeting those they suspected of having criminal backgrounds, in many cases relying apparently only on the youth, skin colour, presence of tattoos and presence on the streets of poor neighbourhoods at night. Evidence in 122 killings contains signs of police having committed an extrajudicial execution.

It was Silva that got this last statistic. It wasn't easy. He had to track the incident records for pretty much every bad guy that was whacked over the weekend. Witness statements were vague. Police records suggested only necessary force. You had to read between the lines. Silva knew what he was looking out for. Access was extreme privilege. A combination of grey-area legal public document claims with insider Militar help. Silva's source is a brute named Carlos. A good brute, though. Staunch and taking something of a risk. He looked up Silva himself, post-weekend. Silva thinks it's a trauma-relief situation. Carlos says it's simpler than that: pure insurance – you fuck or you get fucked.

There is one John Doe that Silva thought stood out. A low-level gangbanger called Sergio Nascimento. Carlos claims the lad was assassinated, that was the word he used, which sparked Silva's enquiring mind. Rumour is that he was a fit-up for a murder charge a few years back, a patsy the PCC put forward, paying off his family in return. So it was better for everyone if old Sergio took his last on his weekend out of the joint. Point is, there was collusion: PCC arranged the hit, Military Police carried it out. No one's going on the record though. Course they're fucking not. This is something Silva's going to have to sniff out for himself.

The report's taken years and some serious heft. Silva partnered up real tasty on this one.

Today, five years later, Harvard Law School's International Human Rights Clinic and the leading Brazilian human rights group Justiça Global release a comprehensive study of the May 2006 attacks. The Report, 'São Paulo under attack: corruption, organised crime and institutional violence in May 2006', seeks to answer several questions essential to public security in Brazil: What led to the attacks? Why were state authorities unable or unwilling to prevent them? Why and how did the police lash out violently in revenge killings? Why have the crimes committed by the state not been investigated, and in many cases, apparently covered up?

Silva did some time in the land of the academia-rich Yank and made some contacts. He was a visiting scholar, year abroad from Universidade de São Paulo, top dog in the Latin American seats of learning. Zero cash outlay, too. Silva appreciates it still.

The result of five years of investigation – including hundreds of interviews; scores of on-site visits to jails, prisons and communities affected by violence; meetings with a broad range of authorities; and

a review of thousands of pages of documents, police reports, and judi-
cial records – sheds new light on the May 2006 attacks. 'Official cor-
ruption, tragically, was a driving force behind the May attacks. PCC
leaders – new information in the study confirms – coordinated their
assault in large part as a response to a series of organised shakedowns
by the police,' said Fernando Delgado, a fellow at Harvard Law
School and the principal author of the report. 'The evidence indicates
that a year prior to the attacks, police were using wiretaps, kidnap-
ping, and other abuse of family members of gang leaders to extract
bribes. The PCC decided to retaliate brutally and brought the city
to a halt.'

Silva thinks the figures here have been smudged a tad. Hundreds
meaning scores, scores meaning several, thousands meaning a fair
few, yeah, but not four-figure thick. Judicial records are a laugh,
Silva thinks.

He flicks through the report itself. It is jargon-dense. It is *dry*.
It is not a page-turner. They're planning on publishing in May, the
anniversary, therefore publicity, therefore media coverage, therefore
blah blah blah. Silva likes Delgado and Silva was keen to help and
he is proud that he did. But he's kept his involvement on the DL, as
they say, silent author. The reason: Silva wants to effect change not
write reports. Reports prompt snail-pace action. Silva's a journalist;
he digs the scoop.

And he reckons he might be onto some scoop and he wants it to
himself. The report will give him some leverage, buy him a meeting
or two, stake his play.

The questions that Silva is interested in are a little different to
those he phrased himself in this press release. The answer to all of
those is simple: no one cares.

Silva knows there is more digging to be done, away from the
Military Police, the state apparatus, digging around the system that
supports the state apparatus.

Silva's first question, which no one seems especially bothered to
ask is:

Why the fuck did they let out so many prisoners on the same weekend?

And related to that:
Who the fuck did all the paperwork?
This is all authorised from somewhere, stone certainty.
Money talks. Money *yells*.

Rafa nudges Franginho, nods to the vacant parking lot. Two cars move slowly towards them. *There are the cunts.*

Franginho clocks them. 'What a crusty, lairy group of little cunts,' he says.

Rafa laughs. 'Considering you can't see them, that is a world-class description, filho.'

'Students,' Franginho says. 'I fucking hate students.'

'Yeah, well, look lively, cara. They've got a big bag of money for us.'

Franginho nods. 'This is going against all my principles, this political activism, entendeu?'

'It's capitalism, porra, pure and simple. Supply and demand.'

'Yeah all right, Night School, just take care of business and I'll stand here looking hard.'

Rafa laughs. He opens the door to the Portakabin they're in that is known to those in the know as The Factory. He steps down. He smiles as a black car spills four characters all dressed in head-to-toe black, caps pulled low, sunglasses, bandanas tied around their mouths.

'Welcome,' Rafa says, 'to my office.' He gives the group the once-over, the amused evil eye. They stay still, tight. 'Which one of you lot is in charge then?' Rafa asks. He points at the largest of the lads. 'You, Metallica. You the boss?'

Rafa's in flip-flops and shorts and his handgun is, if not quite visible, certainly implied by the way he moves, the way his clothes hang. He has favela authority, *experience*. He carries this authority with real authority.

He's been moved up the chain from running the supermarkets and now works out of The Factory almost exclusively. Part of his new role has been cooking up business opportunities away from the traditional PCC drug-slinging and gun-running activities. Rafa has been keen to keep out of that side of the organisation, directly at least.

One of these opportunities has been helping to tie up the site of

The Factory in such endless bureaucracy that it remains a flattened building site, no progress for over five years. That was Franginho's idea. The man has a talent for imaginative admin, what can you say? The Singapore Project committee responsible for the site has given up the ghost. The boys up the hill are *thrilled*.

It feels good to have an office.

Rafa wonders where all the money has gone. He got a little bit of it, but he reckons there was an awful lot more knocking about.

This meeting today, though, is another opportunity:

Rafa and Franginho have decided to go into politics. The contact was made with a student lad they use to punt small amounts of drugs around the college circuit. Now here they are meeting a bunch of anarchists or communists or something. No one's really sure, but it doesn't matter.

'I'm in charge,' a voice pipes up. The speaker steps forward. 'You can address me.'

Address me. Rafa smiles, makes a face: *fair enough, big man*. He grins. He opens the door of the Portakabin. 'This way, sir,' he says, ushering the speaker inside.

The speaker does as is beckoned.

Rafa follows. His office is sparse. There is a table and three chairs. Franginho stands and ushers their guest into one of them.

Rafa raises his eyebrows at Franginho, makes a face: *candy from a baby situation and no mistake*.

The speaker removes a black cap and long dark hair falls over –

Her shoulders. She turns to Rafa, takes off her sunglasses. 'Call me, madam, *sir*.'

Franginho howls and hoots.

Rafa smiles. He says, 'Shall we get started?'

The woman nods and sits down. She opens her backpack. She pulls out a thick envelope. She hands it to Rafa.

'It's all here,' she says.

'I'm sure it is.' Rafa throws it to Franginho. 'You didn't want to see the goods first?'

'I trust you.'

'Thousands wouldn't,' Franginho mutters.

Rafa gives him a sharp look. 'Foundation of any good relationship, trust.'

'Pois é.' *Damn right.*

'My associate here has everything you need. Little Chicken, if you'd be so kind.'

Rafa's enjoying this. He finds he can't stop smiling as he looks into this young woman's eyes. He finds he's not especially bothered about what's in the thick envelope. 'What *is* your name?' he says.

'Carolina.'

'Carolina…?'

'Just Carolina. For now.'

Rafa grins. He nods to Franginho to hand over the sports bag they've filled with a range of explosives. Carolina opens the bag, rifles through it.

'Various tools here,' Franginho says. 'You've got your basic fireworks, something with a little more pop and then some serious heavy metal. You see which is which, okay?'

Carolina rolls her eyes. 'Thank you, Little Chicken,' she says.

Rafa sticks his tongue out in delight.

'Anything else you need while you're here? Bit of weed or powder?' he says.

Carolina shakes her head.

'Fair enough, whatever floats your boat,' Rafa smiles. 'What *are* you lot, anyway?'

Carolina fixes him with a look: *don't fuck with me, querido.*

She says, 'We're anarcho-syndicalists. We're Black Bloc. You'll know what we are soon enough.'

Rafa claps his hands, whoop-whoops. 'I cannot wait to see you again, Carolina menina, linda do meu coracão.'

Carolina, beautiful girl of my heart.

She stands. 'We'll be in touch.'

Rafa opens the door for her, offers his hand to help her down the step. Gives it the old-school gentleman.

She smiles, eyes dazzling, and shakes her head. She leaves.

Franginho roars, slaps his thigh. 'Mate,' he says, 'Carolina menina, that is some nice rhyming.'

Rafa's nodding. He's watching her get back into the car. He's watching her leave and he's nodding and he's grinning.

Ray's back in São Paulo and happy about it.

He has two jobs this year, as he sees it. One: to work out which way the cookie is going to crumble, politically speaking, when the inevitable happens and the left finally implodes. Two: to help make sure this inevitability a) comes to pass and b) is a profitable coming to pass for Ray and the big dogs at Capital SP.

Two jobs, one word: *collusion.*

The weekend riots back in 2006, the civil unrest and economic uncertainty they threw up, worked out *real* well for Big Ray and the big dogs. Taking a short position, hedging, backing the market to re-stabilise: well played, sir, was the general feeling.

And since, Brazil is skyrocketing, economy-wise. The place has struck oil. Lula's administration oversaw a beautiful and fortuitous slice of good fortune: Chinese demand for Brazil's two most valuable exports, iron ore and soya, went through the roof and right at the time of a generally steep commodity price rise; add to this the Yankee dollar that came flooding in from cheap capital imports as part of the old Greenspan put. Ray knew all about these.

What Ray also knows: the government has taken full – and under-standable – credit for the country's turnaround, the influx of jobs and capital, the buoyant mood that almost all Brazilians seem to now have; and yet the government has had nothing to do with this turnaround, zip, nada.

Hence Ray's assertion that political change is not too far away.

Which is why he's meeting young Anna here – Marta's right-hand woman – to identify a target or two, a way in *ahead* of the game.

She's cute, this Anna. Ray's the same age as he always was. He enjoys the game, that's all. And that's what he tells himself.

'Key thing is mensalão,' Anna is saying. 'It's been rumbling for a few years and it joins a lot of dots.'

'I'm listening,' Ray says.

'The word means "big monthly payment" and the thinking is that Lula's been holding his precarious coalition together through the ingenious method of doling out cash to deputies so they'll vote for him.'

'Old-school. You got any insider proof?'

'Isn't that why we're here?'

Ray grins. 'I like your style. Please go on.'

A waiter hovers. They're in Ray's office: the deck bar of Unique.

'I'd say the usual, please, Fernando,' Ray says to the hovering waiter. Ray turns to Anna. 'The usual sound good to you?'

'You look like a man who knows what everyone wants, Ray.'

'Good woman.' Ray nods and winks at Fernando who disappears. 'You were saying.'

'Mensalão is a big deal, but some of these guys are bulletproof, right? Media hysteria is nothing new. They all hate the PT anyway, and since this broke the press has gone full moral, righteous nemesis. They have spared nothing, no noxious conjecture or detrimental detail.'

'That's well put.'

'Perhaps the biggest development over the last few years and especially back in 2006, which you'll remember, is the media have blurred the traditional line between institutional misconduct and individual misbehaviour.'

'You have a way with words, Anna. This is an excellent, and succinct, summary.'

'I know what's what, Ray. And I know what it is that you want.'

Ray grins.

'Rasputin has helped us here. Quietly, certo?'

Ray leans in. 'Mr Favre has been helpful before.'

Anna's nodding. 'He suggests we focus on a certain Antonio Palocci. The word is, Dilma is about to make him her chief of staff.'

The waiter appears with Ray's usual. Three bottles of beer and a bowl of peanuts. Two glasses.

Anna laughs. Ray pours beers into glasses.

Anna goes on, 'You might have heard of Palocci.'

Ray nods.

'Minister of Finance under Lula, the whole "Letter to the Brazilians" architect to get the business community on board, and the guy who made sure all the Workers' Party backdoor deals with the banks and the construction firms were in place pre-election.'

'So something of a fixer.'

'An all-out crook is what Rasputin thinks.'

'Takes one to know one.'

'Easy, Ray,' Anna laughs.

'So how do we get this Palocci on Team Big Ray?'

Anna smiles. 'That shouldn't be too hard. The fucker's got form. They're saying his downfall back in 2006 paved the way for Lula's triumphant second term and, ultimately, Dilma's candidacy for president.'

'The Marxist with the mostest.'

'Point is there may be a quid pro quo situation going down.'

'What, she's scratching his back as he's already scratched hers?'

'He may have scratched hers trying to cling on as he fell from grace, but otherwise...'

'Interesting. So what's the story, morning glory?'

Anna raises an eyebrow.

Ray says, 'I'm young at heart.'

'So,' Anna says, 'here's the kicker. Early 2006, turns out there's this secluded lakeside retreat in Brasília and it's been rented by one of Palocci's aides.'

'Sounds fruity.'

'Only thing in the rooms is beds and mini-fridges. And a combination-locked side table for cash.'

'Ha. What fecund imagination. It's quite glorious.'

Anna smiles. 'They were all at it, apparently. Lobbyists and familiars, the minister himself on a regular basis, kickback recipients, high-office police, all enjoying prostitutes and parties, and swapping tips and favours.'

'Old boys' club.'

Anna nods. 'Rasputin has a list of some of the partygoers.'

'Outstanding.'

'But we start with someone else.'

Ray opens his arms. *Tell me.* Ray grins. He nods at Fernando and the usual appears. Ray pours them both healthy measures of beer. Ray throws back peanuts.

'We've got the housekeeper.'

'Outstanding. Tell me about her.'

'*Him.* Key thing is this happened during the fallout. The kid's twenty-four years old, from Piauí, earns fifty bucks a week, that's US, Ray, and he finds his bank account hacked by none other than the president of the Federal Savings Bank, Jorge Mattoso.'

'Helluva find.'

'Pois é.' *Oh yes.* 'This Mattoso had just paid Lula a visit, and the hack was a digging exercise to see if the lad had taken any dinheiro for his testimony.'

'As I said,' Ray says, 'a glorious business.'

'What happens next is that Mattoso goes to Palocci and tells him this kid has recently taken receipt of ten thousand US in a single deposit. Which is true. Palocci tells the federal police to get the lad on bribery and false witness.'

'So the kid's fucked.'

'Not quite. The money was a payment from his old man.'

'Eh?'

Anna smiles. 'Not your style, Ray, confusion.'

Ray shrugs. 'Drink your beer, sweetheart.'

'The kid's old man owns a bus company, so he's got ready money. He's paying his boy to avoid a paternity suit. He's never acknowledged the kid as his until then.'

'What a gent.'

'So the lad sees his chance and brings criminal charges against Palocci and Mattoso. Which may have been a mistake.'

'I think it likely was a mistake. The old boys' club and whatnot.'

'You've nailed it. Charges reduced and Supreme Court acquits, and now Palocci has the nod to come off the bench to be Dilma's chief of staff.'

'It is an admirably odious state of affairs. And the lad?'

'Hasn't had a job since.'

'Which is where we step in.'

'Grievance.'

Ray grins. 'It's a priceless commodity.'

Hate crime.

Leme and Lisboa slump in their shit-can office. Lisboa has already gone *fuck it* and popped out to buy beers.

It has been a *long* year so far.

Both men look like something the cat dragged in. Their tiredness: existential.

There's only so much horror you can bear in a day. In a life.

The state of play, as Leme has it:

1) The victim is a post-op, pre-ID change trans woman. They ran the ID (male), cross-checked address and known workplace, ran this against medical records and, bingo.
2) The mutilation is deliberate and intended to highlight – with a grotesque and appalling violence – the facts as established above.
3) The autopsy has so far been unable to establish any recent sexual activity, forced or consensual, but it leans to there being none. This ambiguity in itself is appalling.
4) The paperweight was not the murder weapon. It was, however, employed in a good percentage of the post-death physical trauma.
5) The paperweight has no trace of fingerprints. It fits the description of the missing paperweight from the home of the late Paddy Lockwood.
6) Death was caused, the post-mortem suggests, by drugging. Large traces of strychnine were found in the deceased's bloodstream.
7) It is not clear that the mutilation was exclusively performed after death.
8) Pereira Modelling does not appear to exist.
9) The jewellery, according to forensics, was worn by the victim over a significant period of time.
10) The provenance, or ownership, of the shoelace is unclear.

First thing is to find out a bit more about the deceased. Associates, friends, work colleagues. Her prints are clean – no record. Saturday morning, so unlikely to figure on any missing person file. First problem is figuring out what name the deceased is now under. And there's a good chance it's not registered anywhere. The male ID leads down a series of former places of employment, former rented apartment, former gym membership, former life, essentially. And low key, it seems. Office-assistant jobs, stable medical insurance usage, no frills flats in nondescript neighbourhoods. They're missing something but they don't know what. Saturday makes admin cross checking tricky. Leme likes to quiz people. Weekend face-time hiatus.

Lisboa says, 'It seems she was very fucking successful in starting a new life.'

Leme's one step ahead. Mais ou menos. They need to find out the protocol in an ID switch like this one.

What is non-negotiable in life, the day to day?

Money.

Bank records, credit card use. That's the starting point now, surely. That and the last place of work and last place of residence of a Senhor Gerson Anderson.

And the other thing is to work out what Pereira Modelling means. It's got to mean something.

Leme is bone-tired. What a day.

'We need to gather the troops,' he says. 'Brainstorm this head-scratcher. I'd say the level of horrible violence, its social, prejudicial nature, and the trauma of the victim's condition suggest this might not be an isolated incident.'

Lisboa nods.

'Which means we can expedite the caseload.'

Lisboa nods. 'Couple of admin guys is a start.'

'That and at least two juniors to run the checks.'

Lisboa nods. Leme says, 'You sort that and I'll get down to admin and pick out a couple of geeks for us.'

Lisboa nails lager. Leme hits the stairs down to the IT department. Admin, a euphemism meaning: semi-legal investigative work at your service.

Hate crime –

Incarnate.

Renata's hangover is fierce. Truth is she's enjoyed getting over it on her own. Mario's a fidgeter when he's hungover, can't sit still, wakes up *way* too early, gives the impression that he feels he needs to be *doing* something –

It can be exhausting.

She got an extra few hours' sleep, lay quietly for another, made a pot of coffee and shut down any thoughts of New Year dread with the book she's reading, a new translation of a huge, rollicking, nineteenth century French novel from the author of *Les Misérables*. It feels apt to put herself far away from what is happening here and now in São Paulo, namely the commemoration of the inauguration of Brazil's first female president.

She takes her book down to the condominium pool.

The wooden deck is hot under her feet. Saturday.

Waiters from the bar flitting about with drinks and food. Teenagers flirting. Children running. Wobbly toddlers chased by nannies. Parents stripped off and pre-lunch drunk.

Renata orders a beer, lies on a lounger, reads her book –

She swaps gossip with women in bikinis and sarongs as they pass by. Families pad about, eating, playing with frisbees and inflatable toys, cooling off in the pool.

The sun pierces. It ripples the water. The pool pale, a blue storm.

She dives in, the cool shock, swims laps.

Renata's hangover subsides. The world is opaque. Her sunglasses a shield.

The sun swells, gorges, fattens. A chatter-hubbub. Splashing kids. Shouting men, drinking heavily. The thwack of a tennis ball from the court below. The weighty slap of the shower in the sauna hitting the mosaic-tiled floor.

Lunchtime. Families wander off to their apartments. Children drag feet. Bottom lips protrude. The men stay, drink on. The pool calms. Renata finishes her beer, stretches. She wraps up in her throw and smiles goodbyes.

She takes a long shower. She eats a bowl of rice and beans for lunch, washes it down with a cold glass of white wine. Then she drinks another.

Renata switches on the TV to watch the speech. The food and the wine have left her engaged, excited. All the talk down by the pool was not exactly supportive of Dilma and the PT, the left wing.

Renata kept her views to herself.

The news all week has been Lula's legacy and how his protégée is going to continue his incredible work, and even more in fact, she's a woman, look how far we've come, she cares even more than he does, look how far we've come, a woman, a symbol of the new, egalitarian experiment, the social-democrat evolution, economic prosperity rumbles on a tide of optimism, look what a country we have, look how far we've come, look –

In Renata's mind, there is one key thing; and one key thing she has helped deliver:

Bolsa Família, and its message: we, the government, care for every Brazilian, no matter how poverty-stricken, how downtrodden, how pathetic. Every single one of us is a citizen with social rights.

Combine this with Lula's crédito consignado – bank loans for household purchases provided for people who don't even have bank accounts, and with repayment arranged through monthly deductions from wages, pensions – and suddenly you have the disenfranchised well and truly a part of a consumer society.

Social mobility.

Dilma's success is all about the fact that she's a woman, Renata reckons, and not in a mean way. Lula wrapped his arm around her; it was a joint campaign of coronation, effectively. Lula and his anointed successor.

It wouldn't have worked with a man.

The speech begins. Renata pours wine.

My dear Brazilians – To take on this responsibility, I have with me the strength and the example of the Brazilian woman. I open my heart to receive, at this moment, a spark of her immense energy. I am not here to boast of my own life story, but rather to praise the life of every Brazilian woman.

Social mobility is one thing, of course, though it's worth remembering Lula's throwaway line:

———

215

'It's cheap and easy to look after the poor.'

Think about what that means. And think about the fact that he's won the popular vote at the same time as increasing the wealth of the rich.

Clever boy.

My dear Brazilians – I will not rest while there are Brazilians who have no food on their tables, while there are desperate families on the streets, while there are poor children abandoned to their own devices. Family unity lies in food, peace and happiness. This is the dream I will pursue! Social justice, morality, knowledge, invention and creativity should be, more than ever, living ideals in the daily life of the nation.

She's got tasty form, too, Dilma, Renata thinks.

Back in the 60s, she was part of a well-known guerrilla action. A case containing two and half million US was blagged from the mistress of a corrupt São Paulo governor.

Two years later, she was caught, tortured, imprisoned.

Look at her now.

My dear Brazilians – I will be strict in my defence of the public interest. There will be no tolerance of diverted funds or wrongdoing. Corruption will be combated ceaselessly, and the entities that control and investigate these matters will have my full backing so that they can act with firmness and autonomy.

Renata thinks: mensalão. Renata wonders: is this a sly dig at Lula, an admission or a swerve? There's a clever sidestep here, she thinks, a pedalo, as they say in football.

Dilma controls the entities that control and investigate these matters. There is no way she'll ever do anything to compromise her mentor.

My dear Brazilians – It is with courage that I shall govern Brazil.

You're going to need it, love, Renata thinks.

Bocão, Big Mouth, *former escort:*

Guilt.

One night I made it into one of those theatre bars. Paddy decided to take me to see a French play called *The Balcony* put on by someone called Peter Brook, in French with Portuguese subtitles. I spent the week before prickling with excitement. I looked up the play on the Internet and tried to learn a little about it. It was complicated.

'It's all about the difference between reality and illusion,' Paddy told me. 'About revolution and counter-revolution. A lot of it is set in a brothel, but it's a metaphor.'

'What's a metaphor?'

'It's when something is one thing, but is actually something else.' That confused me. 'This play helped invent modern theatre.'

I planned what to wear. Paddy had bought me a black blazer and I matched it with a pair of dark jeans and a pink shirt. I found a cashmere scarf in my sister's wardrobe and though it wasn't a cold night, I decided I'd wear that too.

We took a taxi to the theatre. Paddy seemed agitated.

'You'll enjoy this,' he said, though he didn't look me in the eye and sat a little further away from me than normal. 'I wonder if there'll be anyone I know there.' He took a deep breath. I stayed silent. 'If there is…' he began. 'Well, not to worry. We'll deal with that when we have to.'

I knew what he was referring to, but I was so excited about my first theatre trip that I didn't mind. He would know what to do, whatever happened.

We arrived in good time and though I wanted a glass of wine before it began, Paddy insisted we take our seats straight away.

We were seated in the corner in near darkness. The play was difficult, but I loved it. The thrill of hearing the words spoken in French and the performance of the actors made up for not understanding a word of what was going on. I sat with a dopey grin on my face, leaning forward to laugh or gasp, my hands rubbing hard on my thighs. Once or twice I looked across at Paddy and he gave me a thin smile. I wasn't sure if he was encouraging me or putting up with me. I didn't really care, so pleased as I was by this new experience.

The play ended and I went to the bathroom, Paddy telling me that he'd meet me in the bar at the front of the theatre. I was trembling and smiling so much that a couple of guys in the toilet looked at me weirdly. I was dressed well enough, so it must have been my manner, sabe? I smiled at the men and they shrugged and moved quickly away. As I washed my hands, I looked at my reflection in the mirror and rearranged my hair. I undid a button on my shirt, reconsidered, and did it up again, leaving a light brown triangle visible beneath the pink collar.

I left the bathroom and headed to the foyer bar. I felt my chest expand with pride as I remembered being turned away from this building in the past, ushered on by the guys on the door – vai embora, porra – slinking away down the dark streets flickering red neon that flanked the building.

Paddy was near the bar talking to a small group of people. A lady in a purple hat and dress. A man with a beige overcoat slung over his arm. Another man talking loudly in English with a strong Brazilian accent. A couple quietly sipping at red wine.

As I approached, the man who was speaking faltered and looked at me nervously. 'So, I, erm, I think the, erm… sorry,' he said. His eyes flicked around the rest of the group, as though one of them might be able to explain who I was and why I was interrupting him.

I stood next to Paddy and smiled at the others.

The man continued, with a curious look darkening his expression. 'It will be a tremendous improvement to the school,' he said in English. 'I'm sorry. Do I know you?' He offered his hand.

'Oh, I'm sorry,' Paddy said. 'This is the son of a family friend. He's interested in the theatre and I offered to bring him.' And he reeled off a series of names, but I wasn't listening as I felt a stinging inside, a deep, deliberate wound.

They carried on with the conversation in English and I had difficulty following what was said. The couple with the drinks were English, but the others were Brazilian. Their speech was peppered with a strange mixture of the two languages – 'it's very lamentável.' 'I feel very positivo about it.' 'It's an excellent negocio.' – I couldn't join in. I was worthless, pobre, a favour to a friend.

After twenty minutes or so, we left. 'I'll give the boy a lift home,' Paddy told his friends.

I never did get that glass of wine.

Shame.

After our theatre trip, things changed. In the taxi, I exploded.

'How could you do that to me? You're ashamed of me. I've never felt so humiliated.'

Paddy turned away from me. 'I find that hard to believe,' he said.

'Filho da puta! Desgraçado! How dare you judge me!' I shouted. The driver turned in his seat. 'Stop the car,' I told him and got out, slamming the door.

I walked around for a couple of hours, but my anger wouldn't leave me. I clenched my fists and scratched at my scalp. I swore at cars that got too close when I crossed the road. I cursed couples walking hand in hand. I glared at anyone who looked smaller or weaker than I did.

When I got home, my sister was asleep, graças a Deus. I sat in my room, staring at the blank wall in front of me, muttering – how could he? How could he? – wondering how it was possible that Paddy had reduced me to this. To nothing.

Remorse.

Later, I thought I'd overreacted and that if I did it again I might lose him for good. I resolved to become a better person.

In the morning, as he opened his door to go to work, I was waiting for him, holding two coffees.

'I'm sorry.'

I handed him the drink. He looked approvingly at the brand. I always tried to get the best of things. That was something he taught me.

'I'm sorry too.'

'It was a lovely evening, until…'

'I should've explained. People don't know about us. About me.'

'I didn't know.'

'That's my fault. Things need to be private in my life. That's just the way it has to be.'

This stung.

'I understand.'

'Good. I hope you do.'

'I'm sorry.'

Leme is swaying. He bounces off his bedroom door frame.

Leme slurs. Renata stirs. She says, sleepy, 'It's okay.' She rubs her eyes. 'Are you okay?'

'I'm not,' Leme says. 'No, I'm not okay, really.'

'Come to bed.'

Leme assents. He shrugs off shirt and jacket. He holds the door frame. He slips off shoes. He is unsteady. He unbuckles his belt and pops the zip.

He lies down. 'I must stink.'

Renata wraps a leg around him. 'You do.'

His breathing is heavy.

Lisboa has a briefing scheduled first thing. The troops are thrilled at the Sunday morning shift. Leme talked to admin. He explained their predicament. He handed over details, credentials. He didn't say anything about the potential provenance of the paperweight. As Lisboa pointed out: 'Any fucker can make a batch of misspelt knick-knacks, mate.'

The admin guy said, 'So we're looking for a chick with a dick.'

Leme glared, went *watch it, son.* He said, 'We're looking for a woman whose ID sports a man's name.'

The admin guy spouted contrite. 'We'll try the numbers first then.'

'Pereira Modelling is the other thing.'

'I mean, you could Google that yourself…'

Leme made a face: *you can.*

'Sure thing,' the admin guy said. 'I'll have a dig around.'

Leme and Lisboa went to a cop bar and sat alone and drank. They didn't say much; there wasn't much to say. Neither knew anything that the other didn't already. Talking was futile. What are you going to talk about? Revisit the state of the body? Speculate on why anyone would do that to anyone else? Fuck no.

Leme groans. He buries his head in the crook of Renata's neck. Her hand strays back and he breathes her in.

Home.

Hate crime.

Briefing room. Sunday morning cock-a-doodle-do early. Leme and Lisboa head the table. Two juniors either side: Moreira and Hamuche. Decent lads. Leme trusts them. Lisboa's not sure. Their detail: grunt work, cross check admin leads and systems connections, some low-key doorstepping.

One admin guy, too. Truculent sod Leme briefed the day before. Name: da Cunha. He has a laptop open. Leme's giving him a break after yesterday. These admin guys don't spend much time socialising.

There is a grim look to all of the men. It's not just the Sunday shift work. They've seen the crime scene photos. Their eyes are burned with the images. Their stomachs are yet to settle.

Briefing objective simple: find out the name of the Jane Doe. How?

Leme outlines the day's tasks:

'Moreira and Hamuche to visit all known addresses of Gerson Anderson. See what you can find out. Be aggressive. After this, doorstep the victim's bank and credit card branches and medical insurance offices. There are three functioning bank accounts though we haven't got details of recent activity. There are two credit cards linked to the victim's ID. Chase all this up and see what you come up with.'

Moreira and Hamuche nod. No backchat today, which Leme appreciates.

'Fact is,' he says, 'we have no forensic on the perp. Only thing we can do is establish the victim's circumstances and see where that goes.'

Leme hands round more crime scene snaps.

'See this?' he says. The collection of jewellery, the shoelace, the Pereira Modelling card is circled in red. 'This is meaningful. You –' Leme points at the admin guy – 'your job is to get as much as you can on all this. Anything at all. Do whatever it is you guys do to find it. Certo?'

Admin guy nods. No backchat from him either. Those guys are reliably dark down there, Leme knows, all sorts of weird interests, and yet he is shocked by this crime. And so he should be.

Hate crime.

Lisboa's nodding at the admin guy. Lisboa says, 'Good job yesterday. We'll follow it up today.' He looks at Moreira and Hamuche. 'We think we have the private medical facility. We don't know when they performed the op, of course. We don't know the details of their legal confidentiality agreements and so on. But he – ' pointing at the admin guy – 'he reckons it's this one we have.'

Lisboa circulates papers with the name Emmanuel and an address in Jardim Paulistano.

Moreira says, 'This the name of the company?'

Leme nods. 'Just that: Emmanuel. Classy, ne? Which means it costs, which means it might not fit the profile of the victim.'

'It's known,' Lisboa says, 'for doing high-end tit jobs and filling up the lips of rich teenage girls and their mothers. The old trout pout, entendeu?'

There are grim laughs.

'Other thing is,' Lisboa says, 'we hear they do illegal, pure quality and cash-heavy scrape jobs for society chicks in trouble, right? So we think the operation we're looking into is very likely off the books?'

Hamuche says, 'I didn't know it was even legal.'

'It's a grey area.'

'Yeah,' Moreira says. 'After the op it would be.'

No one laughs.

'Any questions?'

Four heads shake.

Leme pushes another piece of paper round the desk. 'Have a read. From Superintendent Lagnado.'

The gist:

Feel free to use the horrific and upsetting images from the crime scene to help secure cooperation when talking to witnesses and/or making enquiries of any kind; sharing these images with the press will result in heinous career consequences; talking to the press at all will have the same heinous career consequences, with a dollop of personal unpleasantness on top; this is a one-off hate crime and despicable as it is, as gruesome as the murderer's MO appears to be, we must not forget this. Interview technique once suspect is identified: anything necessary employed.

Meaning:

Wrap it up quick and don't be too discerning on who it's pinned on. Hate crime means madman means we can all sleep easy once said madman is locked up and confession signed.

'Reconvene here at 6pm. Keep in touch.'

Three chairs push back, slide noisily on the cheap floor.

'Okay?' Lisboa asks.

Leme nods.

He's thinking about the paperweight. He's thinking about whether it was a one-off fuck-up or a standard batch of tourist tat. He's thinking about whether it has any other distinguishing marks or features that he hasn't noticed. He's thinking about the woman who might be able to ID it. He knows he can't chase that through official channels.

What he can do, he's thinking, is ask Renata to run a name through her Paraisópolis legal aid database and get an address for him.

He can do that.

Ray's told Joãozinho, Little Johnny, he needs an in with a savvy lad who can help with some underground muscle, hook him up with a few political undesirables. Little Johnny's told Ray he knows just the fella, a mid-level Military Police guy, just the right side of clean, but ambitious. Ray knows this means the lad's feeling a little cash-shy. Ray's ready to do business, get his hands a little dirty.

The meet is arranged for Ray's unofficial office. Ray's not sure who he's looking out for, but he assumes the man won't be in uniform. He reckons the Unique deck bar doesn't see too many Militars.

Ray's keeping an eye out for a large man in civvies. The man's name: Carlos.

Little Johnny's reach is quite something, Ray reflects. He's heard that since the famous weekend back in 2006 – in which Big Ray played a significant role, let's not forget – there are Military Police departments across the country linked to various political factions in Brasília. Idea is there's a line of communication open to anyone who needs it. You have a word in the shell-like of a Joãozinho, and the line trickles down and back up again.

Course Ray knows he'll kick something up when the time comes. It's a tab situation at this point: buy now, pay later.

Ray's fave waiter, Fernando, brings him the usual. A moment after that, Fernando brings Ray a big man in polo shirt and chinos.

'Carlos,' the man says.

He looks Ray in the eye. He holds out a hand. Ray grips it. Ray shakes *big*.

They both grin.

Ray gestures for Carlos to sit down. 'I hope you're okay with lager?'

'Very.'

'Outstanding.'

'Saúde,' Carlos says.

They knock glasses. They drink deep.

Carlos looks at his fat watch. 'I've got half an hour, Senhor Marx. Shoot.'

Ray grins. 'Good man. I'll get to the point, then. Why do you think we're having this meeting?'

Carlos raises an eyebrow. 'I'd say there's some political mischief afoot. If I ever get the call, that's what it's normally about.'

'Who gives you the call?'

'One of my boys a little higher up the food chain.'

'And you know where he gets his call from?'

'I can guess. It doesn't really matter. My work is at a certain level. So is yours, am I right?'

'Good man.'

'Então?'

'Então,' Ray says, 'I need two things, eventually. This is an ongoing month by month job, entendeu?'

Carlos nods.

'What I need,' Ray says, 'is the lowdown on one – I'm not

particular which – of the Black Bloc cells currently at work in this fine city. I gather the best way to do that is talk to the people who are trying to stop them.'

Carlos nods. 'And the other thing?'

'I want to donate.'

Carlos makes a face: *you what?*

'Cash,' Ray says.

'I didn't think you were looking to hand over your sperm, son.'

Ray grins. 'I like your style.'

'What's the time frame?'

'I'm going to say this is a three-month project.'

'Reasoning?'

'You let me worry about that.'

Carlos shrugs. 'You know the set-up, I gather, how we play this, ne?'

'It's in safe hands, amigo. First instalment has already gone.'

Carlos raises eyebrows. He nails his beer. 'In which case,' he says, 'saideira?'

One for the road.

'I'll get them to bring over my usual,' Ray grins.

Ray's got one more job to do to make it a decent Sunday.

It's all well and good to puppet-show all this, to pull strings, but you need a forum, you need a public voice, you need an *outlet* to get the news you want the people to read, read.

You need a journalist on the payroll, on Team Big Ray.

Ray's got form here: the way you keep a journalist on side is to keep the relationship very much one of quid pro quo, of the you scratch my back and I'll tickle yours variety, of who you know and where you go. Key point: keep cash well away from it.

To get a journalist in your pocket you've got to hold something he needs. You've got to dangle the goods. And drip-feed at the right kind of a pace.

Or you find something out about him and let him know you know. What they call good old-fashioned blackmail, extortion. Ray prefers: *collusion*.

So Ray's taking his Sunday evening meal somewhere a little out of his comfort zone.

He's at the top end of Rua dos Pinheiros looking for a fat man in a cheap suit.

Ray's been told this man likes to dine alone in one of those brightly lit corner bars. Ray knows a little about these bars. They're the sorts of places that have the TV on, loud, on a Sunday, with that other fat bloke, the famous one, Faustão, yelling over tacky Sertenaja country music about cultural politics while chicks in bikinis and heels dance around him, smiles and makeup plastered across their faces.

Domingão with Faustão the show is called. It goes on all fucking day. *Big Sunday with the Big Man Faustão.*

Faustian pact, Ray thinks. Unlimited knowledge and worldly pleasure abound. He smiles to himself. Not just a pretty face, old Ray.

It's very 2011, Ray thinks. Happy fucking new year.

When he first came to São Paulo, the billboards advertising *Playboy* magazine were immense. They had to take them down in the end. Brazilian men like to tailgate. That makes them accident prone when their heads and tongues are hanging backwards out the window.

Then City Hall put out a citywide ban on billboards full stop. Ray prefers it this way.

Strange: one day you're looking out your hotel window at a pair of building-sized legs in a thong, next day you've got an unimpeded view of green trees and the green spread of the park.

Go figure.

Ray walks past two bars, the sort he's looking for. The bars are *sodden*. Men fall over. Men yell. The bars reek. They seep cheap pinga fumes. They sweat beer.

No sign of a slovenly reporter.

Ray passes a swank French restaurant. Couples eat steak frites. Waiters douse their steaks in a green sauce. Ray thinks it looks muito good this sauce. He's hungry, Ray, given his afternoon beers. He popped two meds before leaving the hotel. They numb his appetite – *just*. The stink of fries provokes abundant salivation.

Next bar along and Ray fancies a stop regardless. A tall lager and a mixto quente would do the trick. A *hot mix*, Ray likes to joke. Ham and oozing grilled cheese. Side of fries.

This next bar is going all out Sunday dining experience. Charcoal glows in a metal bucket. Two men crouch over it turning skewers of stringy meat.

Two men proffer skewers. There are no takers.

Ray scans the outside tables. This bar isn't *too* Sunday soaked. There is at least one couple. There is a table of students, shouting, gesturing, passing round roll-ups. The waiters cackle from the back. Soccer noises come from a radio. The manager nods at Ray to take a seat.

Ray spots his man. The steak and eggs is gleaming. The suit is shabby. Ray chooses the table next to him.

'How's the water?' Ray says in English.

Ray's man raises his eyebrows. 'This isn't really a tourist place, amigo.'

'Good English.'

'Yeah, I did a year at Harvard, post-grad.'

'Medical?'

Ray's man makes a face: *do me a favour*.

'Law then.'

'Bingo.'

Ray snags a waiter. 'Cerveza, obrigado.' Ray lifts a finger. The waiter hovers. 'You want something?'

Ray's man nods at the waiter. He points at his glass of red. The waiter scoots.

'Thanks.'

'De nada.'

The waiter dumps drinks. Ray pours beer. 'Cheers,' he says.

Ray's man wipes his mouth. 'Bottoms up.'

They sit in silence for a minute. The radio screeches. The two men chewing on stringy meat erupt.

Ray says, 'Who scored?'

'Corinthians.'

'Huh.'

'Their fans are a bunch of cunts.'

'And you're not one of them.'

'Palmeiras, mate. Thinking man's São Paulo team.'

'Yeah,' Ray says, 'I've read your stuff. I wouldn't have had you down as a Corinthiano.'

Ray's man does a double take. 'You what?'

Ray leans towards him, holds out a hand. 'Francisco Silva, Ray Marx. Pleasure to meet you.'

Renata's Sunday is a little slow so she decides to go to work, get a jumpstart on the first day back at school, as it were. Mario's working, so will she.

Seeing the state he was in last night and this morning, the hang dog despair, the shocked, glazed eyes, the smell of despondency, death, she's glad she does what she does. She doesn't ask. There's nothing he can tell her.

She shelves it.

She had an interesting email the evening before.

It seemed they'd given up on the Singapore Project build at the bottom end of the favela.

Renata's memories of the day she visited remain bright. That poor kid. Whatever happened to him? She kind of left well alone after that.

The email though is a direct request from the office of the Secretario de Obras: the team that decides on all building work in the state. She's not in a position to refuse.

The request is that she find out the exact land ownership situation as the build *is* going to happen. Bidding is under way for a new contractor. Work is scheduled to start sharpish.

She's not sure she can't answer this question right away: it's state land, but it's *owned* by the boys that run the favela.

It's thorny. Except it's not, really.

It's a headscratcher, though, legally speaking. The technicalities run deep. Your basic favela-ownership scheme means the land is the state's, but anything built on the land is the property of those who built it. So you can sell the land but you can't legally remove the buildings on it. The complication in this case is that there *are* no buildings.

The state department wants Renata to negotiate, is what she reckons it comes down to.

Wonderful.

'So what's in it for me?' Silva asks.

'That's the spirit,' Ray says. 'What's in it for you is a steady flow of useful information.'

Thunder cracks, splits the sky, echoes among the buildings. Windows shake. Evening storm imminent.

'I'll start by giving you a name. Jorge Mendes.'

'Secretario de Obras. So what?'

'I know all about Mendes and the syndicate that funded, in part, the Singapore Project.'

'Now you're talking.'

Ray pulls papers from his inside pocket. 'Mendes is now in charge of a new system of Mutirões – he made his money through the SP and abandoned support for it when politically it was no longer viable – no charges of illegal or improper actions ever brought. With me?' Silva nods. 'I quote: "the failure of the Mutirões – funding given to community groups to build or renovate – led to the adoption of the Singapore model".'

'What's your connection?'

'Easy, son, we're not there yet. Point is look at Mendes. Again, I quote: "favouritism and potential for political corruption in terms of selection of construction companies". That sounds like Mendes, does it not? And: "the housing secretariat apparently demanded compliance with the wishes of the Inter-American Development Bank" – Mendes would have had the financial clout and political influence for this.'

'I mean, it's interesting, but it's conjecture. Right?'

'There were shortcuts and illegal practices. The favelados didn't get what was promised them and the whole thing was a front to ensure re-election. This is a social story, Francisco. Injustice. It writes itself.'

'We're not there yet.'

'You have a nickname at Harvard?'

'Yeah. Fat Frank.'

Ray whoops. 'Well, Fat Frank, I'm just starting you off.'

The sky breaks. Rain falls. Early patter then a torrent. Waterfall and dust. Damp petrichor in a good hour.

The bar staff secure the plastic awnings. They lift and swing in the breeze. The rain hammers, spits in at the clientele. No one is too bothered.

The charcoal in the bucket hisses and dies, smokes.

'And what, so you'll feed me bits like this to be getting on with and I'll be printing stories for you?'

'You'll be *collaborating* on stories with me.'

'Sounds more like collusion.'

'Good man.'

'Why Mendes?'

'Frankly,' Ray says, 'he's small beer. We're looking higher up.'

'How much higher?'

'You'll see. In about a month, you'll have a helluva scoop, my friend.'

'And I just trust you?'

Ray winks. 'Trust is earned, son.'

Silva thinks about this. Ray plays enigmatic. Ray suggests blackmail possibility.

It's a smart move: all journos have something dodgy in their back pocket.

The rain comes down. The sky empties. Lightning illuminates dark, gushing streets. Cars teeter. They're close to floating off.

Silva nods at the street. 'Here's tomorrow's headlines,' he says. 'A social story.'

'Yeah?'

'This is a mudslide downpour, Senhor Marx. Shack-bothering. There'll be a community or two in real trouble down by the Marginal on the way out to the airport.'

'It's a disgrace.'

Silva gulps wine, orders another. 'Injustice.'

The Hotel Unique deck bar glistens post-storm, post-coital.

Ray takes a turn with his caipirinha. The swimming pool is lit purple. Fat drops of water fall from the loungers. Manicured women in thousand-dollar cocktail dresses shriek and giggle. Ray eyes them. Ray feels a longing. Ray *yearns*.

These women aren't a sensible idea, Ray knows this. His work doesn't allow for it. It's a cliché for a reason, the lone wolf. Ray howls, quietly, up at the moon, laughs.

He heads back to the bar area. He beckons Fernando. He makes a subtle gesture, twists his mouth with no ambiguity. Fernando nods, gets on the phone. A few moments later, Fernando approaches. He leans in, whispers: 'Twenty minutes.'

Ray nods. Ray winks. 'Good man.'

Twenty minutes later and Ray opens the door to his room and inside on the sofa is a woman, early twenties, dark hue – not too dark – long legs, hair au naturel, makeup free, eyes shining, dress splayed around her shoulders, hugging her, falling off her.

'Outstanding,' Ray says. 'You, querida, are world class.'

The woman smiles, bites her lip. 'Hola,' she says.

She's just the way Ray likes them. Fernando is a concierge of the highest order.

Lisboa drives. It's Sunday-morning quiet. They're drifting down from Jardins to Jardim Paulistano through good neighbourhoods. Buildings are low-rise, light-brown, red-brick. Green spaces predominate. Glass security booths pepper these well-to-do streets. Flash cars neatly parked in lines of black and silver.

The clinic is open for business: Sunday means discretion *total*.

Leme's reading the admin guy's factsheet. Getting up to speed on the legalities of sexual reassignment surgery. It unsettles him to think about why he's learning this now.

Leme reads:

Changing gender assignment in Brazil is legal according to the Superior Court of Justice of Brazil, as stated in a decision rendered on October 17, 2009. Sexual reassignment surgery is covered under a constitutional clause guaranteeing medical care as a basic right. From the biomedical

perspective, transsexuality can be described as a sexual identity distur-
bance where individuals need to change their sexual designation or face
serious consequences in their lives, including intense suffering, mutila-
tion and suicide.

Hate crime.

Lisboa stares dead ahead. They hit Avenida Gabriel Monteiro da
Silva and a low-ride cruise rhythm through green lights. Men and
women in sports kit drink coffee in swank cafes. They eat eggs, sip at
smoothies. Kids mess with yapping dogs, post-brunch, hopped up
on sugar. Maids leave the posh supermarkets with bags of Sunday
ingredients. Handsome-rich teenage lads amble and lope with tennis
rackets and caps flipped backwards towards exclusive sports clubs.

Leme reads:

Transgender people in Brazil can change their names and legal
gender in the national civil registry and on some identification documents
– but only after undergoing mandatory psychiatric evaluations and surgi-
cal procedures and obtaining a judicial order from the Public Prosecutor.

Lisboa does a left onto Faria Lima.

The shopping mall Iguatemi rises up to the right. Sunday hours, so
quiet, dark, empty. Security guards line entrances. It's not empty of
value, after all. They don't let poor kids in. Only maids and nannies
dressed head to toe in white.

Lisboa says, 'This clinic does illegal abortion work. Know how
much it costs?'

Leme shakes his head.

'It's prohibitive, is the point. Upper class only. That way the illusion of hypocrisy remains.'

'I'm not sure it's an illusion, mate.'

'You know what I mean. And that's our negotiating angle. Fore-
warned and all that, sabe?'

Leme knows what he means. They'll knock some heads if they
have to. Leme reads on, quiet. Nancy Andrighi, the rapporteur of
these new rulings, makes a good point, Leme thinks:

If Brazil consents to the possibility of surgery, it should also provide the
means for the individual to have a decent life in society.

And here's the kicker, Leme thinks: preventing that record

change, that civil registration, for any trans person who's had the op is, basically, a version of social prejudice, just a different one, and an institutional one at that. One that could cause a lot more damage. Integration is the point, right, Leme thinks.

The victim never stood a chance.

Emmanuel is a slick joint.

Clean white lines, discreet. The sign hints at boutique marketing. The receptionist dazzles. Leme badge-flashes and the dazzle fades fast.

The receptionist looks confused and hits a button. The big-lad segurança on the door who clocked Leme and Lisboa going in looks sharp and piles through the revolving door.

Leme sees Lisboa see him and he turns around. Badge up, Lisboa pushes the big lad against the wall. Leme hears a what-the-fuck and calm-down-don't-try-it noise. The big lad huffs and puffs. He realises he's not in a clever situation. He's got his hands up and Leme watches Lisboa growl and front up and the lad's hands down and okay, okay, I get it. Leme nods at Lisboa and goes through alone.

There is a small waiting area – empty. There are three doors off it, fancy doctor-names on each. One is half open. Leme pushes it to and sees a slick-haired, hook-nosed, gym-thin middle-aged man in a white coat sitting behind a Hollywood desk. All wood and green leather and two pens in holders like machine-gun posts. Filing cabinets flank.

'Morning,' Leme says. He shuts the door behind him and sits down.

Dr Slick blusters something about who are you, gives it the do you know who I am? There's a manner to him that Leme does not appreciate. He exudes entitled authority.

Leme smiles. 'We need some info on one of your patients, mate,' he says.

Lisboa pokes his head around the door. Leme raises eyebrows. Lisboa nods, rubs two fingers and thumb together meaning I've paid the goon to fuck off out of it. As you were. Leme settles.

Dr Slick says, 'I really don't think this is necessary.'

Leme smiles. Lisboa comes into the room and stands to Leme's left. He towers over the desk.

'Early start?' Leme asks.

Slick thinks about this. 'I like to work out before work.'

'On a Sunday, too. Dedication, Senhor.'

'Doctor.'

'Excuse me, doctor. And that's Doctor *what*?'

Slick taps a wooden doo-dah on his desk. His name printed on it in expensive-looking cursive lettering: *Dr Emmanuel*.

'That your first name or your last name?'

Slick says nothing, gives it the yes, very funny.

'Both?'

Slick sighs. 'What can I do for you, detective?'

Slick's receptionist is hovering outside the door.

'You don't have to worry, querida,' Lisboa says, 'we're not robbing the place.'

Slick smiles at her. 'It's fine, Adriana, nothing serious.'

Leme swings back in his chair. 'Oh, she can stay if you'd prefer a witness present, doctor.'

A startled look flashes across Adriana's face. Alarm, confusion and something else. *Disappointment*. Leme wonders if old Slick here is leading on poor young Adriana. The cliché of it all, if true, is staggering.

'Adriana,' Leme says, 'I want you to look for a file on a Senhor Gerson Anderson.' Leme turns back to Dr Emmanuel. 'You don't mind?'

Slick shakes his head. Slick looks *real* worried.

Leme's play works.

Slick says, 'Adriana, do as he asks.' Then: 'Let's get on with this, shall we?'

'We're here about the victim of a heinous hate crime, Dr Emmanuel, a brutal murder,' Leme says. 'A post-op trans woman. Next to the victim's corpse, and believe me, you do not want to see any of the crime scene photos just yet, was an ID card registered to Gerson Anderson. Cross-checks indicate the victim had yet to register her new identity. The only information we have on the victim is that of her previous life. We think you might be able to tell us a bit more about her.'

Slick goes white. Full panic.

Slick blusters, 'I'd love to help, I really would, but there's a legally binding confidentiality agreement we go into with all our patients –'

Lisboa leans across the desk and yanks Slick's tie hard. Slick sprawls forward, arms out. Lisboa yanks again. Slick steadies himself, hands on the desk. Leme picks up a tasty-looking paperweight from the Hollywood desk and smashes it down across Slick's right knuckles. Knuckle crunch. Slick yelps.

Adriana hesitates at the door. Leme smiles. 'Can you fetch the doctor some ice please, dear?'

Adriana turns left then right then left, nodding, then goes to give the file to Lisboa, changes her mind, then does give it to him, then scoots off.

Slick clutches his hand. His hand reddens. His knuckles burn and scrape –

He looks up at Leme – no understanding. His face pleads: *why did you do that?*

'It's the shock, mate,' Leme says. 'Just let it throb, feel it, you'll be fine. It's not broken.'

'So you're a doctor too now, detective?' Slick spits.

'Cheaper than you, mate, falou?'

Lisboa scans pages.

Adriana comes in carrying a jug of ice and a washcloth.

Leme gestures at her to go on. Slick buries his hand in the jug. He grimaces. Adriana hovers, dilly-dallies from foot to foot. Slick smiles at her and nods. She leaves.

'Adriana's nice,' Leme says. 'She know about your off-the-books business?'

Slick goes green.

'Look, detective, I –'

'Ricardo,' Leme looks up at Lisboa. 'Get a hold of his left hand, porra.'

Lisboa smiles – broad.

Slick holds up said left hand. 'How can I help you if I don't know what it is you want?'

Leme looks at Lisboa. They shrug-nod, as in: the man's got a point.

'Tell me, Ricardo,' Leme says, 'what did you glean from Dr Emmanuel's beautifully presented and well-kept customer – sorry, I mean *patient* – file?'

'Not much.'

Leme looks at Slick. 'We're trying to identify a body. Help us out.'

Slick's nodding. 'Look, my patient records speak for themselves. I don't have anything else I can give you.'

Leme nods at Lisboa. Lisboa pulls crime scene pics from the inside pocket of his jacket. He lays these out on Slick's desk. He grabs the doctor's slick-backed hair and forces his face down close to the photos.

'Have a real good look,' Leme says.

Slick closes his eyes. He looks. He turns greener. He looks vomit-ready.

'You can see why we're keen to get a quick solve here, doctor.'

Slick looks grim, nods his assent.

Lisboa says, 'File states your patient underwent the operation approximately eight months ago. You were lead surgeon. Payment was made half in advance, half after the fact. Address and billing details as per Gerson Anderson as per what we already know.'

'Seems unlikely,' Leme turns to the doctor, 'that that is simply that, that you let them go off into the world without so much as a follow-up.'

'It's their right to decide,' Slick says.

Lisboa skims pages. 'Two years of tests signed off by state-run psychologist. Then, what, the patient brings you a certificate and you crack on, no questions?'

'It's a legal process.'

Leme nods. 'Business transaction.'

'That's right.'

'Anyone ever not paid up, you know, post-op?'

'That doesn't happen.'

'But it might. Lot of money at stake there, sabe, if you get a dissatisfied customer.'

'It's not like buying a car, detective.'

'Exactly my point.'

'I don't follow.'

Leme stands. He pulls Slick's left hand out from the jug. He bends fingers. He digs his fingernails into Slick's red raw knuckles. Slick groans, cries out.

'See,' Leme says, 'if someone defaults payment to me, I would do this to them. It might not get me any money, but it feels good, entendeu?'

Leme leaves off. He sits back down. 'You do illegal abortions for rich women and the daughters of rich men. We know that.'

Slick says nothing.

'You do extremely expensive life-changing operations for vulnerable people who cannot always be necessarily capable of paying up when the fat lady sings, as it were.'

Slick looks down.

'My point,' Leme says, 'is that there is no fucking way whatsoever that you don't have someone on your speed dial who helps you collect should the need arise.'

Slick nods. He gestures with his hand: a pen, paper, *please*.

Leme nods. He pushes a pad and a pen across the desk.

Slick scribbles.

Leme takes the piece of paper, reads a name, address and phone number. He pockets it.

'This is completely off the record,' Slick says.

'You have a good Sunday, doctor,' Leme says.

Lisboa sniffs, gathers the crime scene portraits.

Slick calls out, 'It's legal, what I do, you know!'

Leme and Lisboa both pause, share a look. Consensus: not worth it.

They leave through the front door. The segurança leans against the wall, cool as you like, smoking. He tips an imaginary hat, nods them on their way.

'You've really got to love these hippies, falou?'

Rafa and Franginho are stretched out on a couple of plastic loungers in front of their office. Franginho is pontificating on the delightful nature of their latest business partners. It is a hot old day. Clouds scarce. Favela hubbub distant.

'I mean, there's all this, what, posing, this fronting they're some kind of Che Guevara-emulating, cigar-chomping, underground international terrorist mercenaries, but they live at home with their mums and go to private universities. It's brilliant.'

Rafa smiles. Franginho's chat remains tip-top and thoroughly thought-provoking. He's a hoot, old Franginho, a total comedian, a philosopher king, Rafa's best and oldest friend.

Concrete bakes. The sky shimmers.

Rafa leans back and lets the hit of weed he's just had circulate a little. He's happy the hippies keep coming back. That Carolina bird: she's an absolute belter, world class. He smiles now thinking about her. She's definitely getting a little friendlier. Might be time to turn on some more of the bad-boy favela charm Rafa has in spades. It's about time he broadened his horizons a touch, pussy-wise. Yeah, he thinks, as the sun beats down on his face, let's ratchet things up a little.

Franginho hasn't stopped giving it the old chatterbox. Rafa drifts back into his drift.

'Basically, we slip them some discount doobie and it's all good, sabe?' he's saying. 'They think we're Scarface. And they're paying well over the odds for the gear we're getting them, as you well know, amigo.'

Rafa does know. The black shirts, as they've been calling them, have been paying a lot more than they even realise. The reason for that is it's pure profit for Rafa and Franginho. And the reason for *that* is it's all boosted gear. Back of a lorry scenario. Turns out some of the favela youngsters, the wannabes and messengers, are very good at locating fireworks with a bit of serious heft to them.

'And they don't even realise what it is they're getting, now, do they?' Franginho's still blathering. 'And when they do figure it out, what are they going to do? Pick a fight with Scarface here? Nem fodendo!' *No fucking way.*

Franginho whoop-whoops with laughter.

Rafa extends his hand for Franginho to slap. Low five.

The scam is that they take the legal, if serious, fireworks, dress them up a bit and flog them as illegal weaponry. Well, illegal *something*. They certainly have a hell of a pop to them. Sounds like a war zone when they snap and crackle.

Rafa feels a bit bad for Carolina, the deception. But, end of the day, he's protecting her. They're not dealing with anything too naughty and nobody gets hurt. They're only kids, after all. This menina Carolina must be nineteen if she's a day. World class.

Franginho's talked out for a moment, has a breather. They pass a bottle of water back and forth. Franginho tips a little into his hands and Rafa hears him wash his face, rinse off some of the jungle dirt.

Rafa's happy to lie back, eyes closed, the world elsewhere. He's thinking about what it is the black shirts are doing with the fireworks they're selling them. He's wondering what it is they do at all, beyond flounce about in their outfits and get high. He's wondering whether he and Carolina might have anything in common, and that's when he drifts off, eases into a well-earned mid-morning nap.

Rafa wakes with what feels like a pointed boot nudging him in his side. It feels nice, soft, like a massage. The sun and dope haze have left him sluggish and he's not bothered about what it might be that's giving him this wake-up call, *who* it might be more importantly.

Rafa hears Franginho muttering, 'What, porra? Que isso?'

This gets Rafa going, the idea of trouble, or surprise, and he sits up, sheds his shades, and whose is the pointed boot but only young Carolina's.

Result.

Rafa grins up at her. 'Oi, oi,' he says.

'Wake up, big man,' Carolina says, 'I want to talk to you.'

'Franginho,' Rafa says. 'What can we offer our guest on this fine morning?'

'Good will.'

Rafa throws his head back and laughs. 'We've got that in spades, querida,' he says. 'Otherwise, agua?'

He hands her the bottle, which she accepts. She drinks deep.

'Thirsty?'

Carolina wipes her mouth. 'Hungry,' she says. She pouts. 'Então, you wanna take me out for lunch or what?'

Rafa considers this. 'Young Little Chicken,' he says. 'Would you mind awfully keeping an eye on the shop while I take a well-earned lunch break with our fine associate Carolina?'

'Bring me back something to eat and you can whistle, son.'

Rafa stands, offers his arm. 'Shall we?' he says. 'Let me give you the tour.'

Leme sits, head against the window. Lisboa drives.

They're heading to the address that Slick gave them. They reckon the man they're after is likely still in bed. They're figuring he's Sunday morning hungover, all frayed edges, no reflexes. They plan on giving him a bit of a going over to help him forget about this potential hangover.

Lisboa for one, Leme thinks, is on a mission.

Leme's letting his mind wander. Renata at home. Their home. Leme thinks back.

He loves living with Renata. The whole process, the to-ing and fro-ing, the negotiation. Compromise is a funny old business, Leme thinks. Where does it end? Isn't that the point?

Leme drifts.

'Building a life together is about accepting the objects, the books, the furniture your partner brings with her,' Renata once said. 'It's not about feeling different or inadequate because they're not yours. Because you would never have thought to get them. They're all ours now, anyway.'

This is true. Leme drifts, feels anchored. Day like today, you need it, the anchor.

The car slips smooth into higher gears. They pass building works. Favela upkeep, upgrade. Shift hicks into tall towers. Renata knows.

Singapore Project.

'The principle of the thing seems sound: tower blocks go up and the residents shift across and the slums are torn down,' she's said. 'Better quality of life. Right. More significantly though, the city looks better to the middle-class voters who drive past the sites every day, entendeu?' Leme smiles, remembers. 'It's an illusion of progress,'

Renata has told him. 'Of safety. A right-wing political ploy to capture the upwardly mobile.' Leme knows what it is, but can't articulate it in those terms. 'I don't want to be with one of those men who teaches me things,' Renata said once, early in their relationship. 'It's so tiresome, being shepherded from car to restaurant to car again, certo? I think I'll be teaching you.'

Leme smiles. He needs to switch off for a few moments. This year, so far, has been a fucking headache.

They pass the swank Astúrias Motel in Pinheiros on the Marginal. Leme raises an eyebrow to himself. Remembers words he's used, thoughts he's had:

Swimming pool, jacuzzi, sauna, wet-room shower to finish. He'd pin Renata against the headboard and try to sort of inhabit her. Bite at her neck, feel her turn to kiss him, feel her want him.

That, and the coursing electric current when they came –

The easy intimacy of the aftermath. He feels they're missing a little of this now. He doesn't know why, exactly. But he misses whatever it is that's missing.

Is it his fault? Can he do something? Can they go back to how it was?

'Free will doesn't exist, we're programmed to do what we do,' she's always said. 'No such thing as choice. No point thinking about what might have been – what might have been is just what never was and never would be.'

When they first started sleeping together, she'd palmed a book on to him. Freud's *The Ego and the Id*.

Fragments, thoughts. Cars slip by. Cars honk and swerve. Drivers have a Saturday night and Sunday morning fuck-you to them. Leme lets it wash over him.

'It's our cultural history,' Renata once said. 'Power struggle. We're conditioned to impose authority. If you're on a motorbike and I'm in a car, well fuck you, I'm in charge.'

Leme chuckled.

'Same at work. If I'm a lawyer, but also something else, and you are just a lawyer, well fuck you, I'm going to show you I'm better than you. It's a sociological phenomenon. Look at our language, the way we talk to waiters: "Bring me this. Get me that." We're brought up on the imperative and that is a display of authority.'

Leme didn't doubt that.

'It's the heart of the Brazilian contradiction.'

'Oh yeah.' Leme always enjoyed her analysis, her theory.

'We're a hospitable, cooperative people,' she went on. 'We go out of our way to help, to be kind, to facilitate things for others, to enjoy life. In a social context. Any other though – like work or in traffic – and we're animals, scrambling over and clawing at each other to get to the top.'

Lisboa grunts something about ten minutes. Leme looks in his crystal ball. What's next? Family. Their family.

'Having children is something to do,' she'd once said. 'We'll get there.' Leme watched his friends with their kids. Renata had pointed out the generational change. 'When we were growing up,' she'd said, 'our parents never gave us a choice. They told us what we were going to do. Here, eat this. Then we're going for a walk. Then this, then that. Nowadays it's all about the child. Would you like some breakfast? Would you like a drink? To play? It's not fair. They're two-year-olds. They don't know what they want.'

Lisboa says something about game faces on. Leme's nodding, he drifts.

The day after his wedding, Leme woke up afraid. And remained so. But each day the fear dissipated. Each year things got better. And they'd started well enough. The lessening fear was a comfort, a sign of progress. On their honeymoon they'd gone to an island off Salvador. Some kind of car-free utopia, an anti-city. He'd felt itchy, struggled to understand what it was to be in the present, to freeze his life for the sake of pure enjoyment. It was supposed to be a celebration.

'There's no such thing as the future,' Renata had told him on their first night there, chewing on lobster in the heat. 'You can mock, querido, but it's true.'

On the last day on the island, Leme was struck down with food poisoning, vomiting prawns cooked in old oil on a deserted beach.

Leme knows what's what and what the future holds. Renata. There is such a thing as the future, Leme thinks. And it's her, that thing is her.

'Smoking is a singular existential act,' she'd say. 'Almost political. It states, "I am aware of my mortality and I am going to live in the present, as the future doesn't yet exist." There is no deeper, habitual, basically prosaic action that shows understanding of our transience and the world's brutal indifference to our fates. And it is delicious, which in itself furthers this understanding. Fleeting pleasure is all we will ever have. The trick is to find what makes us fleetingly happy and repeat it. For me,' she'd say, 'those things are smoking... and you.'

Hearing this for the first time – she would often repeat it to amuse and scandalise at parties – Leme had never felt such validation.

Repeating those fleeting pleasures and finding a practical way to do so in our lives, she concluded, is how we achieve permanence.

Permanence. The future is that permanence, that thing is her.

'To tell someone you know them is a tricky thing,' she said not long after they met. 'It's never that simple. Saying that means you want something. And you'd better know what it is that you want when you say it.'

Leme knows what it is he wants. *Renata*.

Lisboa jerks to a halt.

Rafa's giving Carolina the tour.

'We'll walk up to Dona Regina's for lunch,' Rafa says. 'She's world class. You'll like her.'

'Uh-huh.'

'Meantime, let me show you the neighbourhood.'

'Neighbourhood.'

'It is what it is, querida.'

Carolina smiles. Rafa glows.

They hit the gentle downslope of Rua Rodolf Lotze. Rafa keeps a side-eye on Carolina, curious to see what she makes of the favela. He doesn't know for a fact that she's a rich bitch student living with her folks, but Franginho seems to think she must be so there's a good chance.

'You can see here on the right,' Rafa says, 'a padaria of fairly miserable quality. Note,' he says, 'the empty seats on the concrete terrace, fenced in by red bars. Note the sad-looking photos of sandwiches and juice on the storefront sign.'

'Huh,' Carolina says. 'Nice view of exposed brick across the road.'

Rafa laughs. 'That's not exposed brick, girl, it's just brick.'

'You pay a lot for that in your living room where I'm from.'

'If you do look into the gloom,' Rafa says, ignoring that, 'you'll see a couple of shadowy drunks enjoying their morning sharpeners.'

'You better not be taking me to eat here, young man.'

Rafa grins. 'How old are you, anyway?'

'I'm eighteen, nineteen next month.'

Rafa weighs this. 'And where do you live then? My guess is you're slumming it here with me.'

'Querido, guessing is a mug's game. You can do better than that.'

Porra, Rafa thinks. *Fucksake.*

Women. They're a great leveller.

Doesn't matter where they're from, they're talking in riddles.

They reach the crossroads at Lotze and Hebe. Favela Junction, as it's known, due to its size. Big, fucking exhaust-filled thoroughfare. You can cross the entire jungle in minutes if you hammer this route at night when there's no one around. Rafa shares this piece of local knowledge with Carolina.

She stops and scans. 'A lot of concrete next to your exposed brick,' she says. 'How do you make that choice?'

Rafa sees she's right. There's squares and rectangles of pink and cream, and red and grey, and blue and dirty white hanging from washing lines from the concrete buildings. They look more serious, better put together, these buildings. But the concrete says *unfinished*. Who gives a fuck what the outside looks like when you're in it, Rafa thinks. That's the usual decision you make, the usual *choice*.

'Whatever's to hand, entendeu?' Rafa says. 'Not so much supply and demand as ask around.'

'Capitalism in its purest form.'

'You what?'

'Barter system, convenience transaction, you know? I've got this and want that. You've got that and might fancy this. Trade, yeah?'

Rafa thinks about this. 'Either way the houses look like shit,' he says.

They cross when the traffic allows. In the middle of the road: a huge pile of rubbish, plastic bags and boxes, wooden crates, a mattress, what looks like a pair of bedposts.

Carolina nods at the pile. 'Whatever's to hand.'

'Rich pickings,' Rafa says, all sarky. 'Only the best.'

Carolina smiles – soft. She touches his arm. 'I don't judge, Rafa. I came to see *you*, didn't I?'

Rafa's not sure what to say to that but he likes it. Rafa points up the road which bends away from them. 'This way.'

'I'm in your hands,' Carolina says, all demure-flirty now.

Rafa's hoping that might not be too far from the truth. 'You're a real heartbreaker, menina,' he says.

Carolina tosses her hair. 'Lead on, senhor.'

The road narrows on the other side of Favela Junction. A white van piles towards them. A motorbike zips round from behind them on their right. It has to swerve violently to avoid the van. The driver leans out of the window, swears. The motorbike pauses. The rider gestures with his right arm, gives it the wanker sign. The van driver opens his door, makes to get out. The motorbike revs and guns it, fucks off sharpish, arm raised, middle finger prominent. The van driver shakes his head, tut-tuts loud, lets loose a sing-song chorus of dirty words to no one but himself.

Rafa grins. 'Welcome to the jungle,' he says.

'Charming,' Carolina says. 'How long until we eat then, garanhão?'

Stud. Fair enough, Rafa thinks. *That'll do quite nicely.* 'Not long now,' he says. 'Here.' He points to the right. 'See that? A famous landmark.'

He's pointing at a tropical mural painted on the front and side of a house with no windows. It depicts palm trees, a beach, the ocean, a bar with a sign that says Agua de Coco.

'Paradise, yeah? Right here in Paraisópolis.'

'Paradise City, ne?'

Rafa likes this girl's style. 'That's what they say. France has Paris, we have Paraisópolis.'

'Very clever.'

They push on up the road. It is a gradual climb. It's about a car's width up here, and that narrowed further by bikes and motorbikes left haphazard all over the shop. Piles of bricks. Hole-in-the-wall supermarkets you can't enter for the stacked bottles of soft drinks, the crates of fruit and veg, the gas cylinders. Men lean on cars and swap chit-chat. Dust *everywhere*. Streetlights sag forlorn, bent into question marks, legacy of drunk-driving collisions.

They reach the peak of their little ascent. The road rolls down and the favela opens up. Buildings painted red and green, graffiti, tired-looking pot plants, window-baskets, parched. Water tanks on roofs hoping for rain, getting little.

They walk on in silence for a while, breathing a touch heavier, the sun midday-fat, throbbing. Until Rafa realises where they are. He nods left. 'Church,' he says, 'my grandma's.'

Carolina stops to have a peer. 'Not yours?'

Rafa shakes his head. 'Nah, not my scene.'

A grey gate at the road's edge. A driveway, clear. A hedge. The church set back, giving it airs, Rafa's always thought. A square, white building, light grey façade, angled roof, and its name: Congregacāo Cristā no Brasil.

The bustle of the street is a pertinent contrast.

'What sort of scene is it?'

Rafa shrugs. 'All inclusive, all you can eat, entendeu?'

Carolina laughs. 'So, what, non-denominational with a Pentecostal twist?'

'Put it this way, there's a lot of cheap suits and a lot of noise come Sunday morning.'

'Opium of the people.'

'Say again?'

'Karl Marx, mate. Religion is the opium of the people. Get it?'

'Yeah, well, if we could sell it, we would.'

'More God-botherers than dopeheads in this country. You should look into it.'

Rafa smiles. 'I keep well away.'

He does, too, he thinks. He hardly sees his grandma anymore.

They live separate lives, different timetables. What's the phrase she's been using? *Ships that pass in the night.*

They walk on.

'This Karl Marx,' Rafa says. 'I've heard of him.'

'*The Communist Manifesto*. He wrote it.'

Rafa nods. 'So you'll be a fan then?'

'Mixed feelings.'

'And Dilma?'

'We can talk about that over lunch.'

Rafa smiles. 'Five minutes, tops.'

They turn right and arrow along the corrugated, garage-lined, metal-staircased, brick-balconied squeeze that is Rua Pasquale Gallupi.

Rafa points down the hill. 'See the junction at the bottom? That's where we eat, querida.'

'Maravilhosa.'

It certainly is, thinks Rafa. His mouth waters.

Dona Regina gives Rafa what he thinks is something of a snide, raised-eyebrow look as he and Carolina sit down.

'Dona Regina, bonitinha,' he says.

'At your service.' Dona Regina bows. She hands them menus. 'And what would Lord Rafa like today?'

Carolina is amused. Rafa less so. The back and forth, the banter seems a little *fresca* today, a little fresh, superior. Rafa's used to it, but today he'd like to feel the love, entendeu? He is, after all, something of a lord of the manor. He is a big man in these parts. He wants Carolina to know this, and he reckons it's fair enough for old Dona Regina to show a little fucking respect.

'We'll have two of your world class plates of the day.' Rafa snaps his menu shut. 'And a beer. Why not? Happy New Year and all that, falou?'

Carolina makes a face: right then.

Dona Regina waddles off. Rafa's been coming here for donkeys and the old lady's known him since he was a kid. Doesn't give her the right to mug him off, but still, all right, he'll play the neighbourhood kid done good if he has to. It's charming, in its way, having the mickey taken by a village elder.

'Então,' Rafa says. *So.* 'Why don't you tell me what it is you're up to, Carolina linda?' *Beautiful Carolina.*

'I'm here to see you, Rafa.'

'That's nice, but I still want to know.'

Carolina smiles. Their beer arrives. Rafa pours measures into tiny glasses.

They knock glasses and drink.

'We're a political group,' Carolina says. 'Which I thought you knew.'

Rafa shrugs. 'Define political.'

'We're against the system, that's basically it. We're anti-political.'

'Anti-political?'

'Meaning the old adage is what we follow: all power corrupts, absolute power corrupts absolutely.'

'They teach you that stuff in college?'

'When they teach us anything.'

'So you are at college then?'

Carolina shrugs. 'When I decide I want to learn.'

Their plates of the day arrive. A pork stew, rice, black beans. A sort of basic feijoada without the weight of pig's ears and trotters and the rest of the cheap cuts you get on a Wednesday or Saturday. Some farina and kale on the side. Two shot glasses of pinga.

'Bom appetite,' Dona Regina says. 'Pinga's on the house. Hot sauce on the counter. Help yourself.'

'You're a sweetheart,' Rafa says, but Dona Regina's already walked off and he looks like he's trying a little too hard, which annoys him.

'Dig in,' he says to Carolina.

'Hang about,' she says. 'Toast?'

'Where *are* my manners.'

'To the tour,' Carolina says.

Rafa grins. They nail their shots. They fork up stew and rice and beans.

'Your classic appetite opener, pinga,' Rafa says. 'Works a treat.'

They scoff hearty mouthfuls. Homemade and wholesome. A cracking sun-baked fortifier.

'Então,' Rafa says again. 'I'd love to know what it is exactly you're doing with those fireworks.'

'Not much right now. Stockpiling, I suppose, is what you'd call it.'

'What's with all those black uniforms you lot wear? You've come plain clothes today then.' He smiles. He gives her a look. 'Suits you.'

'Anarchist black, querido.'

'Meaning?'

'Meaning we blend in.'

Rafa nods. They eat on. They knock back freezing lager. Rafa lifts a finger and Dona Regina brings another bottle. He pours more drinks. A light buzz encroaches. Sunglass, tipsy haze. Rafa feels world class.

'All right,' Carolina says, 'I'll give you this. We believe Dilma is the head of a very corrupt government.'

Rafa nods. Tell me something I don't know, he thinks.

'And this government represents a very corrupt political system.'

'Okay.'

'Doesn't matter she's the first female in charge, doesn't matter which party holds the cards, certo?'

Rafa nods.

'It's the system that's sick.'

'Então, anti-political?'

'That's exactly it.'

'And what are you going to do about it?'

Carolina smiles. 'We're not exactly sure yet. And it doesn't matter. I'm here to see you, as I keep saying.'

Rafa's grinning like the proverbial king of the castle.

'You're a heartbreaker, girl, I'll give you that.'

Carolina smiles. Rafa smiles. They eat and drink.

Rafa tells her a bit more about what it is he does. She seems interested, he thinks. She seems pleased his is a sort of office role in the organisation, in the firm. Seems legit, is what she wants to believe.

It's not far off, after all.

'How you going to get home?' Rafa asks when the meal is done, the beer finished.

'I was thinking Moto Taxi.'

'Daredevil.'

Rafa's not a fan of the old Moto Taxi, paying a bloke to sit on the back of his bike. Seems a little dodgy, really.

He says, 'I'll sort one out for you, you know, on the house.'

Carolina smiles. 'What a gent.'

Rafa stands and whistles. A kid scurries over. Rafa gives instructions. A Moto Taxi appears, dawdles, waits for the nod.

As he's helping Carolina into her helmet, kissing her goodbye – *kissing* her goodbye, that is, not really a goodbye kiss – he sees the woman leaving the legal aid office. She sees him. Rafa thinks about nodding hello, about smiling. He's been keeping out of her way, last few years. Best course of action that.

Seated on the back of the bike, her arms hanging loosely from his neck, Carolina says to him, 'You ever want to leave this place?'

'It's not about what you want, querida,' he says. 'It's about being happy with what you've got.'

Carolina makes a face: colour me impressed. Rafa slaps the back of the bike.

The Moto Taxi chugs into action, exhaust fumes black and potent, weaves away, Carolina waving.

Rafa watches the lawyer walk to her car. He remembers the only time they ever spoke, the day his daddy died. He was full of hope that day.

He is again, for very different reasons. He's managed these last five years with pure style.

Renata, that's her name, reaches her vehicle.

Rafa watches her climb into her car, drive away.

Bocão, Big Mouth, *former escort:*
Conscience.

I was sitting at my desk in my new job when I had the Idea. I knew Paddy would like it and it would be a way for me to repay him. Not literally, obviously, he'd still have to pay for it, but in the gesture and what it meant.

I went online during my lunch break and looked at the tourist websites. It was another world, one that seemed welcoming and cultured. Even the names suggested romance: Le Pont Neuf, La

Sorbonne, Montmartre, Notre Dame, La Musée D'Orsay. Paddy had mentioned that museum before, told me about this painting by Delacroix. I felt myself getting excited, my hands twitching in my lap, little rushes of pleasure to my brain. I found a hotel – bem charmoso, *so charming* – in a place called the fifth arrondissement. I was sure Paddy would love it.

I went back to work but couldn't concentrate, images of Paris kept popping into my head. Me and Paddy walking down a cobbled street. Me and Paddy eating dinner in a restaurant. Me and Paddy on a boat on the river, looking at the Louvre. Me making a clever comment on the architecture. Maybe we would end up living there and I could finally leave São Paulo for good. Anywhere in Europe would do, but Paris would be best. Paris, I repeated to myself. Paris. Paris.

Guilt.

I didn't understand my job. Well, I understood what it was I had to do, but not where it fitted into the bigger picture. Basically, I had to match numbers with other numbers, making sure that all the deposits and withdrawals added up. Often I would imagine why a particular transaction had taken place, invent a story behind the numbers. Perhaps a man was buying his lover a present and had to keep it a secret from his wife. Maybe the numbers were a bonus from a man's job, enabling him to put a down payment on a house for his family. Or the numbers were somebody's new clothes or new car. I understood that all these numbers represented something else, that they were actually just an idea. They signified wealth and opportunity, but they weren't real. They were promises.

I suppose I never really got to grips with it.

When I started in the office, I enjoyed dressing up in a shirt and tie, smart trousers. I bought a range of different colours and patterns and enjoyed picking out combinations in the morning. My baby sister would see me off from the apartment with a compliment. 'Very handsome,' she'd say. 'Who's my important executive?' She never really knew what I did, but it was nice to have her share in my good fortune.

And our apartment benefited too. She'd always kept it clean, but now we were able to fix it up a little, add a rug or two, a throw for the sofa, lamps to improve the lighting in our small living room. She began to show off when her friends came over to visit. I felt proud.

I couldn't tell her about Paddy.

There was a tingling sensation in my arms and legs, and I couldn't take the smile off my face. It was definitely a good idea, Paris: I'd have to think about how I could bring it up.

My colleague Fernanda looked over from her desk. 'What are you looking so pleased about?'

'Nothing,' I said, grinning. If I shared it with anyone, it'd lose its magic.

'Whatever.' She gave a little smirk. I laughed. She shook her head in mock reproach.

'Don't be jealous, darling,' I said, 'it doesn't suit you.'

I shivered with excitement and made a list in a Word document of places we would be able to visit. I felt the muscles in my thighs and buttocks tense. I ignored the numbers for a few minutes and imagined the fifth arrondissement and what it would mean for me and Paddy. I saw the grey cashmere scarf I'd need to keep out the cold, the navy-blue overcoat, the brown leather Gucci loafers and matching belt, a stripe of colour on the Samsonite travel bag. Paddy tall and distinguished in a patterned sweater. Maybe that black fedora I'd seen at his house, the one he'd never worn when he'd been with me, streaks of grey hair at his temples. Shopping on the Champs-Elysées, looking at art I could try to recognise and understand. Eating foie gras: I wasn't sure exactly what it was, but it sounded exotic. I'd forget about my weight for a few days. I deserve that.

I made a list in ascending order of places I wanted to visit, names of churches and galleries, neighbourhoods and restaurants. I thought about the number of pairs of underpants and socks I would need for a short trip. The hotel I'd picked out had a website, and it wouldn't cost too much to do laundry there. The turnaround for cleaning clothes was only one day. So handy! I factored this into my plans. I checked the Air France website for flight availability and saw there were regular flights and that Business Class was probably not out of the question. Paddy had half-term coming up in April and we could leave the day he finished at the school and spend an entire week there. If he needed an extra day or two, I felt sure he could arrange it. I wouldn't have to take too many days off work at Easter, though my sister might be unhappy with me being away on the religious holiday. I'd have to think about what I'd tell her. I didn't want to lie, but I was prepared to if necessary. She didn't know if I had to travel for work or not so I decided that this might be the best way to tell her. She'd burst with pride.

My boss wandered over but I managed to minimise the document with my plans before he arrived at my desk. I studied the spreadsheet on the screen, matching the final three digits with a series of transactions.

'I wondered if I could have a quick word? Do you have a moment?'

My boss was a fairly relaxed guy, always well-dressed and friendly.

'Of course,' I said.

'I just wanted to check that everything's going okay. I've heard good things about you over these last six months.'

'Thank you,' I said. 'Everything's fine. I'm enjoying the work. I like being here.'

'Que bom. That's good. We like to make sure that employees feel that they are being well treated.'

'Everyone has been very kind.'

'Good. Do you have any questions about the work?'

I thought about my general ignorance. There was so much I didn't know, so many questions I had.

'I don't think so,' I said. 'It's all making sense to me now.'

Paddy would probably be able to explain to me how the financial world worked. I'd talk to him.

'Just remember that if there is anything you need, you only have to ask.'

I thanked him and he left. I went back to my numbers. I rubbed my legs in anticipation of the conversation I'd have with Paddy when I told him my plan. Our plan. I kept telling myself: that's how I should be thinking about everything now – the two of us together, ne?

Lisboa bangs on the door and there's no answer. He's not in the mood to give up though and he hammers at it until the door's cracked, on a chain, there's a who-the-fuck-is-that from behind it, and Lisboa shoulders the door full bodyweight force and the chain breaks and they're in –

It's curtain-drawn dark and hangover pungent. Lisboa's got a lad up against the wall. He's badge-out and throat-gripping serious. The lad's choking a touch and can't say anything. He's starkers but for his underwear.

'Nice Y-fronts,' Leme says. 'Anyone else here?'

The lad nods.

'Woman, is it?'

The lad nods.

'Bedroom through there, is it?'

The lad nods and points with his chin. The lad's gasping but Lisboa's in no mood to let up.

Leme moves through to the bedroom. A woman is sitting up in bed, naked it looks like, smoking. She seems remarkably unperturbed by the intrusion.

'Morning, love,' Leme says. 'Why don't you get yourself dressed and off to church.'

The woman smiles. 'Don't you want to know who I am?'

'No offence, querida,' Leme says, 'but I think I can guess.'

'Cheeky sod.'

'More of a reflection on him than you, believe me.'

The woman smiles. 'It's a semi-regular arrangement if you do need to know. Here's my card.'

She holds out a business card which Leme takes.

'Don't forget it's in your pocket, big boy, lest your old dear happen upon it.'

It's Leme's turn to smile. 'Sound advice. Now kit on and out.' Leme spots the expression on her face shift a tad. 'He not paid you yet?'

She shakes her head. Her bottom lip protrudes in a full sulk.

'Hold tight,' Leme says.

Leme goes back into the corridor. 'Wallet?' he says to the lad. The lad nods at a pair of trousers inside the front door. Leme raises eyebrows. 'You didn't hang about, did you, son?' He fishes a wallet from a pocket. It's thick with cash. Leme liberates all of the cash. The lad is muffled-groan complaining. Leme winks at him.

He goes back into the bedroom. The woman is now dressed. He hands the woman the wad. 'Christmas bonus a couple of weeks late.'

She takes the money and pockets it. 'Chivalry ain't dead after all,' she says.

'Get out of it,' Leme says.

They're at the kitchen table and Lisboa's making coffee in a swank machine. The lad's sitting in his Y-fronts and smoking. Leme's opened some curtains and windows. The place *reeks*. It's got temporary set-up written all over it. Move in, treat the place like shit, move on. Cheaper than long-term and no one gives a fuck if you get the ceiling dirty.

'How did you get past security?' the lad asks.

Leme smiles. It wasn't hard, that. A classic cop-badge, heavy-mob approach and the segurança let them straight in. In an apartment service like this, there's no loyalty. Like a hotel but with apartment-maid privileges. Does the job if you're a monied transient. Security's not getting any Christmas bonuses from the residents. This one is mid-level reasonable. Tucked just off Faria Lima.

Leme says, 'I don't think they like you very much down there.'

Lisboa pours coffee. He hands a cup to Leme. He glares at the lad. 'You know why we're here?'

'No.'

'Any thoughts at all?'

'None.'

'What if I told you I was looking for someone and you might be able to help me find her.'

'I mean – '

'Would that be more like something you'd be able to understand?'

'I don't know. Can you be any clearer?'

'Emmanuel.'

'Emmanuel, right.'

'You work for Emmanuel, chasing debts, am I right?'

The lad nods.

'I'm guessing to do that properly, given the kind of work they might do at Emmanuel, you have to prepare for the eventuality of a defaulted payment *before* the operation has taken place.'

'Something like that, yeah.'

'And the patient – the *client* – has no fucking idea about you, ne?'

The lad nods.

'So, what, you follow them home, maybe, get a jump on their details, hacking or something. What's your MO?'

'I'm old-fashioned.'

Leme nods. 'Good. You know where they live.'

'That's right.'

'You ever have to collect?'

'Very rarely.'

'Retainer situation, is it?'

'Exactly.'

'Not so bad then, your job?'

The lad says nothing. He lights another cigarette. He gestures around his seedy – if expensive – apartment. 'I wouldn't say it's the height of glamour. I'm a poor man's PI, a rat sniffing around some desperate sod who's even worse off than I am.' He draws hard on his cigarette. 'Not exactly what I had in mind when I was a kid, entendeu?'

'We give you a name, you give us an address, certo?'

The lad's nodding. 'I don't want any trouble. It's all legal, just not very nice.'

'Tailing someone home is not legal, mate, not always,' Lisboa says. 'Bear that in mind, sabe?'

The lad gives Leme the imploring look: keep that fella off of me, eh?

'Gerson Anderson,' Leme says.

'Pre-op name?'

'Yeah, Sherlock,' Lisboa says.

The lad's nodding. 'File's through there. You mind?'

Leme shakes his head. Lisboa escorts. A few moments later and Leme has an address in his hand. Real Parque. Down by the Marginal. Not far from Paraisópolis. Not far from Leme's gaff. Either upmarket favela or swank condo, Leme reckons. Interesting.

'That was where I'd look, right, if the cunt hadn't paid. I didn't have to, as the cunt paid. It's all I can help you with.'

'You followed the client to this address?'

The lad nods.

Leme looks at Lisboa. He nods.

'I hope we don't have to come see you again, lover boy.'

Car-shift ongoing. Leme, again, passenger-seat prone. His phone beeps –

Admin:

I think I might know what Pereira Modelling is about

Leme waits. Another beep.

Allusion to Francisco de Assis Pereira

Leme blood-freezes. Waits. Another beep.

The Park Maniac

Leme goes *fuck*.

The Park Maniac. Serial killer in the 90s. Posed as a modelling agency talent scout. Lured, assaulted and murdered eleven young women. The victims all discovered in park undergrowth. Strangled with shoelaces.

Copycat killer.

Pure hate crime.

Renata is happy enough in the office on a Sunday. It reminds her why she set up on her own in the first place. The fact she's there, in her office, her space, doing her work feels liberating and important. It's been a few years, too. She's established, she's a part of the community landscape; she does a lot of good for the people who live here.

Of course, considering her position is one of influence, and considering her connections to Capital SP, it's not a surprise she's being asked to do this work by the Secretario de Obras.

The question is exactly what work they want her to do.

If they want to go ahead with the Singapore Project build, they need unimpeded access to the land. Land that is currently barren, wasteland, home to a couple of Portakabins and, it's highly likely, some dubious activity by the organisation, as she knows the Paraisópolis branch of the PCC is known.

She thinks back to 2006. She remembers the memo she had, the instruction from Capital SP:

There's a lot of Capital SP numbers tied up in the Singapore Project.

There's a lot of Capital SP product tied up in the enormous loan that went to the government to help fund the Bolsa Família.

The point is that political flux has a direct impact on those numbers and product translating into wealth. It's basically a question of confidence-flogging; if the landscape looks good for the government, the money can move, there is no shortage of international outfits willing to buy in and help out. Everybody gets rich. Well, everybody *rich* gets rich.

She needs the files, needs to cross check Singapore Project background with residency and Bolsa Família registration. Enough people on the Bolsa Família makes the application and justification of a Singapore Project build more straightforward.

She pours herself another cup of coffee – she's hungover; she drank too much all afternoon during Dilma's big speech and beyond – and thinks about popping downstairs to Dona Regina's for some lunch. She'll give it twenty minutes then go eat. She's hopeful Regina will have some of her famous pork stew.

She digs out the Singapore Project information first. The land ownership aspect is torturous. It's a loop, she thinks. State-owned unless other permission given by right of labour by the state. It feels to her that land ownership is very much about what is most convenient at any given time. In other words, you can sell it without actually owning it, is what it seems to Renata.

One company name pops up several times: Casa Nova. Renata notes this name.

She goes to the filing cabinet for the Bolsa Família files from the same period. She's looking specifically for the files for May 2006, before that awful weekend of violence, exactly when she was first asked to look into the Singapore Project by Capital SP. Ray Marx, it was. Big Ray. She shakes her head, smiling. Lucky escape there, she reckons, though she's not sure what from. That was the month when applications and registrations for Bolsa Família peaked, and, in fact, were the final applications that Renata and Fernanda had anything to do with. It made sense; the programme was instituted and eventually everyone eligible for it was signed up. It was a natural ending.

She rifles cabinet drawers. She locates March, April. May though, she can't find. She checks the drawers above and below. She cross-checks files under the same month but in different categories – wedding certificates, birth certificates. Nada. *Nothing.* The files, then, not misplaced. She doesn't panic. This is an archive, there is never a need to go back unless there's a problem with any paperwork and there haven't been any problems for a long time. She's too good, too rigorous for that.

'You're the devil that's in the detail,' Fernanda once told her. 'To misquote a famous line.'

Renata had liked that.

She pulls death certificate files for the months of January to May and places them on her desk. She'll have a look there; it's the likeliest place for a filing error, she thinks, given the way their cabinets are laid out.

She looks through the files. Nothing misplaced here either.

She sips coffee. She's worrying, a little. She's a touch concerned. And part of that is that it's Sunday: she can't call Fernanda – she *won't* – to ask her if she has any idea where the files might be.

The death certificate papers for January are fanned out on the desk. She's gazing at them, not really reading, but not really *not* reading either.

A name leaps from the page:

Maria Regina Vasconcellos

It wouldn't mean much, but Renata remembers processing a Bolsa Família application for the same name later in the year. Very likely in May, in fact. The reason she remembers this: Maria Regina Vasconcellos is Dona Regina's cousin. Or she *was.*

Renata feels something stir. A shudder, a wariness filters through her.

Now she *really* wants to find the Bolsa Família files for May 2006. But they are definitely nowhere to be found.

She leans back in her chair, finishes her coffee.

She takes a deep breath. It is likely an admin error, that's all. It can happen, even to her. The horrendous bureaucracy of this country is what keeps her in business at the end of the day, she thinks.

She decides this will have to wait. She'll speak to Fernanda tomorrow.

She rustles papers, tidies up, washes her cup.

She can look up this Casa Nova company at home.

Ray's feeling rich but cash-poor.

This is not his first rodeo, after all, so he knows that if he's going to take home any real bank, he has to use his own initiative. Salary is chicken feed; the serious dinheiro is always extracurricular.

Play it right and it comes in bags of US and diplomatic flight immunity which means customs and tax are optional.

So what Ray is looking for is a skim job on a roll of overrated loans and credit lines, the sort of favourable situation that Capital SP can set up for large companies. Except the Capital SP cut will be a bag of US deposited somewhere safe for Big Ray.

Deniability is key; he's worked that out, too.

Ray's fixer, Joãozinho, is the go-between. Ray is fairly big news in the sense that he's a mysterious Yank in a gilded pond. Ray's waiting for the nod right now.

He's sitting in his crow's nest hotel room, looking out the porthole window and feeling like he's all at sea.

There's another reason for that. He's out of gear. Which isn't helping the wait. Or helping the day to day, climbing the sanitised walls. Tense as he is, the room feels like a swank medical facility.

The gear situation is a funny one. It's not so much that he needs it, it's that he needs to know he has it should he need it.

Sometimes he wonders if full blown use mightn't be a relief. If there's nothing else you have to do but score, then there's nothing else you have to do.

It's a fundamentalist position, pure and beautiful in its simplicity, its priority.

But it's not Ray's bag. Ray's a high-functioning motherfucker.

The rub is Ray doesn't want to ask Little Johnny for help in this somewhat delicate matter, and Fernando might not be as keen to procure high quality heroin as he is high quality call girls. In fact, regardless of keenness, Ray reckons that a hooker-procurer type might only be able to score street-grade, which does not float Ray's boat. So he'd rather not ask. Equally, he thinks now, his whole shtick would be rather undermined by hotel-wide knowledge of his smack habit. Banging pro chicks is cool and the gang in São Paulo, but mainlining dope is not macho enough to muster any credit, any *prestige*.

Ray will be made for a junkie and that simply won't do. He's at something of a loss and this is not usual for Ray.

It's a pickle.

Ray's phone rings.

'Little Johnny, lad, you're a heartbreaker. Tell me something I don't know.'

'It's set. We have an address. We're going to call it the Bunker.'

'Outstanding.'

'It's in a piece-of-shit town thirty clicks or so out of Brasília.'

'Sounds delightful.'

'It's a nothing place. A room and a fridge.'

'Secure?'

'Very.'

'I won't ask.'

'You haven't.'

Ray laughs. 'And our man? We got him?'

'Our man is very impressed with the numbers you've shown him, Ray.'

'Crunch,' Ray says.

'He's also quite taken with your activities regarding a couple of key politicians.'

'Whose names it would be remiss to mention over the phone given the state's hard-on for wiretapping, but whose names we are both well acquainted with.'

Joe Thomas

Little Johnny swoons. 'Your way with words, entendeu?'

'Hard earned, son, learning.'

Joãozinho laughs. 'Our man is a Renaissance man at heart. He wants to spread himself.'

'Outstanding.'

'The less than subtle implication was if the two politicians whose names it would be remiss to mention were to suffer career setbacks at the same time as our man is making money from us – from *you* – then that might lead to a strengthening of the relationship.'

'Bingo,' Ray says.

'I'll get some balls rolling.'

'Hit it.'

Ray hangs up.

Geddel Vieira Lima is their man. Vice-President of Brazil's National Savings Bank. The deal is old-school: bribes for favourable loans and credit lines.

Ka-ching!

Silva wobbles home. It's not unusual. School night drinking is the only kind. A hungover start to a working day adds an edge. Starting with a disadvantage means a hill to climb, means extra accomplishment, means a well done, old man. Fact is, the buzz of the hours-old red wine sharpens the brain and the pencil. Get in gear, old man, there's much to do. Yeah, yeah, tomorrow's a new day. Silva chuckles on his way home. Playing out a little role play, who's the voice in the old head, the rehearsed diatribes against slights, perceived and real –

The cliché of that line of thought makes Silva laugh. He stumbles, steadies himself on a lamppost. He pushes off, stumbles again, steadies himself on a wall, on the gated fence of a nicer condo than his own. It's late and there's fuck all about. He likes the walk anyway. Sobering. Get a bit of exercise in.

He reaches into his inside pocket for his cigarettes. He's sure there's one or two left. He digs about his inside pockets, trouser pockets, back pockets, shirt pockets –

No lighter.

He is fairly sure he had two when he stepped out earlier. Though that was to get the papers and read them over a grand slam breakfast, a full Brazilian: eggs, ham, bread, pão na chapa, spicy sausage, rice and beans, two coffees, chased down with beer and pinga, double-fisting. Champion-level consumption. The after-effects are *long*.

Silva sees a bloke with a fag on outside his building and thinks hallelujah.

'You're a godsend, cara,' Silva says to this bloke. 'Tem fogo?'
You got a light?

The bloke nods. He makes the shape, lighter in the right hand, the left hand cupping the right hand. Silva leans in. Silva wobbles a tad, misses. He scuffs his shoes.

'You all right, mate?' the bloke asks, pulling the lighter just far enough away that Silva can't reach it. *Snide cunt*, Silva's thinking, but doesn't say it as why would you want any aggro right now, just as you're about to have the perfect last smoke –

'Meu,' Silva says. *Mate*. 'I'm dandy, golden.' Silva sways. 'Here give us the lighter, ne?'

The bloke takes a step back. Silva clocks his smartish clothes, his tight, smartish clothes; he's a big bloke, this bloke.

Silva thinks *fucking light my fag, what's up with you?*

The bloke pivots, throws a left-hand punch, connects above Silva's right eye. Silva's drunk, but he feels this punch. He feels his skin break and blood flow. His cigarette falls from his lips. He staggers but doesn't go down. He kneels, just for a moment. The booze has softened the punch. He feels about six drinks more sober, that's something at least. He sees the cigarette and picks it up. He's not sure why he's done this.

Silva looks up. 'What the fuck?' he says.

The bloke sticks a finger in his face. 'You watch out, that's all, certo?' The bloke wraps his hand around Silva's neck. Silva choke-coughs. Silva's saliva bubbles. The bloke says, 'Don't listen to the promises of charming strangers, entendeu?'

Silva nods but he's not sure he's got a fucking clue what's going on. 'It's a good sentiment,' he gasps. 'Well put.'

The bloke spits on the floor. He throws his lighter at Silva's feet. He stalks off.

Silva thinks *result*.

He lights his cigarette. He leans back against the wall, last-smoke happy.

Leme and Lisboa arrive at the last known address of Gerson Anderson.

According, at least, to the bounty hunter slime ball charged with making sure the poor sod could pay the bill.

It's a bog standard, mid-level, newish build condo. Not a great deal of charm. Materials look some way shy of high spec luxury. The porteiro is Sunday-bored and flicking through the paper. Radio's crackling some new programme or other. A TV with the sound down shows a shopping channel. A girl in a bikini parades perfume bottles, holding them like regal artefacts. Her smile dazzles, her lips shine, her eyes empty.

Leme and Lisboa don't mess around. Badge and a look and the porteiro drags himself out of his chair and shows them to the lift. The three of them stand tight in the pokey lift. The light is cheap-harsh, the mirror glares at them.

The porteiro gestures *you first* with deep sarcasm. He's bowing, mais ou menos, like they're visiting royalty.

Leme and Lisboa ignore him. The porteiro gives it the suit yourselves. He opens the door.

He gestures again with the *after you, gentlemen*.

Leme and Lisboa step into an empty apartment.

'You ever meet the woman who lived here?' Leme asks.

'If I don't know a resident, I'm happy. And that means the resident's happy.'

'So that's a no.'

'I see people come and go. If they've got a car, they don't even need me.'

Leme's nodding.

'Likely this bird's moved then, ne?' the porteiro says.

'You wouldn't know even that?'

'Nope. Not for certain. They might not have told me yet.'

'Who?'

'Management, porra.'

Leme looks at Lisboa. Lisboa nods.

'Então,' Leme says to the porteiro, 'this is what you're going to do.'

The porteiro listens. He yawns. He scratches his behind. He plays the quick draw cowboy, spinning his oversized key ring round his fingers.

Leme grabs his wrist. Leme twists.

'First, you're going to talk to management, find out if the resident has in fact moved on.' The porteiro nods. 'Second, you're going to look at security tapes.' Leme nods at cameras in the corridor. 'And you're going to find us some footage of a woman coming in and out of this apartment. Entendeu?'

Leme lets go of the porteiro's wrist. The porteiro gives Leme a look: *okay okay.*

'Certo?' Leme says.

The porteiro nods. 'Tomorrow morning.'

'Good lad,' Leme says. He hands him a card. 'Call me. Or we'll come back.'

Lisboa slaps the porteiro on the back – hard. The porteiro staggers a touch. Lisboa grins. They leave.

Renata's sitting on the balcony of her apartment, sipping a beer, watching a queue of cars twist and shunt their way around the small streets in front of the building, half-listening to a group of men in the bar across the road talk loudly about football and politics and, inevitably, women. Puta que pariu, she hears. *Fuck me.* Laughter and insults. Vai tomar banho, porra. Você sabe de nada.

Go take a shower, dickhead. You don't know what you're on about.

She shakes her head. She hears: Que filezinha. *What a fine piece of young meat.*

Renata knows that young prostitutes drink in the bar with the older men from time to time. She doesn't know if they're doing trade; she doesn't want to know which of the men might be. Some of them are Mario's friends, after all.

Mario is in the kitchen preparing dinner. Renata imagines him in the bar with the other men from the condominium. She's not sure how well he fits in. He doesn't talk as freely as they seem to, never raises his voice. When they're down at the pool, Mario is considered, withdrawn, but he gets some well-placed jabs in, some banter. Renata always likes it when he does. He's funny, her husband.

When she first came to the building, he introduced her to these older men – a restaurateur, dentist, marketing men, a former cop; all of them were determined to enjoy themselves as much as possible. The condominium is like a club: a huge swimming pool and deck, tennis court, sauna, squash court, barbecuing area, bar, snooker tables, even a disco. It made quite an impact on Renata.

The balconies curve like guitars with Niemeyer elegance, and each of the eight towers is marked by a single stripe of different colour. A sort of art deco utopia.

Not from their balcony though, which is at the building's front. There's something relaxing, oddly, she's always thought, about the traffic noise, the weekday grind, the dissipating heat, the electricity crackling and zipping down the lines that criss-cross overhead. She likes the feeling of being *right there*.

They have friends whose balcony faces the other side of the condominium. There you can step onto it and look out across the dirty greenery that fringes Paraisópolis, see grim-faced men with machetes cutting their way through it towards the favela. There is a municipal swimming pool to the right, and the children's screams die down on late afternoons, parents picking up towels and chasing them away from the pool. These are the residents of Paraisópolis and now their fun is over it is back to the concrete warren and pots of stewed beans and maybe cheap cuts of pork.

These are the people that Renata works for, the people she helps.

Morumbi is not a place with much for the middle class to do, end of the day, and maybe counter-intuitively, she thinks. Place to plonk down roots, to *live* in. It has grown *up* fast. Little to do in the evenings save eat in average, overpriced restaurants or go to the cinema in the shopping mall, or pass the time in the condo bar inside – as opposed to the bar in front Renata is looking at now – listening to bawdy stories and recursive, drunken arguments about politics, a rich lexicon of imaginative swear words, and keeping her counsel.

They say that everything outside of Brazil is better than Brazil,

Renata thinks. She's not sure it is. We have this pride in our country, yes, she believes that's true, and yet are scornful at the same time, as though we don't really trust that we are as sophisticated or impressive as Europe.

It's textbook big city and developing world. Renata smiles.

It's why we're always going on about the fact we're Italian or Portuguese, she thinks. We're fucking Brazilian! It's status. Old world confers status.

These flights of fancy help her relax, these ideas, these little bursts of theory.

Mario joins her. He hands her a beer.

She smiles up at him. She beams at him. 'Thank you.'

'Pasta okay?'

She nods. 'Sunday night.'

He smiles. 'Well, with my old man it was crispy duck down in Liberdade.'

'Pizza for me.'

They both drink. Sunday night tradition: Italian canteen for most families. Football on the radio on the way home. Renata's happy this is theirs. Pasta, at home, together.

'You okay?' Renata asks.

'You know. I'm happy now.'

Renata smiles. She does know.

'I'll bring it out here, shall I?'

'Good idea.'

'I'll open some wine.'

'Great idea.'

He smiles and goes back inside.

She wants to talk to him about work, about what happened at the office, the files, the death certificate and Bolsa Familia overlap that she hasn't worked out at all, the request from the Secreatrio de Obras, the work she's going to have to do somehow, but not tonight, not after this weekend, no, not tonight, they need some down time.

They need to eat, drink and make love, frankly.

She remembered something from law school when she got home: the principle of 'adverse possession', that continual possession of land confers ownership. Confers. That word again. It seems to be the basis for the state's offer to buy the land in the favela with the developer, get the Singapore Project under way.

And it didn't take a lot to connect Jorge Mendes, the Secretario himself, with Casa Nova. But that's all she's got so far, a connection, a name. One day soon, this week, she'll talk to Mario about it. He'll be able to help. It's his fucking job, after all, she laughs.

'Here.'

He hands her a bowl of spaghetti in a spicy, tomato-based sauce, basil leaves torn and scattered, grated Parmesan, bread toasted with garlic and olive oil.

'It looks wonderful.'

He pours them wine. He sits down. They knock glasses.

'I'm famished,' he says.

They eat. They listen to the sounds drifting up from the street. They drink and they eat and they look at each other in the low balcony light, Mario's face sharp, dark in candlelight. She is happy, this will be a good year.

'Can I ask you something?' Mario says. 'A work thing. In theory, sabe?'

'Claro, querido.'

Of course.

'I'm looking for someone who lives in the favela. Nothing to do with an investigation, not directly, but someone who might have some information that might help me, and I can't go through the usual channels, entendeu?'

'Okay.'

'Would you, you know, hypothetically, be able to find someone if I give you the name?'

'Sure, I can try, there's a good chance.'

'And you would, for me?'

Renata smiles. 'Of course I will.'

'Thank you.'

Mario forks pasta. The sounds of cutlery on china. Of wine poured. The crunch of bread.

'Not too spicy?'

'Perfect.' Renata swallows. 'Who is it?' she asks.

Mario looks at her. 'Annette Nascimento.'

Bocão, Big Mouth, *former escort:*
Guilt.

I didn't want Paddy to think that I had to spend every night with him, so I was happy for us to be apart several times a week. He may have wanted to see me more often, but I understood that it wasn't always possible.

My sister was at home when I arrived. She was cooking rice and beans and grilling fish and the apartment smelled pretty bad. I didn't want my nice clothes to smell of fish, so I changed quickly into an old tracksuit in my room.

'Is fish alright for dinner?' she asked.

'Anything you want.'

'But I want you to want it too. You're the one with the difficult job. You need calories to make all those important decisions.'

I was in my tracksuit standing in the doorway between the kitchen and the living room. It could've been any night, this conversation.

I scratched at the paint that flaked off the walls.

'Leave that alone and come and sit down.'

Then we'd sit and have dinner together and she'd talk about her day – she worked as a part-time maid in a few of the apartments in the building – and I'd sit quietly not admitting to my problems at work, not telling her about my relationship, and making no reference to my previous life, the one before she'd come to live with me, after our mother died. But that particular night I was buzzing with the Idea. I came close to telling her. The simple act of confidence would bring us closer, *sabe?* But I didn't know if she'd understand and I didn't want to risk alienating her. It was my apartment, but it was all she had. I bit my tongue: I didn't want her to disapprove of me.

'Have some more,' she'd say, shovelling food onto my plate. 'It's good for you.'

I'd smile and accept, thinking that I should eat fewer carbs: I couldn't rely on my natural energy to burn it off anymore.

2
Orgy

March 2011

_____

You can always get what you want in São Paulo. You get what you need, too. You only have to whistle.

Julião, entrepreneur

It is a civilizational clash. What kind of country do we want to be? The majority of people play by the rules, they work from sunrise to sunset and pay their taxes as much as they can. Yet another portion lives dangling off the state apparatus, living off deals with people who have the keys to the safe.

Eurípedes Alcântara, journalist

Leme's days settle; a dispiriting rhythm.

Homicide – murder – whatever its motivation, is an occurrence in São Paulo.

Hate crime or not, a body is a body. Death is a number; the size of the number determines the dispiriting nature of the daily rhythm, the shuffle. São Paulo is awash, flooded with murder. Cases come and go; you do what you can.

What Leme can do is the minutiae of the procedural business of detection. And what that means is pursuing the only lead they still have: the paperweight. It's flimsy at best. And what this means is an exhaustive, exhausting check of anywhere in São Paulo that makes this sort of trinket. There are, it turns out, a lot of places that do. This does not come as a surprise.

_____

That Leme has to pursue this line of enquiry on his own, an off-the-books job, has by no means expedited the investigation in any way. Every day he tries a new place; every day he is able to rule this new place out. And yet, he is no closer.

It is starting to feel like busy-work.

The only thing that Leme feels at all good about is his refusal to countenance a fit-up to keep his superiors happy. The media, inevitably, got hold of the Park Maniac angle. There were a handful of sensational articles, a couple of opinion pieces focusing on the hate crime, and a few column inches devoted to making the police look bad.

In the end, they spun it into a look-what-we've-become sort of state-of-the-nation metaphor. That *Cidade de São Paulo* crime correspondent Silva was all over it like a cheap suit.

Metaphors don't kill people, of course.

The empty apartment led nowhere; it was empty, after all. The porteiro came good: the CCTV confirmed the victim lived there. Management couldn't illuminate on occupancy. As far as they knew, the apartment remained lived in.

The state psychologist's office confirmed what they already knew: Gerson Anderson was ready, legally speaking, for gender reassignment surgery.

Leme feels like he's chasing ghosts.

And one thing the media has kept at: the possibility of another victim. The serial killer copycat angle.

Leme tries to bury this angle in the procedural detail; it doesn't bear too much thinking time.

He's not especially successful.

And that's partly due to his meeting with Annette Nascimento. She thought, decisively, that the paperweight was Lockwood's. Forensics made it for clean. It strikes Leme that it is symbolic only, not a murder weapon. It strikes Leme that it is a very pointed message. It is a message that tells him that he's got two unsolved cases, not just the one. Which, of course, is not the opinion of his bosses. It tells him that to fit up one patsy is one thing, but to fit up two is a pattern of pragmatic police work bordering on the irrevocably unethical. The message says: mate, stop being a cunt.

And then Lisboa gets the call that takes things forward with an awful finality. And Leme's despondency takes on a new character: to go with the hopelessness, helplessness.

The point is people die, people are killed and there are men like Leme and Lisboa who try to figure out who did the killing, and that's the deal, and it doesn't matter if they manage it, really, as people die and it's all part of the social contract. The illusion of it, at least.

What Leme's been trying to figure out recently: not who, *why*.

The call: a body. Ibirapuera Park. Behind the concert hall.

The sun blistering paint.

That's the first memory Rafa has of the last day he saw his mother.

The sun blistering paint and the cloud of heat, waiting for rain.

Rafa at home with his grandma, waiting for his mum and his dad to come back from the hospital with a new baby brother or sister. The heat weighed heavy, the expectation light. Rafa was six years old.

His grandma took him to the municipal pool on the outskirts of Paraisópolis. The sun violent, malevolent; streaky light sliced through a pollution prism. The water a clear, light blue against the pool's tiles; the eyes of Rafa's little friend, Aninha, sea-coloured. A thought slides into Rafa's head: my brother will look like me; my sister will look like me. Black skin and brown eyes. Aninha is a sun-lit ray, dust-coloured, a smile like a bar of gold, a promise of ice cream, a treat. That's how Rafa feels now, looking at her, laughing, playing together, that she's something like hope.

Rafa's other little friend, Franginho, dirty-faced and muddy-clothed. What was it his mother used to say? If a rat bit Franginho, it's the rat that'd need the tetanus shot.

Bit harsh that, Rafa always thought, not his fault Franginho's mother didn't know soap from sawdust.

They splash and chase each other, throw inflatable balls.

Rafa's grandma sits with her friends, gossiping, half an eye on the kids. Rafa's second memory: bent-backed, topless labourers with long knives hacking their way through the thick brush that circles the pool, grim-faced, making their way into the favela alongside the slow sludge of shit flowing the other way.

They play in the water until a whistle blows time's up. Young men and women in flip-flops and vests, volunteers, harass the kids, hustle them out of the water, corral them to the exit.

Rafa, at this point, pursues his usual game. He runs rings round the volunteers, figures of eight around the pool, dives into the deep end, swims round to the shallow end, splashing and diving out of reach then jumping out and doing the whole circuit again.

He can feel his grandma's eye-roll from under the water.

It's too hot, kid, to argue, come on, the volunteers tell him. His grandma tut-tutting, wagging a finger, a slight smile. Aninha and Franginho, the other kids, cheering him on.

Rafa's trick: he always gives himself up. Right when his fun is about to provoke fractiousness and threat, anger, some righteous revenge on the cheeky moleque, the *punk*, he head-hangs, wrists out cuff-ready, and gives himself up to whichever volunteer he's been tormenting the most.

The style of it is in the timing.

Rafa always nails it, the timing.

The applause is brief, muted; lunch.

Rafa's waved goodbye to Aninha and Franginho. He's tucking into his grandma's rice and beans, two fried eggs and a glass of world class Guaraná Mineira. Post-swimming famished. On another day she might have treated him and his little friends to a plate or two of batata fritas and a coxinha at Dona Regina's lunch stand, but Rafa's grandma wants them at home, you know, just in case, sabe?

It's still very early, she knows this. She's told Rafa more than once. He's happy waiting; it's not often he gets his grandma all to himself.

After lunch they sit in chairs in the cramped, damp living room, the shutters closed, taking well-earned respite from the heat. When the sun, relentless, beats down the favela bakes. The rough stone and brick, the cheap asphalt and cinder block concrete cook the air, like an oven. The air shimmers between houses, pulses, floats above the roads.

On the streets, quiet. This heat, post-lunch, we're not ourselves, is the general feeling, so let's keep interactions to a minimum, eh? The favela, mostly, siesta-slumbers.

Rafa watches TV, Eventually, it puts them both to sleep. The afternoon lopes along. The heat fills the hours like air in a balloon.

At six, Rafa pops out, swings by his friends' houses. Aninha is doing chores; Franginho is eating. Later, he's told by their parents, skedaddle. He takes a couple of turns of the block, finds nothing doing and heads back home, finds there his grandma stewing pork and washing the floors. She waves her mop at Rafa to stay outside, moleque, with those dirty feet! He sits on the steps, flicks stones into the road, the smack-ring as he bullseyes a couple of hubcaps on a broken-down, shit-can, rust-bucket car.

By nine his grandma is fidgety. They eat. Rafa wants to go out, but he's not insensitive to his grandma's mood; she doesn't let him, and he stays home with only a small amount of fuss, pantomime, really, just for form's sake.

They watch her novelas, her soap operas, and Rafa's in bed by midnight. The air has cooled, the night settled. He can hear men in the corner bar jacked up and boisterous, demob-heat happy, as pleased with the breeze as he is, toasting it with cold beers and pinga shots. He hears radios and TVs jabber in other shacks on the block, the crackle and hiss of electricity.

He sleeps only in his underwear. His body cooling down, he feels the warmth in his bones dissipate, the heat sidling off, leaving him. He sleeps, easy.

It's three o'clock in the morning when he's woken by his father's voice in the kitchen. It is flat, dulled, matter of fact. Rafa jumps out of bed and sneaks a look down the corridor. His grandma is holding his father, her son, to her chest; he is sobbing, shaking, and the look on her face is one of silent agony. Rafa goes quietly back to bed.

The next morning they tell Rafa that his mother isn't coming home, and neither is his little brother. They tell Rafa that life goes on.

He is six years old, and they tell him this, and it does eventually go on, Rafa's life.

City Hall.

Anna circulating at one of those political fundraisers where everyone's wearing cocktail dresses and black tie and eating a five-course dinner while deciding who's going to eradicate the terrible poverty in our fine country.

Yeah, Anna thinks, it's an easy target, but still, take aim and let fly. If you don't you get suckered into it all, the glamour of it, the *money*.

She's there with Marta and Luís Favre – Mr Marta, or Rasputin to his friends and enemies – and her role is twofold:

First, to play the protégée eye candy and keep the political folk guessing as to what exactly she's up to, career-wise, in the longer term.

Second, to meet two key figures in Dilma's government, Antonio Palocci, chief of staff, and Pedro Novais, Minister for Tourism, who are both on rare visits to São Paulo and are, ostensibly, being hosted by Marta and Favre.

There's a whole choreographed play going on.

The room has that tacky lavishness Brazilians enjoy. Gold everywhere, bright lights, the national, state and city flags all jostling, tumescent, for attention, thrusting out on poles over the proceedings, unfurled like giant napkins. The amount of cutlery set at each place is startling; at least four glasses to choose from. Anna's snagged a decent snifter of red and has left her table to circulate. No one eats at these things anyway. The leftovers must dazzle.

She's keeping her eye out for Marta's signal to go and join when she has either or both Palocci and Novais at a good moment. This is pure politics: quid pro quo. Or as they say in the more feminist-aware activist circles that Anna sometimes moves in: who you know and who you blow. Enlightened times.

What Marta is offering is access to São Paulo City Hall and a shit tonne of electoral support. What she gets back is an ear to the ground close to the throne and a silver-tongued courtier on her team.

There's a double set-up going on: Anna will get the nod from Marta, and later from Rasputin, and the introductions will involve quite different propositions.

Marta is looking dead-on glamorous and sexy as hell in a politically informed red dress that sits just below the shoulders and just above the knee, just above, in fact, the beginning of her thigh. It's a cracking fit this dress; Anna watched her slide into it only a couple of hours ago. Marta raises a finger, the slightest of gestures; Anna gives herself the once-over in her compact mirror and floats across the room towards her.

They're standing, Marta and Palocci, which makes things easier. They've stepped back, too, from their table, created a keep-clear distance, the vibe very much saying private chat, so do one. They're probably the two biggest dogs in the room, politics-wise anyway, so this no-photos-please, no-autographs stance will most likely be respected.

Marta makes the introductions. Palocci looks Anna up and down. He says, 'I've heard a lot about you.'

Anna smiles. Marta says, 'It's all true.'

Palocci says, 'You've got a great mentor, of course.'

Anna smiles. Marta fake swoons, one hand on her neck, the back of the other across her forehead.

'It's all true,' Anna says.

They laugh, all three of them.

'She's funny,' Palocci says.

Marta places a hand on Anna's elbow. 'Querida,' she says, 'why don't you tell Senhor Antonio here a little of what we've been talking about.'

Anna nods. Paloccci squares up to listen to her.

She says, 'To get straight to the point, senhor, we've been talking about better coordination of the funds from the Ministry of Cities to the overall goal and purpose of the Singapore Project in one or two flagship favela developments which we propose.'

Anna looks Palocci square in the eye. He's nodding, mumbles 'to get straight to the point' to himself, smiling. He says, 'Where do you have in mind?'

'Paraisópolis.'

'Interesting. Why there?'

Marta's thin smile softens, fattens a touch. Anna sees that her eyes are shining a touch more and she is encouraged.

'Biggest municipal favela,' Anna says. 'It's already undergone some work, there is the basis of an infrastructure in place, and, contract signatures pending, a Singapore Project build is scheduled to start work later this month.'

'Okay,' Palocci says, giving it the wizened old master. 'What's the real reason?'

Anna watches Marta turn her shoulders, ever so slightly, away from the conversation in a conspiratorial gesture that says, go on, speak, we're all in this together.

'I've developed,' Anna says, 'a relationship with a legal aid NGO based in the favela. In fact, this NGO has been instrumental in the logistics involved in the sale of the land for the SP site to the Secretario de Obras.'

'Mendes.' Palocci eye-rolls extravagantly. 'What a cunt that man is.'

Anna ignores this. 'And as well as this,' she goes on, 'the NGO has terrific influence in the community. The majority of its work is low-level community help, Bolsa Família, drawing up and notarising legal documents, births, deaths and funerals, that kind of thing, all very wholesome and family oriented.'

Palocci is nodding. 'So the benefits are we get an on-side legal team on the ground to help with greasing the wheels, and the biggest favela in the biggest city in South America voting PT.'

Marta opens her arms. 'You're very clever, Antonio.'

Palocci likes this. He slugs wine. 'Of course,' he says, 'the Ministry of Cities is not mine, but I can have a word. They'll listen.' He looks at Marta and then at Anna. He says, 'What's in it for you?'

Anna holds his look. 'Leverage.'

Palocci roars. He grins at Marta. 'She'll go far, this girl.'

'Woman,' Marta says. 'She's a woman.'

'To-may-toe, tomato.' Palocci gives Marta a quick kiss on each cheek. 'I'll say hi to your ex-husband in Brasília.'

Marta smiles. She links arms with Anna. 'Do,' she says. 'After all, look where it got him, choosing not to work with me.'

Palocci makes a face: mock terrified. *Ooooh*, he goes. He breaks into a grin. 'See you, ladies,' he says.

About an hour later and Rasputin is in a dark corner with Palocci and Pedro Novais. They're sitting down. The table is otherwise unoccupied.

Anna slides into a chair. Rasputin makes the introductions. Palocci says, 'I've already made the young woman's acquaintance.' He looks at Rasputin. 'I think she'll go far.'

'Oh, there's no doubt about that,' Favre says. 'Point is, she's here now as she's going to coordinate this whole thing on the ground, certo? She'll be on site, making the introductions and making sure everyone is as happy as a pig shitting in the woods. A reassuring, legitimate face.'

Novais smiles. He is liver-lipped, liver-spotted; Anna can't believe he can still go to the bathroom without fairly serious help. He says, looking at Anna, 'That's lovely, dear.'

'And she'll send us dates, details, et cetera?' Palocci asks.

Rasputin smiles at Anna. 'She's very competent.'

Palocci nods, twists his mouth into a meaty knot. 'She looks it.'

Rasputin nods at Anna. She stands, gives a little bow, says, 'I look forward to seeing you soon, senhores.'

She glides slowly away, feeling three sets of eyes bore into her back.

What Anna is going to coordinate: off the record meetings between extremely high-ranking politicians and extremely influential construction industry magnates.

Where these meetings are scheduled to take place: Astúrias, a high-class, low-key sex motel in central São Paulo.

The only other invitees: some of the city's finest sex workers.

And who will be bankrolling this business bacchanal, who'll be footing the most likely extravagant bill: the taxpayer. The Ministry of Tourism's budget accounting system is, they have found out from Senhor Novais, vague.

Anna's at the bar. She fingers a glass of champagne. She smiles, the evening a success. What no one else in the room knows: Anna's already arranged to have these meetings bugged. When it comes to the betrayal, she'll protect Marta, but she can't say the same for old Rasputin over there.

Collateral, she thinks, is the only way to look at it.

At home, Anna calls Ray, tells him how the night panned out.

'Outstanding,' Ray says.

'My husband told me never to trust journalists.'

Silva smiles. Renata goes on. 'It's been five years. I wonder why you're here now.'

It's not a question. Renata doesn't much like the look of Francisco Silva. His appearance is not one that invites a good deal of confidence. The tricky thing, she thinks, is that he knows this.

'Your husband probably has a good reason to say that. He's not a politician, is he?'

Renata smiles. 'Detective, Civil Police.'

'I might know him.'

'He certainly knows you.'

This gives Silva pause for thought. They're sitting in Renata's office, the favela spilling away outside the window. Fernanda is out; Renata told her to take lunch, even though it was only half eleven when Silva turned up.

Silva says, finally, 'Nasty case in Ibirapuera Park. Name's Leme. Not very cooperative.'

Renata flicks an eyebrow. 'You obviously make fewer enemies than I thought.'

'I'm right? I normally am.'

Renata makes a face: yeah, yeah. She says, 'What's the expression? It's better to be cleverer than you look than look cleverer than you are.'

'I think in Brazil, querida,' Silva says, 'the saying is that it's better to be rich than it is to be beautiful.'

'Either way.'

'Pois é.' *Indeed.*

Renata shifts in her chair. 'You said on the phone.'

'That I'm interested in the PCC Mothers' Day weekend rebellion. Any idea why I might have called *you*?'

'It's crossed my mind.'

'Point is, I think we might have more common ground than you think we have.'

'So this is, what, advocacy building?'

'Nice lingo.'

Renata breathes out. 'Let's get to the point, né?'

'Você que sabe.' *You're the boss.*

Renata's bristling as she knows that whatever Silva asks her, one sticky incontrovertible fact remains: any information that she has about that weekend, official or otherwise, is seriously compromised by the missing files, the gaping hole in her otherwise pristine archive. Fernanda knew nothing about it; Renata believed her. She didn't so much act dumb as look dumbfounded: she could barely accept, barely *understand*, that this gaping hole existed. There wasn't much else to do. Someone, for some reason, took the files. Likeliest scenario being an organisation pull. One of the boys from up the hill deciding that *anything* to do with that weekend needed destroying. Or, at least, out of the public domain. The balance Renata maintains with them is precarious at the best of times. She can hardly ask around; it was better to pretend it hadn't happened, like it was a computer glitch, something like that – sad, but not the end of the world – and carry on serving the community as per her carefully worded mission statement.

'There's not much I can tell you,' Renata says. 'My husband,' she gives Silva a pointed look, 'came to pick me up when it was kicking off. I shut up the office, went home and stayed there.'

'I'm not bothered about your *whereabouts*.' Silva winks.

She's angry, her eyes flash. 'I don't much like your style, to be fair, senhor. You wanna wrap this up maybe?' She breathes, composes herself, thinks better of making an enemy herself. 'I'd just like to know what it is that you'd like to know.' She softens, tries a smile. 'To help. That common ground you mentioned after all, ne?'

Silva nods. He picks up the coffee she's made him. Renata watches him drink. He gulps it down like a toad, she thinks. She imagines him slurping oysters, coughing and hacking, clearing his throat. Snuffling like a pig in its trough.

'I've done some asking around,' Silva says. 'And it strikes me that this is exactly the kind of outfit that may have helped with all the passes that enabled so many prisoners to get a weekend out of the joint, sabe? There were, what, hundreds? Thousands? Someone had to do it.'

'Well, we didn't.'

'You didn't have to or you didn't do it?'

'I thought you weren't interrogating me.'

'You can prove you didn't file any paperwork?'

'Like you said, you're not my husband.'

'Perhaps I should be asking him.'

Renata tightens her lips. 'Again, like you said, he's not very cooperative. He doesn't like journalists.'

An impasse, then.

They both feel it, Renata thinks. They're dancing around something all right and she's worried, suddenly, that it's not her that's leading. It's not a feeling she enjoys; it's not one that she feels very often.

They sit, for a few moments, examining each other.

Renata stiffens again. Silva leans forward, as if he's about to lay cards on the table.

'I heard,' Silva says, 'about this scam the PCC have been pulling off all over the city. Using fake identities, sometimes the deceased, in fact more often than not, to claim Bolsa Família benefits, the debit cards. Like Robin Hood, except they collect the cash and don't give it to the poor.'

Renata feels a creeping unease.

'You ever hear about anything like that?'

Renata shakes her head.

'So that's two things you can't help me with,' Silva says. 'Not much common ground after all.'

'I tell you what,' Renata says. 'I'll look into both of those things and I'll give you a call, certo?'

Silva goes *fair enough*, shrugs.

'And when I do call,' Renata says – she's bringing the meeting to a close now, she needs some time to think – 'we can talk some more.'

Silva nods. 'Suit yourself,' he says. He stands to leave. 'We're on the same team, you know,' he says. 'I've done my research. Full disclosure is a decent trade, sabe?'

Renata nods. 'I'll call you,' she says. 'By the way,' she circles a finger around her cheekbones, 'what happened to your eye?'

Silva shakes his head, gives her a hard look, goes *no comment, querida*.

He reaches into his satchel. Renata notes that it's battered, faded, light leather, an ink stain where a pen has leaked through. He pulls a thick file. He drops it on her desk. The byline, she notes in a moment:

Report by Harvard's International Human Rights Clinic and Brazilian NGO demonstrates central role of police brutality, corruption and prison mismanagement in major security crisis of May 2006 and today

'Read this,' he says. 'It'll join some dots.' Silva smiles, warm. He leaves.

Renata sinks back into her chair. She has some food for thought. A few things to chew over. Full disclosure. Thing is, she thinks, full disclosure is pretty much what she's given him. Not something you should give away too easily to journalists you don't trust.

Especially when said full disclosure reveals that you know exactly nothing.

He reminds her of a turtle, she thinks. She can imagine him on his back, floundering, little arms and legs waving about, helpless.

Dilma's first few months in office reveal a willingness to root out corruption. The issue with doing that, though, reveals the full extent of the fairly well-embedded corruption that exists in the Workers' Party. She'll get rid of people, that's clear; but corruption is a Hydra, and removing one figurehead means two further down the food chain move up to take his place. It's nearly always a 'he', Anna notes.

The point is where does the buck stop. More and more people seem dead set on finding out the extent. Many reckon Lula governed like he was running a racket. The Mensalão scandal might only be the beginning. The Big Monthly Payments. A pretty straightforward sort of a corruption scheme. The proliferation of so many parties means getting anything through congress is reliant on balancing a fragmented, left-centre coalition filled with all manner of politics and personalities. A simple way to maintain this coalition: cash. A monthly stipend to ensure loyalty. Thinking of the numbers involved and of the greed of your average two-bob Brazilian politician, Anna reckons they must have been shelling out a small fortune every month. Enough to help solve something of the poverty crisis, at least. Enough to gamble and earn a very decent living on the stock market. Enough, is the point.

The thing with corruption scandals: no one ever really bothers to find out where the money came from. That will be the best change, Anna thinks. There are activist groups, students, sector workers making noises. Soon there will be protests. Anna expects the focus of these protests to be the rotten nature of politics in general, which means the government, which means Dilma.

It's not a coincidence, Anna thinks, that they finally get their act together now that a woman's in charge.

A bar: two men yelling at each other about how great they are. A man turns to his wife, says, 'When I talk to you, you don't listen. But when I'm speaking to someone else, you hear every word.'

Silva's thinking about Renata.

Silva did a bit of digging on Jorge Mendes and his construction company. Turns out Casa Nova, a smaller subsidiary of the larger Mendes Construction, is starting the development of the land in Paraisópolis where the Singapore Project building is going up. Lot of money to be made in a contract like that. He's heard that what they do is take the decent materials from the state, plug them into a private, luxury project, pay dirt for shit to build in the favelas. Not like they're going to notice after all.

Silva's been to one of the developments, the verticalisation. It wasn't old, a few months, maybe. It looked like a slum, rubbish and rot. He wonders if he can get a little more on Mendes's business plan, figure out an actual story. This Ray Marx fella's given him the lead; Silva's given *him* nothing so far, and he'll come calling again.

Is he worried about what happened the other night, jumped by a two-real thug and warned off? But warned off what exactly? Warned off *who*?

It wasn't hard to discover that his new friend Renata helped facilitate the land deal in Paraisópolis. He wonders at her role, exactly.

There might be something there. The work's about to start, which should help with his digging. He needs a reason to see her again, to *collaborate*.

Yeah, Silva's thinking about Renata.

Her face, he thinks, could be described as feline. She scraps and squirms in that way, self-reliant, dirty, like a cat.

He admires her for it.

Bocão, Big Mouth, *former escort:*
Fear.

I was at Paddy's house one evening when the phone rang. It was soon after I'd told him about the Idea.

He spoke in English. I only understood a couple of things. 'I can't talk now.' 'Yes, tomorrow. Looking forward to it.' It was his tone that unsettled me. And then his quick explanation.

'That was a colleague. About a problem at school. I'll have to deal with it tomorrow. Sorry. Where were we?'

It was unconvincing: he didn't have to explain himself to me. Where we were: I was talking about Paris, Paddy was distracted. That was the first inkling I had that there might be other men in his life.

There had been other men before me. He'd told me about them. The garotos de programa in the north. Michês who worked in saunas. Paddy was honest about it. He told me that he had always been careful, and who was I to judge? Look where he found me.

There'd been a man in England. I didn't know what'd happened, only that he wasn't around anymore, hadn't been for some time. I felt like I was something of a replacement: in a good way, I mean.

Astúrias Motel, São Paulo. Juliana Mendes, the wife of Jorge Mendes, the state Secretario de Obras, is lying next to Leonardo Magalhães, the Delegado Geral, Polícia Civil:
My face is reflected in the mirror on the ceiling. My body, beneath the covers, curves seductively as I tighten the sheets around me. A hint of cleavage at the top, a tanned leg poking out the side. I'm still able to please Leonardo, who is dozing beside me. I wonder if there is a set of scales in the bathroom. I doubt it. You can get most things

in a posh place like this, but the aim is to make you feel good. Most women who come here don't want to check their weight.

This morning, I was fifty-seven point three kilos, and since then I've eaten a grilled chicken salad (no dressing, just a drop of olive oil and balsamic vinegar), drunk a glass of white wine and spent an hour on the treadmill. I may have burned off a few calories this afternoon too, seeing it was me who did all the work. But I'm not tired. I can't sleep in the afternoons, whatever I've been doing. Leonardo always drops off for twenty minutes or so after he's come a couple of times. I don't blame him; he's quite a bit older than me.

I look around the room. There is the inevitable motel debris: condom wrappers on the floor, two empty cartons of água de coco, clothes strewn about (though Leonardo always insists on carefully hanging his shirt on the back of the door, creaseless, crisp white, a dappled pink tie hanging over it). Through the door is a small swimming pool, a sauna and hot tub bath. I think about going in, but then I remember I don't have a clip and I don't want to wet my hair. I could lie in the sun for a while – the ceiling in the other room retracts – but I have forgotten that there is building work going on next door and the roofs have been disabled.

Can't have lusty builders looking in now, can we? We've made love in the pool before, but without a condom, and that terrified Leonardo. All he did was put himself inside me for a few thrusts, he didn't come. I told him not to worry, but he hasn't wanted to do it again. It's a shame as I enjoyed the intimacy. At his age it's easy to be flippant, to believe that he is somehow immune from such worries, but the consequences would be worse even than if we were in our twenties. There's a lot more at stake these days. He's a very powerful man, Leonardo. Then again, so is my husband. I guess I attract them. They've been friends longer than I've known either of them. They studied law together, São Francisco, Universidade de São Paulo. I've been seeing Leonardo for a couple of years.

Leonardo is breathing softly and he lets out a gentle moan. I prop myself up on the pillows and look down at him. His hair is slicked back – not a single one out of place – and his chest is well-defined for a man of his age. I look at my watch. It's four o'clock. I'll need to wake him soon. My driver is waiting for me at Shopping Iguatemi and I need Leonardo to drop me there in an hour. His own driver is waiting in the little private garage attached to the suite down a flight of stairs. He must be very discreet – the driver – and Leonardo must trust him a hundred per cent. Wouldn't look good for the Delegado Geral of the Polícia Civil to be caught up in a scandalous affair with the wife of a friend and member of the state government. I wouldn't look too good, either, but I trust Leonardo knows what he is doing. He's essentially a selfish man, and I know he would never endanger his position – not for me or anyone else. It took him a long time to rise through the ranks and he is set now until the end of his career, where a healthy pension and well-deserved rest await.

While we can't ensure we get the same room every time, we always opt for the Suite Mansões. It is a little more expensive than the regular rooms, but everything is on one floor and we have the swimming pool should we want to use it. It's only two hundred and fifty reais, so not a great deal and worth it, I think. At least I think I am worth it. Obviously, I've never paid myself. I get up out of bed, wrap a towel around me and wander into the pool and deck area.

Though the roof is closed, light filters through, illuminating the mural on the wall. A naked lady, her modesty protected by her long, dark hair, sits on a rock overlooking a waterfall. In the distance, a green carpet of hills stretches out. Next to the mural, real vines hang from the rock-fronted wall, a sauna behind. I think about filling the enormous bath but decide there is no time. We pay for these comforts but prefer to use the bedroom. Perhaps one day I'll come with my husband, make a night of it – apparently the food is excellent. That's if Leonardo can't do it. His wife, a good friend of mine, is not suspicious of him as such, but I know she wouldn't allow him to spend too much time away on an evening, whatever his excuse.

Leonardo's car has blacked-out windows, but he is convinced his number plate is recognisable and always insists the driver accelerates quickly up to the entrance, off the Marginal just beyond the bridge that leads to Francisco Morato.

The name of the motel is Astúrias. Curious as to what it meant I did a little research on the Internet. It turns out that it is an autonomous principality in Northern Spain, a key area for the Spanish Enlightenment and a loyalist-democratic-republican stronghold during the Civil War of the 1930s. Interestingly – or perhaps not – it is also a brand of Japanese classical guitar. Quite how a motel in Pinheiros came up with the name is beyond me. I had thought – and hoped – that it was the name of some ancient goddess of love or a romantic hero searching for his soul mate in an epic poem. I wonder how many of Astúrias's clients discover they are soul mates as they writhe around between the starched sheets. Difficult when presented with his hairy bottom bobbing up and down in the mirror above your head.

I go back into the bedroom where Leonardo slumbers on. I take off my towel and inspect my body in the mirror. Objectively speaking, I am an attractive woman. It's hard to notice the work I've had done – I only see the best surgeons. A touch of Botox to flatten out the lines in my forehead and around my eyes, a slight enhancement of my upper lip, a breast augmentation, not to increase size but to retain the firmness of my younger days, and a couple of sessions of liposuction to keep my waist. That's on top of a nose job I had over twenty years ago. My nose had always been a source of embarrassment, and as soon as I got together with my husband we decided I would have it done. I was happier with myself immediately: a petite, pretty button replacing an awkward feature. I haven't had anything done for a while – there's been no need – and my diet and regular exercise seem to be enough for now. I finger the slight flap of skin that sits above my hips. I'll have to talk to my doctor to see if I can get rid of it. The scar from my caesarean is faint. It's been fifteen years now.

Leonardo stirs. His eyes open and he looks at me, smiling.

'Amor,' he says. 'Vem cá,' ushering me over to him.

I pull back the duvet and slip into bed beside him. He strokes my hair and kisses my forehead.

'We have to go in a little while,' I say.

He groans. 'There's still time.'

He searches for my mouth with his tongue. We kiss slowly and I feel his hand between my legs.

'You'll have to be quick,' I say, and he grunts something I don't catch.

He eases himself on top of me. I close my eyes and feel him reach for a condom. We make love brusquely and shower together, careful not to get our hair wet.

The first time Rafa sticks his dick in Carolina he calls it lovemaking. To her he says this, at least. He tells Franginho that he fucked her in the Portakabin. Her soft skin. Her small breasts. In a rusted chair, she sat across him. She's tight so that he comes, when he does, quite fast. They both feel enormous relief.

It begins here, then.

After the third time they do it – Carolina pushed up against the flimsy wall, Rafa's pants round his ankles, worrying he'll do himself an injury if she moves a bit sudden – she says, 'I'd like to go to a motel, I think, young man.'

Rafa nods. Nice one, he thinks. Well up for that.

'You been to one before?'

Rafa shakes his head. 'You?'

Carolina gives him a demure, minxy little smile. 'None of your beeswax, porra.'

Rafa finds he can't help grinning.

They decide to go the very next day. Intoxication, Rafa's finding out, means exactly that. He is interested in absolutely nothing but Carolina. Franginho's having a bit of a sulk at doing all the work for a few days, but as he told Rafa himself just this morning: 'One day, mate, once you've shot your load, you'll be straight out of her bed without even a cuddle.'

'What's your point?'

'I'm happy to mind the shop for a bit until you do. It won't be long, son, mark my words.'

Rafa raises his eyebrows at that. 'I'm in love, porra.'

Franginho laughs loud and long, slaps his thigh. 'Love is a drug, mate. It wears off.'

Rafa sucks his teeth and gives Franginho the middle finger. 'I'm off, Little Chicken, to have my rooster plucked. See you later.'

Franginho's laughter follows him all the way out of The Factory.

Carolina's waiting in her car, engine running. Rafa jumps in. He gives it the sullen bottom lip.

'My,' she says, 'don't look overexcited, querido.'

He smiles and gives her a kiss. 'I honestly cannot wait, meu amor.'

Carolina kicks the car into gear, pulls away. 'Good boy,' she says.

They get out of the favela easy and pull across Avenida Morumbi, then wriggle through the backstreets of Real Parque, not far, Rafa realises, from where Dona Renata the lawyer used to live. The roads are lined with big houses, free-standing independent things with high gates and cameras and, on some of the walls, barbed wire. It's very hilly, Rafa thinks, up and down. Be a cracking spot for the old skateboard, that is if he isn't chased away by the private security firm no doubt monitoring some of the cameras.

At the bottom end of Real Parque, they skirt the outsized stores – building supplies, a huge Decathlon sports store, an Extra hypermarket – that fringe the Marginal and the river just beyond. Lines of cars buzz softly along, the Marginal quiet at this time of day. Rafa sits and feels an erotic anticipation. He's well up for this.

The motel is called Swing. Subtle. It's sunk low, the front of it a wall covered in greenery, two garage doors, one the entrance, the other the exit. A great big neon sign, Swing, printed in hot pink. Rafa can't imagine it'll be too busy; how many people are swinging mid-morning, after all. Motel culture's not something he's got much experience in. Busiest day for them is, he's heard, Secretary's Day, when bosses take their administrative assistants for a combo quickie, a special treat of a shag and a decent lunch. The food is, Rafa gathers, quality in some of these gaffs. Other regular patrons are rich kids who live at home with their parents. One way of getting a little privacy. Cheaper than renting your own pad, and room service thrown in. Valentine's Day specials for couples too, apparently. It's another world. There was a time when favela boys like Rafa used to knock these places off, force their way in and rob everyone in every room, empty the till of cash – no one's using their credit cards to pay; bit of a giveaway on the old bank statement, the word Swing. You could make a decent whack but it was risky. And security's got more technical, the CCTV network so comprehensive now that the old bill can tail anyone being naughty all the way back to the favela. You'd have to work very fast indeed to get back into the warren before you're spotted and pulled. No mercy likely if the Military Police are called in. No doubt: shoot first, ask questions later, if at all. Not worth the risk. And not Rafa's game either way, of course. He's here for pleasure, not a research trip. Work can wait. This is his day off.

There are traffic lights just the other side of the entrance, so they're idling towards it. Most cars are turning right to do some shopping, waiting for the cars coming the other way to let them turn, which of course no one fucking does, so there's a queue. Rafa's grinning. Carolina's wearing denim shorts and a tank top and Rafa's eyes are all over her. She's smiling. Rafa wonders how much of this is exactly the anticipation he feels. Is Franginho right? Will the climax roll straight into an anti-climax? Well, if it does, they'll just have to do it again, Rafa reasons. So far, all he's wanted to do is do it again. Pure pleasure.

The traffic does its little shuffle.

'Here we go, big boy,' Carolina says.

She turns onto the shallow ramp and pulls up to the window, kills the engine.

It's like a drive-thru, Rafa thinks. He sinks low into his seat. Instinct, he realises, shrinking a touch from authority. Giving yourself a tiny disguise, shutting out the world. Tight smile.

Carolina's smiling at the geezer behind the window. 'Suite classic, ta bom?' she says. It's low-end on the room spectrum, but still costs almost a ton for three hours.

Peanuts, of course, in Rafa's world. He fingers the roll of notes in his pocket.

They've talked about it already; basic room is still a heinously swank fuck pad by anyone's standards and it's not ostentatious, won't draw any attention.

The receptionist – if that's the term for the gorilla taking the cash – growls something at Carolina that Rafa can't hear.

She says, 'Yeah, we're old enough, course we are.'

The gorilla's shaking his head.

'I've got ID,' Carolina says.

Rafa tenses up. He doesn't like this. It's not a situation he can necessarily get a hold on. He's very much not in control.

The gorilla leans forward, talks into his little mic. Rafa shapes up.

The gorilla points. 'It's not you I'm worried about, querida,' he says.

Rafa bristles, reaches for the door handle. Carolina shoots an arm across, stopping him.

She smiles at the gorilla. 'And why are you worried about *him*?' she says, calm as you like.

The gorilla just shakes his head.

Carolina opens her palms, smiles again, raises her eyebrows. 'Come on,' she says. 'Vamos, ne?'

More headshaking. Rafa seethes. They all know why they're being refused entry. Rafa eyes the gorilla. He says, 'Don't be a cunt, mate. You're embarrassing me.'

More headshaking, resolute, unambiguous.

'This is racial discrimination, pure and simple,' Carolina says.

Rafa sees she's shaking. She fumbles the keys to start the car.

She gestures that she needs to come into the motel in order to leave, loop round as the old drive-in set-up intends.

The gorilla gestures back. He makes a figure of eight in the air with his finger, telling her to sort it out, chin up, querida, you'll have to reverse back down the ramp.

It's a tricky manoeuvre given the space. Snide, the cunt didn't have to do that, Rafa thinks. He leans across Carolina. 'We'll find out where you live, falou,' he says. 'You ain't going to forget me, certo?'

The gorilla nods, goes *yeah, yeah*.

Carolina squeals the car in a rough U-turn.

Rafa burns.

Anna's been working the housekeeper at Palocci's old place in Brasília. The old manor house he rented, threw parties where kickback deals were made over cognac and women. A fridge and a safe in every bedroom, Anna's heard. The housekeeper is the young lad who was screwed over in the investigation; Palocci being done himself over this hub for fraudulent government activity. Their contact on the ground, this poor lad. Bags of cash and prostitutes to seal the deal, so he says. Nice and private.

Working the housekeeper means Anna's been giving him money and letting him try and figure his revenge.

The housekeeper has provided Anna with a written testimony from one Rogério Buratti, Palocci's secretary when Palocci was mayor of Ribeirão Preto. It claims that Palocci is a serious beneficiary in the Mensalão scandal. The testimony claims that between 2001 and 2004, Palocci received a R$50,000 monthly payment from a rubbish collection company, Leão & Leão.

She shares this with Ray, who says he knows exactly what to do with it. She wonders how this might pan out when sex party season begins.

She smiles. That is, of course, the whole fucking point.

'Read this,' Ray tells Silva.

Silva reads the piece of paper he's been handed. Ray watches him, watches his eyes skip, his face flush, his little eyebrows quiver –

'I'll need it back,' Ray says.

Silva nods. Ray rips the paper in half and then in half again and again.

'Okay, sunshine, I get the point,' Silva says.

Ray grips Silva's wrist. 'Behave, son,' he says. 'This is a story.'

'But you're not giving me any actual evidence, are you?'

Ray smiles. 'Your IT guys are supposed to be ninja.'

Silva says nothing.

Ray goes on. 'I've given you a company name and the details of a monthly salary. It's all got to lead somewhere, son.' Ray's palms open. 'Though I doubt this Leão & Leão are taking very much of anything anywhere, am I right?'

'Rubbish collection,' Silva says, standing. 'Apt fucking business, ne?'

Ray grins. 'You're a good man, Fat Frank.'

Silva goes *fuck off*, and middle-fingers Ray as he walks away.

Franginho tells Rafa that they have to leave the Portakabin. The Factory is no more.

'How do you fucking know that?' Rafa says. He's still sulking. He's still angry. He is *not* in the mood to be told what he does or doesn't have to do.

Franginho tells him there's been a message from the Militars. He also tells Rafa that there is one particular Militar who wants to meet. He wants to talk about political activism. Franginho tells Rafa that he thinks this might be a good idea, considering.

Rafa stomps off. He's not being told by anyone today what might or might not be a good idea.

The body in Ibirapuera Park is that of a young man. His ID card has been left next to a pile of jewellery. His name: Guilherme Santos. On top of this pile of jewellery, secured by a shoelace, is a card that states Pereira Modelling. The young man's heart has been removed. The young man's genitalia have been erased. It is unclear as to whether there has been any sexual activity, though the top hedge in this case thinks it is certainly more than likely. This is complicated by the discovery that Guilherme Santos was a sex worker.

The horror, Leme thinks. A bloody orgy of the stuff.

Bocão, Big Mouth, *former escort:*
 Guilt. Hate.
 You see a man leaving Paddy's house.

He's dressed casually, but not with any style, sabe?

Filho da puta. It's too late to be a professional visit. He's not young, either. Does that mean you're not old enough? It didn't seem to be a problem when he wanted a young dick to suck. And you're much more than that now. It's never enough though, for a stuck-up bastard like Paddy.

You keep your baseball cap low and your collar up. You wish you hadn't worn these white trainers. They stand out, not that the security guy down the street is taking any notice. Probably asleep, the fat fuck.

You light a cigarette to calm down. But you can't. It's the eleventh night you've been here and this man must be the third you've seen. You may have seen him before, but you're not sure. But that's irrelevant, anyway: there shouldn't be any men.

There should only be you. You whisper the phrase. There should only be you.

You remember when that was true.

Part Four

PARADISE LOST

São Paulo, 2011

1

Copycat

———

I was possessed by an evil force. I am a person with a good and bad personality. Sometimes I am not able to dominate this dark side. I pray, I pray, but I cannot resist and then I chase after women. I wished that they would not go with me into the park, that they would run away.

Francisco de Assiss Pereira, 'The Park Maniac', serial killer

I have an idea: first I want to say that I want you every night. It's very good. I think you're hot, fiery. You're close to me, inside my heart [...] I want you [...] I love you from the bottom of my heart. Do not lose hope, believe in God, because someday we will meet.

Extract from a letter sent to Pereira while he was in prison.
He was sent over a thousand love letters a month.

He would punch me in the stomach and slap me in the face.

Thayna, a trans woman Pereira lived with for over a year.

It's grim reading, the case study of the Park Maniac.

Francisco de Assis Pereira is born on November 29th, 1967, in São Paulo.

As a kid, pre-adolescent but old enough to get a hard-on, he's raped by a maternal aunt. Not long after this, he develops a pathological fixation on breasts. Leme's not sure what this means. He's not sure he understands the connection exactly, either. But some doctor has mapped it out, joined the dots and crossed the t in trauma –

———

Então, it is what it is. *Fixation* is the key word. Pathology is a subject Leme only knows about when it's used as an excuse for some unspeakable crime.

And it's grim reading.

It doesn't get any easier for the lad, life.

In his first job, he's raped by his (male) boss who then pimps him out to other older gay men. On one of these 'dates', Leme reads, a man – some Goth type, all makeup and tattoos, back-combed hair, *piercings* Leme reads – almost tears off Pereira's cock. It's not clear in the report exactly how he's gone about it, this Goth, and Leme's glad about that.

This provokes another pathological fixation in Pereira: losing his penis.

This connection Leme understands a bit better than the previous.

A consequence of the Goth encounter is that Pereira feels fairly intense pain when having sex.

A different shrink states that it is the impossibility of pleasure during sex that has proven to be a major factor in Pereira's violence, a form of retribution, if you like.

Leme ain't green, but he is well out of his depth here, darkness-wise.

Pereira lives with a trans woman, Thayna, who states that Pereira regularly punches her in the stomach and slaps her in the face.

Leme reads that this is also the case with the victims that survived his attempts to rape and murder them.

Pereira arrows in on women who are suffering from emotional discomfort, low self-esteem, all that. He works as a motorcycle courier, using his bike to take his victims to secluded places. It's a puzzler that they trusted him to do so. Your average rapist/murderer tends to use force rather than rely on persuasion.

It's more persuasive, force.

Equally, less chance of failure and therefore less chance of getting caught.

Pereira uses shoelaces to strangle his victims after raping them.

Leme skims murder files.

Elisângela Francisco da Silva was a twenty-one-year-old from Paraná, who was living with her aunt Solange Barbosa in São Paulo from 1996. She was from a poor family and had left school when she was still young. She had worked, she had *grafted*, for years and years. She and a friend visited Shopping Eldorado, the big west zone mall in São Paulo, not too posh, but not too shabby. She told her aunt she'd be two hours. At the end of the day, Elisângela Francisco da Silva's friend waved her goodbye to go on a date. They'd had a good time. They'd had some lunch, watched a movie, bought some clothes. Elisângela Francisco da Silva's naked body was found in Parque Ibirapuera. It took three days to identify her, the decomposition was so bad.

Twenty-three-year-old Raquel Mota Rodrigues had one ambition, which was to earn money in São Paulo to send back to her family in Gravataí, Rio Grande do Sul. She liked to have a good time with friends, going to bars, restaurants, the odd club, but never stayed out later than midnight. She worked as a saleswoman in a furniture shop in Pinheiros. One night on her way home, she called her cousin Lígia, she was going to be later than expected, she'd met this nice young man who'd asked her to do some modelling work for him and she was going to go for it. It was easy money, a real opportunity. Her cousin told her, in no uncertain terms, that she should absolutely *not* do that, she shouldn't go anywhere with some guy she'd met on the metro, however nice he appeared, whatever work he was offering. Raquel Mota Rodrigues told her cousin she was right, of course she wouldn't go, she was excited and feeling like she needed a boost, you understand. Her cousin did understand, told her to come home and they'd have dinner, a nice time. Raquel Mota Rodrigues's body was found buried in a shallow grave in the bushes of a park on the outskirts of the city.

Selma Ferreira Queiroz was just a kid, the youngest of three sisters, hoping to graduate from high school and then to study accounting or computer science. She had a part-time job working in a drugstore. She was fired, however, and there were complications. According to her boss, she demanded some kind of compensation, there was an argument, and, eventually, she left to go and meet her boyfriend. The '98 World Cup was on, and they were going to watch the Brazil match together. She called him en route to say she'd be late, that the work thing had been a nightmare, she was crying and angry and couldn't wait to see him. Selma's naked body was found in the State Park. She'd been raped and beaten. There were bite marks on her shoulders, her breasts, her legs. She had been strangled. A shoelace was tied loose around her neck, like jewellery.

Patrícia Gonçalves Marinho was twenty-four years old and wanted to be a model. She'd never shared this dream with anyone. She lived with her grandmother Josefa. Not much else is known. Her body was discovered in a secluded area of the State Park. She had been raped, beaten and strangled. Her clothes and her jewellery were the only means by which to identity her.

Leme breathes, shakes, balks.

He greys, his face greys, and he thinks –

What does this tell me about my case?

He doesn't know.

The usual suspects tried to do Pereira in prison, dressed up your basic gangbanger shank job as a minor riot. It didn't stick. Pereira was smart enough to hear about it and hide.

Leme reads that Pereira's married now – a prison ceremony, which must have been charming – some kook who wants to feel his ripped-up cock between her legs. Leme seethes, seethes at his own anger. The kook is some lawyer chick, clever, so it says. Pereira gets thousands of love letters every week. *Thousands.*

What the fuck is wrong with people?

Leme doesn't know. He has no fucking idea.

He gets on the blower to Silva. Time to collaborate.

Bocão, Big Mouth, *former escort:*

Guilt. Hate. Fury –

It's getting pretty late.

You've stood here for hours.

You should go now, there's no one in his house.

But what if someone arrives and you're not here? You want to see what that old fuck is up to. Desgraçado. Vagabundo. How could he do this to you?

You should go in there, confront him.

You can't. But you should.

You might be getting this wrong. You hope so, sabe, it may have all been innocent. But you've been here, haven't you? You've been watching. You've seen and you know you're right. Veado. Velhino. How did this happen? Filho da puta.

How did everything change?

Weekends were spent in Guarujá at Paddy's house in the Marina.

The house was small, but elegantly furnished with a swimming pool in the garden. In the evenings, we'd eat a simple dinner and drink wine in the fading light, slapping mosquitoes and listening to the shrill rhythm of the cicadas.

'Do you want to go out?' Paddy would ask.

'I'm fine here. With you.'

'Good. Me too. The city is always horribly overcrowded at the weekends.'

'It's nicer just the two of us.'

'You're right. There's no need to see anyone else.'

'Don't you ever have other people here?'

'Sometimes. Not often. Occasionally schoolteachers, when they first arrive and I have to be nice to them. Make them feel at home. I've had the governors here. The odd friend.'

'You've never invited me to any of these things.'

'I like to keep you to myself.'

Once, emboldened by wine, I decided to pursue this. 'Do people know about me?'

'Only the people that matter.'

'Who are they?'

'You and me.'

I left it there. I didn't want to think about what that might mean. You and me. I said it aloud. You and me: I liked the way it made me feel.

One afternoon, when I was watering the plants, Paddy's neighbours thought I was a boy who worked in the garden. I didn't correct them. I told Paddy the same evening.

'It's just that normally I'm here alone or with a group of older people,' he said. 'That's all. You're so young.'

I never spoke to the neighbours again. If I saw them, I'd duck my head and keep out of the way.

The best thing about those weekends: Paddy would teach me about books and art and he'd help me with my English, which was improving slowly.

'You see this one,' he'd say, looking at the prints hanging around the house. 'See how the women look predatory, angular. Look at the African influence. It's as if they're wearing masks. The two in the middle are taller, so appear more threatening.'

'They don't look realistic.'

'No, they don't. But they're not an abstraction. That came later in his work.'

'And the colours: they're like carnival.'

'Again, it's an interpretation.' He gestured at the curves in the painting. 'It's supposed to be unsettling.'

'Different.'

'This was painted almost fifty years earlier. It's a development of the traditional nude. Think about most paintings of naked women.' He turned to me and smiled. 'How do they make you feel?'

'Not sure. They're like objects. Soft. I don't really know much about women.'

The truth was that I didn't give a toss about the paintings, but I was thrilled to be asked about them. They represented an opportunity, a different life: one in which I was asked my opinion on things.

'This is a different aesthetic. Look at the background. It is not recognisably anything. And the women are almost frightening. This is a street scene.'

'The women are prostitutes.'

'Yes. And they're judging you. Us. The people looking at them.'

'I know that look.'

'Yes, well.'

'I like this one.'

And I'd feel as if I was offering him something beyond the obvious, giving him a chance to do what he does best: to teach. I didn't think that I was a project of his.

I just felt like I was his.

A long way from the life I had before. When he knew me as Bocão. Talking about paintings together, I really believed that I'd escaped it.

'Your husband called me the other day.'

Renata says nothing, gives Silva the ironic eyebrow.

'Yeah,' Silva says. 'He called me about a case. Ghastly fucking business it is, this copycat serial killer. Real gruesome.'

Renata nods. This is an unwelcome power play and she's not going to let Silva think he's got the upper hand, that he's senior partner in their arrangement.

It's pure wind-up; she's here in good faith.

Renata smiles. 'I don't envy him. I'm proud of him.'

Silva nods. 'That's nice.'

'If you're being funny, you can fetch the horse from the rain, filho.'

Silva laughs. 'Good one.'

'I'm not joking. Let's just get on with this.'

'Good plan.'

Renata shuffles papers. They're sitting in a café in Jardins. She's drinking a sparkling water. Silva's chugging coffee.

Renata says, 'My office played a part in the sale of land in Paraisópolis to Casa Nova, this you know, né?'

Silva nods.

'We acted as mediator, helped with some local knowledge, expedited some paperwork, sabe?'

'Yeah. Local knowledge.'

Renata ignores this. 'Property law's complicated, it's about making sure people are treated right, right?' she says. 'The work's started, viu? It's done. It's what happens next that's interesting.'

'Lot of money in these contracts. Clearing the land, waste disposal, state government materials to organise. Lot of money. Lot of contracts.'

Renata's turn to nod.

'Mendes Construction is an umbrella company,' Silva says. 'Subsidiaries do all sorts of shit.'

'Clearing the land, waste disposal, materials – '

Silva grins. 'É isso ai,' he says.

'You're sure this is how it works?'

'More interesting is how your old employers are involved.'

Renata's heart sinks. She's nodding, she has a good idea.

'Lot of Capital SP interest in Mendes Construction, one way or another. Singapore Project contracts make money. They're also part of the Bolsa Família cash, too. But you know this, ne?'

'Mais ou menos.'

'That's honest at least.'

'We're trying to help the community. A bunch of our seed money was from Capital SP, philanthropy, entendeu?'

'Tax break for helping the poor.'

'Either way.'

'You know one scam that was running a few years ago? Bolsa Família thing.'

Renata shakes her head. She doesn't like this.

'A hell of a number of applications turned out to be for people who didn't exist, the deceased and whatnot. It's a tasty extra income, that bank card you get.'

Renata nods. She understands – Dona Regina's cousin. 'I've heard that, yeah,' she says.

'Question is what you want to do next, like you said.'

'I read that report you wrote,' Renata says.

'But you can't help with that.'

Renata shakes her head.

'Ray Marx,' Silva says.

'Yep.'

They sit for a moment. Renata knows there is an angle here. She can do nothing, officially; Silva can do his job and she does some good. And it appears he knows some things – or can do a little digging. She doesn't know for sure, of course – but still.

She says, 'I can let you have the paperwork for the Paraisópolis sale.'

'I can get hold of that in a number of different ways.'

'Thank you.'

'And the story is layers of interest. Your basic questionable contract bidding. Winner takes all.'

'What happened to your face?'
'You should see the other guy.'
'I bet his knuckles hurt like hell.'
'Okay, querida, turn it in.'
Renata smiles. 'Coincidence, is it?'
'It's not my first barbecue, entendeu?'
Renata nods. 'It's happened before.'
'I've got a tip for you. There's another project, in the centre. Displaced locals need legal advice. Shall I pass on your details?'
'You've got your fingers in a lot of pies.'
'I'm like Batman, querida.'
'Yeah, sure, that's what we do.'
Silva stands. 'See?' he says. 'It's good to be on the same team.'
'Thanks, coach.'
Renata watches him leave. It *is* good, she thinks.

Next day, two representatives from a community group in the Centro favela visit Renata at her office. Her new part-time colleague Gerson takes down their particulars. He's a sweetheart, old Gerson, and Renata's delighted she's been able to employ him, give him a chance to earn some dough after suffering an accident that meant he lost all his labourer work. He's loyal to a fault and it's endearing. Renata reckons he'll do anything she asks, which might come in handy, she thinks, a bit of blind obedience and a desire to help out. A man who knows his way around, knows his way about the place, who might be altogether a bit more *useful* than he makes out, could be very helpful indeed, what with these choppy waters they're now navigating. Renata smiles; she feels powerful having these kinds of thoughts, however half-hearted, however light-hearted they are in truth.

The representatives tell Renata they've heard their homes are going to be cleared to make way for a huge project built in time for the World Cup in 2014. They use the phrase: *complete Centro experience*. Renata knows what that means. *Money*. Very expensive living complex. They might let some of the current residents work as maids and security guards when the building's finished. Though it's a risk, as they'd be disgruntled and with employee insider knowledge. No, most likely these residents are in trouble. Renata sighs.

The representatives tell her they believe they're to be relocated; compensation is minimal and only in financial terms. There is, it seems, no promises to rehouse. There's a lot of families; a lot of children to think about.

Renata doesn't like the look of it at all.

'You better get your old City Hall contact on the phone,' she says to Fernanda.

Fernanda raises an eyebrow, does what she's told.

'You're coming with, mate, end of.'

Rafa looks into Franginho's eyes. He's not messing about, Rafa. No senhor. Revenge is a dish best served cold and all that. It's time to pay the Swing Motel a visit.

Franginho, Rafa thinks, looks uncertain.

'Porra,' he says, 'what exactly are we going to achieve, eh?'

'Not the point, cara. You're coming, certo?'

Franginho huffs and puffs. 'No good, son, will come of this.'

'It's decided. We're doing it.'

Rafa is dead set on doing this, though he's not entirely sure what *this* is just yet. All he knows is he wants to scare the fuckers that run the place and make sure they know that he, Rafa, is not going to be messed about, is not going to *mess about*. He's waited for a long time to do it; he's wanted to make sure that Carolina thinks he's over it, that it's forgotten, his humiliation. He doesn't want her to know he's planning on a little muscle work, a little of the old show them who's boss –

Rafa stung badly that day, a few months before.

It's rankled and burned, and he's been planning on *something* for ages. Today's the day as Carolina is out of town for a little while with family; there's no way she's going to know what he's up to. He doesn't, end of the day, want to disappoint her.

But the desire for revenge is overwhelming. It's closure, is what it is.

Franginho sighs, says, 'Fine.'

Rafa knew he would; course he would, he's a mate, after all. That's what you do.

Franginho sorts out a reliable motor: a rust-bucket, shit-heap of a car they can ditch if they have to, and they head down there at a little before midday.

Rafa drives. They sit in silence, Franginho furiously texting.

'You with me, porra?' Rafa says.

'Meu, leave it out, eh?'

Rafa sucks his teeth. He's nervous; he won't admit it. He feels the cold heft of the handgun tucked into his belt. It's not loaded; it's safer. The pair of them have always been careful not to swing too far, outlaw-wise. They're businessmen, not gangbangers. Gunfire of any sort is dangerous. You don't get tagged, you're a lot more likely to end up pinched. Safety first. Neither of them fancies the death of some schmuck on their conscience.

But the old favela education they've had climbing the ranks means they don't accept it when people take the piss. And the security guy at the Swing Motel certainly did that. Respect, sabe?

Rafa is impressed with his own discipline, waiting this long to return.

He wonders if the cunt will even recognise him.

He'll certainly not forget him after today.

Rafa playbooks it. 'This is what we do. We pull up as if we're going to get a room.'

Franginho snorts. 'You'll be lucky, mate.'

'You keep your head down, right? You could pass for pussy, your frame. Nice little skinny bitch with no tits. Crack whore chic, sabe? All the rage these days, your androgynous type.'

Franginho smiles. Franginho drips sarcasm. 'Good to see you're not taking this too seriously, amigo. Perhaps I can persuade you to rethink. You don't look quite the right demographic for a bird like that, after all.'

Rafa ignores this. 'Nem fodendo.' *No fucking way.* 'I get out the car, you too, show the weapons, tell the guy we know where he lives, know where his family lives, tell him we'll be back to collect, falou?'

'Very original, Scarface.'

'I just want to scare the fucker, that's all. Have the prick on edge for a little while.'

'What if he's holding?'

'It's got to be bulletproof glass. He'll have to come out. He won't.'

Franginho weighs this, goes *sounds about right, I certainly wouldn't*.

They ghost down Avenida Morumbi.

They wriggle through Real Parque.

The condominium buildings thrust up either side –

Rafa says, 'Shape up, porra. Almost there.'

The traffic on the slip road where the motel sits is quiet. It's on their left now, a dozen or so yards up ahead.

Rafa cranks gears. Rafa floors it, pedal to the metal, foot to the floor –

The car screeches up the slope. He hammers the brakes and they squeal to a halt.

Rafa jumps out first. Franginho follows. The same security guy behind the glass, behind the counter –

His hands go up. Rafa's face set in an evil little leer –

Weapons out. Rafa taps the glass with his. The security gorilla backs away, shaking his head.

Rafa's shaking but jacked up, primed –

Franginho behind, head down, arms crossed –

Then:

The crunch of a vehicle slammed to a stop. A single siren wail, a blue-red flash.

Rafa turns, confused, eyes dart –

Franginho panics, Rafa sees, goes for the car.

Rafa turns back. The security guard scarpers out the back door of his office, into the motel, out of sight.

Behind their rust-bucket, shit-heap of a motor: a Militar SUV blocking their exit.

Two Militars, one behind the driver's door, one behind the passenger –

Crouched, weapons drawn, trained on Rafa and Franginho.

Shouts, threats.

Rafa's hands go up. Franginho's hands go up. They place their weapons on the ground. They link their fingers behind their heads. They kneel, heads bowed. They know the drill.

Rafa's thinking: *what the fuck*? Rafa's scared now, terrified, bewildered –

A large, bald bulldog of a Militar climbs out the back of the SUV. 'Hello, boys,' he says.

Rafa looks him in the eye. He *knows* this bulldog. He remembers this bulldog from years before. He saw this bulldog put bullets into old Lanky and Garibaldo. He saw this bulldog put bullets into their backs.

Rafa thinks: *what the fuck just happened*?

What the fuck just happened, Rafa is now finding out, fifteen minutes later, is very fucking far from what he imagined was happening, on his knees, hands behind his head, yelled at by ferocious-looking, automatic-weapon-toting Militars.

Rafa thought it might be game over then, full time, final whistle, tears and permanent relegation, all that jazz.

Now, sitting in the back of the Militar SUV, wedged in between Franginho and the bulldog, he sees that there is most definitely extra time and penalties on the menu.

He ain't happy about it, mind. He doesn't trust this bulldog an inch.

'You can trust me, Rafa, falou?' the bulldog says. 'What choice you got, porra?'

The bulldog laughs. Rafa sits tight.

The bulldog goes on. 'All we need from you is to act as a go-between for us with your little girlfriend. Maybe make an introduction.'

'And say I don't want to?' Rafa says.

'You having a laugh, kid? We've just got you for a botched hold-up job at the Swing Motel, armed and dangerous. Plenty of witnesses.'

Rafa nods. It's a fair point. They could yet pop them both and make the timeline work out, too, of course.

Rafa says, 'This isn't going to work out badly for her then?'

'I'm a perfect gentleman, porra. Chicks are off limits. You don't get your knickers in a twist or your cock in a knot and it'll all be rosy.'

'I still don't understand *why*,' Rafa says.

'Don't you worry about that, son. Your clever little friend here Little Chicken will fill you in.'

Rafa looks sharply at Franginho. 'You knew – he *knew* about this?'

The bulldog barks grim laughter. Rafa eyes Franginho. Franginho does not look happy at all. He looks spooked, distinctly frightened by the situation.

'He didn't know, Rafa, course he didn't. What I mean is that *we* know he's a clever cookie.'

'Yeah.'

'And we also know what you've been up to with your little girlfriend.'

'Pervert.'

'Watch it, son.'

'I am watching it.'

'How do you think we crashed your motel party, eh? We fucking followed you, Einstein. Nobody sneaks out of the favela in a car like that to do a good turn we don't know about it, sabe?'

Rafa bites his lip.

'Rafa, mate,' the bulldog says, a little more gently. 'We're not trying to get in the way of your trading arrangement, certo? You're entitled to make a little bank out of these students, we realise that, live and let live, right? It's free market capitalism, so crack on.'

Rafa nods.

'As for your extracurricular, Romeo, I'm very much a whatever floats your boat kind of a fella. We won't get in the way there, either. Sleep easy. Or hopefully not, am I right?'

The other Militars laugh at this.

'I suppose I don't got much choice.'

'No, you do not.'

Rafa knows he's going to agree to whatever it is he's told to agree to.

He's known it since the proposition was put to him. Well, *instruction*. Hardly a proposition when you're being *told* which way you're going to get fucked.

And you don't walk away from a scene like this unless you *do* agree.

He and Franginho can figure out what they're actually going to do later.

This little performance is all about respect, about showing the world he will not be messed about. At least he can say that about something today.

'All right, chief, you're on,' Rafa says.

'Good lad.' The bulldog opens the door. 'You can walk home, boys.'

'Hey, Fat Frank,' Ray says, 'you know the Dixie Chicks?'

Silva eye-rolls. Ray grins. 'I do not,' Silva says.

'Three cute girls from Texas, Frank, real sweethearts.'

'That where you're from, is it? I pegged you for old-school East Coast.'

'Texas forever, Fat Frank, never forget it.'

'Jesus.'

'Anyway, the Chicks are sweet ole country charm, but with teeth, right?'

'Okay.'

'When Bush Junior decided he wanted to get into a pissing contest with his pa and go after Saddam, the Chicks didn't like it, told the world they were embarrassed Big George was from Texas.'

'Were *you*?'

Ray makes a face: *easy*. 'I was *in* eye-raq, sunshine.'

'Texas forever.'

'Very good, Frank. Anyhoo, point is they make their statement, they get death threats, it's an ugly, unedifying business for us all, they don't need that, they're artists. Damn cute artists.'

'Então?' Silva says. *What's your point?*

'So what do they do about it? They write a song that wins about fifteen Grammys. They go on Oprah. They get to *work*.'

'What's the song?'

'Doesn't matter, Frank, point *is* they write it.'

Ray's grinning wider now. Silva, he thinks, looks a little confused.

'Look, Fat Frank, I'll spell it out for you. Take a look at your face. There's your death threat. Now *you* get to work, certo?'

'Ah, I get it,' Silva says. 'Very clever.'

'Good lad.'

'I'm not exactly sure though that people are going to buy this story. It's too good to be true. Even if it is *actually* true, sabe?'

Ray gives it the trust me, son. 'You ever been to an ice cream truck, Frank, when you were in our fine country?'

Silva gestured at his form. 'What do you think, *Ray*?'

'It's a fair point. Anyway, big guy, those trucks have that sound, you know, telling the kids they're in the neighbourhood and every-one scarpers over and it's a whole white picket fence doo-lah-lah and birds are singing and you get the picture.'

'It's a vivid one.'

'Anyway, a college buddy of mine and I were having a beer one time in the park.'

'Classy.'

'Yeah,' Ray says, 'a real pot kettle black, that one.'

Silva laughs.

Rays goes on. 'So we're having a beer, we're, I guess, mid-twenties, my buddy's from the Midwest, wrong side of the tracks kind of a guy, but a worker, you know?'

Silva nods.

'So we're having a beer and we hear the old ice cream truck jingle, and we see kids scarpering towards the sound and my buddy says, poor kids. And I say what? And he says, that sound means the truck is all out of ice cream. And I say nothing. And he says, yeah, that's what my mom always told us.'

Silva's nodding but Ray reckons he doesn't know why.

Ray says, 'Later, I realise his mom couldn't afford the ice creams and no one had ever told him otherwise.'

'That's pretty extraordinary, that it never came up.'

'Maybe, maybe not. Not once you're all growed up, I guess.'

'Maybe,' Silva says. 'Ray, I'm going to say it again, but what's your point?'

Ray grins. 'My point, Frank, is that people will believe anything you tell them.'

'That's a good pep talk, Ray.'

'Write the story, Frank, that's all I'm saying.'

'Okay.'

'Palocci's a clown. This'll stick. And we've got something else in reserve, too.'

'I still don't really understand your interest in all this, Ray.'

Ray taps his nose. Ray throws notes at the table. He stands. 'Go get yourself an ice cream, son,' he says.

Ray leaves, broad-grinning.

Sex party season is in full swing.

Swing being the right word, of course. Christ, but aren't there a lot of old pervs in this world, Anna thinks? What *is* it about wrinkled old men and young women anyway? What's the *point* of it, really? She's been watching, she can't deny that, as a sort of sociological experiment. The decor of the Astúrias Motel is quite something. There's a lot of faux greenery, tree murals. The experiment goes like this:

If an old, powerful man fails to achieve wood in the forest of the Astúrias Motel, does anyone hear it?

It must be exhausting, all this *failure*. The women go from room to room, the men hammer away at them until everyone's satisfied that no one's satisfied, and the carousel continues.

'I've never seen so many drooping backsides bobbing about in all my life,' she tells Ray.

'I'd hope not,' Ray says.

'How many more times do we have to do this?' Anna asks.

'What Rasputin wants, Rasputin gets.'

So here she is.

The set-up is simplicity itself and all taken care of, cash guarantee. The motel entrance is straight off the Marginal just beyond the shopping mall, Eldorado. Pretty central and easy to find. The swank, blacked-out windowed cars pull in. They give a name at the door – normally an alias, obviously – get a room number and the driver ghosts into a courtyard. The courtyard is surrounded by garages, rooms above, in a square. This number is marked clearly on the garage door. Your usual punter pulls towards their assigned garage, which opens automatically as their car approaches. This usual punter pulls in and the garage door closes automatically behind. Total discretion. There is a single staircase leading up, and when this usual punter reaches the top, they look down on a swimming pool and sauna area, and through to the left, a bedroom, all mirrored ceilings and walk-in shower in the en suite. Not all the rooms are like this; only the best. What your usual punter doesn't realise: each of *these* rooms is connected by a narrow corridor that runs alongside. Entry is only through an anonymous dumb waiter. Point is, you can order a beer, some champagne, a fucking full meal, and a lackey zips down this narrow corridor and delivers a tray through a hatch, either side of which is protected from view. No one sees anyone. That's the whole point.

Which is pretty useful for the sort of scam Anna is running.

What Anna's done is book out all the suites – Suite Mansões, all of them, the best fuck pad options that exist in this establishment, high quality, high price – at the top end of the courtyard. And she's arranged for a blacked-out SUV to wait in the middle of the courtyard. When a partygoer arrives, Anna has a word with the driver, a welcoming smile, an explanation of how the rich old man sitting in the back seat will be assigned his own room, but that various women will be coming in and out, and not to worry, Anna's looking after the schedule and logistics. Also, that should the rich old man sitting in the back seat wish to fraternise with any of the other partygoers, all he need do is send word to Anna via the driver and it'll be arranged.

This set-up is good for the whole day and night, as long as anyone needs. And in the SUV, sit Anna – in and out, clipboard – and an IT guy monitoring everything, recording everything on his laptop, which is connected to the cameras and microphones that have been placed in every room that Anna has booked.

Which is why Anna's been seeing a lot more drooping backsides than she's used to. So far, it's worked a treat. And the reason for that is that everyone trusts Anna. *Everyone.* And that's because everyone trusts Rasputin. Because Anna and Rasputin lead back to Marta. And whether she knows about any of this – which is highly unlikely – there is not a cat's chance in hell that either Anna or Rasputin would compromise Marta.

It's very persuasive, trust, Anna thinks.

That and the money that's changing hands, indirectly, in the contract negotiations going on in dressing gowns and saunas, between bouts of futile from-behind hammering.

Anna's heard a phrase: *don't break the law when you're breaking the law*.

The idea of course is if you're, say, drink driving, perhaps don't put on loud music and do coke in a layby.

This scene is the exact opposite. It's a lot easier to trust someone in a kickback arrangement when you both know where exactly the finer points of the contract were thrashed out.

Rasputin's a clever fucker: complicity equals surety, in business. This merry-go-round was a masterstroke. A total love-in.

Anna's almost sad about the betrayal that's on the cards. *Almost*.

So here she is, again.

Anna slides into the SUV's passenger seat. The IT guy is in the back, laptop-hunched. There's a stern-looking driver beside her. He's said about three words throughout all of this. Seems staunch, discreet, Anna reckons. He's paid enough to be, that's for sure.

Anna sips coffee. She turns to the back seat. 'Anything you want to share?'

The IT guy snorts. 'There's a lot, querida,' he says, 'that you probably don't want to know about.'

'Sometimes,' Anna says, 'I wish your computer set-up wasn't quite so efficient. Bit more buffering, sabe?'

'Buffering. Nice one.'

Anna smiles.

The IT guy says, 'They're each sticking to their own rooms, so far.'

Anna nods. This isn't great news, but the night is young, she thinks. Well, the afternoon. 'Keep an eye on it,' she says.

They sit in silence for a moment. There's a stillness in the courtyard, the sound of traffic on the Marginal distant. A low hum, the tangible buzz of heat and metal.

Anna says, 'How is it you know old Ray Marx anyway?'

'Who?' the IT guy says. 'Ray who?'

Anna smiles, shakes her head. 'Never mind. Forget I asked.'

Of course he doesn't know Big Ray. Sometimes she wishes she

didn't either. That said, this dirty business might produce change, maybe. That's what she tells herself.

A car pulls into the courtyard. A low-rise, sophisticated car, a Jaguar, Anna sees. Black windows, a world class engine growl, idling as it is.

Customer.

Anna pops the door and goes to greet the driver.

The driver's window buzzes quietly down. Anna looks in.

'Welcome,' she says.

The driver's in sunglasses, an earpiece, a well-cut suit.

He says, 'What are you doing?'

Anna hesitates. 'I – '

'I think you're confused, menina.' Menina. *Girl.* 'This is nothing to do with you, okay? Step back, certo?'

Anna steps back.

She shoots a look behind the driver's seat. She sees two figures, a man and a woman. The woman leans forward to say something to the driver as his window rises.

Anna clocks her face. Anna knows her face. She sees the man. She knows him too. Well, she knows who he *isn't*.

Anna turns, bites her lip. Scoots back to the SUV.

The IT guy is chewing messily on a sandwich. Anna smells meat, onions.

He says, 'What was that all about?'

'Nothing.' Anna shakes her head. She's smiling, coy. 'Misunderstanding.'

The IT guy points over his shoulder. 'Yeah, look. Not one of our rooms, love. Just an old-school lunchtime quickie.' He laughs, coughs on his food. 'Lucky sod.'

Anna laughs. She's thinking, yeah, *lucky*.

The woman: Juliana Mendes, wife of Jorge Mendes, former Secretario de Obras, big man in the construction game, a real kickback merchant.

The man: Anna doesn't know him.

But she *does* know that it isn't old Jorge Mendes.

Well, well, she thinks. *Interesting.*

Bocão, Big Mouth, *former escort:*

Anger. Shame.

You see lights switched on upstairs.

Imagine him walking from room to room: using the bathroom, getting undressed, preparing himself for another visit.

You curse.

Picture the details of the house: the books lining the shelves; the shiny appliances in the kitchen, rarely used; the flat screen television, a European film playing quietly in the background; the expensive suits in the wardrobe. These were your details too.

Silver cufflinks left on the hallway table. Your gift to him.

You see the wooden floors and carpeted staircase. You've walked barefoot in there. You were welcome, ne? It could've been home.

You look down the street. There is a faint triangle of light in the window of the security guard's booth. You move behind a tree so that he won't see you.

The light upstairs is switched off and the lamp in the hall shines through the window. He's sipping a whiskey on the sofa, half-watching the film. Waiting for who? You mouth the words. For who?

He should be waiting for you.

You check your phone. Again. Nothing. He hasn't called. He doesn't call anymore. You think about calling him, maybe sending him a message: sleep well, I miss you. That kind of thing.

But that's not enough, sabe?

A car passes slowly. An old Volkswagen, black, coated in dust. Someone has written me limpa on the back window. Clean me. You sink back against the wall behind the tree. The car pauses at the bend in the road up ahead. The driver pokes his head out of the window, looking at the numbers on the houses. He reverses and for a moment you think he is the visitor.

Anger swells. You move into the light. Something startles the driver and the car stops and then moves quickly away. He must have seen you. He must have known who you are.

This can't go on.

Juliana Mendes, at home:

I'm sitting in the kitchen sipping a second glass of wine when Jorge arrives. His top button is undone and he looks tired. He leans down to kiss me and smiles wearily.

'How are you?'

I smile back. 'Okay.'

Jorge goes to the fridge and pulls out the bottle of wine and pours himself a drink. He takes off his jacket and sits down opposite me, placing the bottle between us.

'Are you ready to eat?' I ask.

'In a minute. Let me have a drink first.'

I nod. The maid is hovering in the kitchen. I tell her to leave us alone for ten minutes then come in and serve dinner. She nods, puts a glass she was drying in the cupboard and leaves.

'I had a meeting but it was over quicker than expected.' He takes out his BlackBerry. The red light is flashing. 'Porra,' he says. 'I need to answer this.'

We sit, the tapping interrupting the silence. He frowns and puts the BlackBerry down on the table. Almost immediately, the red light starts flashing again. 'Christ,' he says. He reaches for it and then changes his mind. 'No, I'll leave it until after dinner.'

I refill his glass.

The maid comes back in. She spoons pasta onto two plates and washes lettuce leaves, chops an onion and tomato and mixes the salad in a bowl. We help ourselves and drizzle olive oil and balsamic vinegar on top. With a look, I dismiss the maid. She can clear up when we finish.

We eat quietly. I pick at the food, not wanting to eat carbs so late. Jorge looks thoughtful. He pours wine for the two of us. The al dente pasta is slightly underdone – I'll need to have a word with the maid – but the sauce is excellent, light, a sprinkling of parsley, grated parmesan on top, finely chopped red onion and green pepper, and, if I'm not mistaken, a hint of basil.

We finish eating and leave the plates for the maid to clear. Jorge takes his glass of wine to his study where he needs to do a little work before going to bed. I sit in the kitchen and watch the maid go about her simple tasks. She rinses the plates and puts them in the dishwasher. Takes the remaining pasta and salad and stores it in Tupperware dishes, placing them in the fridge. Washes up the saucepans and leaves them on the rack by the sink to dry. I tell her that she is not needed again and she nods and leaves for her own quarters at the back of the house on the ground floor. We bought her a small, flat screen television for her birthday this year so that she can watch her favourite telenovelas (we often watch the daytime soaps together).

I sip my wine. I decide to go and watch television on the first floor. As I pass Jorge's office, I hear him talking on the phone. A floorboard creaks and I stand dead still. Jorge's back is to the door, but I can hear his voice.

'If it comes to that,' he is saying, 'then we'll take care of it. As we always do. I'll make a call. If he does come snooping around here, he'll find nothing. There's the problem of the woman. I want you to look into that. Cut all ties and cover it up. Write it off as tax. Yes, yes, but we have to pay it occasionally. This'll be a neat way around it. We don't have to worry. To be sure, just do as I say. I'll call you if I hear any news. Stop worrying. Good. Ciao.'

I tiptoe down the hall and slip quietly into our lounge. I find a film to watch and settle into the sofa. The day's exertions pull at my limbs. I doze off, the film halfway through, the lights on.

When I awake, Jorge is carrying me to bed. I remember how much I love him. I would, I think, do just about anything for him.

The next morning, I wake up. Fifty-seven point four kilos. I dress in a pale blue Adidas tracksuit and go down to the kitchen. My breakfast is waiting for me – scrambled egg whites, sliced papaya and mango, a piece of dry wholemeal toast and a cup of black coffee. My driver takes me across the road to Clube Paineiras and I spend an hour on the treadmill, watching the arrests on News Channel 10. I sit in the steam room for fifteen minutes and shower. My driver takes me down the road into Real Parque where I have my nails done – hands and feet, in burgundy – my eyebrows threaded and a full wax.

Back at home there is a text message from Sophia, the mother of one of my son's close friends. This is a surprise. A group of parents are meeting for lunch. Come! I check the time. A little before twelve. I call my driver on the intercom and tell him we'll be leaving in fifteen minutes or so. I go upstairs and change into a Dolce & Gabbana dress and a pair of sandals. Another text message, this time from Leonardo. He wants to see me, and I feel myself smile, blush, my pulse quicken.

I say goodbye to the maid, leave her instructions for the afternoon – I want all the bedsheets washed and changed – and head out the front door where my car is waiting. I give my driver directions and settle back in the leather seats, scrolling through emails on my Black-Berry, the city obscured by the car's tinted windows.

I spend the afternoon at home. I keep an eye on the maid, and she goes about her work satisfactorily. Otherwise, I read *Caras* and *Veja* in the living room and watch soaps.

Jorge arrives a little after seven. He is looking flustered but smiles and kisses me.

'I need to do some more work,' he says. 'I'll be in my study.'

I nod. 'When would you like to have dinner?'

'Someone is coming over at about eight to see me,' he says. 'We can eat after that.'

'Okay,' I say, though there is something about his tone that makes me suspicious, the way he doesn't quite look me in the eye. I think about the phone call I overheard last night and wonder if this has anything to do with it.

I decide to wait in the kitchen where I have a view of the front courtyard and any cars or visitors that will arrive. I pour myself a glass of white wine and spread low fat cream cheese on a wholemeal cracker. I ask the maid what we might have for dinner and she tells me she has prepared chicken stroganoff. I ask if the sauce is a light one and she confirms that it is. I sit and watch the clock, wait for the lights to come on in the yard, signalling an arrival.

At eight o'clock exactly, a car pulls in. A nondescript, black hatch-back. A man wearing a white shirt and black tie gets out and Jorge lets him in. I hear them go up the stairs and down the corridor to Jorge's office.

I drink my wine, wait.

Leme thinks – tell Silva everything.

So he brings him in. Sets him up in the shit-can office Leme shares with Lisboa.

The three of them, cramped, sitting on desks, propped against the door, guzzle black coffee – wary of each other. The light filtered through the dirty glass is urine yellow.

Leme doesn't have very high hopes.

'Look,' Silva is saying, 'copycat crime is all about media representation as much as anything else.'

Lisboa growls something about course it fucking is. *Journalists*.

Leme raises a finger. 'What do you mean?'

'A particular crime might be gruesome as fuck, right? Park Maniac is a good example. Nasty murders, nasty MO, nasty motivation, the lad's backstory is both tragic and awful.'

'Not sure about that, son,' Lisboa says.

'I mean,' Silva says, 'you can *almost* sympathise with one or two of the bad luck stories of his youth, but you are also appalled by his behaviour *outside* of the actual crimes.'

'Which means – '

'Which means you have a character people can believe in. A story that can run and run, like a novel, entendeu? All about believable character.'

'This is bullshit,' Lisboa says. 'He's a real person, an actual murderer. Believable character, what does that even mean? Ta viagando, porra.' *You're travelling, way off the mark, mate.*

'In the media he's a character. He's a story.'

'Fucking journos.'

Leme gives it the placatory palms up, calm down, lads.

Lisboa says, 'The point is the Park Maniac took up a lot of press, a lot of attention, was a sensation and was sensationalised, see the difference?'

Lisboa raises eyebrows. Leme glares. Lisboa says, 'Go on, Marshall McLuhan.'

Silva smiles. His face says: *Really?*

'Yes, mate,' Lisboa says. 'What, you think a brute like me can't dig a little theory?'

Leme's shaking his head. 'Jesus,' he says. He looks at Silva. 'Week one, media training, detective school. Okay?' He looks at both men. 'Chega, ne?' *Enough already.* Both men nod.

'So the point is,' Silva says, 'the copycat criminal is inspired by the media coverage, the *attention*.'

'And the nature of the crime itself is incidental then?'

'Maybe, maybe not.'

'Okay, you copy the crime as you reckon that way you'll get the same or better coverage?'

'Mais ou menos.'

Leme mulls this over. 'What about the fact that most copycat crimes are committed by people who have a pre-existing tendency to criminal behaviour? You know, prior record, mental health problems, history of violence growing up, et cetera.'

'Okay, so it's the nature of the crime. Shock value and horror. I think those are the terms I've read. That's what they're after. High shock, real horror. That gets the headlines.'

Leme nods. Lisboa nods. He says, 'This fits in with your hair-brained theory, Mario.' He shoots Silva a look to say *well, you know*. 'More or less.'

'What's the theory?'

Leme nods at Lisboa. He wants to hear it come out of someone else's mouth.

Lisboa clears throat – serious rattle. 'Okay, so Mario here reckons the Lockwood murder was a stitch-up and that there is a good chance he was offed by a rent boy in a crime of passion.' Lisboa eyes Leme. 'Fair enough?'

'More or less,' Leme says. He looks at Silva. 'It's a simplification, but you know...'

Silva makes a face: *okay, okay.*

Lisboa goes on. 'There's one thing missing from Lockwood's house, a paperweight, suggestion being it's the murder weapon and also maybe a gift from his randy young lover. The same paperweight, at least the same *type*, shows up at the crime scene for this copycat business. Years later. So Mario here thinks it's a message.'

'The message being *catch me*,' Silva says.

'Maybe.'

'Interesting,' Silva says. 'So Lockwood's actual murderer is using these crimes as a cry for help. And he's using Leme as a conduit.'

Lisboa smiles. 'Lucky you, mate. Couldn't he have sent a postcard?'

'It's age-old, copycat crime,' Silva says. 'Nowadays you have psychopaths dressed as superheroes shooting up shopping malls. In the Middle Ages, it was crimes invoking magic, the devil, that kind of thing. Same reason: attention.'

Leme nods.

'And you have nothing, evidence-wise?'

Leme shakes his head. Lisboa says, 'There were leads. They've gone cold. The victims, and this is the *real* point, are a trans woman who'd gone off grid and a male sex worker.'

'Meaning?'

'Meaning no one gives a fuck.'

They sit in silence for a few moments. Leme lets this sink in. He knows it, always has.

The existence of the investigation in itself is enough for his superiors.

There has never been any need to solve the crime.

And, of course, the Lockwood stitch-up –

Who knows how deep that runs?

Silva's talking again, 'Then there's all the psychological profile factors, right, your personality disorders, a lack of identity, social isolation, alienation? The confusion regarding the perceived positive response to violence and crime in society – the media seems to *celebrate* the crime and the criminal.'

'I mean,' Lisboa admits, 'you might not be a million miles away, Mario.'

'I'm not sure how I can help you?' Silva says.

Leme says, 'How about a piece that plays all this down? Writes it off, somehow.'

'Suck the air out of the attention sort of a thing?'

'Yeah, exactly. Maybe focus on the victims and not the murderer, entendeu?'

'At this stage,' Lisboa says, 'we're more interested in preventing any more murders than we are hopeful of catching the cunt.'

Silva nods. He says, 'You know the name of the guy who took the fall for the Lockwood job? One of those unreleased identities, if I remember.'

Lisboa says, 'We don't.' He looks at Leme. Leme shake his head.

Leme watches Silva take this in. Watches his mind tick-tock about.

Silva says, 'Sergio Nascimento. A name I've heard.'

'From Paraisópolis?'

Silva nods.

Leme goes *woah*. Lisboa's eyes wide. *Sergio Nascimento*. Annette Nascimento – Paddy Lockwood's maid. There it is – simple. Favela link, então.

There it is.

'He's dead.'

Leme nods. 'We know.'

'Mothers' Day weekend. Militar snuff, I've heard. PCC collusion.'

'Figures.'

There it is. The patsy –

The lemon.

'No one'll go on the record. I've heard it was a loose-end scenario. I've heard there were a few of those tied up that weekend.'

Leme thinks – that's exactly right.

Silva says, 'You're not going to do anything with this?'

Leme and Lisboa shake heads.

'It's like that?'

'It is,' Leme says. 'It's exactly like that.'

'I can write the story,' Silva says.

Leme nods. 'Go and talk to the lad's mum,' he says. 'Annette Nascimento.'

There it is.

Rafa works out a clever, and fiendishly simple, plan.

After all, what's the difference between investing cash in Carolina's political group and selling them moody fireworks and knock-off gear?

All he's got to do is think of a reason why they would chuck some money into the Black Bloc pot. And the only credible reason is that he's out to make some money for himself – and for the favela firm, too.

He puts the problem to Franginho.

'For whatever fucking reason,' he says, 'Carlos here wants us to give Carolina's gang some untraceable dinheiro that he's going to provide, right?'

Franginho nods. He's working on a particularly big, particularly good coxinha from Dona Regina's. He chews, Rafa thinks, thoughtfully.

He says, 'I wouldn't trust Carlos as far as I could wrestle him, mate.'

'Really not much help.'

Franginho shrugs.

Rafa never told Franginho what he saw, what, five years ago now, that night of the rebellion. Carlos whacking Garibaldo and old Lanky, shooting them in the back and pocketing cash. Rafa never said a word to anyone about that. What good would it do? When asked, he said he'd gone to the boca and they weren't there. It was a lie he could easily pretend was true. And it *was* true, to a point. When he arrived, they weren't there, to all intents, after all.

Rafa's also not sure why any mention of Carlos and Franginho sort of closes up, doesn't really engage. It might be fear – it was pretty fucking scary down at the Swing Motel and Rafa *knows* what Carlos is capable of – but it might be something else and Rafa can't fathom it. It's like Franginho has stopped caring, somehow. Something in him seems dead, like he's lost his spark. He's surly, more cynical than usual these last few weeks – they're just not having as much fun as they used to. And they always had that, their fun. Whatever was going on, whatever the odds, they always had each other.

Rafa wonders if it might not be the fact that Rafa's getting laid and Franginho isn't. That Rafa's fallen in love – and Franginho realises he's playing second fiddle.

Which is true, now. Because Rafa *has* fallen in love, and guess what? Suddenly your mates are just that, mates, no matter how important they are, how far they go back, there are some things *now* where they do play second fiddle, when you're in love. Maybe love means your priorities change. Maybe Rafa is growing up.

He remembers that it was Franginho who passed on the original message that the bulldog wanted to meet, *way* before the whole motel shakedown business.

Rafa doesn't want to think too much about *that*.

After all, he thinks *again*, it wouldn't be the first time a favelado's been approached by a Militar about a bit of work. Happens all the time. It's how the careful balance is kept basically workable.

'So what you're asking,' Franginho says, 'is how we can give your girlfriend a bag of money that seems credible, you know, for *us*.'

'Bingo.'

'Well, that's easy,' Franginho says. 'Tell her you love her and you want to help.'

Rafa doesn't much like his friend's tone. But, he reasons, it *is* the truth.

He does love her and he does want to help and doing this, one way or another, *will* help.

'Yeah,' he says, 'I can do that.'

Renata and Fernanda are doing the company accounts. Their Capital SP funding is healthier than ever. They both know it's your basic tax write-off, this funding, but it remains, and it enables them to do their work, do the good work that they do. And there hasn't been any interference, any requests that really equal demands. Capital SP hasn't used them directly for anything for a long time.

'You haven't heard from anyone there for a while, have you?' Renata asks.

Fernanda shakes her head. 'Nothing for years,' she says.

Renata nods. 'I wonder what happened to old Ray Marx,' she says.

'No idea,' Fernanda says. 'He's – what do you call it? – an enigma wrapped in a puzzle.'

Renata laughs. 'Your big swinging dick,' she says. 'Typical Yank.'

Fernanda laughs a bitter laugh. 'He'll be around, one way or another,' she adds.

'The Singapore Project build is progressing,' Renata says. 'That means they're making money, I suppose. And they clearly appreciate *that*.'

Renata watches Fernanda take that in.

They sit in silence for a beat.

'We haven't done anything wrong there,' Fernanda says.

'We haven't. We've worked for the community, helped facilitate change, sabe?'

'We have.'

They study numbers, tick off incomings, outgoings.

Fernanda says, 'That trip to Brasília, in November, remember?'

'I remember.'

'I'll be gone two days. Meeting our City Hall contact, as I said.'

'I remember.'

'She says there's someone in the Ministry of Cities I should meet, might be useful.'

'It's worth a punt,' Renata sighs. 'Who knows, ne? We're a small part of a much bigger deal and if anyone in power really cares, you might find out who it is we should be talking to.'

'Exactly.'

'Take the time you need. It all takes time, querida.' Renata smiles. 'Next week I'm meeting that community group in the Centro again,' she says. 'They need someone to lobby for them. This Mendes Construction deal is a clusterfuck.'

'See what you can do, ne?'

'Exactly that.'

They smile at each other.

Renata, once again, as she has almost every day since she set up this legal aid office, feels like she's both making a difference and at the same time involved in a futile, Sisyphean struggle to *actually make a difference*.

She's not really sure she'd have it any other way.

Juliana Mendes, at home:

I wake up and Jorge has already gone.

I roll over onto his side of the bed, which is still warm, still fragrant with the smell of his Ralph Lauren aftershave. Last night, he had tried to forget about his visitor. He asked about my day, we ate a nice dinner. In bed he was restless, but from the gentle massage I gave him he became aroused and we made love, quietly and unhurriedly. I luxuriate now in the space left between us. We slept well and I am late getting up. I am not meeting Leonardo until two o'clock, and so will not need to leave until about one-fifteen.

As I had a fair amount of stroganoff last night, I only have fruit – papaya, mango and kiwi – for breakfast with a small cup of black coffee. Up 0.3 kilos. I will have to have a less greedy day today. My driver takes me to the club, where I do my usual hour on the treadmill and then fifteen minutes on the cross-trainer. I sit in the dry sauna for twenty minutes, feeling my limbs relax and my joints soften. I shower and change into a dark green cotton dress that comes on and off easily without getting creased. These little routines give purpose and direction to my mornings. I like to feel the tautness in my muscles, the light punishment of hard work, the reward of having completed it, a task, though self-set, still undeniably a chore; the feeling that one deserves a rest, a treat, an afternoon of pleasure.

I've thought about doing more charity work or getting more involved with the PTA, but I enjoy the time I have alone, and Jorge has always insisted that I don't work, that I remain a full-time mother. This role has changed over the years, obviously, and it has been hard to adapt to having an independent son. I sometimes yearn for the days when he truly needed me, when each little triumph or disaster of his day was reported in bursts of excitement or tears. That's what I have learned as a parent – things level out a little as their character forms and they become accustomed to the way in which they deal with pleasure and pain. If you know how you are going to react to something, the blow is softened; you simply do as your personality dictates. Fabio has reached that age now, and, though that gives satisfaction in itself, I miss the days of his uncertainty. His need.

I meet Leonardo in the valet parking area in Shopping Iguatemi. I get into the back of his car and the driver parks and gets out.

'I don't really have time to go anywhere today,' Leonardo says. 'But I wanted to talk.'

'Can't we go and get a coffee or something?'

'I think it's better we don't.'

We sit in silence for what feels like a long time.

He takes my hand in his. 'I missed you.' He leans over and kisses me and I kiss him back, enjoying the brief moment of passion, a little awkward in the confined space.

'I hear there was someone at your house last night.'

'I didn't meet him. He spoke to João.'

'Did your husband tell you what it was about?'

'He didn't say anything.'

Leonardo nods. 'You're sure you don't know why he was there?' he asks.

'I've no idea.'

Leonardo's phone rings. He looks down at the number, says: 'I have to take this.'

I sit quietly. Leonardo is speaking. 'Yes... yes, that's what I said. Of course. You know that, we all know that already. I've told you before. Look, I can't really talk about this now. No, it's not a good time. Just keep working. But be discreet. We don't need that Silva guy sniffing around.'

I wonder why he feels he can't talk with me sitting next to him. It's never stopped him before.

'I missed you too,' I say. I move closer towards him.

He moves slightly, imperceptibly away from me. 'It's going to be difficult to meet for a while,' he says.

'When do you think we can meet again?' I ask.

'Next week. Maybe Monday. I'll let you know. And you should tell me if anything...' he says.

He's talking about the man who came to visit Jorge the night before.

I nod. 'Sure.'

My voice is soft, almost inaudible. If my husband is hiding something from me, then it wouldn't be the first time.

Leonardo calls his driver and I get out of the car and decide to go down into the shopping centre for a little while. I wander among the luxury labels and feel, in the sterility of the air, a degree of calmness.

The afternoon passes slowly. I think about calling my husband.

In my experience, when you do something impulsive and deceitful, it comes back to haunt you. You need to think of every possible consequence of your action beforehand and how it can be explained away; knee-jerk decisions are harder to undo because the consequences play out before you even realise it. Before you know it, you are cornered into making an inadequate explanation and the implicit trust you have built over years disintegrates in a flash. I've no intention of that happening now.

I sit thumbing through *Hola* magazine, paying no attention to the roll call of the rich and famous who smile for the cameras, failing to notice, for a moment, my own picture, taken at a charity event held last month, smiling, composed, flanked by my husband and my lover.

I pour myself a small glass of white wine to help pass the time. I sit and quietly wait for my husband. My son is upstairs, working, playing, communicating.

I can do nothing. So I do nothing.

The badness in me throbs sometimes, pulses like a muscle spasm. I ignore it.

When Renata gets home, Mario is already there.

She's pleased – it feels, to her, like they haven't had an evening in together for a while.

Renata puts her bag down on the kitchen counter. 'Amor? You here?' she calls.

'Bedroom. Tou indo!' *I'm coming.*

Renata opens the fridge, opens Tupperware, picks out an olive and pops it in her mouth. She thinks about pouring herself a glass of wine –

'Well, well!' she says, laughing, as Mario looms in the doorway.

He grins, spreads his arms. 'What? You don't like what you see, querida?'

Renata's shaking her head. 'Very nice, bonitão. Very nice indeed.'
Bonitão. *Handsome devil.*

Renata says, 'So, you're going swimming, are you?'

Mario is in his sunga, a tight little black Speedo, a small towel
thrown over his shoulder, flip-flops and nothing else.

He says, 'Sauna, my love.' He postures – gives it the hard-bastard
stare. 'Man needs to relax a little, sweat some of this city out of his
pores, entendeu?'

'You wally,' Renata says.

Mario sucks his teeth. 'Don't be hating, sweetheart, it's not becoming,'

'Okay.'

'You wanna come with? I called downstairs, it'll be toasty about
now. Come on, come.' He points at the fridge. 'We'll take some
beers, it'll be fun.'

Renata's smiling, shaking her head. 'You're on, big boy.'

'Get changed. I'll wait.'

Renata kisses him. 'Give me two minutes.'

The condo sauna is a cool cavernous room, tiled in grey, a plunge
pool in the corner, just behind three powerful cold showers. There's
a steam room and a dry sauna. The water from the showers echoes
as it cascades to the floor. There is a row of plastic sun loungers and
they leave their towels and a small cooler bag with their beers on two
of them. Steam, first.

They sit in silence. The ceiling drips. The steam room has been
recently cleaned with the eucalyptus product the funcionarios use.
Renata squirts a touch more of it onto the floor. The hiss and smell
of it is sharp, soothing. It clears her sinuses. Mario reclines on the
top bench; Renata is perched just below. Renata feels Mario's hand
reach down and touch her shoulder. She rolls back into his touch,
murmurs that's nice, and closes her eyes. He kneads her neck in a
light massage, his fingertips firm, a light, insistent rhythm.

They both breathe in and out, and Renata feels herself drift, feels
her mind empty, feels –

'How was – '

'I don't want to talk about work, querido.'

The steam hisses, rises, fills the space.

'Que bom,' Mario says.

Great.

Renata angles her neck to kiss his hand. 'Okay,' she says. 'Shower.'

The cold water is icy violence.

Renata wants to jump back out straight away, but she sees Mario laughing at her, and she sticks to it, tries to breathe into the cold – she knows it takes a few jolting moments and then it's worth it. She moves each shoulder in turn underneath the torrent, steps forward a touch, lets it grip her lower back. She watches Mario in the corner of her eye, jumping from foot to foot, rubbing his body vigorously, letting the water pummel his belly.

She smiles to herself, turns to face the shower, angles first one thigh then the other, lets the water do its work. She ducks her head under the cold, gasps, rinses her hair, closes her eyes as the water hammers down on her face, turns it off.

Above the noise of the water skittering on the tiles, Mario says, 'Beer?' his fist closed, thumb up, jerking at his mouth. The universal Brazilian gesture that says, come on, vamos encher a cara. *Let's fill our faces.*

Renata nods. Yes. Beer.

They crack their cans and knock them, drink thirstily. Mario finishes his in two hefty gulps, crunches the can in his hand and tosses it on the floor, raises his arms, giving it the *come on then*. Renata laughs. They lie on the sun loungers, saying nothing.

It's a warm evening outside the sauna, despite it being mid-June. They can hear shouts and laughter from the condo bar, Mario's friends from the building drinking and telling stories, arguing about sport and politics, a competitive triage of women and manliness, enchendo saco – *taking the piss.*

Mario says, 'Might be nice to go for a jump?'

Renata nods, yes, why not, she thinks, the pool won't be so cold now the temperature outside is dropping.

They gather their things and leave the sauna, circle the low fence that rings the pool, enter through the little gate. There are kids playing in the shallow side, running and jumping from the small wooden decking areas that are half-submerged in the water, normally used by older kids for sunbathing and gossiping.

They head to the deeper part, place their towels and beers on sun loungers.

Mario winks, dives straight into the deep blue of the pool. Renata slides herself in from the side, slips down so that she's up to her neck. Mario is powering through the water, does a lap and turns. Renata floats into the middle of the pool.

The sun is a pink dot, radiating orange-red. From down here, the condo towers – all six of them visible from the pool – stretch up and up, lights on in some windows, the faint noise of food being prepared, parents unwinding, maids and nannies berating children. Clouds streak and glide – it's cool enough there won't be a storm, there rarely is at this time of year.

Mario's hands flap and rest, he flips onto his back, stretches out, kicks with his legs towards her.

She gathers him in her arms, holds him as his limbs reach out, keeping him on the surface.

The water laps at the side of the pool. The men's voices puncture the familial quiet that descends on the condo at this hour.

Mario points towards the bar. A particularly bawdy laugh. 'Nelson,' he says.

Renata flicks an eyebrow. *Oh good, Nelson*, she thinks. Not the most sophisticated of a group of fairly unsophisticated men.

'We could get a quick drink, if you like?' Mario says.

'Sure, in a minute. This is nice.'

Mario swivels, pulls himself up, treading water, pulls Renata into his body, a tight embrace.

His body feels cold, taut, his chest hair soft, his pores smooth – she feels the goose bumps on his neck.

'It *is* nice,' he says. 'I love you.'

Renata feels the insistent familiarity of that truth, her own goose bumps.

'I love you too,' she says. 'I love you,'

Later, they have that drink in the condo bar, the men are funny, their jokes spot on, they flatter-ridicule Mario in front of her, which makes Renata feel proud of him, proud of them.

They sleep well when they turn off the lights.

It was a good evening, she thinks, as she falls asleep.

Bocão, Big Mouth, *former escort:*

Hate.

The first time I saw another man leaving Paddy's house, I stopped sleeping. I got through the days on adrenalin and fear. A voice in my head told me what to do. You're worthless, nothing. Get up. Go to work. Look at numbers. You idiot. You deserve more. You deserve exactly this.

I returned regularly to Paddy's house at night, stood in the shadows watching his front door, watching the lights in his house until it all went dark. And then I stayed longer as the darkness thickened and the clouds glowed as the dawn light filtered through. I'd scuttle off to work and sit in a daze, oblivious to my colleagues, my only relationship a one-sided affair with the numbers on my screen. They couldn't reciprocate, couldn't offer any comfort.

My arms and legs were pockmarked with red blotches where I had scratched myself raw. You're nothing. You're nothing. At home, my sister grew worried.

'I know you go out at night,' she said. 'I can hear you. Sometimes you don't come back at all. What's going on?'

'It's nothing. I'm going out, that's all, *sabe?*'

'It doesn't seem like much of a life.'

'I don't interfere with your life, *sabe?*'

She stopped asking me what I was doing, after a while.

2
Heartbreaker

November 2011

Time doesn't stop.

Cazuza, musician

Bocão, Big Mouth, *former escort:*

Hate.

I went back to see Paddy. It was almost like it had been before, but I felt the creep of uncertainty. We lay in bed. I couldn't sleep. I replayed the conversation we'd had before Paddy dropped off.

'I've got a lot on the next few weeks.'

'Can I ask you something?'

'Very busy time at school. People coming in to look at the building.'

'I'm losing you.'

'And there's a few things I have to go to at the weekends, too.'

'Tell me there's no one else.'

'It'll be back to normal soon enough.'

'Ever since we went to the theatre…'

'Come a little closer.'

'I don't trust you anymore.'

'Closer.'

'It's how you make me feel.'

'Uh-huh. I'm tired.'

'You're not the same.'

'It'll be back to normal soon enough.'

'I don't believe you.'

'Sleep now. There.'

But I didn't. I lay there watching the light change through the curtains. In the morning, I got up before Paddy woke, dressed and went to work.

One evening, we thumbed through one of his coffee-table art books.

'See this one? Look at the way it is structured by the colour. There is no perspective but for the colour. Look where this red borders that red. It creates a change in place. Gives it depth.'

'Do you show other men your pictures?'

'It's by Matisse. *The Red Room*. Look at the objects. Fruit. A vase.'

'Do you fuck them?'

'Now look at the tablecloth. See the way the pattern is reflected on the wallpaper.'

'You do, don't you.'

Paddy laid his hand on mine. 'There's just this line here dividing the two. And the subtlest difference in shade. Can you see it?'

'No.'

'Good. Let's have a drink.'

I watched him leave the room, hoping, strangely, that he would never come back.

Jealousy –

No, something else. Disappointment. Then he called.

'Can you come over on Monday night? I want to talk.'

'You want to talk?' I was surprised.

'There are a few things I need to say.'

'Say them now.'

'Now's not a good time. I'll see you on Monday night? That okay?'

A beat. 'Okay.'

Okay.

It's been a busy few months for Dilma. Anna's impressed by her garra, her bottle. Dilma's hard-line, it turns out, and she isn't suffering fools.

Fool number one: Chief of Staff Antonio Palocci resigns in June after media reports reveal an unreasonably fast accumulation of wealth, much of which, the articles imply, come from Mensalão, the monthly payoff used by Lula to ensure cooperation within the broadly left-centre coalition and a majority in government. Of course, Anna has seen his negotiation techniques, where he conducts his business, and is sad there is no mention of this anywhere. Big Chief Palocci and his little staff. Anna is thrilled to bits that the sexist, miserable old fuck is going down, as it were.

Fool number two: early July, and Transport Minister Alfredo Nascimento takes off for home after corruption allegations fly unheeded in his ministry. Leaving on a private jet plane, no doubt.

Fool number three is Defence Minister Nelson Jobim. He resigns in early August, but it's a pre-emptive strike. He's not under any investigation himself but he's been making some fairly slanderous noises all over town about a whole bunch of other ministers, so he falls on his sword. This is too easy, Anna thinks.

Fool number four: Agriculture Minister Wagner Rossi. His chickens have come to roost, mid-August, with an internal scarecrow whistleblowing on all the money he's harvested as a sideline to the ministry's good works.

Fool number five Anna knows all about. It's September, a few months into the sex party season post-coital glow, and Tourism Minister Pedro Novais leaves office over the alleged misuse of public funds. Bon voyage, senhor.

Fool number six, Sports Minister Orlando Silva resigns in October. His was a dirty little scam, arranging millions of dollars' worth of kickbacks within a fund to promote sport for underprivileged children. Bem jogado. *Well played*.

There are two more fools that Anna has heard are heading for the chop, likely in the next month or so, depending on how deeply they've hidden their crimes.

Fool number seven is Labour Minister Carlos Lupi. Word on the street is, Anna's heard, he and his team have been extracting money from charities and NGOs in a straight-up quid pro quo for ministry funding. Let's see if his hard work pays off.

And, finally, to fool number eight, our good Development

Minister Fernando Pimentel. There are rumblings of a story soon to appear in print about something called 'influence peddling'. Anna smiles. She can't think of a joke for this one.

She doesn't have to –

The whole thing is a joke.

And Dilma, it seems to Anna, might well have the last laugh.

There's one thing though that troubles Anna:

Where, exactly, does the buck stop? At what point down the road will this mean the Workers' Party government becomes untenable?

Dilma might end up cutting off her nose to spite her face.

She's the head of this rabble, after all.

In the taxi to Congonhas airport, where they're getting their short-hop flight to Brasília, Ray says to Fernanda, 'When I first came to São Paulo, there were building-sized billboards advertising *Playboy*, remember them? Huge pictures of incredible women in lingerie looking down at the traffic. And incredible is the right word. They were barely credible, these women, these huge women. What happened to all that, anyway? Seems like a waste of good advertising space.'

'Is this you being charming?'

'I'm curious, is all.'

Ray's sensing Fernanda is not wholly behind his charm today, he doesn't know why. Usually it doesn't let him down, his charm. Must be getting her period, he thinks, with just enough self-awareness and irony to allow the thought – not voice it.

'Traffic accidents,' Fernanda says. 'They were causing traffic accidents.'

'Go figure.'

'Then, a few years ago, there was a state ban on billboard advertising in general, I forget why and exactly what.'

'Huh.'

'You get used to it, right, not seeing them.'

'You do get used to it,' Ray says. 'Funny, you don't realise you do until you realise you do.'

'You're a philosopher, Ray.'

'You are what you are, querida.'

Ray watches Fernanda's reaction to that. It's half-hearted, but it's there, he can see it. This little on-off on-again, semi-casual thing of theirs is a little tiring sometimes. Ray just wants to be loved, all things considered.

Fernanda tells the driver where to stop.

The neighbourhood around Congonhas is an unlovely place. And the airport isn't much better. No such thing as first class in a busy internal hub like this one. Ray thinks – they should have chartered private. That might have helped expedite the whole on-off thing in terms of knowing where they are.

Ray's not too bothered, truth be told. He popped a med at breakfast, and before that shot up the tiniest dose from his Mexican bottle, a dose to see him through the day, the one after that, that's all he needs. That's all his *needs* need. He's, so far, managed to resist trying to score in Brazil. It was easier to make a call international and have a couriered delivery from his beaner friends north of the border. He's used up a couple of favours, but it's led to enhanced productivity and his pal at Capital SP, old Huck, is happy with Ray's work. There's a considerable bonus check inked and waiting to be signed, sealed and cashed.

But that's peanuts compared to what he's banking up in Brasília. Ray's going deep – Ray's paying Geddel Vieira a visit.

Ray's going down to the Bunker.

On the plane, Fernanda's telling Ray a story, which he's only half-listening to, if that. He's got a can of Brahma on the go and a bag of nuts, and he's anxious not to miss the stewardess as there is definitely time for one more beer, maybe two, and that'll see him right through security and the no doubt filthy cab ride through the suburbs.

Fernanda's saying, 'On my first visit to Brasília, I'm taken to Niemeyer's modernist utopia to stay with cousins of my ex-boyfriend. He has millions of cousins. His mother is the youngest of ten or something like that. And they're all married and have millions of kids. Remembering their names is impossible – I identify them according to the manner of their greetings: a handshake, a hug, one kiss or two, even three, depending on the state they're from, or, most weirdly, an arm around the neck and an odd sort of belly rub. From a man. It feels strangely violating, and not in a good way, entendeu? They're hicks, is the point, some of them.'

Ray's still with her. There's something about a plane that allows for this kind of flowing monologue, he thinks. Maybe it's just that they're both facing forward – you're not embarrassed to go on and on.

'So his cousins live in one of the many rough, ugly satellite suburbs that crawl out from the quote unquote elegant Niemeyer centre. We spend a night drinking in a neighbourhood bar with a cousin whose name I forget but who is memorable to me for a recent hair transplant and for going to jail for tax fraud. Yeah, he was quite something. Anyway, okay, there is a desperation to the bar, drunkenness with no *alegría*, a sort of simmering possibility of violence or at least discord. It was not much fun.'

Ray grunts something supportive. This is how she talks.

'So I'm relieved when we head to the centre the next day to meet Ludmilla, a friend of mine from school who is working up there. We tour the major sights and then head to a bar by a lake where young, attractive men and women frolic about on jet-skis and do waterskiing tricks. It is exactly as I describe it, Ray. So Ludmilla lives on an estate not far from the centre. There are, it seems, hundreds of these estates, accessible from slip roads that lead from the main drag. They are all identical, only different combinations of numbers and letters distinguishing them. You've mentioned you've seen them, I think?'

'Sure have,' Ray says. He snags the stew, makes the universal gesture for mais uma, *another one*. He grins. 'They're a little communist in their style, you ask me. A little eastern bloc, eighties track-team digs, you know?'

'Very good, Ray.'

Ray mock bows, pulls an *I'm a funny guy* face.

The stew brings his beer. Ray smiles at her. She flashes teeth through hot pink lips.

'Anyway, Ludmilla takes us to a British-themed sort of castle for drinks, dinner, the place has a portcullis, a drawbridge, what the fuck, right? We're in there about an hour, hour and a half. And during this time, Ludmilla's car windows are smashed, the boot forced and all of our possessions are removed. Including my ex's passport. I might have omitted to say he's one of yours.'

'A man?'

'A Yank, Ray. Half-Brazilian, half-Yank, but one passport.'

'Groovy.'

'So then my experience of Brasília becomes even more fun as we traipse from police station to consulate, to passport office, to photo booth. Even getting a passport photo taken requires a very specific size – which I get wrong – a collared shirt or jacket – which we don't have – and a card which you hold up with the date – making my ex look like a criminal. We row throughout. Ludmilla seems pleased when she puts us on a bus to Caldas Novas – a hot springs resort – with a new bag containing two towels, three T-shirts, two toothbrushes and an Elmore Leonard novel – where we lounge around drinking cold beer. We row there too, on a visit to a waterpark: something about the 'lazy river' and an incident with an inflatable crocodile and my ex hitting on a group of *Paulistana* women on a hen weekend. I storm off and spend several hours drinking caipirinha with old men in Speedos sitting in what feels like filthy bathwater.'

'Sounds my kind of bar.'

'Point is, Ray, I hate Brasília.'

Ray throws nuts into his mouth, washes them down with beer.

'But you like me,' he says. 'It's going to be just fine.'

Briefing –

Delegacia, early doors.

Leme ditches his car in the underground car park. Grease and dirt, oil and engine, boxes of rubbish, damp –

Into the lift. Up and up. Clean air and a/c roaring.

Outside Lagnado's office – Lisboa waits.

Leme sits next to him. They raise eyebrows, touch hands.

They know what this briefing entails.

Lagnado's door opens. That's as much of a welcome as they get.

They shuffle in. Lagnado makes a face: *sit down*. They sit.

'So what do we call this guy now, then?' he says. 'The Park Maniac Two? Park Maniac: The Return of the Park Maniac?'

There's no humour in his voice – no black comedy.

'It's November. There were victims in January and March. Nothing since. You have nothing. I think it's time we put these cases on ice, let them go cold. Issue a statement that says there is no evidence of a connection between them, tragic occurrences of violent, despicable hate crimes, outsiders murdered in some appalling way for some appalling reason – or whatever the euphemism for fuck-ups is. If we're really lucky you might find a suicide case who fits the bill. That'd work, profile-wise. You understand?'

They understand.

Lagnado goes on, 'That journo mate of yours did a decent job in July calming the whole business down. That article sets this up. We issue a statement, get him to do a low-key cover of it and we're done. Certo?'

Leme twitches. Lisboa raises a finger. Leme sees it, nods, says nothing. Leme seethes.

'Public don't care about hate crimes and their victims, boys. Not the public that matter, at least. A couple of weirdos and paedos having their coats buttoned does *not* matter, however sick and disgusting the MO. It doesn't look like we have a serial killer situation. That means priorities elsewhere. It's a manpower thing. We need you doing something more useful.'

Leme stays silent. Lisboa twitches.

Lagnado says, 'You're good boys, know your limits, sabe? You've got success. You helped nail the British headmaster murderer your first case, it's not forgotten.'

Leme thinks: *that's not how it felt.*

He says, 'We think there's a connection between that and the two murders this year.'

Lisboa eye-rolls, tenses. Leme sees him think: *leave it, mate.*

Lagnado smiles. 'Eight years apart, a confession, a very different MO. That was open and closed. You did the right thing. There's no connection.'

'I'm not sure we had the right man.'

'It's a little late for that.'

'There is a connection, a missing piece from Lockwood's house – '

'Coincidence. And I know what you're talking about, lad. You think I don't know every little thing you've been doing on and off for years? It's over; leave it. I'm moving you on, right, to something better.'

Lisboa says, 'It was part of the investigation, senhor, that's all, seemed worth pursuing, dead end, sabe?'

'It's good that you looked into it, leave it there – a necessary part of your job. A job you've done to the best of your abilities.'

Leme thinks: *okay, got it*. He runs it, spells it out:

There can't be a connection, as a connection suggests they got the wrong man for Lockwood, suggests Lockwood was a different man than everyone thought and they can't have that.

Give up, son, he thinks. Lagnado's right –

It's over.

'Jog on, lads,' Lagnado says. 'Have the rest of the week off and come back Monday morning, fresh. You'll be working under Alvarenga for a bit. He needs a couple of sharp minds and I suggested you two. He was pleased.'

They nod. They stand and leave.

At the lift, Lisboa says, 'I like Alvarenga, he's a good man, it's a result.'

Leme nods. Leme says, 'It's a relief, if I'm honest, sort of.'

'Yeah.'

'It was fucking grim, all that. And it's all there, you know, you just have to look. Scratch the surface and it's all there just beneath. And just above.'

'São Paulo, mate.'

'So good they named it twice.'

Lisboa laughs. 'That's funny,' he says. 'São Paulo state and all.'

'Funny 'cos it's true. São Paulo, São Paulo,' Leme half-sings, 'start spreading the news –'

'That's a different song, porra.'

'Come on,' Leme says. 'We're on holiday, I'll buy you a beer.'

Lisboa nods. 'You better.'

Renata's beginning to understand that Dilma's zero-tolerance policy on corruption playing out in the media along with these ministerial firings and resignations, means that Casa Nova and Mendes Construction and anyone involved in Singapore Project buildings or community-based projects are not going to take any risks whatsoever in who they talk to and deal with.

Renata realises that to help the community group in the Centro, she's going to seriously piss off exactly these people.

Why? They don't want anything to get in the way of the project. The goal, so to speak, is the World Cup and the money it's going to generate. Back of the net, she thinks wryly, a Mario phrase, that one.

What she needs to do, she thinks, watching the sky redden through her open office window, feeling the temperature crack and drop, hearing the end of day buzz down below in the bar, in Dona Regina's por kilo restaurant, is make sure she keeps everything about the residents and the legal processes of their rehousing, relocation – and steer well away from any sort of insinuation.

Stirring things up will not be beneficial for anyone, least of all the community.

She needs to tread carefully; she needs to make sure Silva holds off a little with his story. She's lucky he likes her – they both know what they know.

Onwards.

'This will be the last one for the year, certo?'

Rafa nods. The Militar hands him a bag – hands Rafa a bag full of cash.

'And why's that then?' Rafa asks.

'Holiday period, mate,' the Militar shrugs. 'I don't fucking know.'

'That's the word from old Carlão then, is it?'

The Militar shakes his head. 'Porra, don't shoot the messenger, eh?'

'I wasn't planning to,' Rafa winks, 'unless the messenger was planning to shoot me.'

'Very good, son, now fuck off out of it.'

Rafa grins. 'We'll see you in the New Year then, porra.'

The Militar flicks his hand, but he's smiling. He turns back, says, 'Progress report due then, certo?'

'What's a progress report?'

'How the fuck should I know?' he says. 'Don't shoot the messenger, entendeu?'

He mounts his motorbike and guns the engine, skidding down the edge-of-favela road where they've met, in a boca de fumo on the south side of Paraisópolis.

Rafa jumps in the waiting car.

Franginho pulls away. 'What was that about?' Franginho asks.

'Progress report.'

'You what?'

'That's what *I* said.'

They amble down side streets. Franginho raises a finger to each person they pass that they know. It's quite a few.

'Então?'

'They want a progress report in the New Year.'

'What – they've given us bags and we've passed them on, let's call that progress then, that sort of thing?'

'I mean, that'd be the truth of it.'

'But not what they want.'

'Nah, I suspect we both know what they want.'

It's early. Kids are drifting down to the bus stop. They watch mock arguments, boys throwing each other's bags into ditches, behind sacks of rubbish, construction debris. Slinging bits of plywood and brick at each other, well, *towards* each other.

There's been a lot of construction debris since the Singapore Project got under way properly. Rafa and Franginho haven't been back to the Portakabin for donkeys'.

Franginho spins the wheel right and they pull over by Zé Bolacha's bar – *Joe Biscuit's* – for some world class breakfast.

'You best chat to your bird then,' Franginho says, climbing out. 'Find out what the fuck she's been doing with all that cash.'

Rafa knows exactly what she's been doing with all that cash, but he ain't going to tell Franginho – not yet – and he sure as mustard ain't putting it in some progress report for Carlão or anyone else.

Rafa slaps Franginho on the back. 'Grand slam breakfast, amigo, my treat.'

'Lead the way,' Franginho laughs.

Rafa smiles. He'll tell him – *soon*.

Ray leaves Fernanda and Anna chatting in the hotel bar and a car picks him up and drives him an hour or so out of Brasília.

Ray sleeps off the plane beers and the two more he had at check-in. The hotel is new-build swank – it reeks of money. From a distance, Ray thinks, it looks like a giant, expensive ashtray. It's all glass and reinforced steel – like a bank vault. It's a clever fucker, this hotel. With all the glass – and even the rooms are made out of glass – it takes some high-level trickery, some real *chicanery*, to give anyone any privacy at all. It's like an igloo, the hotel – an igloo made of money.

Ray dozes. This is an off-the-books exercise, and neither Fernanda nor Anna knows what he's up to. He told them he was meeting Little Johnny, his man on the lamb, which is true. They eye-rolled and went *yeah, yeah, Ray, you're a real big dog*. Ray let them and winked as he left.

Course, he is meeting Little Johnny – at the gates of the Bunker.

The conversation with Anna was circular and largely satisfying.

Ray runs it; it went something like this:

Anna: The Ministry of Cities is set on kicking some money into
the Paraisópolis project. Idea is long-term community growth.
Basically, they want the favela to no longer resemble a favela.
Ray: So a flagship project?
Anna: Exactly. Success equals further investment in other similar
sites.
Ray: Ka-ching.
Fernanda: How did you make it work?
Anna: Politics, querida.
Fernanda: What does that mean?
Ray: Blackmail.
Anna: I'd call it influence peddling, a term I not long ago learned.
Fernanda: Okay.

Anna: The money from the ministry is going – among other places – into a company called Casa Nova, which you know, and which is connected to Mendes Construction.

Fernanda: Course it is.

Ray: Syndicate-building means always relying on money you can rely on.

Fernanda: Why are you talking in riddles, Ray?

Ray: You put your money into a decent product, like any other commodity.

Anna: The investment will benefit the community, regardless of where it comes from – and where it goes.

Fernanda: How does that work?

Anna: You'll be on the ground to help administer it, to mediate, to make sure that it does.

Ray: At least that some of it does.

Fernanda: And the rest?

Ray: Price of doing business.

Anna: There's just one condition.

Fernanda: I don't like the sound of that.

Anna: They want your boss to keep her nose out of the project in the Centro that Mendes Construction is engaged in.

Fernanda: I'm fairly sure she won't accept that.

Anna: This is lobbying, querida. Negotiation.

Ray: And that will be the next project after Paraisópolis, am I right?

Anna: You are right, Ray.

Fernanda: It'll be too late for the residents by then.

Ray: Tell us again how you got this through?

Anna: Mendes fancies a return to front bench politics what with everyone important turning out to be a scumbag. Rasputin offered a clear run in São Paulo, a clean bill of health.

Ray: He can offer that, can he?

Anna: What he can offer is to keep a certain amount of fruity information to himself.

Ray: It's my understanding that Mendes is no dirty perv.

Anna: No, but his wife might be.

Ray: Outstanding.

Fernanda: I'm going to pretend I didn't hear any of that.
Anna: You didn't need to, amiga. Someone will have a word with
 your boss – if they already haven't. This is context.
Ray: This is politics.

Ray is pleased with that line.

Ray engages his driver with a little political chit chat. 'Who do you like?' he says. 'The gyppo or the slag?' Lula or Dilma is the implication.

Ray's driver smiles. 'It's six of one, half a dozen of the other, am I right?'

Ray laughs. 'You've a career in politics, young man,' he says.

Ray's driver says, 'Why I live in Brasília, senhor.'

'People live *here*?'

Ray's driver drives. Ray sinks back into his seat.

Anna tells Fernanda what she knows about the Ministry of Cities.

'So the ministry is trying to achieve a goal of seven million units to make up the housing deficit, certo? It's brave, it's a noble idea. But to do this, the ministry allocated ninety-four per cent of its housing budget to private construction companies. Which means what? Money. Which means profit, which means no one gives a fuck about the quality of the units or the people in them, ne? They're paying something like up to a hundred thousand reais for each unit, and they're real basic in terms of size and requirements for water and sewerage. Now here's the real kicker: these private construction companies are helping select the sites. How do you maximise profit within the set costs? You build inadequate housing on the edge of town where land is cheap, falou? You slide the municipal officials a taster and they rubber stamp it. Bingo. The ministry is funding roads to nowhere, to wasteland, so that the construction companies can then build on it. And everyone's palms are greased on the way up and down. It's pure bubble right now and it can't last. Some good can come of it, that's true, but it will collapse. Best get in now, is my view.'

'Okay,' Fernanda says. 'A kind of urban utopian dream soured by money.'

Anna smiles. She likes Fernanda. 'That's exactly what it is. It's just not quite turned. I'd give it five more years.'

Fernanda nods. 'Well, we might as well milk it while we can.'

'I think,' Anna says, 'that's what you call a mixed metaphor.'

Fernanda grins. 'Another drink?'

The Bunker is misleadingly named.

Ray's driver delivers him to what looks like a private, low-rise condo. Seguranças man a check-in point. They jabber into radios. A segurança looms his huge bulk into the driver's window. Ray's driver makes noises. The segurança peers. Ray gives it the *howdy partner*. The segurança flicks a look: *turn it in*. Ray winks. The segurança pushes a button and a serious-looking gate swings open.

The car ghosts into the complex. The sun bakes concrete blocks. The tarmac shivers and hums. The houses are uniform basic: white cinder, flat roofs, parched grass in front –

Cars gleam and flash bulletproof windows. One after another, white house after white house, line after line of them like a suburban white picket fence Midwest nightmare. The houses crack faint lines in fresh white paint in the sun.

Ray clocks – no one.

This condo scene is middle-of-nowhere, faux-swank, slap bang in hick territory, Shitsville. Dirty men in big hats toil by security fences. They toss debris onto the back of horse-led carts. The horses look bored. Their tails swat flies. Their shit roasts in the sun, stinking up the place. The carts look precarious.

Ray thinks: new-build chic.

Ray thinks: who the fuck ever comes *here*?

Ray knows the answer to this, of course, to a point.

Ray's driver reaches the end of the complex and drifts to a stop outside the last house in a long line. There is another car parked just ahead. Leaning back against it: Little Johnny.

Ray jumps out. Little Johnny grins. Ray says, 'Nice place you've got here.'

'Let me give you the tour, Big Ray.'

'Outstanding,' Ray says. 'Will there be beer?'

Little Johnny laughs. 'There's not much else, senhor.'

Ray smiles. 'I've said it before, but Little Johnny, you're a heartbreaker.'

'Follow me.'

Ray leans back into his car, pulls his leather grip from the back seat, his leather grip with its false panel.

Little Johnny eyes it. 'We're going to need a bigger bag,' he says.

Ray *grins*.

Anna and Fernanda are still drinking.

Turns out it's a lot of fun, drinking, Anna thinks, when you're sitting with a not-quite friend and confiding, *sharing*.

The hotel bar is air-con cool and the cocktails are punchy and they're going down so smoothly that's it hard to conceive of *not* ordering another one –

'Can I tell you something?' Fernanda says.

Anna nods. They have, after all, prefaced a number of conversations with variations on that question. 'Claro, querida,' Anna says. *Of course.* 'Just nothing about what Ray's like in the sack.'

'I don't think *Ray* knows what Ray's like in the sack, amiga.'

They laugh. Anna smiles. 'Anything you want,' she says.

'Part of the reason why Ray and I are still working together – '

'*Working* together?'

'I'm serious – working.' Anna nods. Fernanda goes on. 'Part of the reason is that I'm kind of in his pocket.'

'Right.'

'Remember 2006, the weekend rebellion, Mothers' Day?'

'I do remember that.'

'Ray pushed a whole load of admin work our way to expedite prisoner furlough weekend passes, certo?'

'How did he do that?'

'I guess he made a connection. There was a recording of a meeting, up here, actually, and, well I'm not sure how, but Ray hooked us up with the work.'

'You got paid.'

'Yeah. *I* did.'

'What do you mean?'

'Ray asked me to keep it a freelance job.'

'Right.'

'But I needed the office resources, so, you know.'

'Your boss doesn't know.'

Fernanda nods.

Anna thinks: *interesting*. She also thinks: *it happens, it's no big deal.*

'And I got rid of the files after the fact. And not just those. We'd been doing a lot of Bolsa Família applications. You know about them, ne?'

Anna nods.

'Well it turns out that we might have been played there too.'

'Huh.'

'Yeah, the favela boys were making up IDs, people who are dead, people who never existed, to get the bank cards and the cash.'

'Seems a lot of effort for not a huge amount of money, ne?'

'It's about being in the system. After that, there's a lot you can do. It's leverage over the community, it's a persuasive thing to have. Useful.'

'So what?'

'I chucked the files that prove we did this, same time I chucked the others.'

'On purpose?'

'Not exactly.'

They drink their punchy drinks. Anna makes a sympathetic face, the right noises. She *likes* Fernanda.

'Why are you telling me now?' Anna says, but soft, being nice. 'It was years ago. I mean, I'm glad to listen, but, you know, I don't know if there's anything to do about it, sabe?'

Fernanda smiles. 'I just feel guilty is what it is. My boss is wonderful, we're doing a good job, I feel bad.'

'You did the right thing, menina, you know.'

'I think I did.'

'You just forget about it, think of the positives. And Big Ray? You could piss on the man's boots and tell him it's raining.'

They both laugh. Anna sees Fernanda breathe deep and knows she's done the right thing. Anna thinks: *my turn.*

'Well, Ray's got me over a barrel too, you know.'

'Really?'

Anna tells Fernanda the whole sex-party shakedown.

'But,' she says, 'we haven't actually had to use it. It's been kept quiet, as back-up, insurance.'

'So you're fine?'

Anna ums and ahs, weighs the question, bobs her head. 'If Marta and Rasputin knew, I'd be fucked.'

'And you care?'

'Marta, yes. But, in the end, she didn't know *anything*, so really it's just Rasputin I might have stitched up.'

'And you don't mind that.'

Anna smiles. 'No, I don't. The man's a total operator.'

'And this way you're doing some good.'

'Yeah, I guess so.'

Fernanda makes a face. 'You did the right thing, menina, you know,' she says.

Anna smiles.

Rasputin is, she thinks, a cunt. He'd let her take a fall before owning up to eating the last biscuit.

She never liked him; he was always a piece of work.

'I think so,' Anna says. She smiles. 'This is therapy is what we're doing.'

'É isso aí, amiga.'

That's exactly what it is.

Renata's ready to go home.

The phone rings before she can.

'Quem fala?' she says. *Who's this?*

'If you continue trying to help the resident community group in the Centro development project,' a cold, calm, female voice says, 'some information you don't want public will be made public.'

Renata bites. 'What information?'

'May 2006.'

Renata hangs up the phone. She knows exactly what that refers to –

Files. Her missing files. She takes off her coat, sits back down.

She's not going home now after all.

Rafa and Carolina are packing their bags and loading her car with provisions. It's a squeeze –

The holdalls full of money are especially cumbersome. Rafa worked a false panel in the back to keep it safe. He's calling it the loot boot. Carolina is not as amused by that as he thought she would be.

Nerves, he thinks.

It takes *nerve* to up and leave.

And however long you've been planning it, when the day comes, it's pretty tense. They're down in the garage of Carolina's parents' condo. The parents are away at their fazenda. Their *farm*.

Rafa's learning that when wealthy families spend time at their country piles, they like to say they're at their farm. Like, you know, they're tilling the soil or some shit. What they're doing is having the help mix their drinks and cut their lawns.

Rafa wants to live on a farm. And that's where this plan came from:

Need and desire to leave this place, this city, this desperate place, this desperate city, leave his home, Paraisópolis –

Get the hell out of Paradise City. That's the plan.

And the money from the bulldog is making it happen.

That was the simple part of the plan: keep the money.

The bulldog didn't seem to give a fuck about where it's going or even where it comes from.

They just sat on it. The plan seemed to make itself.

Love conquers all, after all.

Road-trip romance and see where they end up.

First stop is Carolina's folks' other country place –

A small cottage on a small piece of land near the beach at Camburi.

It's a warren of coast roads down there and a hard place to find if you don't know where it is.

And it's some hours from São Paulo.

Carolina has spun a story that they're going there for a little getaway, a little study retreat. They'll stay a while, sure, but not for long.

Easier to tell her parents once they're gone that they're really gone.

Rafa's not telling anyone anything.

And it's this he's thinking about now. He's folding jackets around bottles to keep them safe and he's thinking that he's not going to see his grandma or Franginho for a long, long time, all goes to plan.

This doesn't feel right.

This *isn't* right.

Carolina appears, arms hidden by bedsheets and towels.

She shovels them into the boot. 'All yours,' she smiles at Rafa. 'You're doing a world class job, amigo.'

Rafa smiles. He nods to himself. He kisses her, holds her for a moment.

'Look,' he says. 'I need to go and say goodbye.'

Carolina smiles. 'I was waiting for you to realise that. We can do it on the way.'

Rafa nods.

It's a good idea.

It's easier to say you're going when you're already on the way – easier to go when you're already going.

It's the right thing to do.

He wants to do the right thing.

Renata sits doing nothing.

There's not much else to do, at this point.

She's thinking, is what she's doing.

She's deciding that she will not be scared off by anyone, will not be blackmailed.

It's all it takes, sitting in the gloom of late afternoon, your resolve stiffening, sitting on your own, that's all it takes, to make that kind of a resolution.

Do the right thing, she thinks. *Do it*.

Mendes is one of these nouveau coronelismos. Renata has heard of illegal payments, cases of intimidation that have never got to court.

He paid off a councillor once who had threatened to prosecute over missing funds in his department. Part of the Singapore Project to revamp the favelas. Make them more palatable for visitors, hide them away behind respectable edifices. (It works like a sticking plaster – after a year the buildings look like shit.) The contractors sell off the materials they get from the state to the highest bidder, then buy in the cheapest stuff to build the projects. Use the original material in luxury apartments and shopping centres elsewhere.

It's why the buildings fall down.

There's a knock at the door –

It opens.

She smiles at the man who has shuffled through it, sheepish.

'Senhor Zézinho,' Renata says. 'Come in.'

The man hobbles in, hat in hand. 'I want to thank you, Dona Renata,' he says.

Renata smiles.

Her job, she thinks, is worthwhile. She helped this man build an extension to his house, his wife expecting another baby, resistance from the tyre shop next door and the bar on the other side. Renata slid into the discussions with easy grace and reason and the man got his space and she helped the business owners feel they'd done the right thing. It's worthwhile, her job.

She is doing the right thing.

Ray loads his leather grip with money. There's a lot of money in Ray's grip. This money is pure profit. Ray has invested nothing in this – it's money for nothing, as the song goes.

Chicks for free, Ray thinks.

Two of them back at the hotel, drinking.

Both of them owe Ray, in a sense.

They are, Ray thinks, beholden to him. So, why not?

Chicks for free.

He's nearly done at the Bunker. They're standing at a white, marble counter, drinking tiny glasses of beer. Finishing up. A job well done. A day's work.

A hard day's night, Ray thinks.

Night time in the day time.

'Keep this cash, Ray, entendeu?' Little Johnny says. 'Take it home as it is.'

'That assessment sounds a little wary, Johnny lad. Do explain.'

'This is a kickback slush fund, you know that.'

Ray nods.

'Credit lines and loans approved for a fee, certo?'

Ray goes *it's not my first rodeo, son.*

'It's not going to stay clean for long, this dirty business.'

'The metaphors, Little Johnny, are not helping.'

'This is the tip of the iceberg. There'll be a reckoning.'

Ray laughs. 'Okay, Shakespeare, what's your point?'

'Traditional means of cleaning this kind of cash are drying up.'

'The metaphors, *please.*'

'The old-school businesses – your hairdressers, your garages, your car wash – can still do it, but there's too much. Investigations are starting, Ray. It's only a matter of time.'

'Your vagueness is reassuring, in its way.'

'What I'm saying, Ray, is take the money and run.'

Ray knocks back his beer. 'I intend to, friend.'

And he does. His ticket home is waiting for him in São Paulo.

Destination: Texas forever.

Renata:

What happens if you hit thirty-five and your career isn't what you were hoping for? Do you give up and start again by having children? Or do you make the career happen? After all, women have children much older these days. We can.

We never got complacent with contraception like those married couples who after two kids mistakenly believe they're in control of their reproductive destiny. That tipsy birthday-fumble. We never slipped into that false security. Maybe the only way to stop worrying about having kids is to have them.

We'd joke in unison when our friends nudged the subject onto family: 'We think it could be the best or worst decision we'll ever make. We just don't know which it is!' Over time, the joke wore thin, our laughter forced and grim. Our friends' reactions changed. Gone was the polite amusement, the hand-on-arm assurance ('for us, it was certainly the best') replaced with something far worse: relief. Relief they weren't us.

Yet I couldn't help feeling that somehow I'd been denied something. Friends talk of unconditional love. 'They only add to your life,' they say. In response we'd convince ourselves of what we'd lose, that this parental keenness to see others procreate was a kind of infatuation. 'Don't you think you're living the most incredibly selfish lives?' We did not. 'It's different when they're your own.' That was a common and believable thread and, some years ago, one that I clung to. But you shouldn't talk of being denied if you've never put in a request, and I never really did.

We hid that behind more jokes, feigned horror at the very weight of children, the baggage. The prams and cots and Tupperware dishes full of slop. The bags full of clean towels and clothes about to be sullied. The endlessly discarded toys. All so definite. The bond, too, I suppose.

Soon, we've said to each other, Mario and I.

Soon.

I really can't wait.

Anna says to Fernanda, 'We should work together, you know, sabe?'

Fernanda says that they really should.

Anna grins – this is one tipsy idea that she's going to follow up on.

'When Ray gets here,' she says, 'promise me we won't have to talk about work, that we can just have a good time?'

Fernanda's big old smile says all she needs to know.

Anna smiles right back at her.

Rafa doesn't call ahead – it'd only be suspicious. Why, after all, would he, entendeu?

He's covered their stuff in the back of the car with a blanket so no one will realise quite how much of it there is.

He's waiting in the driver's seat when Carolina jumps in next to him. She brandishes her parents' keys like some kind of a promise – or threat.

'All done,' she says. 'Vamos embora, ne?'

Let's get out of here.

Rafa kicks the car into gear and they leave. The segurança that monitors who comes and goes waves them off from behind bullet-proof glass. If he knew where Rafa lived, what Rafa *did*, it is unlikely he'd have let him anywhere near Carolina's parents' condo.

A mixed-race guy, Rafa notes.

They're mixed-race and black men, mainly, security.

It's a different sort of a way out – a wage to protect a place from the sort of people you grew up with, which is to say the sort of people middle-class Paulistanos don't trust.

Crooks or otherwise.

What Rafa's learned from dating Carolina is that social problems are self-perpetuating – the poor aren't trusted so they're not trusted.

Not beyond menial work and muscle.

It's half an hour to the favela.

Rafa's quiet, keeps his counsel.

Carolina, wisely, follows suit. She's good like that, Rafa thinks –

She knows when to shut up.

'It's a rare quality in birds,' Franginho once told him, tongue-in-cheek, winking. 'Keeping shtum.'

Rafa's going to miss him.

He's become something of an expert on *birds*, Franginho. His little chicken legs are stronger, his back broad and muscular, his sharp, world class chat –

Makes them laugh. And it turns out that's all it takes.

'You know what it's like when you see a bird,' Franginho said one Sunday morning as they watched families traipse to church, 'and you know you've fucked her already. I mean not her *exactly*, but her, *that* bird. Entendeu?'

'Mate,' Rafa said.

'Cara, I'm joking, obviously. It's ironic. Banter, you know, is the term.'

Rafa feels guilty that this makes him laugh.

He didn't realise he would. Then he met Carolina.

Franginho's right about love, at least. 'It makes you think, love,' he says.

Rafa wonders if he shouldn't ask him to come along.

But then who'd look after things?

Who'll square all this up the hill?

Who'll square all this with old Carlos, the bulldog?

Who's going to keep an eye on Rafa's grandma?

Rafa's not hugely reassured by any of these questions –

It's not surprising.

The favela looks different from the inside of a smart car.

The air-con, for one thing, changes your perception – the heat is *outside*, throbbing.

Gas and diesel fumes indistinct.

There's a distance – the city's at arms' length – when you're sitting high up in a smart car.

Rafa's not sure he likes it.

The darkened windows – he can see people eyeing them up, wary. They can't see him. He *knows* their resentment, their mistrust.

Block after block, brick after brick, rusted roof after rusted roof, foraged wood door after foraged wood door, broken down car after broken down car –

They shunt and weave, brake and beep.

Outside Rafa's grandma's house – *his* house – sits Franginho.

Two-birds situation, Rafa thinks, shaking his head, smiling.

Kill two birds and get stoned, is Franginho's joke: makes for a helluva weekend.

Rafa pulls over. Tyre-squeal urgent.

Franginho jumps up. Steps on a cigarette. By the look of him, it's not the first he's had in the last few minutes.

There's a look to his face, Rafa thinks, that is not healthy.

A sick twist to it.

Rafa hasn't seen this look on his best friend for a long time.

Rafa sees Carolina doesn't see any of this.

'Querida,' he says, 'I'll do this on my own, certo? It's better.'

'I – ' she starts, but thinks better of it. 'Go, go,' she says.

She gives him a look: *I love you and I understand.*

Do what you gotta do, is the gist.

Rafa pops the door and hops down. The SUV height feels VIP. He still notes this despite the situation.

He looks right left right.

He steps up to the makeshift, salvaged wood porch of his grandma's house, his home.

He lifted the beam himself, not three months ago, from the debris of the Portakabin refurb. Nice bit of ply, it was. It looks good. He notes that he still admires it.

He slaps Franginho's hand in their standard, age-old greeting.

'Mate,' Franginho says. 'You need to go.'

'What?'

'You need to *leave*, like now, entendeu?'

'What do you mean, *leave*?'

'What do you mean, what do you mean?'

Rafa shakes his head. 'Meu,' he says. *Mate*. 'Fala serio, ne?' *Come on, stop fucking about.*

'Short version,' Franginho says, 'Carlos knows you've been stowing the dinheiro he asked you to pass on. He ain't happy. He's coming to get it. To get you.'

'And how do you know?'

'He told me.'

Rafa nods. 'Right.' He thinks *yeah, why not? Makes sense.*

'This is a today deal, amigo, like now.'

'Okay.'

'He said something else, too.'

'Oh yeah?'

'He's coming in on the back of a more general raid, certo? It's going to kick off here – soon.'

'How soon?'

'I'd say,' Franginho says, and in his delivery Rafa sees the old sense of humour, the irony, 'any minute.'

Rafa thinks quick. 'And where do I go exactly? You got any ideas?'

'Just go.'

Rafa flicks a look at his grandma's house.

Franginho sees the look, Rafa sees.

Franginho says, 'I'll keep an eye on her. Tell her you've run away for love or some shit like that, falou?'

Rafa's nodding. Here it is. Handed to him on a plate.

'Get the fuck out of here, porra.'

Rafa nods. They hug. Rafa nods again.

'I'll call you,' he says.

Franginho says, 'Give it a week, all right?'

Rafa nods. He gets back in the car.

He thinks *this is the only way*.

'What was that all about?' Carolina is not going to let this go, Rafa sees that quite clearly. Not going to let them go quite so easily as that. 'What about your grandmother?' she says.

'It's okay.'

It's all Rafa can think to say.

And it is, really.

'Franginho's in charge, it's fine,' he says.

'Huh.'

They drive up towards Avenida Giovanni Gronchi.

The traffic will be worse, this time of night, but it's the fastest way out of the favela and they ain't too clever sticking around for more tick-tock than they need to.

There's the bang and fizz of fireworks.

Rafa says to himself *fuck*.

He knows what that means.

He nudges the gas a touch, pushes them that bit quicker along the bump and grind of the unpaved, potholed track. And they do bump and grind.

They hit the junction.

Rafa sees blue-red lights flash.

There's more than there is on a normal day in the jungle.

And they're distant, moving closer.

He sees men move in shadows.

They need to leave, *now*.

He does a sharp right, change of plan: ride straight out through the boca, the boca he rode straight out of years ago, on his board, following –

He sees the lawyer lady outside her office.

He sees her panic.

He sees her drop –

He sees her bend down to –

He hears the first sounds of gunfire.

He hears Carolina gasp. He hears her scream.

He kerb-rides, hotfoots it out as fast as he can. The SUV bumps right left right –

In his rear-view mirror, he sees bodies.

Tiro-teiro. *Firefight.*

They shoot down rock-strewn tracks.

They shoot straight through, straight out –

And they're gone.

They're away, tyre-squeal safe. Down the hill and away.

Carolina sobs.

And they don't look back.

Whose voice can I hear on the breeze.

Leme's sitting balcony-quiet, watching a storm brew, feeling the wind pick up when he hears her voice, Renata's voice.

He smiles.

Ten minutes later his phone rings and his life changes and he howls.

Paraisópolis, Paradise City, early evening. This is what Leme pieces together.

The streets pound with baile funk, and flip-flopped men in dark glasses stand around the car, watching the five dirt roads that join at the junction. The sun slips down out of sight of the favela crater, below the line of the city. Naked bulbs are scattered about the roof-tops of the surrounding houses, each illuminating a few circular feet. Rusted tin doors squeak, open into the gloom and faint rectangles spill onto the street, are still for a moment and then vanish.

Renata leaves her legal aid office an hour later than normal. She's been helping a man with a dispute over land. He is expecting another child and wants to extend the rough house his family live in. But a bar owner and a tyre shop are unhappy with the plans. Renata slipped easily into the space of the disagreement, fluid, empathic, and negotiated a compromise. The man has just visited her office to bless her and offer his respects. He talked for a long time.

She doesn't like leaving after dark.

She scans the street. A cockroach zips out from the back of the por kilo restaurant where she eats her lunch every day. The owner – a large woman – steps out from behind the counter and in three steps crunches it under her plastic sandals. She smiles at Renata, who waves and digs her keys out of her bag.

Fireworks spit and crackle, and the men standing by the car turn, recognising the warning from the top end of the favela. Police. Renata tenses, struggles with the padlock to her office, drops it. She glances nervously at the restaurant owner who stands with her arms crossed, shaking her head, clicking and sucking her teeth, before stepping back behind the counter and pulling down the metal grille. Renata looks over her shoulder, watches as the men skirt around the cars across the road, crouched. Someone is shouting instructions to one of the younger boys. The Military Police will be here soon. These invasions are becoming commonplace, but this one is earlier in the evening than normal. Should she go back inside or try to get to her car? She tells herself not to panic, that she has a little more time. The door is locked now. But better to get back inside, she thinks. Surprised by a single siren-wail and blue-red flash she fumbles her key, watches it fall into the gutter and bounce towards the uncovered drain. The men drinking at the bar flinch then duck under the tables.

She pulls at the padlock.

The maids and nannies walking home carrying their céstas of rice and beans start and scatter down the side roads.

The heat pulses like a heartbeat, the clouds thicken and crack. More shouts. Running. Renata freezes. She looks across the road. The Military Police are advancing. Men in flip-flops run from shadow to shadow. One is carrying a pistol, arm lowered.

Then, an unholy rattle. Renata takes a step towards her car, limbs pushing though water. This is happening.

Gunfire. Strobing light.

And Renata glimpses him – the last thing she ever sees. A teenager with gold teeth grinning, his rifle too powerful for him to control, police moving towards him from all sides.

This is what Leme pieces together.

Bocão, Big Mouth, *former escort:*

Hate.

A man leaves Paddy's house, a little unsteadily. Drunk, you think. It's late Sunday and he's drinking with this man. This fucker.

He's clutching something to his chest, but you can't see what it is. He's muttering and gesturing with his hands as if arguing with himself. He arrives at his car. Places the thing on the roof. You edge a little closer, out into the shadow of the tree in the road. His hat obscures his face.

He reaches up and takes the thing again. What is it? He turns back and crosses the road, staggering slightly. He opens the outside door and wobbles through. Hasn't he had enough?

Come on. *Come on.*

Porra.

He doesn't come out. Why is he taking so long?

Mosquitoes buzz in the streetlamp-quiet. The windows in the neighbouring houses blink then darken. Little domestic routines. They were yours. Rottweilers trigger lights on motion sensors and bark at the sudden brightness, snarling and confused.

On. Off. Light. Dark.

Quiet.

You don't belong here. Not now, not anymore.

Perhaps you never did.

You think about your apartment, with its peeling walls and barred windows; your neighbourhood with its growl of traffic, its michês hawking and shouting, its dizzy amphetamine rush of headlights and noise.

You rub your hands through your hair, slap yourself hard, feel your cheek redden, your brain scramble and expand with the blows.

You breathe and it settles.

Come on.

The door swings open and bangs against the wall. You shrink back behind the tree at the noise. The man looks hurriedly around. The security guard in the booth down the street is asleep. He doesn't stir. The man draws the door closed and heads again to his car. This time his legs are steady and his hands are empty. And then, as he opens the car, he takes his hat off.

He glances anxiously around and pulls his hat back on. As he might. Doesn't look good, this late, this drunk. You know.

Your job. A favour.

Worthless. Pobre.

How that fucker makes you feel.

Vagabundo. Desgraçado.

The man stamps his feet and removes a pair of gloves before climbing into the front seat. The engine purrs into life. Where you live, they splutter and bang, spew smoke and blast tacky forró rhythms, groups of fierce, hardened men and women cheering at the explosions, their hips swaying in time to the music.

The car slides off, quiet as a submarine.

He's alone now.

It's time. Your limbs strain.

Your heart heaves.

You're going inside. Now.

You ring the doorbell. Paddy lets you in, dressed in a red dressing gown.

'I wasn't expecting you. I thought we'd agreed Monday.' He looks at his watch. 'It's late,' he says.

You nod.

'Do you want something to drink?'

You shake your head, loiter in the hallway, wait for him to speak again.

'Why don't you sit down in the living room? We can talk there.'

You follow him, but don't sit down.

'I thought we had planned to meet tomorrow night. I was getting ready for bed. I've been working.'

This is how he talks to you – formal, elegant, restrained.

You look around the room. There are two used whiskey glasses on the coffee table.

'I'm sorry I haven't been as attentive as usual,' he says. 'I've been so horribly busy.'

You know exactly how busy he's been.

'There's something I need to tell you. I think it is best for both of us.'

You're expecting this, but it doesn't lessen the jolt of electricity.

'I'm just going to go upstairs and get some clothes on. Then I'll come down and we can talk.'

You give him a moment, you go into his study, you retrieve the paperweight you gave him on his last birthday, you feel its heft, and you climb the stairs, go into his bedroom.

He is startled. 'Oh, you're here. I was just getting changed.'

His mobile phone is in his hand and he hasn't taken off the dressing gown.

You cross the room, gripping the paperweight behind your back.

'I need you to understand something,' he says.

He turns away from you so he is facing the bed. You take in the details one last time: the crumpled duvet, the book on his bedside table, the clothes neatly folded on his chair, the photo of his smiling nephews, the curtains pulled shut.

Then you raise the paperweight, head high, feel strength –

I remember him lying on the floor. Black spots of blood dotted on the carpet. Thick, patterned, red swirls.

Another drip painting.

I remember the ties I used to secure his hands and feet, where I found them in the closet. I remember exactly why I did it, added that little detail:

Let them know him in death as they didn't in life.

They call it a bala perdida, a *stray bullet*. They call it collateral damage. They call what happened to Renata an accident. Every morning, Leme drives to the favela and sits in his car.

Pilgrimage.

Part Five

GREAT WHITE HOPE

São Paulo, October–November 2018

Document record: phone conversation between
Ray Marx and Dave 'Huck' Sawyer, Region Head,
Capital SP, secure line, 10 March 2016

Ray Marx (RM): So you're telling me don't come?

Dave 'Huck' Sawyer (DS): Big Man, I'm telling you wait,
that's all.

RM: You don't want me back, Huck?

DS: If I had my way, you'd never have left.

RM: Your way or the highway.

DS: Not anymore.

RM: I thought you'd be flavour of the month, with a cherry
on top.

DS: Oh, I'm still golden balls, it's the general climate.

RM: Translate.

DS: What's legit investment, syndicate building and product
speculation, and what's dirty kickback and white-collar
shakedown is no longer so clear.

RM: Sounds sexy.

DS: It means, Big Dog, that we're keeping things very clear
here at Capital SP.

RM: Gotcha. No tickee, no laundry.

DS: Ha, that's some nice mixed metaphor racism.

RM: You know me, Huck. I'm an equal opportunities bigot.

DS: Might be more a no money, no laundry scene right now,
pal. Operation Car Wash, Ray, is the thing. Lava Jato.

RM: Lava Jato?

DS: Means Car Wash.

RM: Okay.

DS: Money laundering from the bottom up.

RM: And Capital SP wants to keep its hands clean.

DS: Capital SP's hands *are* clean, amigo. It's some of our associates who have been naughty.

RM: So you're putting some distance between yourselves and some of your investors.

DS: We're keeping things very high finance, numbers trades only, that kind of thing.

RM: Hedging your bets.

DS: Ha, you're funny.

RM: Yeah.

DS: I guess I'm telling you that the kind of consultancy work you were doing for us is no longer viable. Not at least for now.

RM: Or, it's a lot easier.

DS: There's that, yeah.

RM: Meaning, when the political wind changes and the bad guys are out in the open, it's a whole lot clearer which market to short.

DS: Clever guy, too, aren't you, cowboy.

RM: Any tips for me?

DS: That's called insider trading, big boy. We're taking a number of positions. Whatever happens to Dilma and the left, we'll be all right.

RM: Well played, sir. Spoken like a true diplomat.

DS: We made a lot of money in 2003 and 2006 and 2011.

RM: When I was in town.

DS: It's not going anywhere, money. It'll still be here when you come back.

RM: Question is will I still be here when I come back.

DS: The philosopher.

RM: Adios, Huck. Be lucky.

Document record: Article in OLHA! Online magazine,
16 March 2016
by
Eleanor Boe

What is Operação Lava Jato, Operation Car Wash?
(And why does this particular corruption scandal
threaten to topple the government?)

It began in March 2014 as a routine federal investigation
into money laundering through a car wash and garage complex
in Brasília, the country's capital. Two years later, and
half a million people flooded the streets of São Paulo
to call for President Dilma's impeachment. How did this
happen? And what will happen next?

The discovery that started it all was a Land Rover
illegally bought by Alberto Youssef — a convicted money
launderer of some distinction and considerable reach — for
Paulo Roberto Costa, an executive at Petrobras, one of the
biggest oil companies in the world, a company that accounts
for an eighth of all investments in Brazil, and provides
hundreds of thousands of jobs in construction, shipyards
and refineries across the country.

And what this purchase led investigators to uncover was a
far-reaching mechanism of corruption in which Petrobras
overpaid on contracts to a cartel of construction
companies, and, with the guaranteed business, this cartel
channelled a percentage of each deal into offshore slush
funds. Bribes, leaked documents have shown, were built
into the contracts themselves, which made their illegality
harder to spot.

So far, so your-basic-traditional-corruption model.

However, things might be about to change. Last week, on
8 March, Marcelo Odebrecht, CEO of the international
Odebrecht construction conglomerate, was sentenced to
nineteen years in jail for corruption, money laundering and
criminal association. And it doesn't look like he wants
to go quietly. To reduce his sentence, he's allegedly
been outlining the epic scale of this kickback scheme.
And exactly which politicians — and their parties — have
benefited directly.

Last week, we saw the results of all this: calls for Dilma's impeachment. On Sunday, we'll see the other side of the coin, as hundreds of thousands plan to march in solidarity, in her defence.

If nothing else, it appears that this unfolding scandal runs deep. And the question many people are asking is what's really more important: political ideology and policy-making, or being free of any association at all with corruption in a country in which it is considered systemic.

Brazil, quite clearly, is divided.

Document record: Article in OLHA! Online magazine,
20 March 2016
by
Eleanor Boe

ONE HUNDRED THOUSAND ATTEND PRO-DILMA MARCH

Avenida Paulista turned red yesterday afternoon as a hundred thousand people took to the streets to show their support for President Dilma, who is battling calls for her impeachment.

Earlier in the day, Military Police dispersed crowds of anti-Dilma protestors. They used limited force, including tear gas and water cannons, justified, a statement issued late last night reads, to prevent the possibility of 'serious violence' between rival political factions.

As this took place, a Supreme Court Judge took the step of suspending former President Lula's ministerial nomination. Dilma's critics claim that by attempting to make her mentor part of the government, she is effectively shielding him from money laundering charges, charges he vigorously denies.

Many of the crowd waved red flags, defending the Workers' Party. Banners depicting Lula as a bodybuilder were among many creative displays of support, in stark contrast to only a few days before, when an anti-Dilma protest featured two huge inflatable dolls of Dilma and Lula — dressed as prisoners.

374

Lula, wearing a red shirt, addressed the crowd to rapturous applause. 'There will not be a coup against Ms Rousseff,' he said, to cheers and raised fists. After he left the stage, the rally became a street party, with singing, dancing, and pro-PT (Workers' Party) chanting.

The recent nationwide protests against corruption called for Dilma's removal due to 'economic mismanagement' and her alleged part in the far-reaching corruption scandal based around state-sponsored oil company Petrobras.

Dilma denies all wrongdoing.

More to follow

Document record: Article in newspaper *Cidade de São Paulo*,
29 March 2016
by
Francisco Silva, Crime Correspondent

BODY OF MURDERED DETECTIVE MARIO LEME FINALLY RECOVERED

In the early hours of the morning, the body of Polícia Civil detective, Mario Leme, was recovered after a week-long search. He was found by city workers on a routine maintenance job, buried deep in the city's sewage system. Leme, it is claimed, was investigating possible corruption practices in the world of São Paulo high finance, and the disappearance of a young man believed to be Antonio Neves, a banker at Capital SP. Leme has a distinguished service record and was known as a man of impeccable moral judgement. His death is an enormous loss at a time when there are so few upright characters in authority in our city.

Document record: phone conversation between Ray Marx
and Dave 'Huck' Sawyer, secure line, 12 April 2016

RM: So I didn't get on the plane.

DS: We'll refund your ticket, son.

RM: What's up, Huck, you sound unhappy?

DS: A little mess to clear up here. A couple of youngsters doing some off the books trades with one of our mid-level guys.

RM: Huh.

DS: Yeah. One of them disappeared, and one of them's dead.

RM: That is a mess. Plead the fifth.

DS: What we're doing. Deniability is key, and our mid-level guy knew those principles.

RM: So you're cool and the gang.

DS: Tell that to the kids' parents.

Document record: Article in newspaper *Cidade de São Paulo*, 30 April 2016
by
Francisco Silva, Crime correspondent

INVESTIGATION OPENED INTO LATE SECRETARIO DE OBRAS FOLLOWING *CIDADE DE SÃO PAULO* REPORT

State regulators have begun an investigation into leading political figures including the late Jorge Mendes, the Secretario de Obras, regarding financial irregularities during the now infamous Singapore Project following a report researched and written by *Cidade de São Paulo* journalists. The report alleges that in his role as founder and CEO of his construction company, Mendes pocketed state funds and used state materials in his own luxury developments, replacing them with poor quality materials for development of the Singapore Project. Undeclared bonuses are alleged to have been paid to Mendes for finishing the work in record time.

Only five years on, the buildings in question are in a state of disrepair, current contractors blaming their condition on 'shoddy workmanship and administrative short cuts'. In late 2012, part of one of the buildings collapsed resulting in the deaths of six people, including two young children, as reported by this newspaper.

Mendes was also embroiled in a scandal unfolding at the British School where he was contracted to work on a R$20 million development project. It is alleged that he made unethical payments to an anonymous teacher — we can't name the teacher for legal reasons — to bolster his son's grades and performances at the school.

A spokesman for Mendes explained that the payments were in lieu of work as a political consultant undertaken by the teacher. Mendes's company continues to run the 20 million reais building project at the school, whose Headmaster, Paddy Lockwood, was murdered in an unrelated incident.

Document record: Article in newspaper *Cidade de São Paulo*,
29 September 2017
by
Francisco Silva, Crime Correspondent

**HIGH FINANCE, HIGH STAKES: GEDDEL VIEIRA
ARRESTED OVER SEIZED CASH**

Earlier this month, an apartment was raided near Brasília and $16 million in cash seized. *Cidade de São Paulo* can confirm police have matched fingerprints found on boxes and suitcases in the apartment to those of high finance kingpin Geddel Vieira, former vice president of Brazil's National Savings Bank and, until his sacking in July of this year following corruption allegations, President Michel Temer's top congressional liaison. Vieira was arrested this week and released on bail. It is believed the recovered cash is part of a scheme in which companies paid bribes in return for favourable loans and credit lines. A source close to Vieira claims the apartment was known as the Bunker. Vieira denies all wrongdoing. The investigation continues.

Document record: Memo to Ray Marx from Dave 'Huck' Sawyer,
political summary, 2016–2018, the headlines, October 2018

President Dilma Rousseff is formally impeached on 17

April 2016. She is charged with criminal administrative misconduct and disregard for the federal budget.

The Lava Jato investigation paralyses government: coalitions cannot be built without bribes. Prosecutors suspend Petrobras contracts with all major suppliers, key construction and shipping firms in Brazil. The country faces a devastating recession.

Faith in the political system is eroded. In 2016 a series of huge protests against corruption are staged in over 200 cities in every state in the country. In São Paulo, the largest demonstration in the history of the city takes place, with over 2.5 million in attendance.

The protests, it becomes clear, are about not just the government, but the whole, rotten political structure of the country.

In October 2018, the far-right, populist Jair Bolsonaro campaigns to be elected president. He promises to unite the country, purge the corrupt leftists, and fight crime with a ruthless and brutal no mercy, no leniency policy. He is renowned for his misogyny, and his racist, homophobic views. Weeks before the election takes place, Bolsonaro is attacked and stabbed while speaking at a rally.

Document record: Invitation to memorial service to honour Polícia Civil detective Mario Leme, 8 October 2018

Join us to honour the memory of one of São Paulo's finest policemen, Detective Mario Leme, as he posthumously receives the city's highest recognition of service.

Date: 8 October

Time: 11am

Venue: City Hall

1
Happy Days

October 2018

Make Brazil great again

Jair Bolsonaro

Unanimity is always stupid

Nelson Rodrigues

When Rafa wakes up in the mornings, it's the same thing every day –
The *air*.

It's cool, soft and seems to land on his face like light rain.

He hopes he never gets used to it.

He eases out of bed, careful not to wake Carolina. She breathes messily, a light, wet snore, which just kills him.

Sounds happy, she does, he always thinks.

Something else he doesn't want to get used to.

He closes the bedroom door behind him and surveys their small living room. It's tidy, neat, homely; he likes to look at it.

It means something. It's an achievement, of sorts. Yeah, he thinks, it's something.

He unbolts the front door and slips out. Not quite seven. The sky pink and cracked with blue.

Rafa breathes salty air. He rolls his neck. He cracks knuckles. He stretches. He performs half-assed yoga.

He's getting on a bit, after all.

'You should watch your posture, your back, my love,' Carolina told him.

He didn't like that, no, senhor. Rafa flicked dirty looks her way.

But he *does* tweak his body a little every morning.

He walks at a clip down the bush-fringed, dew-damp sand path to the beach. He whistles. He jangles keys. He feels *jaunty*.

He clocks the other little houses near theirs going through their morning routines. Smoke from wood-burning stoves thin and moist. Outside furniture pulled out from under tarpaulins and snapped upright. Coffee and fried bread in butter makes Rafa's mouth water.

He jogs the last hundred metres or so down the track to the beach.

The sight, as it does every morning, fills him with joy – and something else, too.

Hope is what he thinks it is.

The beach is quiet. Rafa sees a couple out running at the water's edge. An old man walks his dog. Two teenagers silently pulling on wetsuits, wiping down surfboards. The swell doesn't look great. They should wait until the end of the day and the turning tide. It's good surfing, this beach, if you time it right.

Rafa's getting pretty fucking good at surfing.

He's left his skateboard *way* behind.

He arrives at the little shack they run. He unlocks the grille. He vaults the counter. It's one of four concession stands in a row at the top end of the beach, a way in from the car park, shaded by trees when the sun hits its peak, clever positioning.

Rafa is always the first to open up. They do coffee, herbal teas, juice and simple breakfasts. Later, fried snacks and beer, light cocktails, maybe a lunch special if Carolina has slow-cooked a pot of something. He thinks of Dona Regina, bonitinha. He smiles. Theirs is a daytime business; the other stands are bars. Heavy cocktails and loud music. Rafa likes to start early and finish in time for the surf. He doesn't want to spend his life serving drunk tourists.

But he'll happily feed and water the hung-over.

Rafa stacks plates. He checks mugs, flicks switches, opens the fridge. It is fresh-milk happy. He curates a welcoming vibe. The shack makes its money from this vibe –

You gotta be nice in service. People like it when you're nice. They come back.

It all happened fairly easily.

The drift into a quiet, legit life was smooth. They hunkered down at Carolina's parents' beach bungalow until they were in the clear, cash-wise.

Franginho brokered an easy peace –

The favela boys didn't know about the money and their thing was basically: *fair fucks, Rafa, crack on. You deserve a little luck.*

Old Carlos did pay Franginho a visit, but it wasn't his money, end of the day, and his backer had disappeared, so *whatta you gonna do?* was his position.

Happy days.

They spent some time looking for the right set-up, then used the money as a deposit for their little cottage and their little shack. The rent takes care of itself. They do pretty okay, all told, and there's still a bag or two of cash buried under the cottage should they need it.

Rafa cranks the coffee machine. It gurgles and steams. He pours himself a deep measure. The sun pokes through damp cloud. Waves break. Gulls whine.

Life is good.

Rafa feels guilty about Franginho though. It's a guilt that neither of them can acknowledge. To acknowledge any guilt is an admission that Rafa did wrong. And neither of them wants to believe that he did.

Franginho doesn't visit. This helps. He knows he can't. Regardless of the squaring of things, the straightening of Rafa's resignation from the firm, as it were, there can be no trail.

The deal is: Rafa stays gone.

It suits him down to the ground.

This life, as the saying goes, is his praia, his *beach* – his cup of tea.

So he and Franginho keep in touch through a couple of dedicated dumb phones with scrambled numbers. Franginho sorted them and had one couriered to Campinas where Rafa picked it up like some fugitive emptying an airport locker. It took him a day, round trip, and no little stress.

It was worth it.

The morning unfolds. The beach car park fills slowly. There is a limit to how many cars can come down the mile-long dirt road and use it. At weekends, it's jammed full by eight o'clock. But today is a less than spectacular Wednesday, early October. Mainly surfers and dog walkers –

It's one of those protected sites and you need to know about the beach if you're going to find it.

Mid-morning and Rafa's taking a break. He's done a little trade, but it hasn't exactly been brisk, he thinks. It doesn't matter. Slow is good. He doesn't believe in fast food, it's not their style.

The beach curves. The trees bend. The breeze wafts the damp air about the place. Waves slap and hiss. Surfers chat and jostle some way out. Not much action, but it's pretty meditative just sitting around on your board. Been there, Rafa thinks.

He sips coffee, dips bread.

Across the beach, coming towards him: Carolina.

He smiles.

She's hustling a bit, which surprises him. He was expecting her at lunchtime, so she's a little early. There's an odd step to her walk, a shuffle, like she's rushing, but trying not to run.

Rafa straightens up.

He can see her face set in a forced smile.

He can see she's holding something in both hands.

As she approaches, he can see her eyes flash pain, sorrow.

She holds out her hands: she's carrying the dumb phone.

She's shaking a little, crying.

Rafa feels a jolt, a fear. That thump of change.

'What is it?' Rafa says. 'What's wrong?'

Carolina wipes her eyes, her nose. 'Franginho called,' she says.

'And?'

'It's your grandma.'

Rafa closes his eyes. He breathes. He sobs.

Lisboa slides quietly out the back of Leme's memorial. He doesn't want to be there. He certainly doesn't want to go to the drinks party being held in a convention room somewhere in this godforsaken building. That it's taken, what, two and a half years to honour his friend says something. What it is says is:

We don't know which side anyone is on.

October 2018 and things are going to change.

October 2018 and things in São Paulo will stay the same.

The city rides out –

It's better than all this, it thinks –

This city, this dirty city, this dirty, great city.

Lisboa scowls.

October 2018: an election that means nothing to São Paulo but everything to Brazil.

The two years since Leme passed have been a clusterfuck. First Dilma's impeachment, then Lula's arrest, then Temer's ill-fated government, and now a first-round presidential election won only the day before by a stone psycho, a nasty bastard, a real piece of work –

Lisboa thinks: you really do get the politicians you deserve.

Bolsonaro cooped up in hospital, playing the martyr –

Lisboa wonders if the assassination attempt might have been something quite different. It's risky, sure, to have someone stab you and not do you a serious, but it's doable.

He distracts himself with this thought when all he really wants to do is cry.

He misses his friend; life is not the same, never will be.

He saw Mario's girlfriend, Antonia, from across the room, saw her holding Mario's son, a toddler now, saw her standing with her new man, a good man, Lisboa's heard, and fair enough, he won't feel anything but positive about that.

Mario himself once grieved his wife, Renata. Moving on is not leaving behind.

To think that Mario never met his son –

This is what Lisboa has buried. *This.* This thought.

He remembers when his own children were born. The first few days. The irrevocable change – that frantic euphoria.

Nothing prepares you for it –

It's not like anything else.

People talk and talk but there's nothing like your own experience.

A love that builds quickly, unfolds inevitably, replacing that fear and uncertainty about what the future holds with something different.

Lisboa remembers holding his firstborn in the middle of the night. The glare of the TV, the wet purr of his daughter. The contentment. The smell of her. Talking as she slept, about this and that. Her nestling in his neck; her wriggling in his arms.

Yeah, it was something, those first few days.

'You know what it's like, the tiredness?' he remembers asking Mario. 'It's like I've just got off an overnight flight, all the time, but I'm really excited about where I've landed.'

'Maybe take a shower, mate,' was Mario's response.

They laughed.

'You have no idea,' Lisboa said.

Mario shook his head, smiling. 'I don't.'

'No, I mean, *I* had no idea.'

'I'm pleased for you, mate. For all three of you.'

Lisboa remembers that feeling of family, the way the word shifted in his mouth, the way its meaning morphed.

That knowledge too, he remembers: she's going nowhere.

It was exhilarating, liberating.

To put yourself at the mercy of those feelings, of the very fact of the girl.

Life, he remembers, became shift work.

Life became simple, he thinks now, as his heels click in the City Hall corridor.

Lisboa has one rule: don't whinge.

And he never has cause to: it's the happiest thing he's ever done.

Mario never found that out.

For such an unassuming man, Leme certainly collected some serious drama, Lisboa thinks.

Life, he considers, is not fair, end of.

And it changes with a jolt. Things happen to people and you deal with it.

He slips off his egg-stained tie, pulls at his sweat-stained shirt. He wipes his dirty hands on his dirty trousers, wipes sweat from his forehead. He fumbles for his cigarettes, drops his lighter. He bends down – slow. His back creaks, his hamstrings scream.

Age, mate –

He allows himself a wry shake of the head:
Yeah.
Cigarette lit, he skips steps down to the street.
Centro-burn of diesel and gas, hawkers out, sun raw and hostile –
'Hey, Ricardo! Hey! I know you can hear me.'
Lisboa turns. Oh, fuck.
'Ellie,' he says. He smiles at her. 'You.'
She gives him a kiss. 'Always me, querido.'
Lisboa shakes his head. 'What do you want?'
Lisboa didn't much like her when Mario used her in a couple of
cases, including his last. English girl, this Ellie, who Lisboa's known
now for a good few years, he supposes. She was Mario's contact, then
friend, got herself into trouble, out of it again, and fancies herself as
a crusading journo, a real wide-on for the truth, hard-charging and
fearless, all that malarkey. She's got a sense of humour, Lisboa thinks,
a real mouth on her – a *tongue*.
Bit like old Silva, but better turned out.
She was there when it happened to Mario.
She knew nothing about it, but she was there. The trauma wasn't
too hard for her, he's heard. He's not sure what he makes of that.
'I want to talk,' she says. 'About last night.'
'What about it? I don't think we… well, you know.'
'Ha, your famous sense of humour.'
Lisboa shrugs.
'Two things happened. One, a youngish gay man was murdered
in a park near Avenida Paulista in what looks like a straight-up hom-
ophobic attack. Two, a youngish woman is caught graffitiing EleNão
down the road from there by a couple of Militars who arrest her and
take her in and strip her naked and abuse her.'
'Sounds like it was a fun night.'
'Like I said, that sense of humour.'
'Why are you telling me this?'
'I want to know if you're involved.'
'Yeah, sweetheart, I'm a suspect.'
'You know what I mean.'
Lisboa sighs. 'There's a chance I will be, yes. I don't know. I haven't

been given anything yet today, instructions-wise, certo, because of, well, because of this – '

'Right.'

'Last year or so, I basically just help out others.'

Ellie's nodding. Lisboa looks at that antic energy. He thinks: *Is this how you handle it, life?* He guesses it must be. It likely works, too.

She's twitching and hopping from foot to foot –

'You still working with Silva?' Lisboa asks.

She nods.

'Good for you.'

'Look, Ricardo,' Ellie says. 'Do me a favour, if you are on either case in any way, give me a call, yeah?'

She hands him a card. Lisboa pops it into his shirt pocket. He looks over his shoulder. He waves down a cab. The cab jams into a gap next to them.

Lisboa opens the door –

'You take this,' he says. He ushers Ellie into the back seat, smiles. 'I need the walk.'

'This is all well and good, meninas,' Ellie is saying to Anna and Fernanda. 'But we all know that the only thing worth knowing *right now* is the name of the poor woman who was locked up last night by the Military Police.'

Ellie notes the exchange of looks.

Anna says, 'I thought this was an interview about *our* work.'

'Strikes me,' Ellie says, 'the poor woman I mention is *exactly* your work.'

'Advocacy is not the same as legal defence, Ellie,' Fernanda says.

Ellie smiles. She's known Fernanda for a time. Silva made all the connections a while ago, after, well, after Mario. Ellie leaves it at that. Leaving it at that is how Ellie deals with what happened. She knows that Fernanda used to work with Mario's wife, Renata, but they have never spoken of it. This is not a hugely revolutionary coping strategy for Ellie, she knows this.

It is what it is – and it works.

'No,' Ellie says, 'but isn't advocating against the abuse of women in police custody something of a no brainer. Your little organisation's name, too, ne?'

Ellie notes Anna's eye-roll, Fernanda's stoic nod.

The name: Mulher-Poder, which Ellie likes for the rhyme, and the translation's not too bad either: Woman-Power. Funding from big players, Ellie's heard. Influence of Marta Suplicy, no doubt – and Capital SP, too, surely.

'What do you want, Ellie?' Anna asks.

'Quid pro quo, querida,' Ellie says. 'You get the name of the woman – '

'Okay.'

'And I'll write this piece up about all the sterling work you've been doing as the number one socially-conscious, righteous-campaigning, politically-minded legal aid advocacy team in the fine state of São Paulo.'

'No need to take the piss, Ellie.'

Ellie mock fawned. 'Not my style, amor.'

'No.'

'Look,' Ellie says. 'You're doing fine work and I like you girls, but we all know that it's down to the patronage from Marta that gets you the money to operate.'

Ellie notes the silence. She notes annoyed acquiescence.

'Então?'

'Exactly my point. It doesn't matter. Only way to make a difference is from within, ne? End of story.'

'We came today in good faith, Ellie,' Anna says.

'You help me out and the story gets written.'

Anna's shaking her head. 'Sacanagem,' she mutters. *Dirty trick.*

Ellie grins. 'It's called working the source, ladies.'

'Okay,' Fernanda says. 'We can get the name and you publish the piece. Deal.'

'Back of the net,' Ellie says. 'You'll call me tomorrow?'

'We'll call you later today,' Anna says.

Ellie blows kisses. 'You're making me all wet.'

Anna shakes her head. 'Total gringa.'

Ellie laughs.

In a taxi back to their office, Anna turns to Fernanda and says: 'She's a piece of work, that Ellie.'

Ellie's polishing a piece she began writing quite some time ago. Brazil: Order and Progress –

While apparently expressing the basic ambition of any newly independent country, the Brazilian motto has interesting origins. It is adapted from the philosopher Auguste Comte's basis of Positivism: 'Love as a principle and order as the basis; progress as the goal'. Arguably, for modern day São Paulo, the followers of Comte who deposed the monarchy and secured independence for Brazil in the nineteenth century focused on the wrong words. Undoubtedly there is a principle of love in Brazil; and São Paulo represents nothing if not progress as an ultimate goal; but order? It feels that in São Paulo there is little basis of anything, that any order in the city is as irregular as the manner in which the suburbs grew outward from the centre. Some say that the city is a small one: just one surrounded by lots of other small cities. In Positivism – and this is a simplification – introspective and intuitive knowledge is rejected as a means of acquiring justified true belief. It sometimes feels that São Paulo is defined entirely by these forms of knowledge.

Ellie looks out her apartment window.

Traffic and dust.

Briefing –

Lisboa's assignment:

Hate crime.

Here we go again, he thinks. More horror.

Lead detective is Lutfalla who is sympathetic to Lisboa as he liked Leme. He *investigated* Leme too, of course, but in as staunch a way as is possible.

Nothing to do in the end, of course. Thank fuck. The boys upstairs let it all go –

Mario was a good man. Lisboa needs nothing more.

Lutfalla gives basic instructions: *who the fuck is the dead homo?*

That's Lisboa's job. *That* angle.

There's an element of *take care of the big guy having the nervous breakdown.*

On the other hand – why not? It's grunt work.

An hour later –

Lisboa heads to the engine room of the investigation.

There's chatter from Lutfalla and another detective, Alvarenga, about football. Lisboa hears Alvarenga saying:

'What's the difference between Neymar and time?'

Lisboa notes Lutfalla's wry grin. Man of few words, old Lut.

Alvarenga's pre-punchline laughing.

Alvarenga goes: 'Time passes, mate.'

Lisboa nods hello. 'The old ones are the best ones,' he says.

Lutfalla stands. They shake hands. 'Good to see you, Ricardo.'

'Have a seat, big guy.'

Lisboa does as he's told. Lutfalla pours coffee into a plastic cup.

Lisboa nods, takes it.

Alvarenga hasn't finished. 'Why do they call Robinho "The Triathlon?"'

'Not now, eh,' Lutfalla says.

Alvarenga, with a sulk, raises an eyebrow. 'You wouldn't have got it anyway, mate.'

'It's not so much of a headscratcher I wouldn't,' Lisboa says.

Alvarenga looks peeved, gives Lisboa the evils, goes: 'Good for you.'

'Isn't it, no?'

'All right, lads,' Lutfalla says. 'Let's at least pretend to do some work.'

Alvarenga smirks. Lisboa notes something in this smirk, though he's not sure what exactly.

No one says anything for a few minutes.

Lisboa slurps coffee, pops a couple of pastries. He crumb-brushes his suit trousers. They're shiny with overuse and the wrong wash cycles. Cheap patched material. Lisboa pulls at threads. He scratches thighs. He thinks: *just what am I doing here?*

It's air-con heavy and no natural light. Strip bulbs and hard-backed chairs. A round table with nothing much on it. More waiting room than meeting room.

He's known these men donkeys' years so he's not going to just sit still, keep shtum like some lemon, he wants to know what's what, which is fair enough.

Alvarenga is reading the paper; Lutfalla is looking at his phone.

Lisboa says, 'So what am I doing here exactly?'

Alvarenga snorts. He's senior man in terms of age, but he's been a little out to pasture these last few years. Didn't make the promotion grade and a sulky disposition as a result. Lutfalla gives a tight grimace.

'Fact is, mate,' he says, 'there isn't much to do here at all.'

'Right.' Lisboa gestures at the room, the *emptiness*.

'I mean,' Lutfalla goes on, 'there's a case. There's a dead body, a clear murderous attack, and so a case.'

'So what?'

'So it's a tricky one is what.'

'Explain.' Lisboa senses he can push this. Old Lut looks at odds with himself. 'It seems simple enough to me,' he adds.

'Our colleagues,' Alvarenga says. 'Our colleagues in the Military Police, that is, they would rather there isn't too much news broadcast about this murderous attack.'

Lisboa reckons he knows why this might be. 'They're rooting for Bolsonaro, ne?'

Lutfalla makes a face: *no shit, Sherlock.*

'A homo hate crime does not reflect well.'

'It does not.'

Lisboa's nodding. 'We publicise it *as* a hate crime, as an indiscriminate attack, some of the more liberal media might see our friend Bolsonaro's rise to prominence as creating a sort of permission for this kind of murderous attack.'

Alvarenga claps loud. 'That is elegantly put, big man. I am impressed, porra.'

Lisboa mock bows.

'It's a pickle,' is all Lutfalla wants to add.

Lisboa says, 'We call it a mugging and find the cunts anyway.'

'We could.'

'But we won't.'

This is Alvarenga putting in. Lisboa notes that Lutfalla lets him.

Lisboa raises eyebrows.

Lutfalla nods.

Alvarenga says, 'You remember that poor slag Marielle in Rio?'

Lisboa nods. Of course he does. Everyone does.

Marielle Franco: politician, activist, feminist, all that. Real loudmouth about police brutality. She had a point, Lisboa always thought. Campaigned against the use of force in the favelas, spoke out about Temer's federal intervention, sending troops in to clean the place up earlier in the year, February it was. And guess what? In March she's murdered in a hail of bullets in her car. Poster girl for left-wing activism. A genuine tragedy, Lisboa thinks.

'Word is,' Alvarenga's saying, 'that it was ex-Military boys in Rio, certo? Not quite a death squad, entendeu? But not *not* one, if you get my drift?'

'Crystal.'

'Sort of a neighbourhood watch scheme, removing undesirables.'

'Allegedly,' Lutfalla says.

Alvarenga makes a wry face. 'Allegedly, yeah. Fact is, there's word about the place that our own Military boys have a similar operation.'

Lisboa goes *woah*. 'What are you saying exactly?'

'There's a chance,' Alvarenga says, 'that the perps might be low food chain in an ex-Militar-run, or at least ex-Militar-*approved*, organisation.'

'Neighbourhood watch.'

'It is what it is.'

'So no one wants any digging?'

Lutfalla chimes in here. 'Digging is not the preferred approach.'

'And the victim? His family?'

'Tragic robbery. Desperate act of some poor, disenfranchised little thug.'

'Just the sort of thing,' this is Alvarenga, 'that old Bolsonaro will put an end to with his hard-line, no-nonsense business policy: petty, violent crime.'

It's Lisboa's turn to snort.

'Which answers your original question,' Lutfalla says. 'You ID the John and see to it the profile matches with this appraisal.'

Lisboa's shaking his head. 'I thought you two were all right, you know. What happened?'

Alvarenga, playing a tiny violin with his fingers, says, 'I'm getting old. I just want a quiet life.'

'It's only hearsay,' Lutfalla says. 'But think about it. Bruno Covas is mayor of São Paulo. His old mate – his old *boss* – Jonny Doria is running for state governor. These are right of centre politicians who are career driven.'

'And? I'm career driven.'

Lutfalla ignores this. 'They see which way the wind's blowing. São Paulo will be left to do what it does best once Bolsonaro is in office. Until then, don't rock the boat is the message.'

'Hearsay.'

'Do your job, mate, that's all this is about.'

Lisboa stands. 'Lula's in jail,' he says. 'This is a done deal. This is not about politics, entendeu?'

'And who do you think put Lula in jail? The very same federal judges he appointed. Don't matter under whose influence, that fact remains.'

'Just doing their jobs.'

Lutfalla shrugs. 'It is what it is.'

'Yeah.' Lisboa's nodding. 'It really is.'

Walking back to the office he shared with Mario, the shit-can, rust-stained, dingy-lit office that no one chose to move into after Mario, after Mario *left*, walking back to this office, to *their* office, he thinks, do your job, mate, that's all.

First part is working out which ex-Militars might have something to do with Bixiga and why.

He needs a list of the recently retired.

Or, more helpfully, someone involved in locking up this chick activist. Someone in trouble, might be a good place to start.

He should get down to Admin; they'll know how to find that out. Pure euphemism, Admin –

Thin line of the law stuff down there. Real collection of geeks and fuckheads. Checking up on their Militar sisters will be right up their alley.

After that, the autopsy of the poor sod in the wrong place at the wrong time.

The horror, he thinks, once again: here it is, the *horror* – and it stretches on and on and on.

Rafa pulls the car off Avenida Giovanni Gronchi. He idles, bumps down cratered Rua Clementine towards the favela. He slides the roundabout and parks. He bounces out. He backheels the door closed behind him.

A fresh, shit-booze odour.

A couple of mendigos yell out: E aí mano, what have you got for me, brother? then cackle with laughter. Rafa gives them the middle finger, but he's grinning as he does it. They do not, it seems, take much offence.

He's through the gates of Cemitério Gethsêmani and the space rolls out in front of him, green and comforting. The air is clear – like home, he thinks. He loves that he thinks this instinctively. He smiles and considers, yes, that is where home is now.

He takes the path towards the admin office, where he is going to discuss his grandmother's funeral with some technical director or other. He has a fistful of cash and a steely look. And some names to drop if need be – they've been good like that, the boys up the hill. It should be enough for a world class show. She deserves it; he feels he does too.

He stops, though, at the Aviary, a place his dad used to take him when they visited to see *his* dad. It was built, his old man told him, and then the birds just all turned up uninvited a month or two later, hungry and happy, and settled in, so the story goes. Yellow heads and orange cheeks, long grey bodies and yellow-green tail feathers.

Rafa pokes his finger through a hole, makes a kissing sound with his mouth.

The birds ignore him.

Junior's back on the street. In fact, he's on fucking *traffic duty*. That's what comes from trying to do the right thing, he thinks.

It is a clear message, this traffic duty –

Shut the fuck up, son, is the gist.

The interview with his superiors went something like this:

So on the evening of October 7th, your boys Felipe and Gilberto apprehend a young woman defacing public property in an act of criminal vandalism.

Yes.

They take said young lady back to base to charge her.

Yes.

In the meantime, you remain vigilant in your position, monitoring potential trouble with young Rubens.

Yes.

You're a hero is what you are.

Yes.

You return and find Felipe and Gilberto interrogating the perp and consider they're doing a thorough job and reward their initiative by allowing them to continue unhindered by the supervision of a senior officer.

Yes.

To reward you for this outstanding show of leadership, you'll be placed, for one week, on administrative duties, away from frontline stress.

Yes. And now: *traffic duty.*

There's an upside to it: he's not actually working the roads; he's supervising the lads who are. Which means he's doing precisely fuck all, as how are you supposed to supervise lads standing in traffic anyway? So Junior's day – and the rest of the week with it – looks like hanging out in Militar-approved cafes, diners, restaurants and, why not, bars, close to Avenida Paulista, which is his beat for the week, not a snails-pace, stones-throw from where those moleque punks Felipe and Gilberto picked up the graffiti artist and got him into this whole mess.

Caralho, Junior thinks, *fucking hell*, as he sits at the counter of an old-school padaria at the dirty end of Augusta, cursing.

Puta que pariu.

They fucked me, those lads, those *kids*.

Six years he's been one of the boys and he was carving out a position, making a play for captain, sticking broadly to what's right and steering clear of the path to temptation which befalls and befouls so many of his young colleagues.

He's a way with his words when he's angry, young Junior. He grins – wry.

And he knows the state of things, it's all politics – literally.

The deck has fallen trumps high – Bolsonaro, the Militar darling.

So, Junior reflects, it's better to cover up the abuse of a young woman in a Militar cell than undermine the big man's campaign to the big house.

It's easy enough: charge her for something a lot worse and keep her inside, porra.

Junior sips his coffee, picks at a pastry. There's a lefty student paper on the counter and he's flicking through it.

The padaria is mid-morning empty. The breakfast rush is long gone. The students and ravers have passed through on their all-nighters. The whores and the off-duty night shift cops, waiters, security guards have had their early-hours sandwiches, their after-work beers. The dustmen and manual labourers have pounded their shots of cachaça alongside their cafezinho and pão de manteiga, the fortifying breakfast of a long day's hard work – booze, coffee and bread fried in butter. They've all done one hours ago. Lunch will be office types from around, looking for a cheap por kilo option, a long neck of beer or a few shared bottles for the table out of the boss's sight. The students will be back early afternoon to drink off their hangovers.

It's a helluva place, this, Junior thinks. The sort of place he'd never go were it not for his uniform: it's all on the house and why the fuck not, ne?

Bright lights and long nights –

TVs blaring sport and news –

All election, election, election.

Junior's had it up to here, frankly. He signals more coffee, amigo, nice one.

The counter service is Militar-quick. A side of pastries, sweet and savoury, appears. *Why the fuck not?*

'I bet you're happy,' the server says, pouring coffee, nodding at the screen. 'He killed it, am I right?'

Junior shrugs. 'Happy doesn't cover it.'

'Lot to do round here,' he says, meaning outside, meaning the *street.*

Junior nods.

'You'd be able to crack on, wouldn't you? Do what the fuck you want, really have a go, ne? Bet you fancy that.'

Junior goes mais ou menos, *more or less.*

'I wouldn't mind letting a few of them have it, that's for sure. Menos um, ne?'

That's the phrase, right there, Junior thinks.

That's the phrase that's going to get old Bolsonaro into the big house:

Menos um. *One less.*

Meaning: one less crook. Meaning: all force necessary, bang bang bang, medals and honour and anything goes, mate. Meaning: the only good villain is a dead villain.

All that jazz.

Junior makes a non-committal face, like, I'm just enjoying my coffee, son, entendeu?

The server gets it and doesn't like it. Stays where he is.

Junior turns the page of his lefty rag.

The server brings his finger down on it, right on top of an article by a gringa journalist, Eleanor Boe, first published, Junior sees, online, but now already in print –

'I see you've got a head start,' the server says. His smile is ugly. 'Dirty bitch.'

Junior raises eyebrows, shakes his head, watches the server walk away. He flattens the paper a touch, bends it towards him, starts to read –

A hand on his shoulder. Junior turns.

'Hello, mate,' says his old boss, Carlos.

Carlão. Big Carlos.

FUCK.

'Makes for a good read, ne? Fake news, mate. Soon to be discredited.'

Junior thinks: fucking hang about.

'You look like you've seen a ghost, old son,' Carlos says.

Junior grins. 'What the fuck do *you* want?' He shapes up. 'Big dog.'
'Five minutes.'
Junior nods. 'Tick-tock.'

'Well, you're going to have to tell her, because I can't do it, can't let the gringa escrota know we've failed, sabe?' *Gringa cunt* is the idea.

This is Fernanda. Anna is surprised, a touch, by her tone.

She says, 'I thought you liked her?'

They're talking about Ellie.

'Yeah, well.'

'She's all right, vamos, ne?'

Fernanda is nodding. 'She *is* all right. She just fancies herself, that's all, and I don't want to give her the satisfaction.'

Anna's nodding. She feels the same.

They couldn't get the name of the young woman in custody for the graffiti incident, the young woman Ellie seems to know has been abused. Ellie has even written an article about it that's appeared online and now in at least two print newspapers, though student publications, *basically*.

So she feels a failure.

'What did she say exactly?'

This is Fernanda again, this time talking about Marta.

Anna called her and feels embarrassed, too, by this, as it feels to her like a show of weakness, of inadequacy, of well, no, I can't figure things out on my own without you, Marta.

Marta said she wanted nothing to do with anything anymore, was the gist.

'You know she's out of politics, she's had enough.'

Fernanda eye-rolls.

'It's not a place for a woman, is her point, ne?'

'It should be.'

'Which is ours.'

'Which *was* hers.'

Anna knows this is true, feels a bit of shame her old boss has thrown in the towel, not standing for re-election, able to sit the whole thing out from her beach house.

She did take the call, though, at least.

'You know who you should ring?' Fernanda says.

Anna knows the answer but doesn't like it.

'He'll know something,' Fernanda adds. 'He always *knows* something.'

'That's kind of his thing.'

'Call him.'

Anna nods. She phone-scrolls for his number, still filed under R for Rasputin.

He picks up on the third ring. Anna can hear the delight in his voice.

'Well, well, well,' he's going. 'What can I do for *you*, Anninha?'

Little Anna.

She does not like that. She's never liked the nickname and she really doesn't like it when old men use it.

Old men she knows would jump her bones in a heartbeat if they could – and if their heartbeat was strong enough.

'Hello, Senhor Luis,' she says.

'I'm honoured.'

'Can I get to the point?'

The sex motel swinging politico parties were a godsend, it turned out.

Never needed them to go public; they hung heavy like fat, storm-ready clouds. The resignations and the scandals happened without anyone being compromised.

Rasputin was thrilled by it; Ray Marx didn't seem to give a fuck either way.

Anna did very well out of it all, in the end.

And they parted ways on reasonable terms when Marta decided old Rasputin wasn't up to the task of being Mr Marta and canned him, unceremoniously, not long later.

It seems to stick in his craw and Anna isn't surprised.

'Fala, querida,' he says. *Speak on, dear.*

'We're after some information,' Anna says, 'that's proving difficult to come by.'

'This the royal we, is it?'

'Work.'

'Always is.'

Anna sighs. Fernanda makes an encouraging face: *go on, girl.*

'There's a woman been arrested for graffitiing EleNão night of the election. Military Police have her.'

'I've read something about it.'

'Where?'

'Some paper.'

Anna eye-rolls. This act of disingenuousness, this show, is a pain in the backside. 'We want to find out her name.'

'What, get some pro bono work?'

It is what they do, legal help, in various forms.

'Why not?'

Rasputin barks a laugh. 'I suppose you've already asked my ex-wife.'

'What difference does that make?'

'None at all. I've heard she's out of the game and spending all her time and money on her tan.'

'I don't know about that.'

Rasputin's muttering now. 'My fucking beach house, after all, the puta.'

'I didn't catch that.'

'Nothing, nada.'

Anna forces a smile. 'You know where I can find out this woman's name?'

'I'm afraid I don't.'

'Okay.'

There's a moment's silence. Anna can feel Rasputin hasn't finished. She gives him the satisfaction of keeping quiet.

'The question is not where to find her name,' he says, 'but to think about why no one knows what it is.'

'Thanks, Yoda,' Anna says.

'I'll give you a clue: who put Lula in jail?'

Anna thinks. Operation Car Wash – Lava Jato – the chief prosecutor, *him.*

'Sérgio Moro?' she says.

The man's famous now, like Robin Hood or something.

Bringing down the corrupt like an old-school lawman with a six shooter, a horse and a hat.

At least a few cartoons have painted that picture.

'Bingo.'

'And what's he got to do with anything?'

'Who do you think is going to give him a job come January?'

Anna's brain fizzes. 'Bolsonaro.'

'Clever cookie.'

'And this is a clue how?'

'That's national politics, querida. Go local and you'll see the chain.'

'You're such a cunt,' Anna says, fondly.

Rasputin likes this. 'Your old job, sweetheart,' he says. 'Your old boss. My ex-wife. The mayor of our fine city will be making sure this woman's name – this crime, in fact – does not go anywhere.'

'Johnny Doria.'

'Well, his successor, he's stood aside, remember?'

Anna hates Rasputin correcting her.

'Same thing, though, I'll give you that,' he says.

'Okay,' Anna says. 'I'm not sure this helps much.'

Rasputin laughs. 'Querida, this is a beautiful opportunity. You've got to think bigger than pro bono, baby.'

Anna, deadpan. 'You're a heartbreaker, senhor.'

'You call me you get anywhere, certo?'

'Your interest is just darling.'

Rasputin grunts something like *yeah, okay*. 'Ciao, ciao,' he says, and hangs up.

Anna hangs up too. She stretches her neck, rubs her eyes.

Fernanda makes a face. *Well, what?*

'Maybe we call Ellie and tell her the truth. Maybe we think a little bigger, work with her.'

'Jesus.'

'*Maybe.*'

Fernanda smiles. 'Whatever you think,' she says. '*Querida.*'

Anna laughs.

She always nails, it, Fernanda, Anna thinks, knows exactly what to say to make her laugh.

Ellie calls Silva who has been something of a mentor to her since Leme introduced them back in 2014. It's not been easy for her, him leaving. It signified something that she doesn't like to think too much about. What it signifies is it's not worth it, in the end, what we do.

Silva spends his days reading at his beach house. He's drinking a lot less and eating better. He's doing that thing Paulistanos do when they're at their beach houses: exercise-walking. Laps and laps round the gated condo he lives in near Santos. Ellie *loves* to hear all about this, so she calls infrequently.

This time, Silva tells her something useful.

Look to see where the connection is and there's your story.

A hate crime and police brutality –

Join the dots, Ellie.

She says, 'I hope you're well, Francisco.'

She doesn't say: Saudades, cara. *I miss you, mate.*

Of course, old Lisboa's been around the block a few times so he knows what goes on around said block and where to start looking for a renegade neighbourhood watch scheme that might, from time to time, take the law into its own dirty hands.

The neighbourhood Moto Taxi rank.

If Bixiga is the bladder of São Paulo, this is where the bad guys piss.

Lisboa's plan: catch someone with their pants down and yank.

He's left Admin to do their thing and the autopsy was straightforward enough –

The bloke was shanked to death with a long knife through the fucking neck.

Fun and games.

Lisboa's waiting for all the particulars and then it's his job to contact the family and get a positive ID.

Real fun and games.

He's happy as a clam, Lisboa. It's early afternoon and he parks himself in the window of The Blue Pub, a faux-British joint off Avenida Paulista on Alameda Ribeirão Preto, at the top of Morro dos Ingleses, *Englishmen's Hill*, in the heart of Bixiga, and a couple of hundred yards away from Parque Trianon where the poor sod was done. It's not a bad spot, all told. A cavernous downstairs room with a big screen; a discreet bar lined with booths upstairs, which is where Lisboa is sitting.

Happy hour: three pints of Heineken for only R$35. Or two pints of Paulaner for a bargain R$47.

Happy days. This is aspirational drinking, upwardly mobile choices, very discerning.

Lisboa orders a Heineken. The heft of a full pint is something else. Sometimes your regular chopp or frosted bottle with a tiny glass is not enough.

As he takes a big bite into his beer, he wonders, with glasses this size, how anyone ever gets anything done over in old England.

Bixiga's got something about it, Lisboa thinks. It's a *neighbourhood*, local amenities and family-owned restaurants. Italian immigrant and proud. Lisboa went to one of the family-owned Italian canteens every Sunday as a kid: a Paulistano standard. The portions were ominous, could feed a family. It was a clever racket, he later found out, when working Vice near the start of his long and distinguished years of service in the Polícia Civil.

What these places did was insist that every dish was for two people, you *had* to share, but, equally, you couldn't share with more than two. That's a lot of produce. Which means a lot of deliveries. Which means you clear the fridge out every day and cut the right kind of a deal with the wholesalers for meat and tomatoes and you're laughing. There is a shady sort of Italian businessman who makes sure the right deals get cut and who gets cut *in*. Which means delivery truck companies, waste disposal, laundry service, even the agencies that employ the young Italian men and women who wait tables – in their own family's places. Clever business, and the centre of it right here in Bixiga, and all legal – just.

The problems arrive when this shady sort of Italian business-man tries to ratchet things up a little, using the restaurant as a side for a bigger operation – drugs, booze, women, whatever else some two-bit mafioso feels will make a buck. It's when this happens the delicate equilibrium is done for – all the families want the same thing, in the end: their restaurants to run smoothly and profitably.

The appearance of legitimacy is paramount and easy to pull off, too, as it's basically a fair likeness.

Lisboa knows Vice have some decent contacts and there is a blind-eye relationship. He thought about calling someone down there but decided there's a good chance that his solo mission here will not go unnoticed if he follows any sort of protocol.

So he's doing it old-school, a trick his old man taught him. He used to call it chumming, in that you're throwing out bait and watching the scavengers thrash about, fighting for their piece.

Lisboa calls it the old Piranha, in an ode to his dad.

The old Piranha goes like this. Lisboa rings the Moto Taxi number and watches a young lad scurry from behind it to take the call. Lisboa says, 'Do me a favour, son, and meet me in The Blue Pub across the road, I want to talk a little business and don't want to use the phone, entendeu?'

The young lad says sim senhor and Lisboa watches him scurry across and into the door of The Blue Pub. He's not old enough to get served, but the bar staff ignore him and Lisboa notes this and thinks, aye aye, here we go then.

The lad clocks Lisboa and sidles over. Lisboa is plain clothes, but dressed like an aging football hooligan, which is about the dodgiest look he can pull off without looking like a cunt. Idea he wants to communicate is that he might be a general in the Torcida Jovem, the naughty group of São Paulo-based Santos supporters who hang around the neighbourhood.

The lad says, 'You call for a Moto Taxi?'

Lisboa says, 'I did.'

'You want the cheaper kind or the more expensive?'

Lisboa grins, gives it the two thumbs-up. 'Mate, what do you take me for, falou? More expensive.'

The lad nods.

Lisboa says, 'Where do you normally park these Moto Taxis, then?'

The lad looks shifty, but says, 'Apartment service across the road. Downstairs car park.'

Lisboa nods. 'Name?'

The lad says, 'You ask for Michelangelo.'

Lisboa snorts. 'Bixiga, ne?'

The lad says, 'Yeah, tell me about it.'

'How long?'

'Twenty minutes.'

'Good boy,' Lisboa says. He gives the lad a ten-note. 'Now fuck off, eh?'

The lad fucks off and Lisboa notes the smirk on the barman's face. Good, he thinks. We're in here.

The twenty minutes pass and Lisboa devours the rest of his pint.

He stands, wipes his mouth and takes his enormous glass back to the bar.

The barman goes to thank him.

Lisboa says, 'Keep the happy-hour tab running, son. I'm just going for a piss.'

The barman raises an eyebrow and Lisboa returns the look with a *not now, amigo, you know what I mean?*

He leaves through the front entrance and heads for the apartment service, which has the very misleading name of Paradise Rooms plastered across it in pink neon.

He barges through the door all confidence and muscle. The receptionist is a bored-looking student in a great coat with a tatty paperback and a superior look to him. Lisboa delivers the line 'I'm meeting a Michelangelo' with authority and a *don't fuck with me* attitude he is fairly sure the student will defer to.

The student does. 'Take the lift to *menos um*,' he says.

Lisboa nod-smiles. He mutters to himself that *menos um* is an apt fucking phrase.

The lift is tacky-swank like a sex motel, red leather and a dirty mirror. The ride doesn't last long. He exits in the basement. It's a fairly standard, concrete underground car park with more car debris – tyres, spare parts, oil-covered rags, ropes – than actual cars.

A young man sits on a moped. He's wearing a leather jacket covered in chains. He has greasy hair and a ratty tache. He has an unjustified swagger; he is a low-level slinger and looks like he's got nasty breath.

Lisboa points at him. 'Michelangelo.'

The man's nodding. Lisboa's walking towards him sharpish.

The man's smiling and standing up when Lisboa reaches him and before the man has a moment to understand what's going on, Lisboa has forearmed him in the windpipe and kicked him in the balls.

The man goes down.

Lisboa, firmly, stands on his throat. He takes the man's left wrist, pulls his left arm as far as it will go and twists.

'Now get up,' he says.

The young man tries. Lisboa jabs him in the throat and he goes back down.

'Get up, I said,' Lisboa says.

The young man does as he's told. Lisboa rifles pockets and pulls small plastic bags of cocaine and cash.

Lisboa pulls his badge. 'Listen carefully, son,' he says.

'Entrapment,' the young man is saying, 'this is pure entrapment.'

'I'll shut your fucking trap,' Lisboa says.

The young man is snivelling into his ratty tache.

Lisboa says, 'You work for someone. I want to know who. I want to know who runs this neck of the woods, entendeu?'

The young man squirms. He sniffs hard and spits.

Lisboa says, 'I want to know who you pay to allow you to peddle your snide little trade. And you're going to help me find out.'

The ratty tache and the greasy hair look schoolboy on this miserable fuck now that Lisboa's got hold of him.

Lisboa says, 'Here's what we're going to do.'

The young man listens. He understands he has no choice. He will set up a meeting with his boss – his line manager – this evening, late doors, a meeting that Lisboa will witness.

It's a Russian-doll type of set-up: Lisboa will barge in at every meeting until he's at the top of this little food chain.

Meantime, it's back to The Blue Pub and wait. Two pints of Heineken with his name on. Cheers, he thinks. The beer fizzes.

And this, he thinks, is a textbook Piranha.

His old man would be well proud.

The funeral is a success, as these things go, though Rafa doesn't have a great deal of experience.

It's a Sunday, which helps, the whole congregation of grandma's church turning up and making it a celebration. A conga-line of righteous singsong, eyes closed and praise be-ing, snaking through Paraisópolis and across Avenida Giovanni Gronchi, which is quite a spectacle, this mass of hand-clapping fervour and sweating adulation of the Lord queuing for the green light to cross the main road.

It's the first round of the elections, too, which means there is nothing else to do but to celebrate this life.

'Você virou homen, ne, filho?' the pastor tells Rafa, his arm around his shoulders.

You've become a man, haven't you, son?

Rafa wants to squirm.

The pastor adds, 'It's good you went away. She was pleased that you did, in the end.'

No, what Rafa wants to do is calmly remove the pastor's arm from his shoulders, brush off his lapels, look the old coot in the eye and tell him to fuck off.

He smiles, teeth on edge, thinking yeah, okay, big man.

Rafa watches Franginho and Carolina talking quietly on their own and wishes he was with them. The pastor is saying something about a whip round and a memorial service.

'We're all going for a drink at Dona Regina's, certo?' Rafa shrugs the pastor off. 'And this week I'm going to sort out my grandma's things and after that I'm going home, falou?' Rafa's look hardens, his resolve too, though he shakes. 'I want nothing more to do with this place.'

The pastor nods. 'Vai com Deus,' he says. *God be with you.* 'I'll pray for you.'

The boys up the hill decide to throw Rafa a party and Dona Regina's is chocka with well-wishers and hangers-on. No one's putting their hands in their pockets, that's for sure.

Rafa finds himself with another well-meaning arm around his shoulders. It's one of the boys, nickname Fried Rice, a former friend and general of old Garibaldo. Rafa hasn't thought about either of them for some time.

'Point is, Rafa-Rapido,' Fried Rice is saying, 'You were a good boy.'

There are shots of pinga and beers everywhere. Snacks and music. Cars are parked around all points of the junction, so it's sealed off, pedestrianised for a day.

There are two Militar motorbikes in their usual place, but their lights are off. Rafa sees Franginho having a word with one of them. It looks like he's slipping him something. A backhander to keep the peace, show a little respect, no doubt. Good lad.

Rafa's missed him. The first thing Franginho said to him when they arrived?

'You knocked her up yet?'

It said everything.

Rafa scopes his old stomping ground. He notes the lawyer lady's old office. He notes the bar refurb – a paint job and a new fridge. He sees the way the streets look busier, cleaner, modern, aerials and cables and antennas and so on, all official-looking kit rather than the moody knock-offs of the past, more, what's the word, he thinks – *civilised*. That's it: Paraisópolis is more civilised.

Fried Rice is rabbiting on about what a good kid Rafa is and Rafa is busy thinking about how the place has got infrastructure. He'd read something in the papers, few years ago now, it was, how the favela had been earmarked for cash from the Ministry for Cities – looks like it got it. He wonders where this leaves Fried Rice and the organisation. Rafa suspects they helped broker the deal.

'So, mate, you're golden.' Fried Rice toasts Rafa with a shot. 'We'll help with whatever you need.'

'Yeah, cheers, appreciate it,' Rafa says.

He knows Franginho is already negotiating a sneaky cash sale of grandma's house up the hill, and aside from that there ain't much to do. But it's a nice touch, making Rafa feel part of the firm, as if he never really left, as if he never abandoned ship and fucked off with a secret supply of cash.

Yeah, it's a nice touch.

Then an arm round his shoulder that *is* welcome: Carolina. Rafa realises that he is a little drunk. It's hardly a surprise – the world and his wife want to give him a drink.

'My love,' Carolina smiles.

Rafa turns and they kiss briefly and she holds him a moment.

'You okay?' he asks.

She is. She's sad, but she's fine, she tells him. 'I'm just glad we came back – and that you've done this. I'm proud of you. Eu te amo, lindão.'

I love you, handsome man.

'You know you can go see your friends, I don't mind.'

Carolina head-tilts and smiles. 'You mean that? You know I'd love to.'

'Franginho says he'll drive you, pick you up after.'

'You keeping tabs on me?'

This is a joke. Of course, it is a joke: she's funny, Carolina. Rafa laughs. 'I won't be long – it's, you know, it's *today*.'

'I know what today is.'

She says, 'And then we can take care of everything tomorrow and go home.'

This is what Rafa wants to hear. This is all Rafa wants, to go home.

'I love you,' he says.

'You better.'

Later, Rafa watches Franginho drive off with his girlfriend and he thinks there's got to be a way to get Little Chicken out of the Paraisópolis coop.

Junior is not pleased to see Carlos, but he's fronting it out.

He orders a bottle of Brahma and two glasses. He stands, the bottle in one hand, the glasses in the other. 'How about we take this outside?' he says.

Carlos nods and follows.

The table is plastic and rickety. The street is day-quiet. Rubbish trucks roll and crunch by. Dustmen whistle and yell. Their orange jumpsuits evoke clowning, amusement.

Carlos says, 'Been a while since we broke bread, my friend.'

'It has.'

'Happy days, eh?'

Junior knows to what Carlos refers and does resolutely not consider these days to be happy.

'You've done all right, haven't you, son, last few years?' Carlos says.

Junior says, 'Five minutes, ne?'

'Except for one misstep on Sunday night.'

'I wouldn't say misstep.'

'Except for that misstep, you'd be looking at a sweet promotion by now.'

'What's it to you?'

'Just looking out for a former protégé, that's all.' Carlos grins. 'I care about my boys, always have.'

'I'm not your boys.'

'Yes, you are.'

Junior nods – resigned. 'What do you want, Carlão? You do want something, ne?'

'It's not so much what I want as what you want.'

'Okay, chega,' Junior says, *Enough*. But he smiles. 'When did you get so philosophical?'

'Retirement will do that for you.'

'Right.'

Junior pours them more beer. They drink.

'This misstep, I've a way out for you.'

'Okay.'

'Point is I'm semi-retired. I've been doing a little freelance consulting for the firm, sabe?'

Junior nods.

'A job came up yesterday, something I've been tasked with. Something I need your help with.'

'Right, help.'

Carlos ignores this. 'The woman your boys arrested and then did God knows what. I'm in a position to make it all go away, which is what everyone upstairs wants.'

'Sounds delightful.'

'Not like that. I know who she is and I have something on her, something that could cause problems for her.'

'You always were good at networking, Carlão.'

'But owing to my retired status, no one else can have anything to do with my work, right?'

'Crystal.'

'Except you.'

'Except me.'

'And upstairs has deemed – on the sly, of course – your involvement a penance for this misstep.'

Junior nods. Of course they have. This is how it works. This is how he got involved with Carlos and his lot in the first place. A misstep and penance.

'What do you want me to do?' Junior asks.

'They're letting the girl go tonight. As you were the senior officer at the time of her arrest, we reckon you can have the privilege of driving her home.'

'Sounds reasonable.'

'Don't be cheeky, son.'

'And we'll take her somewhere and you'll lay out how it really is.'

'Good boy.'

Junior stands. 'Who's your contact, you know all this? It doesn't sound like one of your snouts.'

'Networking, mate.' Carlos winks. 'I'll call you.'

Junior waves at the waiter and drops some notes on the table. He leaves.

As he reaches the end of the street, an eye out for traffic duty, he sees Carlos and the waiter laughing, Carlos with another bottle, Junior's notes in his fist.

Bolsonaro makes a statement condemning the hate crime murder of the young man in the park. He makes reference to two unsolved murders in São Paulo in 2011; he makes reference to the Park Maniac; he makes reference to other unsolved crimes, and he establishes that under his presidency crime will be beaten, there will be no place for it, murderers, thieves and rapists had better watch out.

Bolsonaro's claim, Ellie reads, between the lines, is that his government will put an end to exactly the sort of hate crime his government will no doubt encourage.

It's such a brazen sleight of hand that it's ingenious: look what happens because of me; only I can solve it. Ellie ponders this. Is this what he's doing?

She's not sure he's that clever.

Her phone rings. Anna.

'Pois não?' Ellie says, half-joking. *Can I help you?*

'We can't get the name of the girl,' Anna says.

'Woman, I think you mean.'

'Okay, Ellie, very good.'

Ellie's smiling, saying nothing.

'We can't get her name, but we do know why not.'

'That might be useful.'

'We think we should work together.'

'We?'

'Fernanda and I – and you.'

Ellie's really grinning now. 'That might be a good idea.'

'But together means *together*, certo?'

'Sisters are doing it for themselves.'

'Something like that.'

There's a moment of silence, of anticipation, excitement. Ellie can feel it. She says, 'So what's the plan, Anna?'

'The plan, querida, is two angles. You look at one, we look at the other.'

'What's your angle?'

'Political.'

'Makes sense. And mine?'

'The cops, querida. You've got history, after all.'

Ellie nods. She has. 'That's true.'

'Good, then that's settled.'

'Yep.'

'We just want to find the name of this woman and talk to her.'

Ellie's not sure that's just what they want to do. She says, 'We're like Charlie's Angels.'

'Speak this evening?'

'Com certeza.' *Absolutely*.

They hang up.

Ellie phone-scrolls contacts down to I.. She gives Ricardo a call. He sounds a little tipsy, she thinks, to be fair.

Meet me in The Blue Pub, he tells her.

'It's happy hour. The pints of Heineken are enormous.'

'I'm English,' she says. 'And it's your round.'

Sunday night, election day, and Rafa and Franginho are kicking back in his grandma's house watching the results come in. They've got Dona Regina's leftovers on the go and they're both a little buzzed from the all-day drinking, but neither of them is stopping.

'You going to be all right to fetch Carolina?' Rafa asks, tossing Franginho a can.

'Yeah, course. I've got a kid to drive me.'

'What, you're chauffeured now then?'

Franginho bows. 'Something like that.'

'Well, I appreciate it.'

'Ah. You can't leave the jungle tonight, it wouldn't be right. And besides,' he gestures at the house, 'some moleque would have all this away if he knew you weren't here.'

Rafa finds this disquieting. 'Really?'

'Oh yeah, things have changed.'

'The place looks different.'

'Let's just say the organisation has less say than it did.'

Rafa nods. He got that impression. The afternoon party seemed like a throwback to the old days, the lawless wild west. Soon as the junction was clear, it was business as usual – legitimate business.

'Military Police are more present, there's more structure, more organisation. Which means more petty crime, ironically.'

'That what ironic means?'

'Close enough.'

Rafa ponders this. 'I best stay put then.'

'We sell this place tomorrow and get the hell out.'

Rafa smiles. 'You're coming?'

'What I was talking to Carolina about earlier. That okay?'

Rafa slaps Franginho on the back, pulls him close. 'Mate, that is world class.'

They drink, quietly. The results are coming in, Bolsonaro all over it like a rash.

'Bet she ain't too happy about this,' Franginho says.

Rafa nods. She's not said much about it, but – well, her past.

'I should go and get her, d'aqui um pouco.' *In a little while.*

'Yeah,' Rafa says. 'Where did you leave her again?'

'Some bar, up near Paulista.'

'Who was there?'

'Bunch of hipsters, you know what her friends are like.'

Rafa does know. A thought occurs, but he doesn't let it settle.

Junior's got the woman in the back of a civilian car and she's saying nothing but that doesn't bother him as he's got nothing to say. All he wants to do is pick Carlos up and get this over with.

They ghost through Jardins and then hit the Marginal. They're headed, she thinks, towards Morumbi. The Marginal is flowing nicely. Junior floors it. He's told her they're going in via Panamby, which is longer as the crow flies, but quicker in the car, which is what matters in São Paulo, after all.

She didn't seem to care. The address she gave was vague. Giovanni Gronchi.

Instead of pulling in at Panamby, Junior turns into the Extra supermarket, just before the exit. He picks a quiet spot in the corner of the car park, which is huge, and not busy. It's dark and he parks in a space by an unlit streetlamp.

He turns in his seat, says, 'Provisions. You can stay here.'

Junior jumps out, locks the doors. Carlos appears from the gloom. Junior gives him the keys. Carlos pops the door and leans in. Junior hears: 'Carolina, it's very good to see you.'

Junior turns away. They'll be off again in not too long.

Rafa's on the phone to Franginho who is telling him, mate, I'm sorry I don't know where she is, and Rafa gets a feeling like he did that weekend in May in 2006, and something else stirs, and he feels –

Last night, hours after confirmation of Bolsonaro's victory
in the first round of the presidential elections, a young
woman was caught by the Military Police spraying graffiti
near Avenida Paulista, São Paulo. Her message: *Ele Não*.
'Not Him', a protest against candidate Bolsonaro. Meaning:
anyone but him. She was arrested. At the Military Police
headquarters, she was, allegedly, refused a phone call or
lawyer, stripped naked, violently abused, thrown in a cell,
and left with no food and water for over twenty-four hours.

With a clear triumph in the first round now under his belt,
the far-right, populist Jair Bolsonaro is campaigning
to be elected as president of Brazil ahead of Fernando
Haddad, the left-leaning Workers' Party candidate, a former
mayor of São Paulo, and the successor to Lula and Dilma.
Bolsonaro holds deeply abhorrent views on women, race, the
LGBTQ community, Brazil's former military dictatorship,
the use of firearms; these views are on show for all to see
in his statements over the years. He is promising to unite
the country, purge the corrupt leftists and fight crime
with a ruthless and brutal no mercy, no leniency policy.
Just weeks before the first round of elections, Bolsonaro
was attacked and stabbed while speaking at a rally. He
survived. It is predicted that he will win the second, and
definitive, election in a landslide.

What, you may ask, is the connection between this situation
and the fate of the poor woman in a Military Police cell?
Or, perhaps, the answer is obvious enough.

More importantly, this question:

How did it come to this?

More to follow.

2

The Cultural Revolution

October 2018

---

*I am in favour of torture, you know that, and the people
are in favour too. Through the vote, you will not change
anything in this country. (TV interview, 1999)*

*She does not deserve to be raped because she is very bad,
because she is very ugly. ('Joke' about Workers' Party
legislator, Maria do Rosario, December 2014)*

*I would be incapable of loving a homosexual child. I would
rather have a son of mine die in an accident than appear with a
moustache next to him. (Interview with Playboy magazine, 2011)*

*Enough of giving the means for more and more couples
to bring people who don't have the minimum capacity
to be a citizen in the future. (Comment on Brazil's poor,
black, indigenous people, radio interview, 2003)*

Jair Bolsonaro

*Este país não pode dar certo. Aqui, prostituta se apaixona,
cafetão tem ciúme, traficante se vicia, e pobre é de direita.*

*This country is not going to work out. Here, prostitutes
fall in love, pimps get jealous, dealers are addicts
and the poor vote for the right wing.*

The Brazilian singer, Tim Maia, born 28 September 1942; died 15 March 1998

Carolina, Monday, 8 October 2018, Military Police cell:

One night in, what, 2007, I'm in the Sky bar at the Hotel Unique. It's a real piece of work that bar, a real nasty piece of work. I'm, like, late-teens/early twenties, no money, but it doesn't matter if you're a chick with a bit of style and I certainly am – there's plenty of drink offers flying around. I'm in the unisex toilet area, washing my hands and checking out the startling range of soap products and moisturisers, when a large, elegant man shuffles in. He joins me at the sink and comes a little too close for comfort. I've had a few cocktails.

I edge slightly away, but his aftershave is pleasant and his bearing somehow noble so I turn to him.

'Oh fuck,' I say, 'you're Al Gore.'

He nods.

'Nice film,' I say.

He's doing a promotional visit for *An Inconvenient Truth* and trying to save the rainforest by plundering rich Paulistanos.

'Fucken a,' he drawls. 'Thanks.'

'Some girls at my university sent you a song they've recorded. A punk song,' I tell him. 'About global warming.'

He looks at me.

I sing it for him. 'It's getting hot in here! Duh-duh-duh-duh! But don't take off your clothes! Not yet! Not yet!'

He smiles: 'Kids,' he says, winking.

We leave together. He shakes my hand. We look down as we shake, and smile, both aware that our hands are as clean as they've ever been.

'Good luck,' I say.

'I'll need it,' he replies and wanders off into a throng of adoring socialites.

I turn to the bouncer guarding the toilets.

'Know who that is?' I say.

The bloke shrugs his vast, suited shoulders.

'Al Gore,' I say.

'Well, I don't know who that is,' the bouncer replies, 'but he's been in there three times already and doesn't like to tip.'

He glares at me so I hand him a five-note and return to my friends.

Thing is, I was one of those girls. I wrote that song. I got that song to Al Gore. This is how I got into politics, into activism. Realising it can be done.

Problem: São Paulo's aptitude for erasing its past. Brazilians talk about our country as young. But never naïve. We mark the contrast with the traditions of Europe, by avoiding nostalgia, existing without sentiment. Ordem e progresso, Order and Progress, is the national motto. But it is progress that is revered, not order, and progress comes at the expense of the past. When you don't have a proud history to celebrate, when your past was defined by colonial ill-treatment, better to brush it aside and live for today.

Cities are paeans to movement, slack-jawed sharks that swallow up anything incapable of progress. But São Paulo actively tries to forget. Graffiti covers the old colonial centre. The attitude of the construction industry is knock down and build again. In fact, we see it all over Brazil – the degradation of the Amazon rainforests; the urban regeneration for the World Cup and the Olympics, which legitimises tearing down favelas and any structure built before this century, this decade, shunting the residents out of sight, like the Sun King in Paris – but São Paulo leads the way with its unremitting desire for growth. The city is being fattened up and groomed for the global markets.

São Paulo is the future; but notice the tense. Is. It's already there. Forget the past.

Context: I taught a little, when I was studying at the University of São Paulo. It's arguably the best in South America, but it's plagued by strikes and lack of funds. The private universities have a much weaker academic reputation. The very expensive ones, sometimes considered finishing schools for the wealthy, have terrific facilities. For the working classes in search of social mobility, there are the so-called shopping mall colleges, which have popped up all over the city and offer courses in everything from accountancy to hair and beauty.

There is a clear need to translate the desire poor children have to study and learn into a reality where it can be achieved. There is not the same desire among the ruling class. I get it: I was part of the problem teaching where I did.

Election night: This is what happened to me.

My partner's best friend accompanied me in a car driven by an associate of his to a neighbourhood bar on Alameda Santos, where a gathering of my friends watched the election coverage. My partner's grandmother's funeral had taken place that day; I was upset by this and upset for him. He encouraged me to see my friends. We no longer live in the city and there are rare opportunities. This is a testament to his good character and one of the reasons why I love him.

At the bar, my friends were indignant and upset with what was – what is – happening to our country. My friends are a highly politicised group. At university, many of us were part of a left-wing society. We would meet every week, distribute leaflets, write manifestos – that sort of thing. Kids, eh? Well, some of my friends were very drunk as the evening wore on. Angry and drunk. And one of the group is a graffiti artist – a celebrated artist, an *artist*, viu? – and he had his paints with him. He distributed aerosol cans to a few of us. We were laughing, joking, this was a prank, you see, a little harmless protest in a moment of real – in our eyes – tragedy. It made us feel better to do something silly – silly but meaningful. My partner's grandmother's funeral had left me tipsy and emotional – and determined not to let the bastards get me down, sabe?

I was wearing black trousers, a black shirt, black shoes – I'd been at a funeral. I carried a black rucksack, yes, but look at it – leather, small. I was cold. A friend had earlier lent me his black hooded top. I suppose, yes, at first glance I might have looked like someone in a black bloc. But, look at me: look at the clothes I wore underneath the hooded top, look at my face. I am a woman, not some hoodlum girl, not anymore. People choose not to see this.

I chose the bookshop in the Conjunto Nacional mall for two reasons: irony and convenience. Spraying EleNão on a place that sells learning, reason, erudition, liberty and so on – seemed apt. Also, it was a window – not hard to wipe it off. Finally, it was round the corner and very close to where my partner's best friend was due to pick me up.

This is what happened next.

As I was applying the finishing touches, from nowhere two Military Police officers grabbed me from behind. They secured my arms behind my back, picked up my rucksack and the aerosol can, and frogmarched me to where their boss was waiting.

Their boss. There's a funny bird.

He was not impressed with his boys' actions. And yet.

And yet, they took me to the MP HQ down towards the Centro and booked me in for the night on vandalism and sedition charges.

Sedition.

This is what happened after that.

The two officers entered the cell and goaded me over my political affiliations. Well, one of them goaded me, took the lead – the other stood by the door.

I couldn't tell if he was covering the door in case I bolted for it – or keeping it closed so that no one could get in.

I did not rise to their taunts; I said nothing. I believed I would receive my statutory rights, my phone call; I didn't.

After the taunting, they stripped me naked. The man by the door looked like a reluctant participant in this. I appealed to him to stop, to help me; he did not.

They stripped me naked and continued to taunt me. They made obscene sexual gestures. They made detailed sexual threats. They placed their hands on me in a grotesque sexual manner. They did not penetrate me. I believe that they intended to do so.

They did not, as their superior, that funny bird, appeared in the doorway and pulled them out, pulled them off me. He physically restrained the more eager of the officers, slamming him into the cell wall and throwing him through the door. The other officer, the more reluctant participant, left of his own volition with a look of horror on his face.

I spit on him now, for that look of horror, of shock, of *how could I*.

I spit on him.

I was naked, sobbing, curled in a ball.

The superior officer gave me my clothes and brought me coffee and bread and water. He made sure that I was physically unharmed, that I was okay despite the trauma, the abuse. I was okay. His manner was firm but sensitive. He said little. He gave nothing away.

I asked him when I could speak to a lawyer.

He didn't answer.

I asked him when I could expect to be let out.

He didn't answer.

I asked him did he know what it is I had done.

He didn't answer.

When he was sure I was okay, he left.

I haven't seen him since. I have heard nothing since, I have had no recourse to a lawyer; I have not been allowed to inform anyone where I am. Trays of food and water have been pushed through the cell door. That is the only contact I have had with anyone at all.

And here I am almost twenty-four hours later and none the wiser.

This is my story; who is going to tell it?

Junior sits in the front seat. Carlos is next to the woman in the back. Carlos is getting quite close to the woman in the back. Junior knows that the woman trusts Junior, to a point, and he knows, too, that his silence, his complicity, is breaking that trust quite definitively.

Yeah, well, it is what it is, ne?

Junior's listening as Carlos is laying things out. It's a classic bite your tongue and here's why kind of scenario. See no evil, hear no evil, speak nothing whatsoever.

Carlos is saying, 'So here's what you're going to do, querida. You're going to go home to lover boy and you're going to tell him you went out and got good and drunk, lost your phone and stayed with a mate. You're going to make that work as I'm sure a little minx like you won't have too much trouble doing, certo?'

'Why should I?'

'You'll remember when you and your fella were stashing cash a few years ago, cash you ran away with, cash that really was not yours to make house with. You do remember that cash?'

Junior's watching in the rear-view mirror, sees the woman nod.

'Where do you think that cash was coming from, sweetheart?'

Junior sees the woman shake her head.

'It came from me. Well, it came from someone else who gave it to me who gave it to your fella's best mate, who gave it to your fella who squirreled it away for your little love nest.'

The woman, Junior thinks, looks different. She doesn't look scared. There's a look there, on her face, that spells out, ah, okay, I *see*.

Carlos says, 'The boys in Paraisópolis don't know much about this money. How do you think they'd feel should they find out?'

The woman bites her lip. Junior sees her nodding.

'It's simple, really,' Carlos says. 'You say nothing about what happened last night, and the favela hoodlums learn nothing about their former protégé keeping his slush fund private.'

'Okay.'

'You do what you got to do tomorrow, next day, tops, and you head back to your little love shack and all this unpleasantness goes, like you do, puff, into the ether. Entendeu?'

'I understand.'

'Good girl.'

Carlos is smiling now. The woman, Junior sees, is not.

Carlos says, 'My associate here will take you home. You want your fella alive and well, you want your idyllic little life together intact, I suggest you do what I say.'

'Okay.'

'Good girl, you're smart.'

'One thing,' the woman says. 'How did you know where I'd be last night?'

Carlos taps the side of his nose. 'Everything always gets out, querida, bear that in mind.'

Carlos climbs out the car. Junior does the same, locks the doors.

'We good?' Junior says.

'Not quite. Drop her close to the favela. Not too close, not so far she's mugged on her way in, falou?'

Junior nods.

'And there's one more thing you're doing for me.'

Junior glares.

'I've got a thing back over the river in an hour or so. I need you to come with, falou? It's a five-minute meet and greet, piece of piss.'

'I got a choice?'

Carlos slaps him on the back. 'Next couple of days,' Carlos says, 'you'll find your career is back on track, son.'

'How *did* you know?' Junior asks. 'I mean, where she was.'

'Networking, amigo. It wouldn't hurt you did a bit yourself.'

Carlos laughs, he's pleased with that line. He leaves, arm raised in farewell.

Junior sighs. He unlocks the car. Without looking at the woman, he says, 'I'll take you home.'

'Mate, *you're* enjoying happy hour.'

Lisboa smirks. 'These drinks, girl, are mountains.'

'What am I doing here, Ricardo?'

Lisboa breathes heavily. Ellie watches his shirt heave. She spies a heavy booze-sweat. Lisboa tugs at his belt.

'You rang *me*, querida,' Lisboa says.

'I did. But you invited me to this dreadful place.'

Lisboa laughs. 'Ah, vamos, ne?' *Come on now.*

'It's a pure gringo sugar-daddy honey trap.'

'You young women and your lingo.'

'Rich gringos come here to try and fuck Brazilian women,' Ellie says. 'And the women come to try and pick up a rich boyfriend, is what I said.'

'Prices in this place,' Lisboa says, 'I could use a sugar daddy myself.'

Ellie laughs. 'I guess what I'm wondering is why you've been in here so long.'

'Didn't want to lose my seat.' Lisboa points through the window. 'The view is spectacular.'

Ellie watches him shake with laughter at his own joke. She thinks: *this guy.*

They haven't exactly seen eye to eye over the years, but enough shared experience will create affection – especially considering the experiences they've shared.

He's a bit wobbly, she thinks, and hardly surprising. Mario's memorial will have dredged up all kinds of memories, good and bad. It certainly did for her – to a point. She simply doesn't let things get to her. Ellie knows how close the two men were, like kin. She will always respect that.

The bar heaves and sways. Loud guitar music plays over pidgin pick-up attempts. Pink Floyd, 'Wish You Were Here'. Dead romantic, Ellie thinks. It's funny what these pricey fun pubs think is cool, classy – cover bands doing bad versions of 'Have You Ever Seen the Rain', that kind of thing. There's a lot of flesh and teeth on display. A lot of white shirts and black shoes. Ellie throws back her Heineken.

'I'll get a round in,' she says.

'Happy hour, baby,' Lisboa calls after her. He's laughing, again, at his own joke.

Ellie smiles. *This guy.*

'I'll give you one thing about this place, though,' she says when she's back with their pints. 'They do a good burger.'

But Lisboa's not listening. 'This is why you're here, why we're here.' He points across the road at a taxi rank. 'Look.'

Ellie looks. She sees a ratty little bloke sniffing about the taxi rank. He's pacing up and down and has a mobile phone to his ear.

'Who is – '

'Just watch. I need you to watch, that's all.'

'Okay.'

Ellie takes her phone from her bag, carefully sets it on the counter, checks the angle and hits record. Lisboa doesn't notice; she doesn't tell him.

Ellie watches. The ratty man sits on the taxi-rank bench. He jitterbugs his knee. He smokes cigarettes like he's drawing breath.

Lisboa says, 'Another man is about to turn up. I need you to get a good look at him. I want you to go outside, walk down the road, go to the pharmacy or something, and come back. Be discreet, but get a good look, certo?'

Ellie nods. She leaves her phone filming the ratty little man smoking away.

She leaves the pub, she turns left, walks slowly. She bends down to tie her laces. She window-browses desserts in a gelato joint. She hovers outside the pharmacy. She goes in, keeps her eye on what she sees now is a Moto Taxi stand. Interesting – or not.

She runs her hand over pain medication. She stands on the scales, pretends to weigh herself – this gives great scope-elevation.

She sees another man approach the stand. She exits the pharmacy and goes to cross the road. The man hands something to the ratty little man. Ellie is halfway across the road. The man jabs a finger into the ratty man's chest. A message, it seems, is being given here. A lesson maybe. Ellie takes two steps, stops, her eyes wide –

FUCK.

She recognises the man; she knows this man.

But from where?

Ellie pivots, ducks her head, walks quick-time back to The Blue Pub.

'You get a good look?'

Ellie picks up her phone, stops the recording. She scrolls through, finds a clear view, pauses. She takes a screenshot. She finger-thumb enhances it. She shows the image to Lisboa.

'I know this man,' she says.

'Who is he?'

'I don't know.'

Lisboa nods. He slides off his seat.

Ellie's shaking. She drinks her beer. Lisboa brings her a shot of pinga, which she gulps down, gasping.

She settles.

'Sit tight,' Lisboa says. 'Let's think this through.'

Ellie nods.

Junior meets Carlos again in Bixiga. They park at the top of Morro dos Ingleses, outside a seedy-looking apartment service called Paradise Rooms. Junior thinks: Paradise City, Paraisópolis. The good old days, something like that.

Carlos says, 'See that nasty-looking cunt at the Moto Taxi rank?'

Junior nods.

'You're going to give him this.'

Carlos hands Junior an envelope.

'Inside,' Carlos says, 'are three bus tickets. You tell the guy to make sure they use them.'

'Who's they?'

'Doesn't matter.'

'Right.' Junior thinks a moment. He brandishes the envelope. 'Why'd you tell me what's inside, porra?'

'Because then you know, mate,' Carlos says. 'And you know what it means.'

Junior does know. It means: complicity. It means: silence bought.

When he gets back in the car, he tells Carlos, 'Funny thing, you remember that gringa journalist, Ellie?'

Carlos goes, 'How can I forget?'

'She was crossing the road just as I made the drop.'

'Interesting,' is all Carlos says to that.

Junior decides, for now, to park this information.

He just wants to go home.

Lisboa drives Ellie home. He sobered up a treat when Admin got back to him with an ID for the lad in Ellie's phone and the list of recently retired Militars –

The ID: Junior something, a mid-level guy whose nose is generally considered clean. On the list: Leme's old friend, once upon a time, before a lot of water under the bridge, Big Carlos, whose nose, quite definitively, is not.

When he drops her off, he tells Ellie, 'Don't write anything – yet.'

She nods. He notes a steely look to her. Good girl, he thinks.

He looks again at the list. Carlos, you are having a fucking laugh, old son.

He guns the car and heads straight back to the Paradise Rooms.

Ellie gets online and sees a statement from the Military Police supported by state deputies – and, implicitly, the mayor's office – discrediting her article as a fabrication and part of an online fake news political campaign against – implicitly, which is enough – candidate Bolsonaro.

Impartiality seems to be the point; no objective advantage through duplicitous means.

The statement is already being batted back and forth in social media echo chambers.

Anna and Fernanda are running into dead end after dead end. Fernanda had the clever idea of approaching the problem from a missing person perspective. So she's been on the phone at the channels where you would expect to report one, or locate one – hospitals, mainly. It takes a real sleight of hand, though, to find out if a missing person has been reported when you don't know their name. She's been cut off more than once and is making no discernible headway.

It seemed like a good idea; but the point of a missing person is you do know who they are, even if you don't know where they are.

Anna leaves her to it and decides to knock on doors.

First step: she checks the Tribunal de Justiça de São Paulo.

She draws a blank there: nothing filed nor set for assessment even.

This is where the legal aid route normally winds up and it is likely too quick anyway, but it was worth a shot.

Her contact in the office over there told her, laughing, 'Você ta viagando, querida.'

Viagando, *travelling,* abbreviation of *travelling in the mayonnaise,* a phrase Anna loves, but in this case it means she's dreaming if they have any info on something like this.

Second step: figure the protocol when the Military Police make an arrest.

Turns out there isn't one.

They can do what the fuck they like.

Anna does some research and it turns out the United Nations Human Rights Council recommended that Brazil get rid of the Military Police entirely, not that long ago. There have been a number of international groups that are not especially happy with the beating and torturing of detainees, surprise, surprise. So this isn't new, but Anna knows this. Thing is – and here's the political climate coming into play, the post-Lava Jato landscape – human rights organisations are basically apologists for criminals: 'Some believe that investigating and prosecuting police abuses would weaken the hand of law enforcement, and thereby strengthen criminal gangs,' says Human Rights Watch. This is exactly the ticket that Bolsonaro is running on: elimination of crime, the causes of crime – and the criminals themselves.

Then there's the question of why the Militars behave like they do. First point Anna learns is that the execution of criminals is a fairly simplistic response to being fed up with arresting the same faces over and over again. The civil justice system is too unwieldy, too complex, too much red tape and too much obfuscation, so it's easier to simply eliminate them, to use Bolsonaro's word. (One nice story Anna reads is that there was a drop in Militar-related murders when a rule was passed forbidding them from helping or tending to the wounded; before this, they'd pick up the wounded, ostensibly to take them to hospital, and finish the job on the way.)

Then there's the other side. The average Militar works long hours, long shifts, in dangerous areas for fuck-all money. They're forced to take on other work – which is illegal. So, if it's illegal anyway, Anna thinks, why not take on work that is illegal. It'd pay better than private security, though private security can also be something of a euphemism. And there's no way to air any grievances, they're not in a union, they can't strike. It's all military principles, treason and special courts. The really interesting line though is this one: Military Police officers are not allowed to reveal 'facts or documents than can discredit the police or disrupt hierarchy or discipline'.

So talking to one is a non-starter, then, Anna thinks.

This is when she decides to go and knock on doors.

She heads to City Hall, her old office, as she likes to call it –

If she can't find out who the woman in the cells is, then she might be able to find out why she can't find out.

Why the Military Police are able to get away with it. The answer to that is that they can get away with it if no one complains.

And no one's complaining.

There are still people at City Hall who know Anna; she'll get an audience with someone.

First, Anna's been doing a little more reading.

The mayor is Bruno Covas and all you need to know about him is that he voted 'Yes' to begin impeachment proceedings against Dilma. Oh and two other things are useful: he was part of the investigation into Petrobras connected to Lava Jato; and he was a member of the Special Committee of Criminal Majority. And you can believe that he wasn't trying to get the age any higher, that's for sure. Kids equals crooks equals jail time. Which connects him to his predecessor, João 'Johnny' Doria, a real piece of work. They were elected together, Doria as mayor, Covas as deputy. Earlier this year, Doria stepped down to run for state governor, the election for which takes place next year. Doria is a rich fucker and host of the Brazilian version of *The Apprentice*. He was a hard-line right-wing mayor representing a centrist party. A wolf in sheep's clothing, is the phrase, Anna thinks. His policies can be reduced to five key points: anti-abortion, anti-decriminalisation, pro-reduced age of criminal responsibility (hello, Bruno Covas!), pro-Operation Car Wash, pro-electoral reform. His net worth, give or take, R$180 million. His hair is plastered neatly across his forehead. He's almost certainly had work done to his face; his teeth *gleam*.

Anna makes a call, arranges to meet Roberto, an old friend at City Hall. She tells him a lie: she's interested in switching sides, from PT to the Brazilian Social Democracy Party, the PSDB, the party of João 'Johnny' Doria and Bruno Covas, and wants to chat, get some off the record advice.

He tells her, 'You know which way the wind is blowing then, amiga.'

'I'll see you in an hour,' she says.

'Now you don't have a pass, we might have to book you onto the guided tour.'

'You're funny,' Anna says.

Lisboa, hungover, is trying to work out what they know about the victim of the horrendous hate crime on election night. His return visit to the Paradise Rooms yields little. The ratty dealer is nowhere to be found; the kid at the Moto Taxi stand is saying nothing. Lisboa reckons it's this Junior and, principally, Carlos that he needs to talk to.

Now, he's looking at autopsy reports and other evidence so far gathered and filed.

The autopsy detail is grim: the victim received traumatic blows to the head and body suggesting he suffered a sustained and vicious attack from more than one assailant. His left eye socket is dislocated. There are at least three broken ribs. There is deep bruising around the jaw. There is internal bleeding in both ears. His abdomen is discoloured and there is damage to his kidneys and bladder. It is likely, the report states, that he received over a dozen blows to the stomach and groin area, consistent with being kicked with heavy boots. There is evidence of blows to the back of the head; the cranium is depressed in two places. But none of this did for him. The fatal wound was caused by the insertion of a knife – at least six inches long – into the victim's neck, which severed the jugular causing death by suffocation.

There is the standout, superficial – in terms of depth – but significant – in terms of motive – detail: a swastika scratched into the victim's chest. The report states the belief that this act was performed with the same knife that dealt the fatal blow; the lacerations are consistent with the entry wound. The report states the belief – though hard to corroborate – that this act was carried out *after* the fatal blow was delivered.

The report, in its detail, outlines significant lifestyle possibility: the victim, the physical evidence suggests, was a homosexual, and had not long before engaged in sexual activity. CCTV footage pieces together some of the story, though it's incomplete and the murder scene itself is a blind spot, beneath the trees and shielded by the thick undergrowth of the park. A man is captured on camera leaving a well-known homosexual hangout in Frei Caneca. He heads up to Avenida Paulista and crosses towards Jardins. He is last spotted at the northeastern edge of Parque Trianon. The southern side was, until a few years ago at least, a notorious hotspot for cruising, generally for young men. Although this is an activity that has lessened considerably, Lisboa reads in a note from Vice, it still exists on specific days and at specific times.

Lisboa draws two possible conclusions from this: the victim was on his way to become involved, somehow, in this activity; the perpetrators were waiting to attack him or another homosexual man.

The conclusion, the thing that nobody else seems too bothered by, is the incontrovertible fact that the attack was carried out by between two and four people, according to the report. This was not some individual vigilante; this was, Lisboa's hunch, an opportunistic, group attack on a gay man. The man wore a T-shirt with the EleNão slogan printed across it. It was this that provoked the attack, at least in part.

Lisboa thinks: a group of assailants means it's harder to hide.

The rest of the team are busying themselves IDing the John and figuring out the next of kin so that muggins here, Lisboa, can inform them of this tragedy. It's not proving that simple, apparently.

Lisboa leaves them to it and heads to the Paradise Rooms.

Neighbourhood watch schemes aren't lone wolves. Group dynamics. There's got to be something in that.

Hate crime.

He'll swing by Parque Trianon on the way –

Crime scene.

Just because you want to believe something, doesn't mean it's not true.

This is what Rafa is telling himself. On Monday, when she finally got back to his grandma's house, Carolina told him:

'I'm sorry. I was drunk and stupid. I should have asked Alessandra to take me home. She looked after me.'

Rafa was so relieved to see her that for an hour or so he was just that: relieved.

He stayed up late watching TV and drinking, blotting them out, his fears. He'd never doubted her before, and deep down he doesn't doubt her now, it's something else.

On Tuesday, as they pack up his grandma's house, there's an air of calm, of anticipation – of *home*.

There's not much to do; the house is sold with everything in it – which isn't much – so they're tidying up, packing personal things, some keepsakes, and throwing the rest out.

It's intimate, Rafa thinks, *going through someone's stuff.*

Franginho's got a small fire going on the front step and Rafa's feeding old bills, bank statements, documents into it.

'Wasn't that long ago,' Franginho says, 'she wouldn't even have had *this*.'

It's true. She worked as a maid for cash, for years. Then her boss at a British school, Rafa thinks, set her up with a bank account, made sure she was in the system. Then came Bolsa Família, all the admin for that, getting Rafa secured, too, even if he was fleecing the system himself with help from the boys up the hill.

They've shown their gratitude by buying this house in cash and letting Rafa get the hell out again. Franginho, too, this time.

He told Rafa, 'It's no longer what it was, porra, like I said. They don't have the means to keep just anybody on the payroll. You've got to do a lot more than I am prepared to do, entendeu? They're happy to see me go.'

It's a funny thing to think of austerity measures in the jungle. A legit cash injection has actually done something, Rafa thinks.

There are photos, in a box, of Rafa's dad. There's a letter too, a short one. Rafa reads it again and thinks, *yes, papai, yes, Daddy, I am doing exactly that.*

The letter's last line: *Leave this place and be happy.*

He doesn't think about his father too much; he never knew him well enough. His grandma shielded him, he knows this. His dad was a two-bit guitar player and a low-level crook. Whatever happened to him, Rafa is fairly sure he was responsible, in part. That night, some twelve years ago, Rafa changed, changed *again*, he hardened and his resolve hardened, and it made him, to a point.

Leave this place and be happy.

His old man only followed half of his own advice.

'Anything you want to keep?' Rafa asks. 'From the house, I mean.'

'That's kind of you, mate.'

'Fiche avantage, ne?'

Help yourself. Or, *make yourself at home*, Rafa thinks, both meanings pretty apt.

That morning, lying in bed, Carolina turned to him and said, 'You know, I'm late.'

He was waking up. 'Late for what?'

'No, silly, *I* am late. My period. It's quite late.'

Rafa wanted to say something about why the fuck were you drinking then, but thinks maybe that's why she *was* drinking, so he says –

'I love you.'

'You're happy?'

'It's world class, meu amor, if it, you know.'

'And if not?'

'We can have a lot of fun trying again…'

Carolina gives him such an almighty smile that nothing else matters, and yeah, he knows now that it really is true –

Just because you want to believe something, doesn't mean it's not true.

'That question you asked me when I got back,' he says now to Franginho, 'first thing you said.'

'Yeah?'

'Answer is maybe, you know. Might be.'

Franginho cracks a smile, it's his first smile for what feels like a long time.

'Porra, meu,' he says. *Fuck me, mate.* 'Que maravilhosa.'

They hug, slap each other's backs, hold each other for a moment.

'You're going to be an uncle,' Rafa says. 'One day.'

Franginho is grinning. 'Lucky kid, ne?'

Later, Rafa sees Carolina and Franginho talking.

They're in the kitchen, Rafa's out the back and he sees them talking through the window. He's told her he's told him, but there's something that's not especially joyful about their exchange.

Later still, Franginho says, 'Mate, we need to talk, the three of us.'

Rafa nods. What he feels, he realises, oddly, is *relief.*

Just because you want to believe something, doesn't mean it's not true.

Ellie finds that she's gone viral. The article about the abuse of the young woman in a Militar cell. The article – *her* article, the online version and photographs of the print version – is being shared widely on social media, while the Militar statement is all over the place, too. Their denial that it happened, their denouncing of her credentials. Both sides – left for and right against – are speculating on where Ellie either got the information or found the garra – the bottle – to make it up.

She's at home, following it online. It's thrilling to be the centre of something. And what's even more thrilling is the discipline she's showing in doing nothing, saying nothing. This fake news business is pure profit.

Bolsonaro has been coordinating most of his campaign via social media from a hospital bed, after all.

The martyr, the great white hope, the chosen one.

Biggest comeback since Lazarus.

There are requests for clarification; there are requests for interviews; there are requests for further articles, opinion pieces; there are dozens of requests building in the inbox of her email account. The lefty student rag that first published in print is having a whale of a time, and playing the game with skill, working their hand. The editor is a sometime friend of Ellie and he loves the idea of a stage, of being a mouthpiece. He's making outrageous statements without actually committing anything concrete in print or online. Fuelling the fire. He hasn't bothered giving her a ring; it's better, she thinks, this way.

Who has rung her is Silva. 'Hold fast, querida,' he said. 'Do nothing and wait.'

It's good advice. It's thrilling to be empowered like this, to feel *power*.

'Francisco,' she says. 'I do hope you're not stitching me up.'

'Trust me,' he tells her. 'Your piece is watertight, it's pure suggestion.'

'Beyond the claim of the facts, mate, maybe,' Ellie says. 'Facts that you provided, let's not forget.'

'We never reveal our sources.'

Ellie laughs. 'This plays out well, it's my investigative journalism. It goes tits-up, and a former mentor, a real patriarch figure, forced me to do it.'

'Suits me.'

'I'm grateful, Francisco, I am.'

'I know. But don't be too grateful, I've got my own stake in this, entendeu?'

'I don't want to know.'

'You're right, you don't.'

They hang up.

Anna and Fernanda are ecstatic. Fernanda is tying up the legal side of things and Anna, she's told Ellie, is getting some sort of explosive bigger picture, party political perspective.

Yeah, okay, Ellie thinks. So far, she's carrying this team.

She wonders, again, how Silva found out in the first place. Again, she doesn't want to know. He's got moles all over the place and he keeps his cards firmly up against his apparently shrinking belly.

Ellie's checking her email and one message stands out. The address is pure late-90s detective fiction:

militar@hotmail.com

She's laughing when she opens the message and reads –

I saw you outside the Blue Pub and you saw me. We should talk. You need corroboration.

Ellie's not stupid enough to ignore this – or to think it might not be entirely safe. She's been in similar situations. Leme was always on hand.

She thinks – call Lisboa.

She replies and sets up a sit-down.

Anna's on her way to City Hall and she checks her phone to see how the social media storm is brewing. Their own tweet – from their legal aid office handle, quoting Ellie's article; pointing out the legal implications of the slander of the Militar statement – has been retweeted over 12,000 times already –

It's not been two hours since they posted.

Anna realises, very quickly, that it suddenly doesn't matter what's true and what's not. Apart from for the woman, of course.

Fake news is something, but don't lose sight of that –

Ellie's not making this up. This is not just a political firestorm.

She's in a cab on Avenida 23 de Maio.

This road, she thinks.

The hours she's sat on it, chugging along from Ibirapuera to the old centre.

The road is pure apocalypse highway; ten lanes across at its widest point, Anna sometimes can't quite believe a city can contain such a beast.

There's a text from Roberto, her friend at City Hall.

Not joking about the guided tour. Meet in the roof garden

Nice spot, at least. There's a little way to go yet.

She's crawling towards the eastern tip of Avenida Paulista. Up above, on either side, nice neighbourhoods leak west and east. Anna's heading north.

The taxi swings left under the overpass and the road splits, surges like a river. It floods and bursts.

The road is sunken, carved through the city.

They talk about a city's veins, its arteries –

23 de Maio is São Paulo's *spine*.

Once upon a time in São Paulo.

History embedded in its name: the date, May 23rd in 1932 when four students are killed by government troops protesting Getúlio Vargas. President by coup d'état, he rules by decree, unbound by constitution. The coup erodes state autonomy.

São Paulo stands up.

This road, Anna thinks, as she does every time she travels it, is built deep *inside* this city, her city.

São Paulo's motto: *I lead, I will not be led.*

It doesn't feel like it today.

Where will this election fit, she wonders, when measured against the 1930 coup, the constitutional revolution of 1932, the dictatorship years, the Brazilian Miracle –

What are they seeing, *now*?

Here, the road swells, the ten lanes become twelve in rush hour, but today, mid-morning, it's clear enough. Either side, trees bank up and overhang; the walls scrubbed clean.

This, one of Mayor Doria's initiatives.

The Beautiful City project, meaning Doria dressing up like a worker and being photographed painting bus stops and scouring walls of graffiti.

And on top of the clean walls, a carpet of grass planted, now growing out, the Corredor Verde, the *Green Corridor*.

It's vast, the road at this point. It's as if you're bowling through the earth's core, its heart; the buildings in the old Centro hover in the distance, ominous.

It's coming along, the old Corredor Verde, and it looks okay, Anna thinks.

But here lies the problem with the likes of Johnny Doria, and why she will never join her old friend Roberto:

Doria didn't distinguish between graffiti and graffiti *art*, the murals, the neighbourhood-defining images that formed a part of the character of the city, of the neighbourhoods. The graffiti art tradition had become that: a tradition. World famous, too, the artists in demand, the tropes and lifestyle aspirational. What Doria did was clumsy and divided the city; he reinforced the prejudices of some, erased the identities of others. This is what right-wing politicians who want the popular vote, want to appeal to the working class, this is what they do –

They divide.

Traffic thickens. Motorbikes dart between lanes, like mice.

Doria is a classic coxinha, a rich right-winger, uptight, socially conservative. Coxinha, a tasty, deep fried chicken thigh snack: the joke is that these men – and they're always men – wear shorts in the summer to get their little thighs tanned. The pointlessness of their bourgeois values, the emptiness, the *whiteness*.

She's not sure she sees it, *exactly*, but Anna does like it as a term.

They're barrelling through Liberdade.

The taxista, silent until now, says, 'I used to like Japa-town, ate down here a lot. Now it's just knock-off Korean markets and crack addicts.'

Anna gives a tight smile. 'Hm,' she says.

'You know why?'

Anna gives a shake of the head.

'That Doria's fault,' the driver says. 'He sends in the Military Police to clear out Cracolândia, and he only goes and spreads the noias all about the place. Should have left the cunts where they were.'

Cracolândia: *Crackland*. A downtown hell inhabited by desperate noias – addicts – and ruthless dealers.

Anna visited once for work, a guided tour it was, like going to the zoo. Except there were no cages and the animals had no teeth.

'Liberdade's still got character,' Anna says.

She eats there herself, a lot, Japanese and Chinese canteens.

'Maybe.'

They drive on in silence. Anna scans left, right.

Red flags and Chinese lanterns float between smaller streets.

The taxi driver's opinions, Anna thinks, say something about old Doria.

She's not sure exactly what. She texts Roberto:

ten minutes. Order me a coffee and a dish of farinata

Farinata: reconstituted, expired food made from pasta and flour. Dog food, really. Doria's solution to the problem of feeding the poor and homeless.

Anna's phone shakes. Roberto.

I'll get you a coxinha, querida

She remembers he's funny, Roberto.

Her phone shakes again. Fernanda.

we get some sort of proof, we can serve notice on the militar statement, on behalf of ellie, certo? would be a symbolic process, that's all we're not going to go through with it. but we do need proof.

Yes, Anna thinks.

When Franginho is through telling Rafa what he had to tell him, Rafa boils –

Rafa *burns*.

'I'm okay,' Carolina tells him. 'We're – all of us, amor – okay.'

For a while Rafa fails to maintain any sort of perspective.

He calls Franginho names. He spits these names.

Desgraçado. Filho da puta. Escroto. Vagabundo. Seu caralho.

Franginho hangs his head. Franginho says, 'What can I do to make this right?'

'You can never make this right.'

'Amor,' this is Carolina. 'Listen. This is not his fault.'

The idea that Franginho and Carolina have discussed all this, have worked out that this is not Franginho's fault, is a serious block to Rafa's perspective –

His best friend and his girlfriend in cahoots.

He'd rather, he thinks, in a black moment – and later he understands that this is not of course the case – he'd rather that his best friend was fucking his girlfriend.

'Don't tell me whose fault this is,' Rafa says.

He goes for a walk, clears his head. Slowly, one or two things dawn on him.

Firstly, it's not Franginho's fault that he and Carolina were followed from the favela on Sunday night.

Secondly, it's not Franginho's fault that Carlos threatened him again and again. A simple instruction, mais ou menos, the threat from Carlos to Franginho:

You tell me your boy ever comes back; if I find out he does from someone else, you're fucked.

Rafa realises it's his fault, that's whose fault it is.

This threat, and Franginho's diffusing of this threat, this was a large part of Franginho covering for Rafa and Carolina.

'You were just keeping us safe, right?' Rafa says when his head has cooled, his head has cleared.

'Mate,' Franginho says, 'I've only ever tried to do that.'

'What happened to me after that,' Carolina says, 'was nothing to do with Franginho.'

Rafa's not sure how she knows this, but she seems to know it.

Just because you want to believe something, doesn't mean it's not true.

She must have her reasons; she's clever.

'We should do what Carlos says,' she goes on. 'All he has to do is talk and we're in real trouble, querido.'

'What do you think?' Rafa asks Franginho.

'I think if our boys knew what you'd done, they'd be very unhappy,' he says.

'It was nothing to do with them.'

'That's not how it works,' Franginho says, 'you know that.'

Rafa knows he's right. There's a cooperative element to the firm: you share your dividends from any activity with those higher up, or they simply take them from you. And do to you whatever they consider the fairest – and by fairest they mean what sets the best example for their future profit – punishment.

'I also think,' Franginho says, 'that Carlos the bulldog is about as trustworthy as a Paraguayan mail order bride.'

Rafa smiles. World class, Franginho's chat. Always has been.

'Okay,' Rafa says, 'here's what we're going to do.'

And Rafa lays out a plan:

Tomorrow, with the sale wrapped up and the house cleaned and cleared, he and Carolina – publicly, notifying the Militars on duty as they do it, a little farewell parade, effectively – will leave the favela and head home.

A day or two later, Rafa will come back, discreetly.

Franginho will set up a meeting with Carlos, telling him that Rafa wants to square things with a straightener, a sizeable cash donation to Carlos's pension, which will guarantee Carlos's diplomatic position.

At this meeting, Rafa will put a bullet in Carlos.

'We'll do it in the old boca,' he says. 'Same spot he killed Garibaldo and Lanky. That's settled.'

Carolina and Franginho say nothing. The three of them are, again, a team and they need to hold onto this uneasy peace, Rafa knows this, he knows they'll do whatever it is he says – for now.

'And then,' he says, 'we'll all three of us meet up again – at home.'

Franginho, Rafa thinks, looks a little sceptical.

Rafa says, 'Então, cara?'

What you thinking, mate?

'It's all good,' Franginho says. 'We just need to find a bit of hardware that no one else knows about, sabe?'

Rafa nods. 'I trust you, porra.'

They both know that whatever happens, there's going to be reprisals and they need to make sure that they're well in the clear.

They ponder this for a while. It's easy to get hold of a gun, but it's very difficult to get hold of a gun you can trust from someone you don't know. There are only so many networks, after all. It'd just be a question of asking around. Or, you take a huge risk on some rusted piece of shit from some desperate chancer – and even then you've got to find said desperate chancer.

They're tossing reasons back and forth as to why one or other of them might need a gun, you know, *innocent* reasons –

Maybe Rafa's got a bit of bother down by the beach.

Maybe Franginho wants to protect his property.

Maybe they're doing a little sidearm arms dealing themselves –

None of these ideas swing. Then Franginho goes *Eureka* and has an absolutely outrageous idea.

Rafa's laughing it's so brilliant. 'So you call him, tell him you need to buy a gun, go and meet him in his manor, and when buying the gun you tell him about the other meeting, set it up. That about right?'

Franginho grins. 'It's world class, mate.'

'It's all good, truly.' Rafa looks at Carolina. 'Though it'll slow things down a touch.'

'Not necessarily a bad thing,' Franginho says.

'Like I said, I trust you, porra.'

The person they're going to buy the gun from –

Carlos.

Ellie arranges the meet in a bar –

Ellie's been to this bar before.

Back when she first came to São Paulo, working for *Time Out*, little bits of writing, doing the listings. She's chosen this bar to meet this Militar as it's swank-casual, in the middle-class, affluent, professional neighbourhood of Itaim, and plenty of people, a decent terrace, no chance of trouble.

On my first day at the office, she remembers, now, less than fondly, *my colleagues invited me out for a drink. We went to a local bar called Vaca Veia. Old cow, ne? They drip-fed me caipirinha. There was a man outside the ladies' toilets, handing me a shot. I staggered back to the apartment with him and passed out in my clothes, threw up a few hours later. Fuck me. The hangover. My mouth tasted of limes and aftershave, my skin raw from stubble.*

The good old bad old days, she thinks.

Lisboa's standing at the northeastern end of Parque Trianon and he's thinking, who is this guy?

Lisboa's second fiddle on the investigation, which means everything he's found out is through reports and his own guesswork. No one wants anything much to do with the case; there's no ID yet and no real hurry.

There's a cold, battered stiff on a slab and that has to mean something.

Lisboa's trying to think like Leme: there's a dead body, so there's a victim, so there's a crime, so there's something to be done. The unsolved cases they worked on together were unsolved as there was scant actual physical or forensic evidence and they weren't clever enough to take the imaginative leap that was needed to think themselves into the perpetrator's – or the victim's – shoes.

The question that's screaming at Lisboa is why does this man have no ID card, no credentials? Figure that out and maybe he can figure who the guy is. One detail from the autopsy he didn't believe and double-checked: the victim was mid-thirties, forty tops. Not much trade for that demographic, surely. Lisboa doesn't want to cast aspersions, and he's very much a whatever floats your saddle kind of a fella, but he's pretty sure your older rent boy ain't thumbing lifts out on the street. So what was he doing there?

Question number two is: how can it be so easy to ignore a victim?

So far what Lisboa's done is put out an appeal. But one head-scratcher is what fucking mug shot do you use? He hasn't puzzled that yet. He's cross-referenced missing persons reports. He's got Vice to look at any, unlikely though it is, related solicitation beef.

What he's doing next is going to a well-known Frei Caneca homosexual hangout and asking a few questions, something no one else has bothered doing.

The victim, literally, is on ice.

First, the park. On the way, Ratty sends him a text:

bus tickets. three

This is either a little misinformation or the kid is genuinely worried Lisboa's going to shop him. Either way, what he and Ellie saw outside The Blue Pub was three bus tickets changing hands. Lisboa lets this settle.

The park itself is crime-scene empty.

Lisboa buys a bottle of upmarket, cheap pinga from a convenience store nearby. He buys a pack of cheap smokes. At the south-eastern edge of the square – outside the park – sit three mendigo drunks, two men and a woman. Lisboa brandishes the bottle as he approaches.

'Any of you here on Sunday night?'

There is cackling through toothless mouths, catcalling and jostling for attention. There is scrapping and squabbling, a heavy reek of shit and booze, piss and tobacco.

One of the men beckons Lisboa to come closer. 'Ah, meu, Ypioca!' He's talking about the brand of drink; the glass bottle is wrapped tight like a wicker basket, looks classy, artisanal. 'Fancy,' he says.

'You can have it if you help me.'

The guy's nodding now. His friends have shut up.

'Sunday night, Sunday night. Yeah, we were here.'

Lisboa points at the crime scene tape, the cordoned-off area. 'So you know what happened?'

'Give me the bottle, porra. Vamos, ne?'

The mendigo's eyes dazed, his mouth open, his palms spread, like a goalkeeper, ready to catch.

Lisboa tosses him the pack of smokes. He fumbles them, drops them, scrambles to grab the pack before his friends can.

'We'll do this bit by bit.'

The mendigo unwraps the pack and takes out a cigarette, which he sniffs. The brand – Free – is also cheap, but upmarket cheap, Brazilian. 'You could have bought American, ne, cara?' the mendigo says.

Lisboa goes *don't be cheeky, son*.

'Okay, okay,' the guy says. 'You got a light?'

Lisboa tosses him a box of matches. The guy strikes one, lights his Free cigarette and pockets the matches.

'Where were you exactly on Sunday night?'

The guy points.

'In the park itself?'

'Sim, senhor.'

'How many of them?'

The mendigo hacks and coughs, spits and sniffs. He gives Lisboa a look. 'Meu,' he says, 'vamos, ne?'

Come on, mate.

Lisboa nods, all right, then, have it your own way. He unscrews the bottle top. He goes to drink, but, instead, he pours a slug of the cachaça onto the ground.

There are howls of protest, the injustice.

'How many?' Lisboa asks again.

Lead mendigo holds up a hand. Lisboa nods. The three of them huddle up a touch, conference call.

Lisboa waits. The three mendigos, he thinks. *The three amigos.*

'Three, there were three of them.'

'Three? Tem certeza?' *You're sure?*

'I can count.' He points at Lisboa, his two friends. 'One. Two. Three.'

They all fall about laughing.

'You seen these three around here before?'

'Ah, you know, sabe?'

Lisboa tilts the bottle.

The three amigos are all going woah, calm down, no need to waste anything. Another quick huddle.

'Yeah, we've seen them around.'

'Doing what?'

'They're young, kids. Keeping an eye out, you know?'

Keeping an eye out. *Neighbourhood watch.*

'You ever see anyone talking to them, giving them instructions, entendeu?'

'No.'

Lisboa believes this. 'And the other guy. Why do you think they did it?'

Heads shake, mouths grimace, dirty faces crease unhappily.

'Come on,' Lisboa says. 'It's not a trick question, there's no right or wrong answer.'

'Maybe the guy was something they didn't like.'

'I'll ask a different question: what the guy do to provoke them?'

'Nothing. He was walking across with his, with his... ah, his shopping bags, porra, minding his own business, falou?'

'What kind of shopping?'

'I don't know, his fucking lingerie.'

Laughter at this.

'So bags from a clothes store?'

'Yeah, why not?'

'How old would you say he was?'

'Older than us, amigo, but younger than you.'

They hoot and cackle at that, the three amigos. Lisboa feigns good humour. He hands lead amigo the bottle of Ypioca.

'Don't drink it all at once,' he says.

Lisboa walks from the park to the bar in Frei Caneca they've put the victim at minutes before it happened.

Lisboa walks the inverse route. It's about the same time of night – a little after eight – and the streets buzz with traffic and a nice after-work vibe. Paulista is a queue of taillights and horns. Men and women in work clothes walk and chat, heading to bars and restaurants at the top of Rua Augusta. Others, dressed the same in suits and shirts, skirts and jackets, clip along at a good pace, talking on their phones, walking to their bus, their metro, their homes. The lights in the skyscrapers beam bright messages across the city –

We're all still making money, is the gist. *We're all still working*.

Very different on a Sunday night; a lot quieter.

The man could have walked this same route and barely seen a soul.

Lisboa has studied the CCTV footage and he was struck again by how much more helpful it would be if it were at ground level.

Then again, that might defeat the point – if you don't know you're being watched, but think you might be, you're going to think twice – but you still might well do it.

Problem is you don't get a clean shot of a man's face. He's wearing a cap, your man, and the angles make a positive ID tricky. They know it's him from his clothes, route, the timing, the shopping bags – and when he drops off the CCTV radar.

Lisboa's going to the bar to see what they might have on any private internal cameras. Lisboa wants to get a proper look.

He wonders, too, about these shopping bags – have they been booked in as evidence?

The feet-dragging in this investigation is criminal –

It's an embarrassment.

Even if the message from way up above is to be half-arsed about it, do it *right*.

Gather the evidence and stall the conclusion.

This way, they're all going to get a bad reputation: one thing to be a little shady; quite another to be unprofessional, incompetent.

The bar is a happy hour sort of a place, with a heavy gay-friendly clientele, but by no means unwelcoming to a man like Lisboa. No one flutters an eyelid as he heads to the bar. He's noted the camera at the entrance; he's not going to waste any time with small talk.

He also reckons the community round here will be ready to help – and that it's likely no other representative of the law has bothered to show any interest.

Lisboa's banking on these things to expedite this visit so he can get off to the Paradise Rooms with a bit of concrete progress.

He smiles at the barman. 'A chopp,' he says. 'And bring me the manager too, certo?' Lisboa's pointing at his badge. 'Look sharp, kid,' he says.

The barman nods. 'I'll be right back.'

'You can pour me the lager first, son.'

'Yeah, sure.'

Lisboa smiles. 'Good lad.'

When he comes over, the manager is equally helpful. 'Anything we can do. Terrible, disgusting business.'

'I'm guessing you don't know the victim was here just a few minutes before.'

The manager gasps. 'No.'

'It's what we believe. Why I need to see your security footage.'

The manager has a look that Lisboa thinks is one-part horror, one-part thrilled: this is quite an anecdote for the lad.

Problem is, it's early in the week, no need for security, so the manager has to call their regular guy, but he's tied up with something, something he can't get out of just like that, mate, entendeu? So the manager hisses down the phone the urgency level, gives it the big one, the big I am, and what it means in the end is that Lisboa's going to get through a couple of beers on the house before the cavalry arrives.

They're quite good, the beers.

Course, you're supposed to have a warrant to have a gander at private security tapes if you're going to use them as evidence in any way, but no one seems too bothered and Lisboa's only having a gander and there's nothing wrong with that – if you're not going to use them as evidence.

And he's not, not directly. Technology creates loopholes, is the thing –

Use your phone to take a photo of a photo and who's to say who needs a warrant for that.

Lisboa's waiting in the back room when security comes in. Lisboa says, 'Let's make this snappy, son.'

The guy nods.

Lisboa gives him a time and a date and the guy rewinds and fast forwards and in not too long, there's an image on the screen of the victim, leaving the bar, alone, carrying in one hand his shopping, and the key detail here – his cap in the other.

'Pause,' Lisboa says. 'That's perfect. Can you make it bigger without losing too much of the clarity?'

'Sure.' The guy clicks and zooms. 'That do you?'

'What a worker.'

Lisboa pulls his phone and snaps a few photos of this paused image of their man.

'You ever see this guy here before?' he asks.

'He doesn't ring any bells.'

'What's that, a euphemism?'

'Ha.'

'Do me a favour and ask around a bit, quietly, certo?'

'Sure.'

He takes the security guy's number; he takes the manager's card from a box on the desk.

As he leaves the back room, the security guy says, 'What do I say if another one of your lot comes by?'

There are a few levels to this question, and Lisboa knows the guy knows this. Security detail at any place has got a little shade to it. They *know* is the point, always know *something*. Lisboa thinks: *be honest.*

'I doubt you'll see anyone. Keep the tape somewhere safe, though, as I'll be back.'

'Combinado,' security says. *Deal.*

The next thing Lisboa does is email the photo to Ellie and tell her to put it out and get ready to do some work –

The red tape and the general laissez-faire attitude to the investigation means this will get the quickest result.

You didn't get this from me, Lisboa adds.

He walks up the road to the Paradise Rooms. He does the I'm here to see Michelangelo routine and takes the stairs.

And lo and fucking behold, waiting for him with Ratty, is Carlos.

'Why am I not surprised to see you, old son,' Lisboa says.

Carlos grins. 'Disappointed, but not surprised, eh, mate.'

'I'm not your mate, Carlão.'

'Let's get this over with.'

Lisboa nods.

'Follow me.'

At City Hall, Anna's being told a few home truths.

'I really don't know how you expect me to help you,' Roberto is saying, 'or even *why* you expect me to, but it's not on, right – '

They're up on the roof of Edifício Matarazzo and the garden is spectacular, Anna will give it that. It's definitely improved since her day; there are tourists at every other table.

The building's a big concrete square, but it's tall, and she's looking north, trying to spy the city limits as Roberto's giving her something of an earful.

' – and it's not right of you to lure me into a meeting under false pretences, sabe?'

'*Lure* you?' Anna says. 'Deus me livre.' *God help me.* 'Who do you think you are, James Bond?'

'Yeah, Anna, I think I'm James Bond.' Roberto sighs. 'I see that delightful sense of humour's intact, at least.'

Anna smiles. 'I only tease people I like.'

'How enigmatic.'

'Look, I just want to know what you know, that's all.'

'And not much is the truth of it.'

'What about this business about the woman in custody? What's the position here on that?'

Roberto fidgets, Anna notes. He slings a look over his shoulder. He says, 'I don't know what that is.'

'Come on.'

'I don't, really.'

Anna takes out her phone. She opens her social media accounts. She shows him how popular their messages about Ellie's article have become.

'Now you know,' Anna says.

'Okay, I know, of course, I know, but I don't *know*.'

'You mean officially?'

'I mean that there is no position yet – that's the position. While the article says one thing and the statement says the opposite, City Hall can't have a position.'

'That's convenient.'

'It is, actually. If this is fake news, well, we'd be making a big mistake going after the Military Police.'

'We.'

'Yeah, I know, I get it, I'm not James Bond. I mean my office, who I work for.'

Anna smiles. 'I'm just teasing.'

Roberto, she sees, smiles at that; coyly looking down, unable not to. She notices all this.

She says, gently, 'So no one is doing anything, no one's allowed to?'

The *allowed to* is a clever turn of phrase.

'Officially, there are people looking into what's real and what's fake, and until that's established, you're right, no one's allowed to do anything.'

Anna's nodding. 'What I've heard,' she says carefully, 'is that top man here and former top man are both in line for tasty government jobs when Bolsonaro is confirmed.'

'I don't know about that.'

'As long as São Paulo remains open for business for a right-leaning coalition, so it can go about *its* business.'

'Like I say, ne?'

'Lula's in jail, put there by right-leaning collusion.'

'I'm not sure you can – '

'I can't. But it makes sense, doesn't it? I mean, forget loyalties, you can agree with that, ne?'

Roberto's nodding now.

'We think that Sérgio Moro, the chief prosecutor, helped the *public* prosecutor, Delton Dallagnol, guide the case against Lula. That Moro gave him considerable advice, made sure the case would stick. That they were in it together, nas fim das contas.'

In it together, *at the end of the day*.

'And you can prove this how?'

Anna can't, of course, prove anything of the sort.

She just has names and motives, that's all. Rasputin couldn't – or wouldn't – offer any more than that.

She says, 'What we're looking for is a specific link to Bolsonaro.'

'I don't think he's that clever.'

'It was you who mentioned the way the wind is blowing.'

'Look, Anna,' Roberto says, firmly, 'the Lula imprisonment, Lava Jato, all of it, all of this change of wind direction, as it were, it's all down to one thing and it doesn't matter how legal or shady it is.'

'Okay, really?' Anna says. She bristles at his tone. 'What *does* it all come down to? Why don't you tell me?'

'Years and years of PT incompetence and corruption, that's what.'

Anna's silent.

'If there was collusion, so what?' Roberto is on a roll. 'It demonstrates how much people want them out. Their corruption has fucked this country in the ass for fifteen years under the guise of changing the country for the better, of rubbing out inequality, and people are sick to death of their lies, their self-righteous, left-wing lies.'

'But – '

'All of this is down to the mess the PT made of the country.'

'And this will clean up that mess, will it?'

'Bolsonaro isn't clever enough to swing an election he barely knew he was in by making sure Lula was in jail and out the picture. That's the story you want, ne?'

Anna nods.

'I'm not sure that story isn't fake news, querida.'

'And the woman in custody?'

'I don't know. Only thing I know is why everyone's doing and saying nothing.'

'And why's that?'

Roberto smiles. 'Remember that thing we were always told when we were kids? Don't make that ugly face; if the wind changes direction, you'll be stuck with it.'

'I remember.'

'Well, the wind's already changing and you don't want to keep pouting and snarling like you are, is my advice.'

That might be good advice, Anna thinks.

Junior barrels into the locker room.

His boys, inside.

Felipe and Gilberto.

His boys, Junior believes, in cahoots with old Carlos.

Neighbourhood watch scheme.

Junior remembers it is here, two and a half years ago, here in the locker room, where his whole story with Carlos began.

Apt, he thinks, that it can begin to end here too.

Junior says, 'Hello, boys.'

Felipe and Gilberto look up from tying their boot laces. Felipe sniggers. Gilberto looks down.

Junior says, 'I need the name of the woman you brought in here Sunday night.'

He decides to leave it at that, at them bringing her in.

'No one knows her name, you know that.' This is Felipe. 'It didn't happen, porra. You know *that* too.'

Junior nods. 'What I know is what you two malandros are doing in Bixiga.'

Junior notes the flick of the eyes, the *glance* between *his boys*.

'What we heard,' Felipe says, 'is your career is back on the railroad thanks to a little involvement of your own.'

Junior's ready for this. 'You give me the name or it comes out what I saw you do to her.' He pauses. 'My imagination is filthy, mate, if you're in any doubt.'

Another shared look, a moment to weigh this thought. Junior's in here, he thinks.

He looks at Gilberto. 'Didn't feel to me you were into it, son,' he says. 'We can have a chat, sabe? We can iron this out without any perv rep coming your way, entendeu?'

Another shared look. Junior notes Felipe's glare, Gilberto's pleading

'Okay, okay,' Felipe says. 'This is off the books, though, yeah?'

Junior nods. It's all off the books for now, he thinks.

Felipe goes to his locker. He fishes a piece a paper from inside. He hands it to Junior.

'We're good now, yeah?'

Junior nods. Scribbled on the piece of paper is a name, Carolina Meirelles, and an RGE number, her ID.

Bingo.

Rafa, home, is on edge until Franginho calls and tells him: 'It's on. Sunday, 28th. The bloke was practically wetting himself when he delivered the hardware.'

Rafa is reassured by Franginho's buoyed attitude.

Sunday, 28th October is election round two –

There will be a lot happening. The city will be partying – and drowning its sorrows.

Clever boy, Franginho.

'I suggested the date,' he told Rafa. 'And he said we'd do it down our end, where it would be quieter.'

Clever.

Lisboa follows Carlos to a ground floor suite in the Paradise Rooms. He fingers the phone in his overcoat pocket.

The room is a delight.

There's a bed and a chair and a shitter –

Real suite.

'Suite as a nut,' Lisboa says.

Carlos roars. 'I heard you were funny.' He points. 'You want the bed or the chair?'

Lisboa shakes his head. He shapes up to remain standing.

Carlos shrugs. 'Você que sabe.'

You're the boss.

'Your little friend not joining us?'

'Be best if you forget about him, full stop, entendeu?'

'Judge a man,' Lisboa says, 'by who he does business with, is what they say.'

'Who's they?'

Lisboa grins. 'Shall we get on? I think we've done enough flirting.'

'Again, você que sabe.'

'I think you know who is responsible for that nasty attack election night in the park.'

'Straight to the point then?'

Lisboa nods.

'Why do you think that?'

'Militar-approved earner is why. You help run the neighbourhood and you get a cut.'

'What's that got to do with election night?'

'Means you know what's happened, who done what.'

Carlos nods. 'Say that's not far off, what if it's me sorting out the mess that I had nothing to do with?'

'Very honourable, mate.'

'I thought you weren't my mate.'

'Three lads is what I've heard. Three lads, which is consistent with the autopsy. Three lads who keep an eye on the area.'

Carlos grunts.

'Keep an eye on things for you, I expect.'

'You've turned into a right old Sherlock Holmes.'

'I saw one of your boys hand three bus tickets over to rat-face here at the Moto Taxi rank which doubles, it seems, as a little HQ for your operation.'

Carlos looks at the door. 'You must have really got the wind up the little cunt out there,' he says. 'I think he might be off the firm, shortly.'

'You're fired, right?'

Carlos laughs. 'Olha,' he says. *Look*. 'Reason we're here is this: I'm squaring things with you so you leave off, certo?'

'I'm not sure I follow.'

Carlos smiles – patient. 'There's a general feeling from both our employers, well, my former employer, *officially*, that we don't need to look closely at the heinous hate crime that occurred night of the election.'

'Good police work.'

'Point is, the bloke they nailed is a transient fag who shops his arsehole for cash, right? Who cares?'

'That's a rhetorical question, I imagine.'

Carlos makes a face. 'Clever fella.'

Lisboa gestures *well then*.

'Overexuberance from a few lads. Boys will be boys and all that.'

Lisboa shakes his head.

'Your lot are doing nothing, as you know, son. My lot are waiting for the next election round, then they can do anything they fucking like.'

'What's your point, Carlos?'

'It's taken care of, justice will prevail. It'll just be off the books, as they say.'

'And you've taken care of it, have you?'

'Three bus tickets. The bus stops at some service station or other. Three tickets get stamped, entendeu?'

Lisboa nods. 'So the idea is you tell me this and I think, okay, fair play, that'll do and I'll stop sniffing around?'

'You really are clever, big man.'

Lisboa thinks *he's got a point.* Lisboa thinks *focus on the victim.*

Lisboa nods. 'Always a pleasure, Carlão.'

'So you're on board?'

'Aye, aye, captain.'

Carlos roars. 'Funny guy. Enjoy the suite. It's yours for as long as you want it.'

'One thing,' Lisboa says. 'The victim was carrying some bags, shopping. I want to see them.'

'Your lads don't have them?'

'Not booked in anywhere, far as I can see. Word is, your boys cleared the scene.'

Carlos is nodding. 'And this squares it?'

Lisboa nods.

'I'll sort it for you, though it might take a few days. I'll call.'

He slaps Lisboa on the shoulder and does one.

Lisboa waits five minutes. He pulls his phone. He tests the recording.

There are other ways, he's understanding, to do the right thing –
Clever fella.

Ellie sets up a new email account to handle the responses to her photo of the victim. It's working. It's a simple missing persons beef, she says, a friend of a friend of a friend, there's no mention of what happened to him –

And she's got deniability: she's a journalist, helping a friend of a friend. It's the first thing she's posted since the article, and it's a clever move, profile-wise.

She comes across as a real crusader, absolutely not stopping the good fight to cash in on a little success.

There's a lot of right-on concern and a lot of sharing of the image. Shouldn't be too long until the emails roll in.

As she's waiting for her Militar, she gets another message from Lisboa. An audio file.

Have a listen, but do nothing – for now.

She thinks it's cute the way he punctuates his messages properly.

Lisboa logs a bit of misinformation of his own.

He gets some Vice grunt on the nightshift to check back on known sex workers and cross-refer with missing persons' cases, see if anything comes up that's been reported but not resolved.

The grunt says, 'This a hunch, is it?'

'Let's call it that,' Lisboa tells him.

'I'm going to have a good night, then,' the grunt says.

'Dinner's on me.'

All by the book, now, he thinks. Mais ou menos.

Junior knows the bar the gringa journalist is talking about. He's been there before, with old Carlos, jumping rich kids for kicks. *Fun*. He remembers:

Clientele: young, good-looking, professional. Cash flow: heavy. Tables dotted inside and out. A lunchtime buzz. Some drinking. Plates of food picked at. Not much on them, Junior thought. Memorabilia on the walls, hanging from the ceiling.

Bit different this time.

Ellie takes a table on the terrace at Vaca Veia. It's covered, so no smoking –

Stupid rule.

And after two quick beers – she's early, of course – she wants a smoke. She steps out from under the awning into a roped-off area on the street.

Well worth it, she thinks.

The angle from where's she's standing means she sees the Militar arrive and watches as he hangs back, not seeing her –

She smiles. Advantage me, she thinks.

She sashays back to her seat and raises a finger to attract a waiter who brings another glass of the excellent chopp –

She's sunglasses on and a middle-distance, glamour smile. Her hat is broad enough to hide under, narrow enough she doesn't look like a cunt. Well-chosen –

Incognito.

Then the Militar sits down. He feigns an old friend hello. He waves at a waiter and points at Ellie's drink.

Quite smooth, she thinks.

He waits for the drink, saying nothing. The beer arrives and he gulps it down. He reaches inside his jacket pocket and pulls out a piece of paper.

He places it on the table and pushes it across to her.

She glances at it: a name, Carolina Meirelles, and an ID number.

He says, 'That's who you're looking for.'

He stands. 'Good luck.'

'Wait,' Ellie says. 'Why do I recognise you?'

He shakes his head. 'Best you don't remember, I think. Okay?'

Ellie nods and he's gone.

And only left her to pick up the bill, of course, the fucker.

Price of doing business, she supposes. She can't place him. It doesn't matter.

She calls Silva.

'Guess what I've got?' she says.

'Pick your moment, querida,' Silva says. 'Don't waste it.'

She tells him about the audio file.

'Jesus,' Silva says. 'I never thought Lisboa would have the balls.'

'I've got two friends working the political angle, too.'

'It could be quite a cocktail. Know what they say about cocktails?'

'I do not.'

'A dish best served cold. Bide your time, certo?'

Ellie smiles. She will.

20 October: Disinformation is everywhere. Millions of messages flying around on encrypted platforms. The best one that Anna has seen is a photo of Lula, and next to him the number 17. But Lula is in jail, not standing for election, and the number 17 is the candidate number for one Jair Bolsonaro. Someone's done a study: of a million Whatsapp messages, around half contained misinformation, disinformation, fake news – lies. It goes both ways: messages exaggerate Bolsonaro's hard-as-nails, military heroism, true; but they also suggest he faked his own stabbing. Anna wonders why and thinks of two possibilities: first, just how good does it look! The chosen one, here to save Brazil. *Hard to Kill*, as the T-shirt slogan tells you. Second, lying in a hospital bed, he is going nowhere near the presidential debates.

So far, in the second round of elections, debates planned for 12 October, 14 October and 15 October have been cancelled. The reason given: Bolsonaro's health. You can't argue; it's a respectful position. What Anna's hearing is that the debate scheduled for 21 October is in jeopardy too as the campaigns are somehow – somehow! – unable to agree terms. Now that's a surprise! Clever tactic: sick leave and then refusal to cooperate and blame the other side – terms, my arse.

There's a story in *Folha* that big business is getting involved, spending millions on huge text message bundles and planning to unleash them – hundreds of millions of messages – a week before the election, which is tomorrow. Anna thinks: if *Folha* reckon it's happening tomorrow, then I don't think anyone's going to stop it happening.

Anna reads widely. What she's realising: Ellie's story about the poor woman is but a drop in the ocean. It flared, for a moment, but then it settled into the echo chamber. The first round went as it did and there is no shortage of opinions. Anna likes this one, from Clara Araújo, a sociologist: 'The dissatisfaction over the economic crisis, it seems to me, was channelled along with a discourse about conservative morals.'

It's mob-rule happy, this election. Polls suggest about 25 per cent of people want Bolsonaro in simply to punish the PT for their years of misrule, just like Anna's friend Roberto suggested.

Anti-politics.

22 October: Ellie reads a newspaper snippet about three youngsters murdered in a hail of bullets at a service station not far from Santos. They were travelling on a bus, rest-stop situation. Some kind of gangbang execution is the gist, no biggie. State Military Police say it is classic turf war and drug related. Thank God no civilians were injured. This terrible affliction on our society – God bless Mr Bolsonaro is the general implication. He'll stamp this out.

Ellie notes the article, bookmarks it and searches for more on the subject. It's there, a snippet, in *Folha* and *Estadão*. *Cidade de São Paulo*, Silva's old rag, doesn't even run it.

She sends Lisboa a text with a photo image of the snippet. She does the same for Silva. Both men write back along the lines of *patience, querida*.

Yeah, yeah, she thinks. Without her, this team of theirs is struggling; she's carrying this team.

26 October: the Bolsonaro juggernaut rolls on, unimpeded. They, on the left, are saying that only Lula would stand a chance against him. Six months ago, Anna thinks, before he went to jail, the same people on the left were saying this was Lula's election to lose.

It doesn't really make any difference what they've done, Anna realises now – fake news or real news she doesn't really know, and it doesn't make any difference: Bolsonaro wins with a fuck-off majority, a landslide. Everything changes; everything stays the same. The old story.

28 October, at an election night street party on Avenida Paulista, São Paulo, supporters of Bolsonaro respond to his win. Ellie reading this on a live blog from UK newspaper the Guardian:

Viva the Military Police! Viva the Military Police! Viva the Military Police!

A drop of hope has arrived! Now there will be order in this country! The streets will be safe. There will be no pornography on the TV.

It's a moment of renewal, of cleansing and starting from scratch.

He doesn't care about the presidency. He cares about the country. That is what it means to be a Bolsonariano.

We were a country without rules and with him we will have some rules... I feel so proud to have been part of this change.

Together we are stronger and with God we are unbeatable.

Our country is going down a path it has never been down.

Our flag will never be red! The captain won!

We think he can get the train back on the tracks.

We don't know exactly what it will mean – but he symbolises hope.

28 October, night: Christ, it's a fucking rave, Junior thinks.

He's on Avenida Paulista, just after ten, moments after Bolsonaro's win is confirmed.

And it is going off.

He can't tell how many people are on the street; it must be thousands and thousands. This is not an official get-together; there's darkness and light, and the skyscrapers loom, and the shadows are long.

Car headlights and music blast.

Junior's on crowd control duty with his team. Fact is, there's nothing to control.

Why?

Because everyone packed into the street at the very heart of São Paulo, its main artery pumping blood and guts and emotion, is there to celebrate.

And what they're there to celebrate, it seems to Junior, is the São Paulo Military Police.

There is a lot of showboating going on. Some serious grandstanding.

Six motorbikes abreast, headlights on, red flash and sirens, inching up the road, revving, surrounded by a crowd, chanting –

Viva a PM! Viva a PM! Viva a PM!

Long live the Military Police.

The riders growl and glare. They give it the hardman stare. Men and women snap photographs with them, on their phones. Junior sees one couple perch their toddler on the handlebars and pose.

Junior's being slapped on the back and congratulated by every man and his wife and their dog. He looks to his right. Felipe and Gilberto are shades on and a ferocious look about them, playing to the crowd.

They are, Junior sees, bloody loving it.

A makeshift DJ sets up around a circle of cars. Beers are sold from makeshift coolers, bins and bags. Men and women toast and shout. They jump, they sing, in snatches, the old É Campeão! football chant.

We are the champions.

Then a familiar voice, a refrain, and a heavy guitar riff –

Tropa de Élite.

The theme song from the film, *Elite Squad.* A film Junior has seen – everyone's seen it – and is conflicted about.

A film that tells the story of the elite Military Police group in Rio, the BOPE: Batalhão de Operações Policiais Especiais.

Their logo: a skull with a knife running from top to chin, and two crossed guns, one through each ear.

Their motto: Faca na Caveira – *knife in the skull* – which symbolises victory over death, apparently.

Brutal, they are, the BOPE, a take-no-prisoners approach to urban warfare. Pacification of the favelas by going in mob-handed and murdering as many dealers and wide boys as they can.

Tactically, they are top notch, trained to the very highest level and it's seriously hard to get in. The sort of unit Junior has never really aspired to, and yet the sort of unit his superiors seem to think he's exactly cut out for.

The film is problematic.

The hero, Nascimento, is fighting some heavy demons, about to become a father, guided by violence and a righteous hatred of drug dealers. There's a whole plot line showing the hypocrisy of middle-class drug users, which Junior thought spot on. Campaigning for human rights while buying weed and coke from a friendly favelado – wankers.

But the film, Junior thinks now, watching people catapult themselves about to the soundtrack, yelling the words, punching the air, celebrates the violence, in the end. And what's connected to the violence is the corruption.

The film's contention is that the elite squad is not corrupt; and the rest of the Military Police clearly is.

So who are these jokers in São Paulo venerating exactly? Junior thinks, sucking his teeth.

The Militar gorillas lining Avenida Paulista and showing off on their motorbikes are very much not the elite.

Babacas, todos, these dancing goons.

Wankers to a man.

They've missed the point of the film entirely. Worse, they've missed the point of the election result, too.

Junior is finding this whole business thoroughly depressing.

The music changes, a funk ostentação with verses about Bolsonaro's opponents, references to how Maria de Rosario doesn't know how to wash dishes, to how Jandira Feghali has never lived in the favela.

Classy.

Junior's had enough. He waves Felipe over.

'I'm needed back at HQ,' he lies. 'You're in charge.'

Junior doesn't give a fuck anymore. This whole business has got way out of hand.

28 October, same time, Paraisópolis: 'What the fuck is everyone so pleased about?' Franginho says to Rafa.

Rafa's not really in the mood, but he humours his friend. 'I'm sure you know the answer.'

'Mate, it's a joke. We've just voted in a complete buffoon. This lot,' he points at the party that is going on around Dona Regina's and the bar opposite, 'haven't got a fucking clue. They're not going to get a sweet centavo out of Bolsonaro. And this idea that he's going to crack down on crime? There isn't any fucking crime where we live.'

'That's not what you said the other day.'

Fireworks spit and crackle. A whine and burst, like gunfire. Red and green flashes. Cheers.

'You know what I mean.'

Rafa does know. He pours beer from the bottle on the table set back from the road, back in the shadows, into two glasses. They brought the table up from Rafa's grandma's place a few weeks before and just left it there. It's their own private bar.

Franginho says, 'Best leave it at that, entendeu?'

Rafa nods. It's all set up. The old boca de fumo where he watched the bulldog Militar off old Garibaldo and Lanky is even more perfect for their purposes –

It's no longer used as a boca, as a place to deal drugs.

In fact, it's pretty much decrepit now. The same cover, the same couple of light bulbs, straining. They were dead when they went by yesterday – Franginho fixed that. They don't want the bulldog to get suspicious.

Rafa remembered tailing the lawyer lady from there. Feels like a long time ago.

Anyway, he's not too tense right now. Fact is not a sausage goes on up there at the boca anymore and they'll not be missed at the party. Rafa's been keeping his head down, his baseball cap pulled low, no one needs to know that he's here.

This is very much an undercover job; the reprisals will be mean.

Both men know how selfish they are doing this and getting out.

They both know they deserve it, in their way.

'It's putting an end to the tyranny of our lives, porra,' is how Franginho frames it.

It's taking a chance and being bold, grabbing what you want with both hands, giving it the sharp elbows and see you later.

'When the poor vote for the right wing,' Franginho is saying, 'it all ends tits-up.'

The lad's chat remains world class, it really does.

28 October, same time, Militar HQ, near Avenida Paulista: Lisboa's delighted to get off the main drag.

He's pretty sure Carlos will be late, loving the whole business, drinking and flashing his old badge – his *gun* probably – and posing for photos, but Lisboa does *not* want to party.

Carlos took a little while to get in touch and Lisboa was beginning to doubt he'd come through. But it's happening now – he's going to get to see exactly what the victim was carrying in those shopping bags.

Quite an intelligent plan, to do it when the rest of the city is celebrating – or in mourning.

Shouldn't be too many Militars knocking about HQ is the theory. Carlos has promised Lisboa a free hand.

The night is balmy enough it makes you want to be out and about, at least.

Outside the Militar precinct is dead quiet. Up the road a bit, bars teem and hustle. Down the road, the Italian canteens do a brisk Sunday night trade. Tradition holds fast whatever the political weather.

Conservative place, São Paulo, Lisboa's always thought, which goes against the grain of the progressive mob who are vocal in the city, if not getting anywhere votes-wise.

Lisboa reckons he's pretty much done with the whole shebang, just wants to do his job, if he can.

There's Carlos, bowling down the street, jabbering into his phone.

He gives Lisboa the nod, keeps talking, leads him inside.

Security wave them through. Carlos hangs up.

'Lisboa, old son, second floor, room fifteen. Here's the key. Drop it off at the desk on your way out, it's all good.'

'I'd thank you, but you know.'

Carlos snorts. 'Yeah, I do know. On you go, big man.'

Lisboa turns to the lift, pushes 'up'.

Carlos says, 'I'm heading back out. You going to be okay?'

Lisboa nods. The lift arrives and the Militar Lisboa saw outside The Blue Pub steps out –

Lisboa keeps his head down.

Carlos goes, 'There you fucking are. I've been looking for you.'

The Militar shrugs. 'What now, eh?'

'You're coming with me.'

Lisboa steps into the lift. As the doors close, he hears, 'And then that's it, Carlão, certo?'

Lisboa hears Carlos laugh loud.

28 October, late, at a house party in Vila Madalena: Ellie scans the room and thinks: losers.

She is not in a generous mood, to be fair. Anna and Fernanda are snaking through the crowded living room towards her.

She thinks: *oh, good, the cavalry*.

Fernanda gives Ellie an evil look. 'I think there's something you're not telling us, amiga,' she says.

'Don't get your knickers in a twist, querida,' Ellie says.

'Ellie – '

Anna, palms up, makes a calm-down gesture. 'Let's have a drink, ne? No need to argue.'

Ellie smiles. The *drama* of it all. It's quite entertaining. 'Balcony?' she says. 'I want to smoke.'

The three of them shoulder and elbow their way out onto a huge balcony with a view over the bars and restaurants of Vila Madalena.

'Whose party is this, anyway?' Ellie asks. 'This deck is *Roman*.'

'What does that even mean?' Fernanda bites. 'Roman? You really are full of shit, sabe?'

'Grandeur, cash-money is what I mean. Empire.'

'Jesus.'

Ellie sees that Anna is smiling now. She's got a bottle of red wine and three plastic cups and is pouring. They move to the railings where there's a bit of space. A group of serious-looking actorly types sitting on the floor by the French windows. There's a couple smooching in the dark by a tall pot plant. Otherwise, everyone else is inside, bitching about how stupid people are.

Delightful atmosphere.

The balcony curves, the wind drops.

'Here,' Anna says. She hands round cups of wine. 'To not giving up, right?'

They gulp wine. Ellie is a little buzzed. It's been a beer here a beer there kind of a day.

She offers cigarettes and they all smoke.

Ellie looks down. Sunday night in Vila Madalena is a mess. Bars on every corner, bands competing to be heard, the smell of barbecuing meat, a mass of bodies swaying across the roads, weaving between honking cars, the drivers knocking beer cans as they pass. This is where it starts, the Pauliceia Desvairada, and you rarely know where it will end. It's a good phrase, she thinks, and an apt one for today.

They thrive on the mess here, the chaos, the Pauliceia Desvairada.

'Nice to be above all that,' she says, pointing at the street. 'Higher ground and whatnot.'

'What is it you're not telling us, Ellie?'

'What I'm not telling you is relax.'

'That's helpful.'

'This story – or whatever it is – this starting point, is going to be good, is what I mean. I've got people who'll go on the record and I've got evidence, too.'

'Então?' Anna says. 'Fala, ne?'

So tell us.

'We just need to bide a little time, pick our moment.'

'And us?'

'Big-picture political context is what it'll need. And you get first dibs on any legal work that comes from it, obviously.'

'How generous of you,' Fernanda says.

Anna shoots a look. 'You know what she means.'

'We can talk properly in the week,' Ellie says. Her phone's ringing. Lisboa. 'Hang on.' She answers the phone. She says nothing and listens, nodding, murmuring agreement. She's enjoying watching Anna and Fernanda watch her.

'Interesting,' she says, pocketing her phone.

Anna makes a face. 'What is?'

'More evidence,' Ellie says. 'Quite a bit more, actually.'

Military HQ The shopping bags are laid out on the table, their contents in plastic and labelled.

Cheers, Carlão, Lisboa thinks.

Lisboa examines the goods. There are some new purchases – a T-shirt, shorts, flip-flops – and one or two bits of pocket detritus – a wallet, empty, a cigarette lighter, a few coins. There is a battered paperback book, an airport thriller, but Lisboa doesn't recognise the name of the writer. And there –

In plastic, tagged and wrapped –

There, on the table, in the middle, sitting in plastic –

Tagged, wrapped and just sitting there –

A paperweight.

A paperweight with the words Feliz Aniversario etched on it.

A paperweight Lisboa has seen before. One like it.

There it is, on the table, in the midst of all this stuff.

———

Lisboa thinks back, the bodies in the park, old Lockwood's swank study –

He retches, the bodies in the park, the study –

Lisboa heaves. He steadies himself.

He turns, checks the door.

Wearing gloves, Lisboa pockets the paperweight, the evidence.

Vila Madalena: Ellie's phone goes again. Fernanda raises an eyebrow. 'Miss popular, ne?'

Ellie feigns flicking her hair. 'Prom queen,' she says.

It's an email, an alert she set up. An email in response to her posting the photo of the victim of the awful hate crime on the night of the first round of elections.

She's had some real kooks getting in touch, a couple of lonely hearts, a couple of well-meaning but misplaced thoughts –

It's not been too-heavy traffic.

This message, Ellie sees, is promising.

First line:

The man in your photo is my brother.

Fuck me, Ellie thinks.

She thin-smiles at Fernanda and Anna, raises a finger to say wait a sec.

She calls Lisboa.

Lisboa goes *We'll meet tomorrow morning.*

Ellie thinks this might be a little more than I bargained for.

Marginal, a little before midnight, Junior driving: 'Why do you need me for this again, Carlão?'

'I don't need a reason, son. For now, you're still in my pocket.'

Yeah, yeah, Junior thinks.

'I mean,' he says, 'you can't pick up a drop on your own anymore?'

'Olha.' *Look.* 'We're going to the edge of the jungle is why. I chose the spot as it's quieter than Lula's family Christmas – but that doesn't mean I don't want someone to come with.'

Junior nods. *This is it* he thinks. Last roll of the dice and leave this place.

'You'll get a cut.'

'I could use the cash.'

'Good boy.'

Junior drives, picks up pace.

They do a right just past the Extra supermarket and head up towards Paraisópolis.

Boca de fumo, Paraisópolis, right before midnight: Rafa's crouched almost exactly where he was the night Garibaldo and Lanky were killed.

Franginho is a little further into the favela; the idea is that Carlos will walk past Rafa so Rafa will do him from behind, as it were. That's the idea.

They're bang on time; Franginho is getting the script in his head straight.

Rafa's taken off the safety and feels the heft of the weapon, its curves, its power, its slick machinery.

They know there's going to be fireworks at Dona Regina's at midnight, which will cover the shots. Franginho's planning to keep it short. He'll hand over a combination lock briefcase, give Carlos the code, and as he's checking it, Rafa will shoot him dead.

That's the idea. It's a good plan. Rafa thinks the combination lock case is clever, professional. And it's a case, not a holdall: much easier to disguise what's inside.

Wooden crates are piled high. Plastic rubbish bags seep contents like poison. There is an ooze-odour to the place. Toxic waste bubbles and steams. There are still some who will chuck their sewage into the gutters of the unused pockets in the favela. Stagnant puddles of shit and mud.

The bulb Franginho sorted out sways in the breeze a few feet above his head. He's positioned himself right underneath.

They've checked and rechecked – Rafa's invisible. Key thing is he moves fast, slips out like a ghost.

Rafa hears a car hop the kerb and pull over close to where he's waiting. Headlights stay on. That's a giveaway. He listens: two doors slam. Two.

That's a worry. It's too late to call out to Franginho. Two doors. Fuck.

The crunch of boots on stone, the rough concrete scrape. Heavy breathing and the light of a mobile phone.

Rafa hears muttering. 'Jesus, the stink of the place,' he hears. 'Fucking animals.'

Rafa thinks this is the bulldog talking to himself. But he heard two doors –

Two car doors close.

He's sure he did.

Maybe he didn't.

The bulldog wheezes and shoulders his way along the narrow path, past Rafa –

'Hello, son,' he says to Franginho.

'Carlão.'

'I gather your mate's bird is all right.'

'She's fine.'

'I had a word with the lads, they're sorry about that.'

'Yeah, well.'

Rafa thinks: hold on.

'They were overenthusiastic. Won't happen again.'

'No, it won't.'

Rafa's not sure what this means, this little chat.

'You never told me, Carlão, what the deal was.'

'I didn't know, son.'

Rafa thinks *get a wriggle on*, vamos, ne? *Let's go*.

'Então,' says Carlos.

'Let me show you,' says Franginho.

Boca de fumo, Paraisópolis, midnight: Carlos tells Junior to wait by the car.

'Give me two minutes, then follow me in, certo? Quietly and look sharp, entendeu?'

Yeah, Junior knows what that means. Fuck this, this is it for me, he thinks. Too many years of bad business.

Junior sighs. He's standing by the door, checking his watch.

Fireworks soar and whine – cloudburst.

Two minutes pass –

He edges into the boca, rubber-soled shoes tread soft. He slows his breathing; he lets the gloom settle his eyes.

He hears Carlos saying, 'Combination lock? You're having a laugh,' and then laughing.

Junior gets close, he sees –

Movement, to his left. A shadow, eyes, an arm extended –

Boca de fumo, Paraisópolis, midnight: On Franginho's combination-lock cue, Rafa stands up and moves –

He looks right. He sees –

A man, moving slowly, purposefully, a gun in his hand –

Rafa, startled.

Carlos hears something. Swings round, raises his phone –

Rafa a rabbit in headlights. Carlos says, 'Do him for fuck's sake, Junior.'

Rafa looks at this Junior. Rafa makes a face, his eyes plead –

What should I do?

This Junior lowers his pistol, holsters it.

He looks at Rafa, gives a nod, raises his palms and backs away.

His look: go ahead, mate.

Rafa gathers himself; this all happens in a second.

Franginho's pushing at Carlos.

Carlos is swearing bloody murder.

Rafa straightens up. Pulls the trigger three times: two in the chest and one in the head. Three times, not too messy.

Carlos, the bulldog, crumples.

Rafa hears a car door slam, an engine burn and tyres squeal.

'Drop the gun and come the fuck on,' Franginho is saying.

Rafa's staring at the body. It looks huge, down there, unmoving.

A slab of beef, bleeding out.

29 October: President-elect Bolsonaro nominates Operation Car Wash all-conquering hero Sérgio Moro for Minister of Justice and Public Security. Sérgio Moro, Anna notes, who put Lula in jail.

1 November: Sérgio Moro meets Bolsonaro and accepts the nomination and will join the cabinet in January. The old story. It doesn't matter what's true or not, this is hardly an act that inspires faith in the fair-dealing, straight-shooting, anti-corruption line the president-elect peddled all through his campaign.

The same old story, Anna sighs.

15 November: A story in *Folha* about seventeen PCC gang members killed in Paraisópolis after a Military Police raid. Eyewitness reports mention a line-up and an execution; this was not a raid but revenge. A tit-for-tat job for the murder of an ex-Militar captain a couple of weeks before, which itself was a bait and switch, old-school killing. Reports suggest this raid is the first of a sanctioned operation in the favela of the sort supported by President-elect Bolsonaro.

Ellie knows this ex-Militar is Captain Carlos.

Silva tells her, 'Bide your time, querida.'

Part Six

DECLINE AND FALL OF THE ROMAN EMPIRE

São Paulo, January 2019

1

It's a shame about Ray

January 2019

Não existe amor em SP

Criolo, *musician*

---

1 January, Zona Sul: It's taken two months, but on the very first morning of the year, on the very first day of Bolsonaro's new government, with a low-level hangover and reluctant to leave his family, Lisboa is on his way to what he believes to be the last known address of Gilmar de Santos, murdered 7 October 2018, in a hate crime attack on the night of the first round of the presidential elections.

After his sister came forward and identified the body, the work really began.

Lisboa did most of it himself. Gilmar's sister provided an address where they both had lived back in 2003. She provided a birth certificate and an RGE, an ID number. She told Lisboa that she hadn't seen her brother in more than fifteen years, but that, occasionally, she would receive a postcard or letter that gave some sense of how he was. She provided Lisboa with these pieces of communication.

It was then a case of cross-checking and cross-referencing and visiting address after address to try and piece together the movements of the young man.

The paperweight – he had to know, he had to see if there was any clue at all, and the only way was to find Gilmar de Santos's last place of residence.

Here, the work of the grunt in Vice became suddenly and

---

definitively relevant: it became clear that Gilmar de Santos had lived something of a double life and had, for a period in 2003 and then again in 2006 and 2008 and, suspected but unconfirmed, in 2011, been active as a sex worker, with a street name of Bocão. *Big Mouth.*

Gilmar's sister had never reported him missing; he had always been in touch just before she started to worry about him.

They had fallen out in 2003, when she began to suspect that he was deceiving her over money and his whereabouts at night, and had stopped speaking several months before he eventually left their shared apartment.

The last time she had seen him was New Year's Eve, 2002.

Lisboa notes this now as he approaches a run-down apartment building –

The night before Lula's first day in power.

Doesn't half communicate an ominous message: political power changing hands, officially, on the first day of the year.

Later, Lisboa has planned to avoid Bolsonaro's inauguration speech, visit Mario's headstone at the cemetery, and then go home to his wife and two kids, have a drink, cook something nice, try to relax.

He can't wait.

But his day has been interrupted; it's not the first time he's dragged his sorry arse to a situation on New Year's Day.

A text message, from his Vice grunt, the one person who has shown any sort of dedication to finding this man, this poor man's past.

The text message: an address and a line:

I really think this is it.

Lisboa likes his Vice grunt. Part of him, if he's honest, is going to miss the dogged work of tracking down Gilmar de Santos. The rest of the team were very much job done and Bob's your uncle, until Gilmar's sister came forward and they got the positive ID.

They've basically humoured Lisboa ever since Leme died, and he was given a bit of space. Out to pasture –

It won't be long before he takes voluntary severance.

Criolo's song about how there's no love in São Paulo is playing on the radio when he cuts the engine. Something about the city being a bouquet of dead flowers.

Happy days.

Lisboa's phoned ahead and the building super is waiting for him.

The super says, 'No one's been in or out for a couple of months. I thought the guy had done one and skipped rent. It's slow round here, the admin, entendeu?'

Lisboa understands. He shows the photo of Gilmar outside the Frei Caneca bar.

'This him?'

The super nods.

'You're sure?'

'Certeza, cara.'

Sure am, mate.

Lisboa nods. The super hands him keys. 'Fifth floor.'

In the lift, Lisboa thinks the building even worse than the Paradise Rooms.

The room is your basic shithole. A bed, a desk, a clothes rail and a sink. Rusted brown taps. A toothbrush and a tube of toothpaste. A threadbare blanket. Clothes scattered around a washing basket.

Lisboa pulls on gloves and examines the desk.

Papers and cheap biros. Some loose change. Yellowing newspaper snippets –

Dates: 2003, 2011.

The place screams weirdo. The place reeks of bitterness. The place smacks you in the face with its loneliness, its emptiness, its *lack*.

There's a musty, damp feeling, but Lisboa reckons this is not new. He opens the window. The view: an air-con unit on the side of a concrete building that flanks this one. A sheer drop between, fast-food wrappers festering in the tiny space on the ground. Lisboa clocks two rats, feasting.

Happy days.

Lisboa rummages through the one bookshelf. There are self-help pamphlets, two paperback novels, second-hand, he thinks, some trinkets, from the northeast, sort of ethnic, spiritual bracelets –

A notebook. A journal.

Lisboa pops it open. Scans words, pages, sees the name: *Paddy Lockwood.*

His heart thumps, his head gasps. He thinks: *I knew this*. He thinks: *the horror of it all*.

He flicks to the last entry, dated 1 January 2003:

Then you raise the paperweight, head high, feel strength –
   I remember him lying on the floor. Black spots of blood dotted on the carpet. Thick, patterned, red swirls.
   Another drip painting.

I remember the ties I used to secure his hands and feet where I found them in the closet. I remember exactly why I did it, added that little detail:
   Let them know him in death as they didn't in life.

Lisboa breathes slowly. He thinks: Mario was right. He exhales, he inhales, he lets this settle.

There is a terrible inevitability to what he thinks.

Lockwood, firmly shut years ago. Sixteen years ago –

And covered up.

Mario was right.

It doesn't matter, he realises. It doesn't matter, now. Nothing matters anymore.

Mario was right.

There is nothing to be done.

1 January, Austin, Texas: Ray Marx is kicking back with a morning beer and watching old Bolsonaro on the TV giving it the big one in his inauguration speech.

Ray goes *I knew it wouldn't end well*.

Ray thinks about his score down in São Paulo and is pretty pleased with himself. He's been pretty pleased with himself for some time.

He's glad he took his own advice and scrammed and never looked back.

The white man's privilege.

Good ole boys. Ray's in the pink –

Texas forever.

Same time, offices of Cidade São Paulo: Ellie watches her editor apply the finishing touches to her article. It promises to blow things wide open; she's got a handful of international publications primed and ready to run it. She's got eyewitness reports and insiders on the record: her Militar, Lisboa, to name just two. She's got an incriminating audio file. She's got Anna and Fernanda's work gathering anonymous statements on the less than wholesome relationship between City Hall and the president's office. She's got the lot. And, in about four hours, when the article goes live, Ellie is getting on a plane and going home.

Silva read the final draft that morning: *I'm proud of you*, he told her.

That'd been a long time coming.

Later: Lisboa at the cemetery visiting Leme's headstone. He goes when he can. He spends time with the man, is the way he sees it. He kicks around memories; he focuses on the good times, and there were many of them.

Time, he puts in time; he always did.

Leaving, he sees Antonia, Leme's old girlfriend, partner, the mother of Leme's child, Leme's son, the son he never met.

Leme's son, in Antonia's arms.

They stop, face one another.

The light cracks blue sky, the heat-pulse and cemetery-stillness.

Lisboa smiles; Antonia smiles.

And the little boy –

Afterword

Brazilian Psycho is a work of fiction based on fact. Much of this fact is recognisable in terms of certain names, places, statistics, institutions, events, laws, and policy, which have been adapted and, in some cases, changed for dramatic purposes. I lived in São Paulo for ten years; this experience accounts for much of the information, and many of the anecdotes, in the novel. Friends, colleagues, associates and contemporary media outlets all informed the writing of the novel, both directly and indirectly. During the writing of the novel, I consulted a number of sources to clarify particular facts and timelines; in general, these sources are news media, notably, the *BBC, Guardian, Folha de São Paulo, Reuters, New York Times,* among others. What follows is a list of instances where fact and fiction meet; I've provided information as to which is which – as far as that is possible in the context of a work of fiction – as well as where further information can be found, key sources I've used, and any quoted material. All articles by Francisco Silva and Ellie Boe are fictional; the newspaper, *Cidade de São Paulo,* is also fictional. As stated in the Author's Note, factual quotations are attributed, while fictional quotations are attributed to fictional characters. Excerpts from the speeches of well-known politicians are a matter of the historical record; any conversations they have with my characters are entirely invented. This is, I stress, a work of fiction, and all of the names, characters, places, incidents, organisations, and events portrayed are either products of my imagination or are used fictitiously. Where real-life figures appear, the situations, incidents and dialogues concerning those persons are fictional. I want to thank the authors of works I have quoted or referred to; more often than not, there were several sources, and frequently contradictory.

The acts of violence and abuse that open the novel are based on similar acts that took place around the time of the election in 2018;

year after year, Brazil records the highest figures in the world of violence against women and the LGBTQ community.

The character of Paddy Lockwood – headmaster of the fictional British School of São Paulo – is based on Casey McCann, former headmaster of St. Paul's School, São Paulo, arguably the most prestigious international school in the city, where I worked for a number of years. Tragically, McCann was murdered in his home, in similar circumstances to my character, Paddy Lockwood. McCann was a hugely respected figure, and some of Lockwood's achievements are his; details from his biography, too, including the two quotes from 'friends' (from contemporary press reports) and the incident in 1981 where he rescued a number of pupils from the Moonie cult in San Francisco.

Marta Suplicy was mayor of São Paulo from 2001–2004. The excerpts from the speech Marta made on taking office that my character Anna references are from a BBC news report from Tuesday, 2 January 2001.

The Singapore Project that Renata investigates was a well-known, and largely unsuccessful, construction project in São Paulo, riddled with corruption problems. The notes that Renata takes on the project are from *Lessons on Public Housing from Singapore for São Paulo* by W.E. Hewitt, 2002, with some fictional additions. Ray is quoting from the same source when he talks to Silva over drinks.

The notes on São Paulo Zoning Laws that Ray Marx reads are well-known in terms of the history of urban planning in the city. For further information, a report from the 14th International Planning History Society Conference, entitled *Regulating Inequality: Origins and Transformations of São Paulo's Zoning Laws* is instructive, especially on the 'controversies, contrasts and challenges' that the city faced.

I first read the line *I'm rent, not bent*, in a Jake Arnott novel. Thanks Jake, for the loan.

I was living in São Paulo in 2006 when the Mothers' Day weekend rebellion took place and remember well how frightening and confusing the city was for a few days. Much has been written in the Brazilian and international press about this incident. The documents I have included in the novel are a mixture of fact and fiction. I made use of a timeline from a particular online encyclopaedia which informed my fictional police report of the weekend. I have quoted from two [redacted] *New York Times* articles, the first by Paula Prada, from 17 May 2006, and the second by Larry Rochter, from 30 May 2006, as they offer, I think, the clearest headed versions of what happened, and of the conspiracy and corruption theories that abounded at the time. In the novel, my character, Francisco Silva, helps to write a report on the events of the weekend by Harvard's International Human Rights Clinic and the Brazilian NGO, Justiça Global. The report exists; his involvement is pure fiction. I have quoted from the report's press release, 9 May 2011, from Human Rights @ Harvard Law. The report itself, *São Paulo sob achaque: Corrupção, Crime Organizado e Violência Institucionel em Maio de 2006*, IHRC, 2011, (*São Paulo Under Attack: Corruption, Organised Crime and Institutional Violence in May 2006*, my translation) is available online in Portuguese and is a thorough and fascinating analysis of the events.

The installation *Penelope*, by Tatiana Blass, in the Morumbi Chapel, which Renata visits on the morning of the Mothers' Day weekend was, in fact, exhibited in 2011. More details – and some terrific images – can be found on the artist's website.

Brazil continues to be the world's deadliest country for trans people. Since Bolsonaro assumed the presidency, the already appalling number of hate crimes committed against the LGBTQ community has worsened. In 2019, according to a dossier produced by the National Association of Travestis and Trans People (ANTRA), there were 124 reported cases of the murder of trans people in Brazil. ('Travesti' is 'a typically South American gender identity describing people assigned male at birth who take on a feminine gender role and gender expression.') To give some perspective, Mexico, in second place, reported fewer than half the number. Although most reports come from the northeast, São Paulo, at 21, has the highest number of murders by state. The dossier: 'Assassinatos e violência contra travestis e transexuais brasileiras em 2019' (Murder of and violence against Brazilian travestis and trans people in 2019' [my translation], by Bruna G. Benevides and Sayanora Naider Bonfim Nogueira can be found online. ANTRA has been active since 2000, bringing together organisations to promote citizenship for travestis and trans people; their website is informative and their work vital. For an overview of the dossier and ANTRA's work, see the article 'At least 124 trans people killed in Brazil in 2019: report' by Lu Sudré for Brasil de Fato, which I have paraphrased parts of here. The torture and disfigurement of the victim is common in the murder of trans people and travestis. The horrific and appalling details of the crime scenes in *Brazilian Psycho* are based closely on real-life crimes. In Brazil, the LGBTQ community has suffered some of the most dehumanising treatment and horrendous violence it's possible to imagine. There are countless examples spanning far more than the time period depicted in this novel.

Further perspective is gained by considering that Brazil only criminalised homophobia and transphobia in 2019. An article by Julia Carneiro for the BBC, 24 May 2019, provides a sense of why it has taken so long. The ultra-conservative, Catholic community is both enormous and enormously influential. Terence McCoy's article for the *Washington Post*, 'Anyone could be a threat', 22 July 2019, provides further insight into the levels of homophobia and transphobia through the lens of LGBTQ self-defence courses.

For an insight into the nature of male sex work in Brazil, the relevant chapters in 'Men Who Sell Sex: International Perspectives on Male Prostitution and AIDS' (UCL Press, London, 1999) edited by Peter Aggleton are illuminating. The outreach project and NGO Programa Pegação has information based on its work raising awareness of the risks of HIV and AIDS among male sex workers through 'peer education' and 'community outreach'.

The discussion of, and changes to, Brazilian gender reassignment surgery is informed by, and quotes from, articles from The Associated Press, *Brazil: Free Sex Change Operations*, 18 August 2007, and *Brazil Boosts Transgender Legal Recognition*, by Graeme Reid for Human Rights Watch, at hrw.org, 14 March 2018.

Francisco de Assis Pereira, The Park Maniac, is a notorious, real-life Brazilian serial killer. His crimes and life story held a particular and gruesome fascination over the Brazilian public, and he was something of a media sensation. I first heard about him from friends; this was a famous and disturbing case. There is plenty of salacious information written about him freely available online. The few details of his biography I include in the novel appear, as best I can tell, to be accepted as fact. The victims named in the novel are, tragically, real life victims, their biographies and the circumstances of their deaths adapted from public record information. Extracts from the letters Pereira received after his arrest, referenced in the novel, can be found, apparently, in a book by journalist and writer Gilmar Rodrigues, *Loucas de Amor – Women who Love Serial Killers and Sexual Criminals*, but I was not able to track down a copy or publication reference. The three quotations I have used connected to Pereira appear in various places online, including the encyclopaedias Wikipedia and Murderpedia. Perhaps the definitive, published work is *Caçada ao Maniaco do Parque, (The Hunt for the Park Maniac*, my translation), Editora Escritura, São Paulo, 2000, by Luisa Alcalde and Luis Carlos dos Santos.

The line *who you know and who you blow* that Anna reads is one I read in a James Ellroy novel. I owe him far more than this one line.

The plot line in the novel involving The Ministry of Cities is fictional; the department was not. For more information, there is an excellent article by Gregory Scruggs, *Ministry of Cities RIP: the sad story of Brazil's great urban experiment, Guardian*, 18 July 2019.

Ray Marx uses the words 'Texas Forever'. This is, originally, the catchphrase of Tim Riggins, a recurring character in the TV series *Friday Night Lights*. My partner and I watched all six seasons while I was writing the novel. The song by the Dixie Chicks that Ray is talking about is 'Not Ready to Make Nice' from the album, *Taking the Long Way*.

The list of ministerial sackings that Anna makes is based on a list from a BBC news article, *Brazilian Minister Negromonte resigns over 'corruption'*, 2 February 2012. The lyrical additions are Anna's own.

The fictional article by Francisco Silva about the arrest of Geddel Vieira is based, in part, on a Reuters article, *Brazil police arrest ex-minister Vieira Lima after cash seizure*, from 8 September 2017. The plot line is, of course, entirely fictional. 'The Bunker' does not exist and never did, so I believe.

Anna's research into the São Paulo Military Police includes an excellent article by Vanessa Barbara, *Pity Brazil's Military Police*, *New York Times*, 19 February 2014.

The death of Marielle Franco in 2018 was a terrible tragedy. There are numerous articles about her life and work, and the circumstances of her death. I urge you to read about her.

To read about alleged links between Operation Car Wash and Bolsonaro's election win, see The Intercept, a 'Secret Brazil Archive' of previously undisclosed materials. The plot lines in the novel that relate to the investigation are fictional.

During the 2018 presidential election, there was a lot of fake news. For a sense of how this played out, and the consequences, the Comprova project put together a report on misinformation circulated on WhatsApp throughout the campaigns. This is gathered in *An Evaluation of the Impact of Collaborative Journalism Project on Brazilian Journalists and Audiences* by Claire Wardle, Angela Pimenta, Guilherme Conter, Nic Dias and Pedro Burgos. For a summary, see

Burgos's article for First Draft News, *What 100,000 WhatsApp messages reveal about misinformation in Brazil*, 27 June 2019.

A quotation Anna notes from Clara Araújo, a sociologist – 'the dissatisfaction over the economic crisis, it seems to me, was channelled along with a discourse about conservative morals' – is from *New York Times* article *Brazil Election: Jair Bolsonaro Heads to Runoff After Missing Outright Win* by Ernesto Londoño and Manuela Andreoni, 7 October 2018.

The quotations from the live blog that Ellie is reading on the night of Bolsonaro's win are from the *Guardian*: *Far Right candidate Jair Bolsonaro wins presidential vote – as it happened*, 29 October 2018, by Kate Lyons, with associated articles by the Brazil correspondent, Tom Phillips.

Junior's views on *Tropa de Élite*, the film and the soundtrack song, are his own.

Dramatis Personae

Adriana, a receptionist at Dr Emmanuel's private practice.

Al Gore, former American Vice-President.

Alfredo Nascimento, a politician, the Minister for Transport.

Alvarenga, a detective in the Civil Police. Alvarenga appears in *Paradise City*, *Gringa* and *Playboy*.

Aninha, a childhood friend of Rafael Nascimento, lives in Paraisópolis.

Anna, aide to Marta Suplicy, mayor of São Paulo, 2001–2004, based in City Hall.

Annette Nascimento, Paddy Lockwood's maid and Rafael Nascimento's grandmother.

Antonia, Detective Mario Leme's girlfriend. Antonia appears in *Paradise City*, *Gringa* and *Playboy*.

Antonio Neves, a banker at Capital SP. Neves appears in *Playboy*.

Antonio Palocci, a politician, Chief of Staff of Dilma Rousseff's government.

Assis, a middle-aged businessman.

Aurelio, an estate agent.

Beto, **Andre** and **Fat Pedro**, The Bixiga Boys, a group of teenage thugs with right-wing connections, Bolsonaro supporters who police their neighbourhood for undesirables.

Big Daddy, the nickname for a low-level, anonymous figure in the organised crime syndicate First Capital Command, the PCC.

Bloke, a thug.

Bocão, Big Mouth, a former escort and male sex worker.

Bruno Covas, mayor of São Paulo, 2018.

Carlos, a Military Police officer, and an associate of Mario Leme. Carlos appears in *Paradise City*, *Gringa* and *Playboy*.

Carlos Lupi, a politician, the Minister for Labour.

Carolina Meirelles, a student activist, a member of a Black Bloc political organisation.

Cazuza, a songwriter and musician. Cazuza appears in *Paradise City*.

Cláudio Lembo, governor of São Paulo State, 2006.

Criolo, a songwriter and musician.

da Cunha, an admin guy at the Civil Police.

Dave 'Huck' Sawyer, Capital SP region head, and long-time associate of Ray Marx.

Dilma Rousseff, 36th President of Brazil, and leader of the Workers' Party. Dilma appears in *Paradise City*, *Gringa* and *Playboy*.

Driver, a driver who works for Ray Marx.

Eduardo Suplicy, Marta's ex-husband and a high-ranking politician in his own right.

Eleanor 'Ellie' Boe, a young English woman, a journalist, associate of Detective Mario Leme, and colleague of Francisco Silva. Ellie appears in *Paradise City*, *Gringa* and *Playboy*.

Elisângela Francisco da Silva, a young woman.

Emmanuel, a private surgeon.

Eurípedes Alcântara, a journalist.

Evandro, a young man from northeast Brazil.

Fabio Mendes, Jorge and Juliana Mendes' son.

Felipe, a Military Police officer.

Fernanda, a lawyer at Capital SP and legal aid colleague of Renata Sanchez.

Fernando, a concierge at the Hotel Unique.

Fernando Delgado, a fellow at Harvard Law School.

Fernando Pimentel, a politician, the Minister for Development.

Francisco de Assiss Pereira, a real-life serial killer, 'The Park Maniac'.

Francisco Silva, crime correspondent for newspaper *Cidade de São Paulo*. Silva appears in *Paradise City*, *Gringa* and *Playboy*.

Franco and **Martina**, Anna's colleagues at City Hall.

Franginho, **Little Chicken**, Rafael Nascimento's best friend, lives in Paraisópolis.

Fried Rice, a mid-level figure in the organised crime syndicate First Capital Command, the PCC, based in Paraisópolis.

Garibaldo, a mid-level figure in the organised crime syndicate First Capital Command, the PCC, based in Paraisópolis.

Gerson, Renata's part-time colleague in the legal aid office in Paraisópolis. Gerson appears in *Paradise City*.

Gerson Anderson, a young man.

Geddel Vieira Lima, Vice-President of Brazil's National Savings Bank.

Gilberto, a Military Police officer.

Gilmar, a young man.

Goon, a Military Police officer who works for Carlos. Goon appears in *Paradise City* and *Playboy*.

Gorilla, a security guard at the Swing Motel.

Guilherme Santos, a young man.

Guy, a security guard at a bar in Frei Caneca.

Housekeeper, employee at Antonio Palocci's Brasília pad.

IT Guy, a geek who is helping Anna.

Jair Bolsonaro, 38th President of Brazil, a right-wing, populist politician.

James, a disillusioned, alcoholic teacher at the British International School.

Jim O'Neill, Goldman Sachs economist, creator of the B.R.I.C economic concept.

João 'Jonny' Doria, a former mayor of São Paulo, now running for state governor, presenter of the Brazilian version of *The Apprentice*.

Joãozinho, Little Johnny, a political fixer and friend of Ray Marx.

Joe, an expat teacher.

Jorge Mattoso, President of the Federal Savings Bank.

Jorge Mendes, Secretario de Obras, a political position in charge of construction in São Paulo. Mendes appears in *Paradise City*.

Juliana Mendes, the wife of Jorge Mendes, the state Secretario de Obras. Juliana appears in *Paradise City*.

Julião, an entrepreneur.

Junior, a Military Police officer. Junior appears in *Playboy*.

Lagnado, a Superintendent in the Civil Police, Leme's superior. Lagnado appears in *Paradise City*, *Gringa*, and *Playboy*.

Lanky, a low-level drug dealer in the organised crime syndicate First Capital Command, the PCC, based in Paraisópolis.

Leonardo Magalhães, the highest-ranking officer in the Civil Police. Magalhães appears in *Paradise City*.

Lúcia Sousa da Silva, a greengrocer who lives in Paraisópolis.

Ludmilla, a friend of Fernanda who lives in Brasília.

Luís Favre, Rasputin, Marta Suplicy's new lover and husband elect. Favre is a political mover and shaker.

Luiz Inácio Lula da Silva, 35th President of Brazil, and leader of the Workers' Party. Lula appears in *Paradise City*, *Gringa* and *Playboy*.

Lutfalla, a detective in the Civil Police. Lutfalla appears in *Playboy*.

Manuela, a friend and colleague of Bocão, when he worked a legit office job.

Marcos Williams Herbas Camacho, Marcola, leader of the organised crime syndicate First Capital Command, the PCC. Marcola appears in *Paradise City*.

Maria, an administrator.

Maria Elisa, a cleaner at the British International School.

Maria Regina Vasconcellos, Regina Vasconcellos's cousin, lives in Paraisópolis.

Marielle Franco, a journalist, activist and politician.

Mario Leme, a rookie detective in the Civil Police (Polícia Civil). Leme appears in *Paradise City*, *Gringa* and *Playboy*.

Michelangelo, a low-level drug dealer working out of a cheap motel in Bixiga.

Militar, a Military Police officer who works with Carlos. Militar appears in *Paradise City* and *Playboy*.

Moreira and **Hamuche,** Civil Police detectives.

Nelson Jobim, a politician, the Minister for Defence.

Nelson Rodrigues, a playwright.

Orlando Silva, a politician, the Minister for Sport.

Paddy Lockwood, headmaster of the British International School.

Pastor, a priest based in Paraisópolis.

Patrícia Gonçalves Marinho, a young woman.

Paul Wolfowitz, a former president of the World Bank.

Paulo Maluf, a notorious São Paulo mayor, appears in *Paradise City*, *Gringa* and *Playboy*.

Pedro Novais, a politician, the Minister for Tourism.

Porteiro, a doorman.

Rafael 'Rafa' Nascimento, a young boy who lives in Paraisópolis.

Rafaela, a cleaner at the British International School.

Raquel Mota Rodrigues, a young woman.

Ray Marx, a former CIA operative, fixer and consultant for high finance firm Capital SP.

Regina Vasconcellos, a restaurant owner in Paraisópolis.

Renata de Camargo Nascimento, heir to the Brazilian multi-billionaire Camargo Correa Group.

Renata Sanchez, a lawyer, runs a legal aid office in the favela Paraisópolis. Sanchez appears in *Paradise City*, *Gringa* and *Playboy*.

Ricardo Lisboa, a detective, Mario Leme's partner and best friend. Lisboa appears in *Paradise City*, *Gringa* and *Playboy*.

Richard Hullah, a chaplain based in San Francisco, and an associate of Paddy Lockwood.

Roberto, an old friend of Anna's at City Hall.

Rogério Buratti, Antonio Palocci's secretary.

Rubens, 'Chatterbox', a Military Police officer.

Selma Ferreira Queiroz, a young woman.

Sérgio Moro, the chief prosecutor in Operation Car Wash, the corruption scandal that features in *Playboy*.

Sergio Nascimento, Rafa's father, a musician and a low-level figure in the organised crime syndicate First Capital Command, the PCC.

Sophia, a friend of Juliana Mendes.

Thayna, a trans woman.

Wagner Rossi, a politician, the Minister for Agriculture.

Wilton, a Brazilian teacher.

Y-fronts, a low-life debt collector who works for Dr Emmanuel's private practice.

Young Lad, a messenger boy for drug dealers working in Bixiga.

Zézinho, a client of Renata's, lives in Paraisópolis.

Acknowledgements

Piers Russell-Cobb, Martin Fletcher, Will Francis, Angeline Rother-mundt, Kid Ethic, Joe Harper, Rosie Stevens, Lucy Caldwell, and Martha Lecauchois

Read on for an extract from

WHITE RIOT

By Joe Thomas

Available January 2023

1978

The National Front is gaining ground in Hackney. To counter their influence, anti-fascist groups launch the Carnival Against Racism in Victoria Park. Observing the event is Detective Constable Patrick Noble, charged with investigating racist attacks in the area and running Spycops in both far-right and left wing groups. As Noble's superiors are drawn further into political meddling, he's inveigled into a plot against the embattled Labour government.

1983

Under a disciplinary cloud after a Spycops op ended in tragedy, Noble is offered a reprieve by an old mentor. He is dispatched in the early hours to Stoke Newington police station, where a young black man has died in suspicious circumstances. This is Thatcher's Britain now, a new world that Noble unwittingly helped to usher in, where racial tensions are weaponised by those in power.

Supercharged by the music and counterculture of the era, *White Riot* weaves fiction, fact and personal experience to record the radical tale of London's most thrilling borough. Politics, music, police corruption, institutional racism and the power of protest all take centre stage in a novel that traces the roots of our current political moment.

Locker room, West End Central police station.

Detective Constable Patrick Noble is kitting up for the day. He's off to Victoria Park to have a look at this festival so he's in his civvies. Seconded to Hackney –

Racist attacks and all hands on deck.

And this is what, Noble thinks, a fact-finding mission?

Giving up his Sunday.

The Clash are all right, he's thinking, what Joe Strummer said the other day makes sense –

'People ought to know we're anti-fascist, we're anti-violence, we're anti-racism and we're pro-creativity. We're against ignorance.'

'Oi, Noble.' A yell from across the room. 'You better pack your handkerchief, son.'

Noble turns. It's Big Ron Robinson, Detective Constable and all round 'character'. A real charmer is Big Ron.

Noble says, 'Leave it out, eh, Ron.'

'And keep an eye on your wallet, too,' Ron says.

'What are you on about?'

Big Ron leers. 'Punks and blacks, mate,' he says. 'At your little concert this afternoon.'

Noble shakes his head. Noble mutters, You wanker.

Big Ron leans in. 'One'll spit in your face and the other'll lift your cash while he's doing it.'

'Fuck off, Ron.'

Noble closes his locker, heads for the door.

'Be lucky, Chance, old son,' Ron is laughing. 'Be lucky, Paddy boy.'

Chance Noble: one small bit of good fortune, *once*, one lucky break, and the nickname stuck.

Doesn't help his name's Patrick –

Luck of the Irish ain't a phrase you hear in a London nick.

Same day, a few hours earlier.

Suzi Scialfa's at a squat party on Charing Cross Road.

At four in the morning, someone puts on Junior Murvin's 'Police and Thieves'.

The party ripples quiet. Reggae vibe.

Someone shouts, Isn't this a Clash song? Everyone laughs.

Suzi's looking out the window. There's a procession, hundreds of people making their way down the road.

Suzi, quite drunk, leans out of the window. She calls out, 'Where you guys headed?'

'Where you *from*, love?' someone yells back.

Laughter. Shouts: oi, oi!

Suzi laughs back, hams up that all-American drawl of hers. 'New York, New York, darling.'

She takes her camera and snaps. 'You're not going to tell me where y'all are going?'

Another voice says, 'Trafalgar Square, sweetheart. March against racism.'

Suzi goes, 'Now? It's four in the fucking morning.'

'May as well get there early,' someone else shouts.

Junior Murvin's bass player rumbles through the night.

Someone puts on The Clash.

Suzi's boyfriend joins her at the window. She points at the crowds. Fucking hell, he says.

Mildenhall Road, Clapton, a little later.

Jon Davies lies in bed with his six-month-old son, Joe, his wife Jackie downstairs making the tea.

She calls up. 'You going to want to go to the march, love? Or just the music?'

Jon's been thinking about this for a few days. The march is Trafalgar Square to Victoria Park, a decent few miles. They'd be going a long way west to come back east again. What would the boy make of it all? Jon never knows what he'll make of anything. He seems happy enough with whatever's put in front of him, until he's not.

It's a hassle, the march, is what it is. But it's Anti-Nazi League and the music's Rock Against Racism, and Jon works for the council, so it might be diplomatic to do both –

As if anyone cares.

'Just the music, love,' he shouts downstairs. 'I want to make sure we see Steel Pulse.'

'Steel who?' Jackie yells.

Noble knocks on DS Foreman's door and goes in.

Foreman's smiling. 'Got your glad rags on, Chance, I see. Very trendy.'

'Very funny, guv,' Noble says.

'At least you'll fit in.'

Noble's not sure how true that is.

Foreman says, 'Take this.' He hands Noble a piece of paper. 'These are a few names to look out for.'

'OK.'

'This is a recon exercise, Chance, that's all. You're just there to observe.'

'Yes, guv.'

'And this,' he hands Noble an envelope, 'is some ready money and a backstage pass.' Foreman smiles again. 'We thought you'd like to knock boots with the glamour crowd.'

Noble nods.

'We want you at Trafalgar Square, do the whole route. Get a sense of it, OK?'

Noble examines the piece of paper.

At the top, a title: PERSONS OF INTEREST ON THE LEFT

And a list of names:

Red Saunders, founding member Rock Against Racism [RAR]
Syd Shelton, central RAR committee member
David Widgery, central RAR committee member
Ruth Gregory, central RAR committee member
John Dennis, central RAR committee member
Wayne Minter, central RAR committee member
Kate Webb, central RAR committee member

Roger Huddle, Socialist Worker Party and central RAR committee member

Peter Hain, founding member, Anti-Nazi League

Paul Holborow, founding member, Anti-Nazi League

Halfway down, another heading: PERSONS OF INTEREST ON THE RIGHT

But there is no list of names.

'Guv,' Noble says. He gestures with the piece of paper. 'What's this?'

Foreman smiles. 'You're supposed to fill that in yourself, son, that's what this is.'

Noble nods.

Foreman softens. He says, 'You've got your skinheads and your headbangers on one side, right? On the other,' and here he raises his left hand, 'you've got your subversives. Easy enough to keep an eye on the skinheads. They're hooligans, end of.'

'And the National Front?' Noble says. 'They're not of interest, guv?'

'They're an official political party, DC Noble,' Foreman says. 'Legit.'

'I thought, guv,' Noble says, slowly, 'that I was looking into racially aggravated assault, GBH, that kind of thing.'

'You are, son.' Foreman breathes out.

He's all right, Foreman, Noble knows this, he's just –

Well, he's just more worried about his job than anything else.

Foreman says, 'A word of advice, Chance.'

'Go on.'

'The skinheads won't fancy this lefty mob marching straight through their patch, know what I mean?'

Noble nods. 'Brick Lane.'

Foreman shakes his head. 'That's not a problem.'

'No?'

'You know Gardiner down at Whitechapel, don't you?'

Noble nods.

'He'll be at the top of Brick Lane with the uniforms. Go and say hello.'

'Right.'

'And when you get close to Bethnal Green,' Foreman says, 'I'd get near the front, if I were you.'

'In a manner of speaking,' Noble says.

Foreman laughs. 'Good one, Chance, clever boy. Arrivederci.'

Suzi's half-listening to a man talking loudly about how the stage at Victoria Park has been occupied all week by some old-school dockers and like-minded West Ham fans, and it's already been attacked three times by National Front thugs, but they were seen off no problem, sounds like it was a laugh –

Suzi turns to her fella. 'What time is it?'

'Six-thirty.'

'*Six-thirty*? How did that happen?'

Her fella taps his nose, gives a big sniff. 'How do you think, love. We better go soon, eh?'

Suzi nods that they should. They'll both be working all day, after all.

She's grinning and wired in a good way and checks her bag for camera equipment, notebook, pen.

Pats down her pockets for keys, money, fags. Check check check.

'Let's go,' she says. 'Let's go!'

People are already leaving the squat and the stairwell echoes excited chatter and shouted slogans:

'The National Front is a Nazi Front, Smash the National Front.'

People are singing in the street. They hear 'London's Burning' by The Clash.

Suzi leans into her fella's shoulder. She likes the word fella, makes her feel more English, somehow.

'You excited, babe?' she asks.

Keith, her fella, wraps his arm around her. 'I am, love. It's a big deal, today. You excited? You should be, girl.'

Suzi smiles, she noses her way further into Keith's corner, the crook of his neck.

She can't wait, truth be told.

There's a dampness in the air – it's rained three days solid – but the light's bright and cuts through it, and the streets *gleam*, and there's a bounce in everyone's step. A West End Sunday morning is a bleak business, normally, Suzi thinks. The patches of vomit. The *debris*. Not today though. Today, it feels, they're all on a mission.

Keith is the sound man for The Ruts, and The Ruts are set to perform on a truck the whole way from Trafalgar Square to Victoria Park, and Suzi is going to be on that truck, on assignment, taking photos for *Temporary Hoarding* magazine and making a few notes, getting a few quotes.

Someone's bounding down Charing Cross Road yelling 'here we go, here we go'.

They turn. It's Syd Shelton, one of the organisers and the graphic designer for *Temporary Hoarding*, so, in a way, Suzi's boss.

He slaps Keith on the back and gives Suzi a big kiss.

'All right, Sweetheart,' he says, grinning.

So many people called Suzi sweetheart when she first arrived on the scene as a seventeen-year-old, she took it as an official nickname, half-ironic. Suzi 'Sweetheart' Scialfa. Co-opting it, is what she said she was doing. It stuck.

They do that, nicknames, they stick.

Keith says, 'You're up early.'

'Couldn't sleep.' Syd winks at Suzi. 'You Suze, you lose, get it?'

'I'm American, Syd, I'm not stupid,' she says. 'I've lived here all my life – *man*.'

Syd laughs.

'You're looking very pleased with yourself, Syd, if I may,' says Keith.

'Hear that?' Syd stops them, cocks an ear, puts a hand to it.

They're halfway down to Leicester Square and it's too late – or early – for any Soho carousers, and the tourists are still tucked up, but there is a lot of noise coming from somewhere.

Suzi says, 'That sounds like a crowd.'

'There's about ten thousand here already, we reckon,' Syd says. 'Coach loads from Scotland, Manchester, Liverpool, Sheffield, Middlesbrough, South Wales, all over. They wanted to beat the traffic,' he deadpans.

'Ten thousand?' Keith whistles. 'Well, we shouldn't have any problems today then.'

'Unlikely, mate,' Syd says. 'I just chatted to a load of punks from Aberystwyth. They're rugby players, most Sundays.'

They laugh.

Suzi feels a touch of relief. She wouldn't admit it, but she was a little bit concerned about the possibility of trouble. Sham 69 are playing later – well, Jimmy Pursey is rumoured to be doing *something* – and there's been a lot of it, trouble, she thinks, at their gigs. National Front skins at Middlesex Poly causing a ruckus was the worst of it.

Suzi's been thinking that the truck on the march might come in for a little attention. But ten thousand *already*? They'll be dandy.

'It's not just punks,' Syd adds. 'There's all sorts. Young, gifted and black, white, brown. Teds, mods, bikers, punks, greasers, disco kids. All ages. The reggae sound systems are setting up in the east. And it's not even seven.'

'Fucking hell,' Keith says.

'Look,' Syd says, 'I need to get a wriggle on. See you on the truck, my lovelies.'

They watch Syd fly down the road.

'Where the fuck is Aberystwyth?' Suzi says.

'Babe,' Keith ignores her. 'I don't know about you, but I fancy a cup of tea and a bacon sandwich before all the fun begins.'

Suzi squeezes Keith's arm. 'Lead on, squire,' she says.

Keith takes her hand and they swerve right into Chinatown.

Suzi makes a face, confused. 'Love?' she says.

Keith grins. 'I know a place.'

'Course you do, love.'